THE EXPERIMENTALIST

THE EXPERIMENTALIST

Nick Salaman

THE
DOME
PRESS

Published by The Dome Press, 2018

This is a work of fiction. All characters, organisations and events
portrayed in this novel are either products of the author's imagination
or are used fictitiously.

A CIP catalogue record for this book is available from the British Library

ISBN 9781999855925

The Dome Press
23 Cecil Court
London WC2N 4EZ

www.thedomepress.com

Printed and bound in Great Britain by Clays Ltd, Elcograf S.p.A.

Typeset in Garamond by Elaine Sharples

O Rose thou art sick.
The invisible worm,
That flies in the night
In the howling storm:

Has found out thy bed
Of crimson joy:
And his dark secret love
Does thy life destroy.
William Blake

'…Of the 100 prisoners you despatched to me, 18 died in transit. Only 12 are in a fit state for my experiments. Therefore I require you to send me a further 100 prisoners between 20 and 40 years old who are in good health and in a state comparable to able-bodied soldiers.

Heil Hitler.'

Dr E. Haagen

15 November 1943

Prologue

From the papers of Professor Felix Mittelberg, 29th April 1945
I found the couple as I made my way out of the battered western edges of Berlin on roads choked with people, traffic and rubble, towards the oncoming American or British armies, whichever came first. I had taken off my SS colonel's uniform and was wearing the armband of a Reserved Occupation medic. An SS officer would not have been a popular travelling companion at that stage of the war.

Somewhere, stray remnants of our troops were straggling, sometimes fighting, their way westward to try to reach the Allies before the Russians overtook them. Every now and then detachments of diehard fanatics were firing on them, and on civilians too, trying to stop them.

I carried papers on which I had not changed my name or qualifications, since it would only arouse suspicion among my captors. I was a professor with various medical (especially psychiatric), psychological and scientific degrees. I was a behaviourist – as you would expect a psychiatrist to be at that time – though recently I had begun to feel that one could not exclude the influences of early childhood. You only had to look at some of our leaders. I was specialising in the new sciences of aviation physiology and psychiatry

1

(survival under extreme stress, high altitude, speed of sound, extremes of uncertainty, heat and cold etc.) in which we had recently achieved significant breakthroughs in research – the development of drugs and strategies through experimentations – some of it dangerous but urgently necessary, at the edge of physical toleration. It was something the Yankees would almost certainly want to hear about. They would not want it to fall into the hands of the Ivans.

The couple were young and good-looking, dark-haired, possibly Jewish though they had to be the last Jews living in the Third Reich, or what was left of it. What were they doing here? How had they escaped? There was no point in asking questions like that any more. It was now each man for himself.

They had a baby with them – young, only months old – which they wheeled in a big old-fashioned pram like an antique Daimler. It made me think how lucky I was to have no family. Every so often there would be trouble on the road, a truck blocking the path, a broken down Opel; and now and then a rifle or machine gun would open up. There were still crazed gangs of Hitler Youth about who were fighting beyond the bitter end, and were now infuriated to see the unending stream of Germans leaving the country like rats, to avoid falling into the hands of the Ivans.

It was in one of these mindless acts of rage that the couple were hit. The man died immediately. The girl, mortally wounded, was still conscious. The baby, however, was gurgling merrily. I did not want to waste time. The Russians were not far away, and the sounds of distant fighting seemed to be gaining on us as we fled. But in all conscience – and I have to admit, curiosity – I could not leave the girl and her child. Even then an idea was flickering through my head. It was quite unbidden; I had never thought of it before. In these dire circumstances – unexpected, unpredictable – all manner of new ideas were flooding in, like particles into a vacuum. The notion vanished as quickly as it had arrived when the girl groaned. She had been shot through the stomach and the lung.

'Please, sir,' she said, painfully, through a bloody mouth, 'I am dying, aren't I?'

I was moved by the 'sir'. It would be interesting to do a paper on the habit of formality, even at the extreme edges of life. I suppose I do have a medical look; you take it on with the white coat at university. I felt her pulse and looked at her wounds.

'Yes, my dear,' I said. 'It does look that way. I am sorry.'

People jostled and flooded past us as we stopped there, like rocks in a torrent. Behind us, the sounds of warfare were growing.

'Please,' she said again, speaking with a great effort, but almost sibylline in the way that the imminence of death sometimes promotes, 'I will bless you and give you good luck in this life if you look after my child. Don't let her go. Watch over her. Guard her. Make sure she is educated. She will be clever and beautiful. Will you do that for me? Her name is…'

Her breath failed her and I leant forward to catch a sound softer than a moth's wing, a name she whispered into my ear. I readily agreed, as one does when faced with someone leaving this world. How could I not? Naturally, I had no idea about babies or how to make them happy, or not unhappy. We have all been babies, but it is one of the few things that personal experience does not teach us.

I gathered up the baby, and the woman gave me the most beautiful smile you ever saw.

'God bless you,' she said, and died.

There was no time to be lost. The baby immediately became a

kind of talisman as its mother had predicted. Wherever I went with the child, I seemed to prosper. We hitched a lift on a passing lorry. That in itself, to stop and help a walking refugee, was unheard of, but there it was.

'I thought I'd stop, mate,' said the driver, a little, wizened fellow in his fifties, 'seeing as you had a baby with you.'

'Thank you very much,' I told him. 'It's good to know in this troubled time that someone has a kind heart. You're a good man. I hope you find what you want when you get out of this.'

'This is my wife Ilse. She was the one who spotted you.'

He indicated the sad-faced, younger woman who sat next to him. She smiled at me and the baby.

'We lost ours,' she said.

'I'm sorry,' I said. 'What terrible times!'

Babies had been dying like flies – no, no, not like flies, since flies were thriving in Berlin – like our soldiers on the Russian front, but it was the same problem. Too little food, too little medicine, too few doctors.

'Where'd you get the truck?' I asked him. 'They're like hen's teeth.'

'I just finished a job, medical supplies, when my boss says turn round and get out. I put my family in the back and we hoofed it. We're making for the American army 'cos they have more food than anyone else.'

'Good plan,' I said.

And in due course I found myself being interviewed by an overworked American army captain who wanted to know all about me before sending me on to someone else. I was overcome with sudden rage that it had come to this, a rage I was careful to dissemble to the captain, but I cast about in my mind to find something, someone, anything – life itself – from which I could exact compensation. It gets to you in moments like this. Not a quick solution, you understand; it did not appeal to my academic instincts. No, something more like a project that I could still pursue many years from now, its heat not dissipated by time but growing quietly from within like silage, or cancer. A project to make up, in its small way, for everything I had lost.

The baby started crying. The idea that had crossed my mind when I was tending the woman on the road now came back to me. Yes, that might do very well; very well indeed.

PART ONE

The little girl had crept up behind the box hedge that ran around the rose garden, so the grown-ups did not see her.

'Such a tragedy for the child, of course. Her mother dying so young…'

'Of shame, they say.'

'Possibly. She was a sickly woman. They gave the cause of death as pneumonia, but I daresay shame came into it. To have a monster as a husband…'

'I'd rather have a monster as a husband than as a father.'

'I'd always be worried about bad blood coming out.'

The little girl had been meaning to pounce out at her great-aunts, Claire and Bertha, and their friend the Abbess but, hearing the words, she paused and crept away.

She took the subdued atmosphere of the castle for granted, of course. She could not remember anything different, and she was used to the way the grown-ups lowered their voices when they thought she could hear their conversations, but she had never heard the mention of monsters before. She thought about it all day, and raised the matter with her nurse at bedtime.

'What is a monster, Nanny?'

'Why it's a bogeyman, a bugaboo, or a troll if you like. A bloody bones. The sort that'll get you if you don't clean behind your ears.'

The nurse gave her a hug to show her she didn't mean it. The child was short of such affections.

'What do they look like, Nanny?'

'Well, they're sort of knobbly, with warts and such. They have squashy faces and big, hairy feet. They've got teeth like portcullises.'

The little girl thought about it. She didn't see how she could be the daughter of a monster because she didn't have any of those things.

The nurse saw she was looking thoughtful, and hastened to explain.

'They can't get in here,' she said. 'We've got a great big portcullis of our own.' The little girl sucked her thumb.

'You're a funny little thing,' said the nurse. 'Why d'you ask about monsters?'

'They said I was the child of a monster,' replied the girl. 'But I think they may have been wrong because my feet are quite smooth.'

'Who did? Who said that?' asked the nurse, crossly. 'Silly duffers. I should like to hear them say it in front of me.' Some boy about the kitchens, she thought, or gardener's lad, no doubt. They needed a good drubbing.

'It was the Abbess and Aunt Claire. I heard them in the garden.'

The nurse was silent. They should be more careful what they said with a child around but it was hardly her place to tell them.

'Why did my mummy have to die?' asked the little girl.

'She caught a bad cold and couldn't breathe,' said the nurse, on safer ground here. 'She's with the angels now.'

'Is my daddy with the angels too?'

'It's all in God's hands, little one. Don't you worry your head about it.'

'And what's bad blood, Nanny?'

But Nanny had a look on her face that meant the subject was closed.

'Chatter, chatter, chatter. Have you said your prayers yet, that's what I'd like to know? Let's have no talk of blood before bedtime, what with your birthday tomorrow and all.'

'Sorry, Nanny.'

'That's better. Now, what are you going to thank God for today?'

The little girl slipped into the comforting litany which made sure only nice things could get into the bedroom and had the bogeymen running for cover, tails between their legs, far into the darkness beyond the whispering moat.

It was the Old Midsummer's Eve, the 24th of June, 1950.

* * *

Occasionally, the gardener's lad would steal across the lawns when his father wasn't watching, and show her a worm or a grub. One day he even brought her a baby hedgehog which Nanny had allowed her to feed with warm milk and keep in a little box until Aunt Claire discovered it. At which point of course it was returned to its owner because Aunt Claire had a horror of ticks and fleas.

'Hedgehogs are full of fleas,' she said. 'And TB.'

Apart from the boy, and a little snot-nosed girl – who was something to do with one of the kitchen maids and occasionally escaped round to the front, but did little when she got there except stare and eat bogies – she had the choice of her dolls or the grown-ups. Her dolls were on the whole more communicative.

On Sundays, her aunts took her to church. The service was long and for the most part boring, but she enjoyed it because she could look around at all the people. The trouble was, she had to sit in the family pew which was right up at the front, so it wasn't so easy to get a good look at everyone. It meant you had to turn right round, which Nanny said was rude.

'But everyone stares back at me, Nanny. They all seem to want a really good peek.'

'I expect they do,' said Nanny. 'I expect they're wondering who that funny little monkey is, sitting in the family pew.'

Marie giggled. She was a pretty little girl, with pale skin, curly hair and distinctive, very bright, pale-blue eyes. But the looks on the faces weren't exactly admiring – it was almost as if they were sorry for her – and a few of them seemed angry or even frightened. She noticed that when she followed her aunts out at the end the other people kept their children well away. She asked her aunts why this should be, and she was told it was because they lived in the castle. It was about this time, around the age of four, she started talking to the Man in the Wall.

The Man in the Wall was her friend. He was just a face. He had the ability to appear in any wall, outside or in, and had even been known to manifest in trees. Because he was so good at moving around, he became her constant companion and confidant. On the whole, she kept him to herself but Aunt Bertha caught her once, muttering at what appeared to be a blank piece of stonework in the East Wing.

'Come along, Marie. Head up, shoulders back! Mustn't stand around mumbling at nothing. Hasn't your governess got any books for you to read?'

Aunt Bertha was the more masculine of the two old ladies. For some time, when Marie had been little and was first brought to the castle, she had simply caller her 'Bert'. 'Bert' hadn't stood for it for long.

'I'm not mumbling at nothing, Aunt Bertha. I'm talking to the Man in the Wall.'

'Man in the wall?'

Aunt Bertha had peered closely at the stone, searching for delineation. Finding none, she had become vexed. The aunts' father had been a general in the army and Bertha had a soldier's shortness of temper. She thwacked the wall with her stick.

'Ow,' said the Man in the Wall.

'You hurt the Man in the Wall,' said Marie. 'Horrid Aunt Bertha.'

'There's no man in the wall,' cried Aunt Bertha. 'Look! See? Nothing.' She jabbed her stick savagely right up the Man in the Wall's nose. 'He is a figment of your imagination.'

'There is, there is, there is,' shouted Marie.

'Insubordination. Truculence. You shall go to your room if you don't mend your manners. Repeat after me: there is no man in the wall.'

'I won't.'

'Marie.'

'I won't.'

'I'm giving you one last chance.'

The child hesitated, then made up her mind.

'There is no Man in the Wall.'

'That's better. Cut along now. No mooning. And do not ever call me horrid again or you'll go to your room and eat turnips.'

The Aunt watched Marie run off to the centre of the keep where a sundial stood among the daisies. The little girl started to make a daisy chain.

'The old timekeeper and the child make a charming juxtaposition, do they not, Bertha,' babbled Claire, advancing paunchily to meet her sister. 'One could almost make a poem about it.'

The little girl looked at the Man in the Wall who had taken up his quarters in the pedestal of the dial. She placed her daisy chain carefully over the corner of the dial so it hung over his head like a halo.

He very slowly closed his left eye and opened it again.

Later, she told her nanny about the Man in the Wall.

'Aunt Bertha says he is a figment of my imagination but I don't think he can be because he winked at me. Do you think he can be, Nanny? He wouldn't wink if he was a figment.'

'Poor little soul,' said the nanny to her friend the cook afterwards. 'They don't give her any friends and they go and take away the one she invents for herself.'

'All the same,' said the cook, 'sins of the fathers and such … I hope it's not one of them departed spirits come to wreak vengeance on the child.'

* * *

Sometime after her ninth birthday, her aunts sent for her to come to the great dining room. There was a stranger standing behind them when she came in. He was middle-aged with grey-brown hair, a long nose and a look of pained surprise. He had a kind of gloss to him which Marie later learned to associate with great wealth.

'This is Mr Brickville,' said Bertha. 'He was your father's solicitor, and he has been looking after our affairs. He is a very busy man so we are most grateful.'

'How do you do?' said Marie. 'We are most grateful.'

'Indebted,' said Aunt Claire.

'Come here, child,' said Mr Brickville, drawing her to him.

He peered deep into her face, holding her hands tightly so she could not get away.

'Yes,' he said at length. 'I see the father.'

'She is a quiet girl,' said Bertha. 'We do not countenance rackety behaviour.'

'Friends?'

'We have thought it best to keep away from society,' said Aunt Claire.

'There is a governess who is satisfactory,' said Aunt Bertha. 'She is taught English, French, history and mathematics. She learns the piano.'

She pronounced it pee-ano.

'She should meet other children in due course. We do not want her to grow up into an eccentric. We know where that can lead.'

The man exchanged glances with the Aunts. They all shuddered. Marie had the impression that they were a little frightened of him.

'Would you like to go to school one day?' he asked Marie.

She could tell it wouldn't make any difference whether she expressed enthusiasm or not. As it happened, she thought school would be rather fun. She sometimes saw, through the castle gates, the children swinging their satchels as they walked down to the village. She thought they looked jolly and she would have liked to have asked them in, but when she had mentioned it to the Aunts they had pursed their lips and looked grave. Now it seemed they had changed their minds.

'Thank you, Mr Brickville,' she said, curtseying as her aunts liked her to do. Perhaps he wasn't as bad as he seemed. On the other hand, perhaps he was worse.

'Well, that's enough of that, then,' he said. 'Run along now.'

Marie hated to be told to run along now, so she let him stand as bad after all.

'Now tell me,' she heard him ask as she left the room, 'how is the financial side?'

There was something about his voice when he spoke of money that sounded like a man in love – a chilly sort of love of course – but passionate nonetheless. Tell me, how is the financial side, she mouthed to herself in her looking-glass. It was her first meeting with Mr Brickville but it was not to be her last.

* * *

The years passed slowly in Castle Cowrie. Her aunts had found teachers for her who gave her instruction in the castle schoolroom, a dour, north-facing chamber with little to distract her outside the window.

Mam'selle was a dry old French prune who spoke and taught the French of yesteryear, and made a strange rustling noise when she moved, as if her bloomers were made of leaves. Nevertheless, she had managed to teach Marie to speak passable French, because learning French was less boring than not learning French.

Another woman, known as her governess because the Aunts liked the sound of it, but really the local Church of Scotland vicar's wife who had been a teacher, came and taught her English, mathematics, history from *Our Island Story*, and even the rudiments of Latin. She roped in a friend of hers called Betty, also known as Mother Nature, to come and teach Marie about biology: pond life, flowers, trees, birds and beasties.

Marie was reasonably good at maths and French, wrote essays on *Alice's Adventures in Wonderland* and *The Hobbit*, and played solitary games punctuated by visits to the countryside for biological studies, and trips to the seaside to sample the bracing air and cold waters of the North Sea. She was allowed to ride a small pony which she loved very much. It belonged to the gardener's daughter who was now away in Edinburgh, so Marie could not completely call it hers. She was discouraged from riding it too much, because it gave the gardener extra work.

She also read a great deal, not just to pass the time but because she loved to sink herself into a book. The castle's library was classically well stocked for some bygone Edwardian child: George Macdonald, Rudyard Kipling, Henty, Charlotte Yonge, Captain Marryat, E. Nesbit, Lewis Carroll and Edward Lear. There were the *Red, Yellow, Blue* and *Green Books of Fairy Stories* and *The Golden Treasury*. There were more modern authors too, intended for grown-ups, that she had begun to read: the eerie Algernon Blackwood, Somerset Maugham and Kipling, M. R. James, Sapper, John Betjeman and a Scottish writer called Bruce Marshall.

She was nearly eleven now, and it was April again, with the almost unbelievable surprise of spring after a hard winter. Windows were left open, hyacinths wafted sudden drifts of sweetness and birds dodged like little dark punctuations in the white pages of the cherry blossom.

For some days, Marie had noticed the Aunts in a huddle talking darkly about something – it happened on several occasions, always stopping meaningfully when she came in. Such secretiveness had always been a feature of their relationship with her, so at first she had taken no notice. But at length she felt something special was up. When pressed, however, they frowned discouragingly and changed the subject. That was their way of saying it was something to do with her.

She noticed another thing. When the family went to church now, she was aware of a new interest in her presence. There would be a little stir when she came in. She had thought it might be the fact she was growing up, that she might even be growing pretty, but she wasn't altogether convinced by this explanation. Whatever it was, it seemed the Aunts noticed it too for they decided to worship in the castle chapel for a while.

'Why, Aunt?' asked Marie when they told her. She had enjoyed the variety provided by the church, even though some of the looks she had been getting seemed puzzling, uncomfortable.

'There are unfortunate elements there,' said Bertha. 'It is becoming increasingly vulgar.'

'We have such a pretty little chapel here,' twittered Claire. 'I always used to think it was the Grail Chapel when I was a little girl. I used to think I'd come in one day and see Sir Lancelot.'

Next day, Mr Brickville arrived on a flying visit, and there were three people talking earnestly and stopping meaningfully when she came in.

'My poor child,' Aunt Claire exclaimed once.

'Leave us, Marie,' said Aunt Bertha. 'Come in when you are called.'

'What on earth is going on, Nanny?' asked Marie.

'It is better not to ask, darling.'

'Give me some idea.'

'My poor Marie.'

'Something *is* going on.'

'I'll tell you this. But you must promise not to say.'

'I promise.'

'It's about your father.'

'Father? But ... I thought he was dead.'

'He is dead now. He was ... very ill...'

'Why did they tell me he was dead?'

'They were trying to spare you.'

'Did he suffer much?'

'I think he suffered dreadfully. He would not have wanted you to see him like that.'

'Poor Father.'

It was strange to hear about a father she did not know. Once she had thought she needed him, but it was too late now. She didn't really feel sad about his death. It was like someone else's father dying, not hers at all. A thought struck her.

'What was wrong with him, Nanny? Did he have bad blood? Was that what they were talking about? Did he die of bad blood?'

'I expect so, darling. Now you must forget about it. And forget I told you. All right? Mum's the word.'

'Yes, Nanny.'

Later the Aunts sent for Marie, looking grave as they greeted her round the table.

'We have news for you, Marie. You must prepare yourself,' said Aunt Bertha.

Marie knew what was coming and tried to look prepared.

'Your father is dead,' said Aunt Claire, tears running down her cheeks. 'Our nephew Giles is dead. The last of the Lavells.'

'I know he's dead, Aunt,' said Marie. 'I always understood so.'

'He has been dying for some years,' said Bertha. 'Now he is dead indeed.'

'Was he … very ill?'

'Very, very ill. He could not see you.'

'Oh,' said Marie, 'was he blind?'

'Blind … deaf … sick…' burst out Aunt Bertha. 'He could not live.'

'Ah,' said Marie. 'I'm sorry.'

'Sorry? Sorry?'

Aunt Bertha was going to say more, but Mr Brickville interrupted smoothly.

'Now you are going to be an heiress, my dear.'

'Not that there is anything left,' said Aunt Bertha.

'All gone … those lovely chateaux…' sniffed Claire.

'All that lovely fortune…' corrected Bertha

'That is not quite true,' said Mr Brickville. 'There is considerable

19

doubt in many people's minds – including the courts' – as to the legality of some of the appropriations. There is a residual estate, too, of your mother's. You are the one now. There will be papers to sign in due course. We have to keep you going.'

She thought it was a strange thing to say.

'Mr Brickville is going to see what he can do for us,' said Aunt Bertha.

'Thank God we have such a staunch friend. That will do now, Marie. You may go. Curtsey politely to Mr Brickville.'

Marie did as she was told, resenting the man all the more now she was going to be an heiress. She hadn't asked for him. He was a lawyer.

'Goodbye, Mr Brickville. And thank you.'

'We shall see what can be done, Marie,' said Mr Brickville, rubbing his chin thoughtfully as he looked at her. 'It may take time, mind. Patience is the thing. Wind and tide, wind and tide. Run along now.'

He had a strangely metallic smell she had not noticed before. She thought it was the smell of money.

* * *

A week or so later, the Aunts summoned her again.

'School,' said Aunt Bertha. 'We have come to a decision.'

'O goody, when can I start? Does it mean Mam'selle will stop teaching me? Will I wear a uniform? Can I have a satchel? And walk with the village children?'

'You will start school at the beginning of autumn term in September which is the usual time to enter. Mademoiselle and the governess will terminate their duties forthwith. You will indeed wear a uniform. But surely you did not think we would allow you to attend the village school? That is a disgraceful idea.'

'Sorry, Aunt. But where will I go? There's no other school nearby.'

'You won't be going nearby. You will be going to a convent recommended by the Abbess. It is on the coast, I believe, some two hundred miles away. The air is bracing.'

'Two hundred miles? But how will I get there every day?'

'Come, come, child. You won't be going every day. You will be boarding. It is a boarding school.'

The full enormity of the news sank in, slowly.

'A boarding school? Where I'll sleep?'

'Boarding means a school where you live day and night. That is the usual definition of the term.'

'But I don't want to go away, Great-Aunts,' said Marie. 'I am very happy here, thank you. Though I am grateful to you for thinking of it.'

'It is not a suggestion, Marie. It is an order,' said Bertha. 'It is time you mixed with girls of your own age. Your Aunt Claire and I are no companions for a growing girl.'

'But what about Nanny? She's a companion. Can she come with me to school?'

'Certainly not. What would Nanny do at school? Nanny has been to school.'

'She could help with my clothes and things.'

'The whole purpose of going to school is to learn to fend for oneself, Marie; fend, I say. Not whistle up Nanny when things go wrong.'

Marie's lip was trembling.

'What sort of … things go wrong…?'

'You will start in the autumn.'

21

* * *

It was not uncommon to send girls to boarding school at the tender age of eleven or twelve, or even earlier, at that time, though it argued either a premature independence of spirit on the part of the child, or a certain austerity in the parent.

In nearly every establishment, particularly the convents, the food was bleak, the dormitories cheerless, the nuns stern to the point of mania.

A proximity to the sea was particularly sought out by these places since it ensured a healthy air – though so much of it was encouraged to blow through the open windows that it was a miracle so few of the children developed serious respiratory infections. St Saviour's was fairly typical of such establishments, though its emphasis on fresh air and hardiness was perhaps more rigorously applied than in some of its southern counterparts. In winter, the windows were left open as they had been in summer. Ice formed in the ewers that stood on the long white washstand which stretched down the centre of the room. Each bed had sheets, of course, and three red blankets that looked warmer than they were.

The convent that had been selected for Marie was in other respects no different from the general rule. It was a large, beastly sort of building, erected in the mid-nineteenth century and situated on a cliff overlooking the North Sea near Scarborough. Aunt Claire delivered her to the place, spent a few minutes talking in a low voice to the Mother Superior, kissed Marie perfunctorily – admonishing her to be an outstanding example to those around her – and disappeared down the steps into the waiting limousine.

A nun with a face like a lozenge, introduced as Sister Veronica, took Marie by the wrist and led her through a dining hall that smelt of floor polish and cooking grease – when she came to taste the food it was apparent that the one might well have doubled for the other. From here, she led her up a great flight of stairs, not offering any help with her night-case (the trunk with all her school things had been left for the porter), to a dormitory where twenty bleak little beds with red blankets lay stiffly with their heads to the wall.

The sister pointed at one and indicated it was for Marie.

'Leave your cases now, child. You may unpack later. I will take you down now to meet your school fellows.'

She led Marie back down the stairs to the assembly hall where some ninety desks sat to attention in front of a raised dais with a piano on it. Some of the desks were already occupied (though the majority of the girls, she was told, would be arriving later). Sister Veronica clapped her hands.

'Girls. This is Marie Sinclair, a new girl like the rest of you.'

The new girls stared miserably up at her and Marie stared miserably back. She had been trying to suppress her tears all day and she knew she wouldn't be able to hold them back very much longer, but it'd be awful to cry when everyone was looking at you. Sister Veronica pushed her in the direction of a desk at which sat a small, dark-haired child with a pretty little pouting face. Marie noticed that while the desks were separate, each pair was joined together by a single form.

'This is Harriet, your form-mate. Harriet, this is Marie. You will be sitting together this term. Don't let yourselves down, don't let each other down and don't let the school down. And now I must get back to Mother Superior. There'll be someone along in a minute to tell you all about St Saviour's.'

The nun scuttled off. Marie opened her desk, stuck her head inside and started to cry. She felt utterly helpless and desolate. She thought of her nanny and cried some more, remembering how Nanny herself had sobbed when she had said goodbye.

'It won't be long, my love,' Nanny had said, snuffling like Aunt Bertha's Pekinese. 'You'll see. You'll be back at home in time for Christmas before you can say bangsmashums.'

Bangsmashums came from a game you played with a sixpence that Nanny had taught her, called Up Jenkins. The thought of Up Jenkins momentarily cheered her. She felt something plucking at her sleeve. It was the small, dark-haired girl, Harriet.

'I say, don't blub,' said Harriet. 'I did at first, you know. But when you arrived and started blubbing, I felt better. I expect you will too when somebody else arrives and starts blubbing. Don't you think this is the most awful place in the world? I'm going to escape at my earliest possible convenience.'

Marie liked Harriet. There was something brave and good about her, the way Nanny had described the Red Cross Knight.

'Do you know how to play Up Jenkins?' Marie asked her, blowing her nose and mopping her eyes in the wrong order.

'Can't say I do,' said Harriet, 'but anything's better than sitting here waiting for the next new bug to come in blubbing. Mind you, it'd be awful if they came in skipping and smiling because then you'd feel worse.'

As it happened a large, slightly podgy girl with fair hair and close-together eyes came in just then doing exactly that, escorted by another nun whom Harriet said was called Sister Julian.

'Girls, this is Teresa, another new girl like you. But Teresa has two sisters already in the school. Her mother and her grandmother came here too. So she's hardly a stranger, are you Teresa?'

'No, Sister Julian,' smirked Teresa, and proceeded to make the little girl she was directed to share with change seats so she could be nearer the radiator.

'What a pill!' said Harriet. 'I feel worse.'

'So do I,' said Marie, suddenly remembering her twizzler, the piece of satin cloth she used to rub between finger and thumb as a baby and which had always been a source of support at home in moments of stress. Aunt Claire, who had supervised her wardrobe, had made her leave twizzler behind, on the grounds that she would be teased.

'But don't let's blub, though,' said Harriet quickly. 'Teresa will see us and smirk some more. Tell me about this Up Jenkins.'

'I'd need a sixpence to show you how to play it, and I haven't got one. It's no good.'

The Mother Superior had told her that no money was the rule of the school.

'I have,' said Harriet. 'Here.'

So Marie explained that one person had to hide a sixpence in between her fingers, and when the other player said, say, 'Five Bar Gates', she had to bring her hands up from below the desk and put them up like gates on the surface, with the palms facing in so the other person couldn't decide where the coin was hidden. If her opponent couldn't decide exactly where the sixpence was, she could then use one of the various other commands.

There was 'Lobster Pots' – both hands resting on the tips of the fingers and jigging up and down – or 'Coffee Pots' – one set of fingers resting on top of the other with pointing motions to left and right. There was 'Butterflies' – a crafty flapping of the hands taking especial care not to let slip the trembling sixpence.

And finally there was 'Bangsmashums' – a straight palms down slap on to the surface whereupon, if the coin was heard to strike the wood, it could help the opponent guess its exact location.

Harriet proved surprisingly handy with a sixpence and there was much laughter as Marie explained the intricacies of the game. Some of the other children started to crowd around, but Teresa stayed aloof, looking thoughtful.

When Sister Veronica brought in the next new girl, Teresa put her hand up.

'Yes, Teresa? What is it?'

'Someone's playing with money, Sister Veronica.'

'Money? There is no money in the school. It is a rule. A rule of the school.'

All eyes turned on Harriet and Marie.

'Who is playing with money? What possible games can be played with money?'

'It's those two, Sister Veronica. I think they may be gambling.'

* * *

Throughout the rest of an uncomfortable term, Harriet and Marie remained close friends. The nuns, of course, did their best to keep them apart, and Teresa always seemed to be around spying on them, although they tied her shoes together in the refectory and put a grass snake in her clothes locker to try and discourage her. Harriet was good with creepy-crawly things. She told Marie that her parents were actually divorced which was a frightful blight, and made her something of a dangerous freak. Marie hadn't yet been able to analyse her own freakishness but she knew it was there all the same.

Winter was late that year. Early November was mild but then, around the fifteenth, the weather suddenly turned, bringing clear blue skies and a north wind straight from the Arctic. The cold froze the water in the ewers in the middle of the dormitory. Legs turned blue on the sports field. The school cook who had been hired because she couldn't cook (said Harriet) provided what she called 'cold weather food' which turned out to be burnt stew with globular clusters of fat and gristle in a sort of gelid brown gravy.

Even so, when the end of term finally came in sight – the nuns permitted an austere degree of Christmas jollity, and the last week of term featured a school play, a carol service and even mince pies for tea – Marie found, to her surprise, that she almost didn't want to go home. Christmas spirit at the castle was kept on a low burner, with Christmas dinner being the nadir of awfulness. The aunts were more interested in their food as they gobbled down the feast, but felt duty bound to ask Marie questions whose answers were of no interest to them. There were long intervals of succulent absence of dialogue, punctuated by Aunt Claire's rowdy digestive system.

It would be good to see Nanny again, though.

'Where are you going...?' asked Harriet. 'Anywhere frantically wonderful?'

'Just home, I think,' Marie said. 'What about you?'

'I'm going to New York to see my mother. She's married to this businessman.'

'Lucky you,' said Marie. 'I'm just going back to the Aunts. It's a bit drear.'

'Drear to say the least.'

'Nanny's all right, though.'

'But Nannies only go so far. Why don't you come with me to New York?'

'They wouldn't let me.'

'You haven't asked.'

'You don't know them. Their idea of a good time is giving me a bad one.'

'Try them. Go on. You'd like New York. They have wizard ice creams and things. Tell you what, I'll get my mother to write to them. She's not a bad old witch.'

But even Harriet was mystified when her mother, who was usually indulgent, failed to respond to her daughter's prompting. They both cried a little when they said goodbye to each other, and Marie returned to the castle with low expectations of entertainment, sadly missing her friend.

Predictably enough, Aunt Bertha received her gravely and remarked that she hoped she would keep quiet as Aunt Claire was indisposed with gout.

There were bright features, though. It was good to be in her own bedroom again and to be able to tell Nanny all about the awfulness of the school and the wonderfulness of Harriet. Nanny said there was going to be goose for Christmas dinner which at least was a change, and real silver sixpences in the Christmas pudding which Marie could keep. And one of the few neighbours was having a children's party in their castle to which Marie had not been invited. Children's parties were the worst things of all. So, though inevitably cast as a social outsider, Marie was very happy to fulfil that role.

Nanny was cautious about Harriet.

'Now, you don't want to get setting too much store by that one, you know, dearie,' said Nanny, looking thoughtful. 'There's no knowing how things might turn out. You know what it says in the hymn book, "Our earthly friends may fail us and change with changing years".'

'Harriet won't fail me, Nanny. She's decent. She's not the sort.'

'I don't know, dearie, I'm sure. No doubt she means well.'

'Anyway, *you* haven't failed me, Nanny.'

'That I haven't and nor will I. But even Nanny can't go on for ever. You've got to learn to be self-sufficient in this world.'

Marie didn't like to think of Nanny not going on for ever, so she reverted to her theme.

'And the Man in the Wall hasn't failed me.'

'You still talking to that old stone? Don't tell your aunt. Funny girl. You're too old for all that. Still you always were fanciful…'

It was true that the Man in the Wall had been dropped by her for Harriet, but passing down the book-lined corridors of the library at a loss for something to do – it was a rainy new year when it arrived – Marie found herself once more staring at the strange configuration of lines that flawed the masonry.

How strangely like a face it seemed: goat-like, eyes narrowed, with pointed ears.

'Hello, Man in the Wall,' she said to the stone. 'I expect you missed me last term.'

The stone said nothing but continued to gaze at her through narrowed lids.

'It would be nice if we could be friends again and you would talk to me like in the old days. Harriet's away in New York, you see, and I don't suppose there'll be much else to do these holidays…'

She had learned long ago that the Man in the Wall never replied in words, but if you emptied your mind and allowed your thoughts to run on a loose rein, you could start to see a whole jumble of visions and notions that seemed to come from somewhere outside you.

She spent much of her time in the library over the course of the holiday, ignoring the pale winter sunshine and the snowdrops that sprouted in the grass among the damp hedgerows, and lost herself instead in banks of misty thought.

Her Aunt Bertha expressed no more than routine caution about eyestrain – caution was the nearest she ever got to approval – and hazarded that school might have inculcated some sense of scholarship in her niece. But the Man in the Wall was the kind of instructor that showed Marie colours she had never seen and feelings she did not know – experiences which would be of no possible use in any syllabus.

One day, as she was sitting in the library as usual, with a book called *Great Cities of the World* open in front of her – she'd got it out to look up New York so as to be near Harriet and was now floating pleasantly along a great avenue between skyscrapers – she felt an inexplicable stab of pain right in her centre, accompanied by sensations of the utmost dread and depression.

She almost called out, the feeling was so intense; whether it came from mind or body she could not determine. However, there was no doubt about the fact that she was sitting upon something warm and sticky that turned out to her horror to be blood.

The Man in the Wall gave no indication of concern.

She rushed in a panic to the lavatory and discovered she was bleeding. She thought that she was probably going to die. However, after a while she decided that she wasn't bleeding fast enough to die immediately, and cleaned herself up as best she could, putting her handkerchief inside her knickers to stem the flow.

It seemed to her that she must have done something terrible to bring on such a bleeding. She searched for a reason. Certainly some of the sensations she experienced under the gaze of the Man in the Wall had been oddly exciting, particularly when she had thought of

Harriet. It had made her feel warm and wriggly between the legs. Perhaps these were the thoughts that Mother Superior called lusts of the flesh, but they hadn't seemed very fleshly, not, anyway, as fleshly as Dawn the kitchen maid who had bosoms the size of butter churns and a roving eye and was no better than she should be, according to Nanny, but she didn't walk around bleeding like a plane tree.

Then she thought of the phrase that Aunt Bertha had used so long ago in the garden to the Abbess.

'I'd always be worried about the bad blood coming out.'

That must be it. Her aunt's worries were well founded. The blood was bad – it even smelt funny. Whatever happened, she had to conceal it, otherwise – the way they had talked about it – they might send her away somewhere for good because it was so terrible.

She crept to her room – Nanny was visiting an old friend in the village, thank goodness – and changed her skirt and knickers, soaking the blood away in cold water and preparing a fib about falling in the wet grass down by the lake.

She rinsed out the handkerchief in the same manner and put another one in its place. The flow of blood seemed to have slowed a little.

Then she lay down carefully on her bed and cried.

* * *

As it happened, no one guessed that there was anything the matter, though Nanny did say something about getting the roses back in her cheeks and took her out next day for a walk round the lake to look at the coot chicks.

Marie was still convinced that at any moment she would spout

31

blood like a fountain and keel over and die, and the handkerchief made it difficult to walk, but she waddled round bravely and Nanny didn't notice.

And next day the bleeding stopped.

It was towards the end of the holiday that she was summoned to Aunt Bertha's sitting-room where she found the two old women looking grave. Aunt Bertha had a telegram in her hand. She told Marie to sit down. Claire was dabbing her eyes.

'Child,' Bertha said, 'brace yourself.'

Marie looked at her with a sort of slow dread of she knew not what gathering under her belly-button.

'Your friend Harriet.'

'Yes, Aunt Bertha.'

'Harriet has had an accident.'

'Accident?'

Why should they tell Aunt Bertha? Harriet was always having accidents. Her knees were always scratched and bruised. Her hands were always scarred. Harriet went too fast.

'Accident, Aunt Bertha? Is she all right?'

'I'm afraid not, my child. Harriet is dead.'

'Dead?' repeated Marie. 'She can't be dead.'

'Nonetheless, I tell you she is, child. Do not contradict.'

'There must be a mistake.'

Harriet could not possibly be dead. She was so full of life. Marie could see her now – sparkling brown eyes peeping out of a fringe of dark hair, skinny legs poised to dart towards some new escapade.

Escapade was one of Harriet's favourite words. She could hear her now: 'Come on Mary-Mary. What about this for an escapade?'

'She was knocked over by a car, Marie,' said Aunt Bertha, more gently. 'She darted into the road without looking. They drive on the other side of the road there. There was nothing anyone could do.'

It was some five minutes before Marie could take it in. The only friend of her own age she'd ever had was dead. She'd darted into a new escapade all right. She'd darted right out of St Saviour's and out of everything. Marie felt almost cross with her while at same time succumbing to the most dreadful guilt and grief. She too wanted to escape out of everything.

* * *

For three days she felt – and was – violently sick. Nanny tried to console her.

'Don't take on so, darling. She's with the angels now.'

'Why are the angels so selfish? They keep taking everyone. Mummy, Daddy, and now … I hate angels.'

'Shhh. Don't say that. Angels are kind and good.'

'They can't be good if they've taken Harriet. Why don't they take me too? I don't want to be here any more.'

'Marie!' Nanny sounded shocked and angry. 'Never say that. I shan't be your friend if you say that again. There are other people who care about you.'

'Who?'

'Your aunts care about you in their way.'

'They only care about me because it's a way of caring about themselves.'

'Well, there's me, then. What would I do without you?'

Marie hugged her. 'Sorry, Nanny. But there's only you. And the way the angels are, how do I know they're not coming for you next? It's too many eggs in one basket.'

They both laughed.

'That's better,' said Nanny. Now I don't want to hear any more talk like that.'

Marie suddenly blurted out what had been troubling her since she'd heard of the accident.

'I think it was me,' she said, starting to cry again. 'It was my fault.'

'You? How could it have been you?'

'Bad blood,' said Marie. 'She was my friend. I killed her with my bad blood.'

'Such nonsense. You couldn't have done it. Bad blood's just a phrase. It doesn't work like that.'

'It wasn't a phrase I had. I was having it when Harriet got knocked down. It was because she was my friend. To punish me. It was my fault.'

'You were having it? What d'you mean?'

'It was coming out of me. Bad blood ... wickedness. My wickedness. But I don't know what I've done.'

'My poor child,' said Nanny. 'That's not bad blood. Do they teach you nothing at school?'

'They teach us to feel wicked.'

'That's not what I meant. Oh dear. I'm such a silly. I should have told you, but somehow ... Oh, never mind. What you had was, well, because you're growing up.'

'Growing up? I'm only twelve!'

'You're becoming a woman, my darling.'

Nanny told her the facts of life as best as she could. Marie suddenly remembered little huddles of older girls at school, giggling and looking furtive. So that was what it was all about. She realised now that she'd had nothing whatever to do with Harriet's death.

It made her feel a little better, but no less lonely. At the back of her mind, though, in spite of what Nanny had said, she still had the feeling of being tainted. Why had Harriet's mother not wanted her to come to New York? Why did she never seem to get asked to the children's parties she heard the other girls at school talking about?

'What's wrong with me, Nanny?' she asked.

'There's nothing wrong with you, darling. It's people who are wrong…'

But somehow Marie had the feeling there was more to it than that. The other thing was, the Man in the Wall had gone. It wasn't like the other times when he'd vanish and then reappear after a month or two. This time she knew he was gone for good.

* * *

For the next few years, Marie kept herself to herself. The other girls at school left her alone; it is the child who desperately wants to join in who generally gets persecuted. The great school weapon, sending to Coventry, has no effect on the solitary. Marie did not want to be popular; to have been one of the gang would have been a travesty. One or two schoolmates – usually girls new to the place – would try and strike up a friendship, but Marie discouraged it. It would only go wrong.

As for the nuns, they only bothered you about lessons and religion and, as she was good at the former and enjoyed going to the ugly little chapel because it allowed her to think in peace, she was generally considered to be a good pupil. She had developed a talent for painting which excused her self-sufficiency.

Not that she felt self-sufficient. She knew that what she needed was

Harriet back alive again. She built Harriet up into something even Harriet had never been.

She wanted someone to love her. Not that grubby love that little groups of girls snickered over when the nuns weren't about, but love how deep, how broad, how far; the marriage of true minds; a love that would excuse, and unify and transcend. But if she could not have that cake, she certainly could not bear to survive on callow bread. Meanwhile she painted, and waited for school to end.

The holidays passed in the same way. Solitary excursions with her easel, or painting in the studio that she had been allowed to set up in the attic over her bedroom or reading art history in the library. This drew no adverse criticism from the Aunts who had their own troubles to contend with. Claire was going deaf and Bertha's hip was seizing up. It was inevitable that their control would slacken, but it gave way completely when Bertha had a heart attack after Marie's sixteenth-birthday lunch, which they held in July on her return from school for the summer holidays.

Bertha had always tended to indulge in the pleasures of the table. The doctor had indicated to her that she was badly overweight, which was putting extra strain on her hips, but the heart attack was unexpected and, as it turned out, fatal. Bertha lingered for a few days then died without regaining consciousness.

There was a funeral in the castle chapel to which various retainers and a few local dignitaries came. Marie did not feel any great sense of loss at the departure of the hard old woman.

'You must be brave,' said an old general who lived nearby. 'Chin up, chest out. Don't be upset.'

She was so surprised at being addressed by anybody but the immediate household that she committed an indiscretion.

'It's all right. I'm not upset at all, thank you,' she said.

The general looked at her oddly. Later she heard him telling someone of the exchange.

'Extraordinary girl,' said the general. 'But you have to look at the family. She's a Lavell, you know. The shame…'

Marie was familiar with shame. She knew it as she knew the particular cold, stony, rainy smell of the castle. It was always there. But Lavell was another matter. She had overheard the name in her aunts' conversations but hadn't known it referred to her.

One of the guests was the thin-faced lawyer, Hubert Brickville, who always cropped up on matters of family importance. He spent some time afterwards with Aunt Claire and went away in a black car. Aunt Claire sent for her that evening. Sitting in the drawing room, dressed in black, she seemed to have put on some of the authority that Bertha had wielded. She was also eating chocolate, non-stop.

'Sit down, child,' she said, 'and listen. I can't hear what you say so there's no point in talking. Now your Aunt Bertha's gone, I suppose I should be the one to hedge you round and see you don't get into trouble. But I'm no good at that sort of thing. I'm not bossy and I can't learn to be at my age. I know that Bertha might have seemed a trifle harsh to you. She was, for that matter, more than a trifle harsh to me. But she cared for the family, d'you see? Indeed, it could be said she held us together by sheer will, my dear, in the days of our disgrace.'

'What disgrace, Aunt?'

'Don't interrupt. I can't hear.' Aunt Claire ran a finger round her teeth to get out a piece of one of the stickier chocolates. 'Where was I?'

'Disgrace.'

'It's the name. Your name.'

'Marie?'

'No, of course not. Your other name.'

'What about it?'

'It's not really Sinclair. We used that because we are Sinclairs and it was easier for you to be too. But you are really Lavell. Your father was Lavell. A great name. But now … unsuitable.'

'Unsuitable?'

'I mean that Lavell is not well thought of at the moment, but it will pass. Everything passes.'

'Is your name well thought of? Sinclair?'

'Yes, I should think so.'

'Well, I don't care if they don't think well of Lavell. That's their problem. I couldn't care less. I shall be Lavell.'

'Your Aunt Bertha felt the shame very keenly. I felt it keenly too, but I never had the stamina. It all seems a long time ago. You will learn about it, child, but don't be in a hurry. When you are eighteen, that is what Bertha said. Meanwhile, enjoy yourself. You are young and in health. Attend to your studies. You have some talent at painting, I believe. I envy that. I never had any talent whatsoever, unless it was for chocolates. Bertha was unsympathetic on that score. You may kiss me. Hand me that box of Suchard before you go.' Later, in Nanny's sitting room, Marie asked what her aunt had been talking about.

'Come on, Nanny. You must know.'

But Nanny shook her head. 'It's something I promised your aunt,' she said. 'And especially now she's dead. I couldn't go back on it. It's a family matter. Nothing you've done, my precious. Don't bother your head about it now. When you're eighteen. That's when she said. I say, what's in a name? A rose by any other name would smell as sweet. And you are a rose, a lovely rose, my darling.'

Nanny was looking older too. There was a greyness about her skin, though the eyes were still as bright as ever. As Marie looked at her, a shadow seemed to pass across her face and she noticed the work-worn hands clench a little.

'You're all right, aren't you, Nanny?'

''Course I am. A little tired, that's all. It's just you and your questions. When you're eighteen. Time enough till then.'

Marie prayed for Nanny that night, although she knew she was really praying for herself as well.

'Dear Gentle Jesus. Make Nanny be all right. Let me die before Nanny does. Let me know what the secret is. Don't let me have spots or unsightly blemishes…'

* * *

As it happened time passed, and the last two items of her prayer were answered.

She did not have spots. Indeed her complexion seemed to glow ever more blemishless, and her mirror indicated to her that her general appearance was at least satisfactory.

She stood naked in front of the mirror in the castle one morning and examined herself – something the nuns at school had expressly warned the girls against. They were even made to bath in their bathing knickers – the girls as well as the nuns.

'Love of self is unclean,' said Sister Bridget. 'Filthy thoughts can come jumping out of a mirror. Leave your body to the eye of Heaven.'

But Marie liked showing herself to herself. It was as if, just for a moment, she had that loving counterpart she so longed for.

So here she was again, she thought, loving counterpart with such shiny, bright hair and bright pale-blue irises; slim waist, flat tummy, long legs joined at the top with a little sealing of hair; breasts a little too big for the slender frame; anemone-pink nipples that stiffened a little as she looked at them as though they had a life of their own and might trap a passing plankton. She ran her hands over herself, touching her secretness, anticipating the lover but on the look-out for devils.

I'll paint myself, she thought. Self-portrait. Nude. That'd show the Mother Superior.

After breakfast, she lugged an old full-length mirror from one of the attics into the studio, locked the door and took off her clothes. It was a sunny day. The studio was pleasantly warm. She pirouetted in front of the mirror.

She felt unspeakably wicked. Devils were popping out of the glass like squibs from a bonfire. She adjusted the easel and started sketching. Around mid-morning there was a knock on the door.

'Marie? Marie. What are you doing?'

Her heart turned a cartwheel in her mouth. Had she locked the door? Yes, the handle was turning vainly.

'It's all right,' she shouted, struggling into her dress. 'It's a secret. Coming!'

She turned her sketches over on their faces and substituted on the easel a self-portrait she'd put aside, of her face only.

Nanny was reproachful. 'Locking me out like that. Whatever next.'

'It's a surprise, Nanny. Your birthday's coming up, remember?'

She felt guilty about deceiving her old friend.

'You shouldn't be wasting your time on presents for me. You should be out in the sunshine. Get some fresh air in your lungs. It's springtime. You shouldn't waste the spring. When you're as old as me you'll realise how few there are.'

'There's plenty more for you, Nanny. But all right. I'll stop. Only if you'll come with me, though.'

'I ... won't, my dear, if you don't mind. I've got a touch of indigestion. It's nothing really. But you go. It'll do me good to think of you cutting your capers. Off you go now.'

Marie left the castle grounds and walked down by the river, through a wood, underneath eaves of sweet chestnut blossom. The sun was so strong that she lay down beside a pond in a clearing, kicked off her shoes, and studied her reflection in the water.

'Loving counterparts,' she said, 'you who know me so well, now come out of the water and embrace me upon the grassy bank.'

Sister Bridget had not specified as to whether devils might come out of rivers as well as looking glasses, but, whatever the origin, Marie was startled by a pleasant voice that now spoke from somewhere very nearby.

'I'm not sure that I qualify for the first part of your invocation. I will study to become so. But I should certainly like to take you up on the last section.'

Marie sprang up, more in confusion than alarm – the voice, which had an American accent, had sounded so good-natured. At the same time, she could not help laughing.

She turned in astonishment and saw a young man watching her from the shelter of a willow tree. He had his back against it and his legs were crossed and his arms folded as if he had been there for some time. She sprang to her feet, blushing.

'Who are you?' she asked. 'Have you been there long? How dare you spy on me? Why have you come all the way from America?'

'One question at a time,' the boy laughed.

He had a cheerful, roundish face with a fine, straight nose, reddish hair and browny-green eyes. Although she put on a stern face, she could not altogether feel angry with him.

'My name,' he went on, after a charitable pause which allowed her to catch her breath and compose herself, 'my name is The Great Collapso. When I appear, people go weak at the knees. Who are you?'

'I am Impervious,' she said. 'Now answer the second question.'

'I was there just ten seconds,' he replied.

She knew he wasn't lying, and felt better about it. Five minutes of being observed would have been shaming. He had looked so settled under that tree. He read the relief in her face and was encouraged to give her the third answer.

'And I dared spy on you because I thought you were quite the most beautiful girl I'd ever seen.'

No one had said anything like that to her before. It was true, a girl at school – one of the new girls, fattish with glasses and no friends – had, when Marie had shown some kindly interest, developed a crush on her and told her she was beautiful; and the gardener's boy had taken to mooning around with his wheelbarrow early in the morning, gazing at the window of her bedroom, but this was something altogether different.

She blushed again, felt like looking down, but instead gazed upon the youth intently.

'I know who you are,' she said. 'You are Mephistopheles. Don't try to deny it. You've jumped out of *Dr Faustus*.'

'Right,' he said. 'That's just who I am. And I have come all the way from America just to see you. Now you have conjured me up. What is your wish?'

She thought for a moment. Then she surprised herself. 'I should like you to fall in love with me.'

But the young man was not in the least surprised. 'Nothing simpler,' he said. 'There. It is done. I love you with every fibre of my being.'

She looked at him closely. Was he teasing her? 'Do you worship the ground I tread on?' she enquired.

He looked at her feet. A daisy had somehow contrived to peep up between her toes. 'Yes,' he said. 'As a matter of fact, I do.'

'Excellent.' She clapped her hands. 'And now, Mephistopheles. I should like you to conjure a picnic so we can take refreshment here beside the pool, and you can teach me the language of butterflies.'

He bowed solemnly. 'Your wish is my command.' Turning, he ran off lightly between the trees.

She closed her eyes and felt the breeze play with her hair and the sun with her skin. In what seemed a moment, the boy was back with a fishing-basket.

'See,' he said. 'Refreshment as ordered. French bread, tomatoes, cheese, cucumber, oranges and wine. Oh, and chocolate biscuits.'

It was too extraordinary that he should have produced such a feast. She began half to believe that he really was some kind of supernatural agent. Well-stocked baskets didn't materialise just like that.

He spread a rug on the daisies and they sat down. He opened the bottle of wine and gave her a mug.

'Meursault,' he said. 'Only the best. There'll be the devil to pay if they find out I've taken it.'

Again she couldn't tell if he was being serious. She wasn't very used to wine, but she knew that this was the best. It was absolutely delicious.

'It is nectar,' she said.

'We call it something different where I come from.'

'Devil's brew?' she asked.

'Of course. French bread?'

She wanted to ask him where he really came from, and what an American was doing in Fife. But she didn't want to spoil the magic by saying something too down to earth.

They drank, they ate, they watched the butterflies, they spoke to the butterflies who seemed to understand perfectly, she told him something of her life, and they talked energetically about what afterwards seemed nothing but at the time seemed the most interesting things in the world. It became very hot and she began to feel drowsy.

A fat fish flopped in the water. A little dust-devil of midges swirled about among the shadows of the bushes at the water's edge. A sun-drunk peacock butterfly, freshly awakened, flapped lop-sidedly over a bank of periwinkles to her left. She closed her eyes again and felt the sun burnishing her hair.

He was indeed like some spirit, she thought, only not a bad one. Nothing so beautiful could be possibly be bad. She hadn't told her aunt that she would be out to lunch but these days no one seemed to care what she did. Aunt Claire would lunch alone reading her *Lives of the Saints*; she would read them anyway whether Marie were there or not.

When she opened her eyes, he was standing there still looking at her. She smiled and closed her eyes again. She must have slept for some time because, when she awoke, the sun had swung across the glade and the shadows had crept out of the other edge of the lakeside underwood. The midges had disappeared. And so had the young man. She sat up in a panic.

'Mephistopheles,' she called, feeling slightly ridiculous because that couldn't possibly be his real name, but she didn't know any other.

'Mephistopheles.'

But there was no answer. A feeling of absolute despair swept over her as she realised she might never see him again. She rushed to the edge of the trees and called to him once more. He wasn't there. He had vanished into thin air, leaving only the tartan rug on which she had slept. That at least was a comfort. Devils didn't leave their rugs and nor did young men who intended to disappear for ever.

As she walked back towards it, however, she saw something white lying on it that she had missed in her distraction. It was a note. She picked it up feverishly, squinting her eyes to read in the brilliant sunlight.

It said: 'Didn't like to wake you. Had to go. Meet me next Sunday, same time, same place! Love, Mephistopheles. P.S. Bring the rug.'

She walked back full of the most unaccustomed happiness. The first thing she proposed to do was to go up and tell Nanny about the strange encounter in the wood, but, arriving home, she found the house in turmoil.

* * *

Aunt Claire, during her solitary lunch, had choked on a piece of steak and had expired at the table, alone, in the middle of the life of St Rosa of Lima. She had been found dead by the gardener's wife who helped out at mealtimes. The doctor and the ambulance had come and taken her away. Now the gardener's wife was weeping and Nanny was in a bate.

'Really, Marie,' she said, 'going off like that. You should have told us. There's a pretty pickle here. Your poor aunt was quite vexed at having to eat alone. I don't say it brought on a choking fit but it may have made her snatch at her food. And if you'd been there you could've thumped her on the back or something. It's too bad!'

Nanny wasn't looking too good herself. Her face was yellowish under the powder she'd hurriedly dabbed on, and her eyes were red, like little cherries in a cupcake, thought Marie. She didn't feel all that upset at Aunt Claire's demise – they had not been close and there was something slightly repulsive about her greed – but she did regret not having been there to help her. It was bad luck on the old girl. She was much more worried about Nanny. She couldn't manage without Nanny.

'I'm sorry, Nanny. But honestly she never seemed to notice much if I was there or not. Anyway, you look awful. You shouldn't have got up.'

'Someone had to hold the fort if someone else is gadding around,' she grumbled. 'Anyway, I've sent for Mr Brickville, not that I like him but there you are, beggars can't be choosers. Mr Brickville will do the necessary. That's solicitors for you.'

Marie helped her back to her room.

'What you need's a holiday, Nanny. When did you ever have a holiday? I shall be rich now Aunt has died. I'll take you for a holiday.'

'Don't count on being rich, lovely. Those two old girls were living on capital. It's expensive running a place like this. They only inherited money. They never made any. They were too interested in the...' she paused.

'In what?'

'Oh, nothing. Shouldn't speak ill of the dead.'

'In what, Nanny? What were they interested in?'

'In the problem. They were too interested in the problem to think of a solution.'

'In what problem, Nanny? What was the problem?'

But Nanny wouldn't talk about it any more. She said she was tired and it was time Marie went and shouldered her responsibilities.

Marie didn't think now was the time to tell her about the young man and the picnic. Aunt Claire's death had cast a shadow over the encounter. Perhaps he really was a devil. And yet she still felt buoyed up by the meeting. It was as though everything in the world was now sharper and finer, as if she'd spent all her life twiddling at binoculars and now at last, miraculously they had come into focus.

She kissed Nanny on one of her wrinkles and went off to her responsibilities, shoulders at the ready.

* * *

She had never had to deal with Mr Brickville by herself before, there had always been an aunt to give him sherry in the library; but now she found herself in the front line.

Mr Brickville arrived at seven o'clock, and she took him into the library and pressed the sherry upon him. She splashed it a bit but he didn't seem to mind. She gave herself one too. Mr Brickville looked slightly pained.

Looking slightly pained was Mr Brickville's stock in trade. He looked slightly pained at parties, at weddings, commissioning oaths, drawing up wills and winding up estates. He probably looked slightly pained when he was having a pee. He slept looking pained. If he ever made love, you knew how he would look.

'A tragic occurrence,' he said, looking slightly pained. 'I understand you were not present?'

'It was such a lovely day,' she said, blushing and feeling guilty, 'I was out walking and completely forgot the time.'

47

'I see,' he said. 'Quite so. Walking ... with anyone?'

She tried very hard not to blush again. He might be a dry old stick but he was no fool. That sharp right-angled triangle of a nose of his had an instinct for human weakness.

'No,' she replied. 'I was walking alone.'

It was strictly true.

'She walked alone,' he repeated. 'I hope that is sensible. There are some funny people about. We must look after you now. You are in a small way an heiress. In a small way. Or you will be when you inherit. You are, I believe, seventeen?'

He knew perfectly well she was seventeen. He was the family solicitor, wasn't he?

'Yes,' she said. 'Seventeen and a bit.'

Then he said something that took her completely by surprise.

'Until you are twenty-one, you are my ward.'

'Your ward? I didn't know that.'

'It wasn't necessary for you to know.'

She didn't like the idea of being his ward at all. She looked at him with new eyes.

'You mean ... you're my guardian?'

'Precisely.'

In the books she'd read, guardians seemed generally to have a bad press. In fact, looking at him now, she thought Mr Brickville perfectly fitted the category. He was cool, he was polite, he was stiff, he was nosy, he was disapproving. She wondered if he went to bed in grey pinstripe pyjamas looking slightly pained.

'When you are eighteen,' he said, 'there are certain things of which I must apprise you. Until then, we must rub along as best we may.'

'I shall continue to live here.'

It was not a question but Mr Brickville took it as such.

'That is for me to say. But I think for the moment it may be suitable. It would not be appropriate for you to live with me.'

She shuddered at the thought of his house – which would be full of shuttered rooms and ticking clocks; a place where a laugh was like a rude noise in church.

* * *

She told Nanny about the strange young man next day, not because Nanny was looking better, but because something terrible had happened. Aunt Claire's funeral had been arranged for Sunday at the very hour of the assignment by the pond.

Nanny, anyway, was dubious about the encounter. 'He could be up to no good,' she suggested, shaking her head. 'He could be a ne'erdoweel.'

'What would a ne'erdoweel want with me?'

'Well, he might be after your money.'

'Mr Brickville says I don't have any money till I'm of age and even then I won't be rich.'

'Your young friend may not know that. Besides, one man's modest means are another man's more than sufficient.'

'I don't think he's after money, Nanny. I think there's money where he comes from.'

She didn't like to tell Nanny she wasn't quite sure he wasn't a pretty devil from Hades.

'And then there's another thing he might be after,' said Nanny.

She knew what Nanny meant all right, because she'd had a dream about the young man herself last night just when she should have been feeling sombre about Aunt Claire. He'd shinned up the drainpipe and come into her studio just when she was doing a self-portrait and the whole thing had become extraordinary!

'And he might not be the only one,' Nanny added, her wise old eyes noticing the blush. 'It's time you were back at school thinking about games and exams and whatnot.'

It was going to be her last year at school. No one seemed to be quite sure what she was going to do after that. Aunt Claire had talked vaguely about finishing school. No one mentioned university. Suddenly at Nanny's words the future fell open in front of her like a precipice at the end of familiar hills, giving on to beckoning and yet troubling misty vistas.

'What's going to become of me, Nanny?'

She turned to the old woman, her eyes filling with tears. Why was she so strangely upset today?

'You must never worry about the future,' Nanny said. 'One thing's certain. It'll happen. Buck up now. You can go and leave a note for your beau and arrange to see him another time.'

Marie went up to her room, scribbled a note, tore it up, wrote another and tore that up too. Her wastepaper basket filled up. Finally she wrote: 'Dear Mephistopheles, my aunt has died unfortunately and I must go to her funeral. Please don't think that I do not want to renew our acquaintance. Besides, I have your rug. Could you come again on Wednesday? I shall bring some devilled chicken. Yours, M.'

She thought it struck a balance between eagerness and decorum.

It was cloudy today with a fresh wind from the west. She put on a coat and hurried out. The first person she met was Mr Brickville.

'Ah,' he said, slightly pained, 'my ward. Good morning, ward.'

'Good morning, Mr Brickville.'

She tried to walk on, but he detained her.

'You are posting a letter?'

'Yes.'

It was true in a manner of speaking. She tried to hide the envelope but her attempt at secrecy encouraged him to extend his hand.

'Shall I take it for you? I am going past the box.'

'No thank you. I ... I would like a walk.'

She held on to the envelope tightly, almost afraid that he would snatch it away from her.

'Then we shall walk together. But I believe you have no stamp.'

'I do not need a stamp.'

'Not need a stamp? Have you some kind of ah ... deal ... with the post office?'

She had never heard Mr Brickville make a joke before. She thought she preferred him slightly pained.

'It is a note I am taking for Nanny.'

'But I thought you said you were posting it.'

His legal manner made it seem like a cross-examination.

'In a manner of speaking,' she said. Her guilt made her suddenly angry. 'Is there anything wrong with taking a note for Nanny?' she asked.

'Wrong? Good heavens, no. Wrong? Should there be? Is there any wrong afoot?'

'No,' she said.

She could see him debating whether or not to ask her outright to whom she was taking the letter, the note for Nanny, but in the end deciding that it would seem like bad manners. He was after all a solicitor.

'Well,' he said, 'I am taking a walk. You are taking a note for Nanny. How is she, by the way? I understand she has been poorly. I feel we should ah ... make some arrangement for her, give her a holiday?'

'She'd like that, I expect.'

She didn't like the sound of making an arrangement for Nanny but she was too eager to be off to take it up now.

'I shall see you at lunch, no doubt,' he said. 'Meanwhile I wish you a pleasant errand.'

He took his leave and she hurried down the path and across the fields toward the wood. Every now and then she thought she was being followed, and stopped, listening for the forensic step of her guardian, but there was nothing to see and soon she was hurrying down the glade towards the pond.

The place had a different character today. A chill wind ruffled the surface of the water and there was a brooding quality about the undergrowth that fringed it. The butterflies had gone and the trees swayed moodily. There seemed to be eyes, not the puckish ones of yesterday but eyes of surly and malevolent spectators that begrudged her intrusion. It was stupid, of course, because she'd been to the place before and she'd never had such intimations. It had to be Mr Brickville's baleful influence.

She looked around quickly for a place to leave her note – somewhere sheltered from the rain but where Mephistopheles would see it when he came. Finally she selected one of the nearest trees which had an overhanging branch at just the right angle for protection and display. She stuck her envelope to it with stout bands of Sellotape, wrote MEPHISTOPHELES on it with bold letters, and stood back to inspect her handiwork.

It was perfectly visible to anyone who might be looking for a message. At the same time, it wasn't so obtrusive that the casual passer-by would notice it. Not that there were many casual passers-by in the place – Mephistopheles was the first person she'd ever seen there. But one couldn't be too careful.

Satisfied, she set off home again, bracing herself for a boring lunch in the mahogany dining room alone with Mr Brickville.

* * *

On Sunday, it was fine again for her aunt's funeral. Not too many people attended but there were enough to do justice to Aunt Claire and the Monsignor who came to give the sermon. There were some refreshments afterwards at the castle, which Mr Brickville had ordered.

Indeed Mr Brickville seemed to be flexing his guardianly muscles a bit too much for Marie's liking. Not that she herself wanted to do the ordering but it was a bit thick having someone who didn't even live there calling the tune. When she returned with him after the service, Marie could see that the cook and the housekeeper had their noses out of joint.

The housekeeper was a Mrs McGarrigle – someone with whom Marie had had very little contact – but this was one of her great assets as far as Marie was concerned. She didn't want a great deal of contact with the housekeeper, but she and the cook were looking so thunderous that she asked them what was wrong when she went to warn them the guests were on their way. Even that was odd. The housekeeper would normally have been at the front door on the look-out, not lurking in the kitchen.

'That Mr Brickville says we're spending money like water,' muttered Cook. 'I'd like to see how he'd manage. He always wants the best when he comes here. His fillet of beef and his fresh salmon. We'll have to have savoury mince for weeks to make up for his dainty living.'

'Officers' wives eat puddings and pies, soldiers' wives eat skilly,' said Mrs McGarrigle, darkly. 'And there'll be other economies, mark my words. The staff's already pared to the bone.'

'I'm sorry,' said Marie. 'I'll see what I can do. But he's my guardian now, you see.'

'I know, Miss Marie. It's not your fault. But I can tell when the writing's on the wall.'

It was now exactly the hour that she and Mephistopheles had appointed for the rendezvous at the pond. She kept thinking of him, as the Mother Superior of the neighbouring convent and the various catholic dignitaries moved forward gravely to press her hand and urge her to be brave.

'Poor child. All alone now.'

'No. I have Nanny still.'

'I mean without family. But always remember. You are part of God's family. May we look forward to seeing you in church?'

He would be there now, waiting for her, turning sparkling eyes which had seen so much of her in that ridiculous dream to look for her under the trees, coming to meet her perhaps, and then turning back to sit beside the pond not wanting to seem too eager, throwing a stone, disturbing a butterfly with the splash or scaring a frog as it flippertyflopped between those beds of blue watermint, even now perhaps noticing that unmissable envelope winking whitely at him under the bough.

'I beg your pardon?'

Mr Brickville was saying something to her, looking at her, looking at her intently as though he read her thoughts, as though he could feel the excitement working like a mole beneath her breast.

'Something on your mind, Marie? A little secret perhaps? Another note from Nanny, ha ha. Marie has her mother's features, don't you think? Marie, may I introduce Mr Sully? Mr Sully is our stockbroker in London. He has always taken an interest in your affairs.'

He turned to a plump, smooth-featured man beside him whom Marie had not seen before and who went through the motions of a smile as he shook her hand.

'At Marie's age, financial affairs are not the principal ones on a girl's mind,' said Mr Sully, slyly, pressing her hand.

'Quite so, though I think perhaps we're a little young for that.'

'Not as things go in London. My own daughter…'

'Yes … well … perhaps now is not the time.'

'Of course.'

The two men moved off. Marie watched them go with distaste. Why had she been saddled with such creatures? They had put a blight on her conjectures about Mephistopheles and the clearing. She tried to go back but a cloud hung in front of her imaginings and a feeling of foreboding gathered round her heart. She wanted to go now to find him there, to gather up sandwiches and vol au vents and wine, cram them in a basket and run across the fields to him, to smother him in treacle tart; but she knew she was a prisoner. She could feel Mr Brickville watching her from the corner of the room. He was talking about her still, making careful points with his hands, making sure that Mr Sully understood that insofar as, heretofore and notwithstanding, he, the aforesaid Mr Brickville, was now master of the castle and all its inhabitants.

She turned and smiled dazzlingly at a very old priest who was so surprised his salmon mousse slid, in a savoury parabola, onto the Persian carpet, adding an unplanned pink curlicue to the writhing greens and crimsons and blues of the designer's fancy.

Mr Brickville was still looking at her, slightly pained. Although she knew it was not the thing to do at a funeral reception, she blew him a kiss and waved. It was an action she would live to regret.

* * *

By Tuesday, Mr Brickville had departed. Nobody seemed to know where he had gone. He left a telephone number with her which he said would find him in emergency. He had business interests in France, Italy, London, New York, Los Angeles and Sydney, he said. Exactly what they were was not discussed. He had left instructions with Mrs McGarrigle as to the running of the place and arranged a money order to be made payable to the agent he had helped Aunt Claire appoint some time previously – a bleak man called Bain whom Marie had taken an instinctive dislike to. He lived in the village, wore a distrusting expression, had grizzled red hair, and looked out at the world with weaselly eyes, the sort of eyes – wary and implacable, with something between a glare and a peep – that she had felt watching her in the wood. He wasn't liked in the village. Nobody is liked who likes nobody, Nanny had said.

At any rate the running of the castle was looked after. Nothing seemed to have changed apart from there being no Aunt Claire, but you didn't see much of Aunt Claire even when she was alive. And Brickville was gone.

Marie could scarcely wait for the rendezvous on Wednesday, and when the day dawned with blue sky and irrepressible sunshine, her happiness nearly went off the gauge.

She would have been perfectly happy to meet Mephistopheles in a cloudburst but a sunny day was more conducive to conversation. She had much to ask him: where he lived, what he did, who he was. She had kicked herself that these obvious questions had seemed too obvious to ask at the time of that first fatal interview.

She had tried from memory to make a sketch of him but it was hopeless. There was something uncatchable about the animation of his face. This time she must try and get him from life. She packed a drawing pad and some charcoal in her fishing-bag and turned her attention to the picnic itself. She had pondered long and hard about what she should say to the kitchen on this issue. A picnic for one would be no problem, but a picnic for two might raise eyebrows. It might even – perish the thought – get back to Mr Brickville. Mrs McGarrigle knew on which side her bread was buttered. Marie had seen her and Brickville walking up and down between the box hedges in the formal garden, deep in conversation. So she consulted Nanny as soon as she was up.

'I'm going to meet him today and I want the picnic to be nice – not just for me, I mean, but a proper one for two, with napkins and glasses and things. Would you say that you're coming with me?'

'But that's a lie, dear. We don't tell lies.'

Marie thought hard. She knew there were some things that Nanny dug her heels in about.

'Well, then. Could I say that I'm planning a surprise for you because it's such a lovely day, and I need a picnic for two?'

'You could say that, lovey. I daresay you will. You don't have to say what surprise. I daresay you will surprise me. You usually do. It's not exactly a lie but it's a bit of chop logic.'

Nanny was satisfied, however, and Marie went off to see Cook after breakfast. She knew that Nanny usually made her own meal in her little kitchen, so no one would be any the wiser whether she came with her or not. In fact, Nanny seemed to live on almost nothing these days and rarely left her sitting-room no matter what the weather was doing.

Cook was in a good mood and promised to put a nice picnic for two in a hamper with all the trimmings. 'That's good of you, Miss Marie. She needs to get out more. She looks so pale. We never see anything of her these days.'

Marie felt guilty but nerved herself to the next question. 'Could you put in a bottle of wine?' she said as casually as possible.

'Wine, Miss Marie?' Cook looked momentarily shocked. She had known Marie since she was four and still considered her a child. 'Do you mean…?'

'Wine, Cook, please.'

There was something very appealing about Marie when she was entreating. Startling blue eyes went very deep and liquid.

'I expect Nanny needs the iron,' Cook said at last.

'Oh yes, she does,' agreed Marie, feeling bad about lying to a friend, but in too deep now to draw back.

'In that case I'll see if there's some burgundy in the store room up from the cellar,' said Cook. 'Mr Brickville likes his burgundy. We don't want to disturb Mrs McGarrigle, do we?'

'No, we don't,' agreed Marie, guilt and excitement giving her the most delicious sensations.

She passed the morning in a fever of expectation. She picked up a book and put it down; she went up to her studio and tried to paint; she ran out into the garden and paused, irresolute, kicking the gravel; she mooched down to the fountain where the big fat carp wallowed placidly among the lily pads like retired bank mangers moving between restaurant tables. Nothing seemed to calm her or to accelerate the sluggish minutes.

At last the station clock struck twelve. It was time to go and collect the hamper from the kitchen and start on her way. As luck would have it, Mrs McGarrigle came into the kitchen while Cook was going through the contents.

'There's ham and chicken and tomato and cucumber. There's your salad dressing. Then for afterwards there's ... well ... There you are!' she finished hurriedly, seeing the housekeeper. 'It's a lovely day for it.'

'Picnicking?' asked Mrs McGarrigle, nosing nearer. 'I didn't know.'

'Yes,' said Marie. 'Bye now. I must be off.'

'I like to know these things,' she heard Mrs McGarrigle saying to Cook as she hurried out. 'Mr Brickville left instructions. I insist on knowing.'

'Fiddlesticks,' said Cook. 'It belongs to her now, doesn't it?'

Marie left them to fight it out. If there was going to be trouble, she could deal with it when she came back. The most import thing in the world could not be put off for Mrs McGarrigle.

* * *

Swinging her hamper gaily by the handle, but not without consideration for the good things inside, she set off across the meadows, went over the river by the old packhorse bridge and entered the wood where the chestnuts were beginning to show the green spiky fruits that would turn into marrons in the autumn.

She had covered perhaps a mile and a half – no small distance carrying a heavy basket – but it might have been the length of a tennis court so buoyant was her step and so lively her imaginings.

Would she sit down and look at the water as she had been doing when he first appeared, sit there knowing that he was watching her,

59

waiting to be surprised again? Or would he this time be sitting there himself, mimicking her original position, studiously addressing himself to the deportment of the butterflies? Or would it be quite different, some magical conformation which, at the moment, escaped her?

She was drawing near the clearing now. Between the fuzzy new green of the trees she caught a glimpse of shining water. Her pace slackened. She stopped and then, very quietly, she began to steal forward again, keeping off the main path and following a subsidiary tracklet to the edge of the clearing where she would spy from an unexpected vantage point.

It wasn't easy with a heavy hamper, but she accomplished it with a silence worthy of a pirate of Penzance. She parted a frond and peered out.

The glade was almost exactly as it had been before. It was a little greener. There were a few more butterflies. And there were a couple of ducks on the water. Mephistopheles would like that, she thought. But where was he, the devil?

She debated whether to stay and wait for him to show himself, but she reflected that he might be doing exactly the same thing himself, and it would just be a waste of time. And it was already one o'clock. So, parting the saplings, she stood up and walked quietly out, hoping her appearance wouldn't disturb the mallard.

The ducks were none too keen at the invasion of their privacy, and retreated up to the further end of the water, making low, disparaging remarks to each other. They did not, however, fly off, which Marie took to be a good augur. As for her envelope – so carefully stuck under the bough – that had well and truly flown.

Spreading the rug, she now seated herself in her previous position at the water's edge, and amused herself trying to coax the mallards up from their retreat by throwing pellets of white roll out to the surface immediately in front of her. It was infuriating. They would make as if to approach, swim a few yards, look at the bread, look at each other, and then swim back to their safe water. She simply could not get them to come and take it. They reminded her of one of those middle-aged couples who drive miles to the seaside but finally can't bring themselves to get out of their car.

So engrossed did she become in her seduction of the duck – *seduckshion*, she thought, another one for Mephistopheles – that in spite of the pressing nature of her business there, she lost track of time for a while. There was, after all, no hurry; the sun was hot, this was the best place to be on a beautiful day. But after a while she looked at her watch. It was half past one.

She sprang up, suddenly dismayed, and the ducks rose as one and beat their way across the water, climbing almost too soon, walking upon it with the tips of their wings in their desire to get away from this pellet-throwing precipitator.

She watched them go, a horrible sense of loss beginning to overcome her, not with the tips of its wings but with great hobnail boots in her heart. He wasn't coming. If you invited people to lunch at one, it was rude to turn up at half past. He had either been annoyed when she hadn't shown up on Sunday, or he simply didn't want to see her again, or both. He couldn't be bothered. And yet … she could have sworn that he'd really liked her. Perhaps he was a devil after all.

A tear began to meander down her cheek, followed by another. She knew she shouldn't cry but she couldn't help it. A tear for Aunt Claire; two tears for poor Nanny; tears for being alone in the world; and tears for lost love.

* * *

Mrs McGarrigle greeted her with a long face that evening.

'I understand you lied to Cook.'

'Lied?'

'Lied about wanting a picnic as a surprise for Nanny.'

'I didn't say I wanted a picnic as a surprise for Nanny. I said I wanted to surprise Nanny, and I wanted a picnic. The two weren't necessarily connected.'

'Now look here, Miss…'

Suddenly Marie lost her temper. She had had enough. To lose one's love and nearly lose one's honour all in one day was too much. 'No, you look here. If I want a picnic, I'll have a picnic. I am the mistress of this place now.'

'No, you are not. Mr Brickville is legally responsible.'

Marie stamped her foot. 'I am the owner. If I want a picnic, I'll have one. If I want to lie, I'll do it.'

Mrs McGarrigle pursed her lips. 'Well, we know where we are, then. May I enquire what you were doing in the wood alone with a picnic for two? Not of course that we can be sure of a straight answer.'

'*The lovely lady, Christabel*
Whom her father loves so well,
What makes her in the wood so late,
A furlong from the castle gate?
She had dreams all yesternight
Of her own betrothéd knight;
And she in the midnight wood will pray
For the weal of her lover that's far away,' said Marie.

It was in Nanny's book of favourite verses.

'Lover?' snorted Mrs McGarrigle. 'What sort of talk is this? Lying again?'

'Just a friend, Mrs McGarrigle. Not a lover yet, worse luck.'

'Really. I shall have to tell Mr Brickville. He may have to take certain steps.'

'Tell him what you like,' said Marie, coolly, though inwardly dismayed. There was no knowing what arrangements he might have in mind for her. She wished, not for the first time, that she had a real father to love her.

Bloody hell, Mephistopheles, why didn't you show up? She began to hate him for this betrayal of her trust.

* * *

She spent her last term at the convent in a state of scarcely subdued impatience. The nuns were, with certain exceptions, generally not good teachers, the discipline had become irksome and the other girls were taken up with the picnics, politics and petty jealousies of summer term at a girls' boarding school.

One girl, it was true, had developed a considerable liking for her. Rather than the usual crush, this girl's affection seemed to want to take a more physical form. There were rather too many sidlings up in the changing room for it not to be mistaken for something seamy. Marie agreed once to being fondled in a shower just to see what it was all about but she didn't like the fixed look in the girl's eyes and the heavy-breathing noises that went with it so she turned the hot tap on, accidentally on purpose, and that was the end of that.

The odious Teresa who was still at school and was now in fact Head Girl, did her best to impose her will on Marie, sensing that she had scant respect for the little ritual lunacies of the place. But on the whole Marie kept out of the way, revised, went off by herself with a sketching pad and her set books and lay in the sun and dreamed the dreams of the half-innocent; of shapeless pleasures and opportunities, and the beckoning imminence of life and love.

She was taking three A-level exams: English, Art and French. And, because she had nothing else to entertain her, she worked hard at them. It was almost unheard of at the convent for anyone to take one A level, let alone three. Higher knowledge was regarded by the Mother Superior rather in the manner of the tree of Good and Evil in the Book of Genesis. The fruit was there but it was of doubtful benefit to pluck it.

On the eve of her first exam she received two letters. One in a typed envelope, the other in a blue one with Nanny's handwriting. She saved Nanny's till she'd read the other one – it looked strangely official and it was in fact from Mr Brickville.

'Dear Marie,' it read, 'I hope you are working hard for your examinations. I fear the subjects you are taking are not exactly those most likely to be of benefit in the modern world. Even such qualifications, however, are better than none. I regret to say that Nanny is not at all well, and I am sending her to a nursing home in Dunfermline which I hear is well spoken of. You may of course visit her there when term is over but I feel we should do as little as possible to disturb her. Meanwhile, to provide some entertainment for you during the summer – and because Mrs McGarrigle says she is finding you something of a handful – I would like to suggest you join me at a villa I am taking near Cannes. My secretary will send more instructions as to what you should bring and details of how you should get there in due course. Meanwhile, I send my best wishes for a successful conclusion to your schooldays. We shall be able to discuss your future at length in the pleasant circumstances of the Côte d'Azur. Yours, Hubert Brickville. PS I understand you are known at school as Couldn't-Care-Less. Is this quite wise?'

Marie's first reaction was one of shock. She had known that Nanny was not well, that she was getting thinner and greyer in the face, but it had happened so gradually, and she hardly ever complained; somehow it had never really seemed serious. And now she was moving out of her cosy little room in the castle's East Wing, and going to some horrible place smelling of death and antiseptic. And what was she, Marie, going to do without her friend and counsellor – her only friend, her only counsellor?

She started to cry. Then, remembering that she hadn't read Nanny's version, she opened the blue envelope.

'My Little Marie,' she read, 'I hope this finds you well. By the time you read this, you may have heard from your guardian but I hope to be first. The doctors say I have a lump that has to come out – you know I have been a bit off colour. I never trust doctors. But anyway your guardian says I'd be rather better off in hospital so that's where I'll go. I'll be back soon sure enough, right as rain. Now, I don't want you to worry with your exams coming up. If you want me to get well, the best tonic I'll have is to hear you've got good results. So don't mope. Remember, least said, soonest mended. But there's just one thing I want to say. Just in case anything goes wrong which I'm sure it won't. I want to say, whatever happens, wherever I go, you'll always be my little Marie. I shall be there watching over you. I know that. Life has not been very kind to you. To have no father is bad and to have no mother is worse, and there is more that I cannot tell. But I can and I do tell you that nobody on earth could have loved you more than I, so it is not at all bad. You were such a funny little thing when you were small. Remember that "Man in the Wall"? He was your invisible friend. I shall be your Man in the Wall. Buck up now and get on with it. Quick's the word and sharp's the action. And remember to get those potatoes out from behind your ears. I must close now, your ever loving, Nanny. PS You can come and see me in hospital if you like, but I don't want to see any misery-mopes.'

By the time she had finished reading, Marie was in floods of tears. She became conscious of the dreaded Teresa standing near her.

'I say, the famous Couldn't-Care-Less is blubbing!'

Marie sprang up and gave Teresa the most resounding smack on the cheek which made the obnoxious girl cry almost as hard.

'Ooh. I shall report you.'

Marie felt guilty, but only because she could hear Nanny saying 'Temper, temper.'

The exams proved to be difficult but not impossible. She left the convent afterwards without regret. They didn't give her a farewell tea-party in the Prefects' Room, which was almost unheard of.

'Tough titty, Couldn't-Care-Less. No Pre's Tea,' they chanted.

But, quite honestly, she couldn't care less. She was nearly eighteen.

* * *

The castle was strange without Nanny in her little sitting-room. Everything still looked just the same but without her comfortable reassuring presence, it did not feel like home. Marie sensed the old walls reverting to some chill she recalled from a time she could not possibly have remembered. The shadows now seemed longer. The tapping of the creeper against her window was not friendly any more, but sinister and threatening. Her eighteenth birthday passed without celebration or comment. It was the age when Aunt Claire had said she could be a Lavell. She felt comfortable in the name no matter what the world said. It was hers and her father's whom she knew must have been at heart a good man. They could be two against the world. The age of Sinclair was over.

It was a rainy July. The dark days sapped any urge she felt to paint. She mooched around the familiar places feeling like a stranger, so it was with rather less dread than she had anticipated at the thought of spending a whole month with her guardian, that she began to pack the things so carefully enumerated in a typewritten letter from Denise Tweddle, signed for Mr Brickville in his absence.

The list included swimsuits (decorous), evening dresses, tennis things (rackets to be provided), a ball-gown and even five changes of summer underwear. It was rather like those lists that schools send out to new girls.

She did not need her guardian to tell her what sort of, or how much, underwear she should bring. As for decorous swimwear, did he really think she was going to look like a strumpet? Mind you, these days the strumpets looked respectable and the respectable took everything off, so you couldn't tell where you were, at least that's what Nanny had said. Marie's only setback was a minor one: her passport said Sinclair. Fine. She could wear that and take it off when she got through customs at Nice.

Nanny had been moved to a hospital in Edinburgh, so the first thing Marie had to do was visit her. But when she arrived, her old friend was heavily sedated and all Marie could do was smile at her and hold her hand. Nanny managed to give a little smile in return, and press her hand weakly. She murmured something which Marie could not hear, and fell asleep. The nurses said she had had one operation and was going to have a further one shortly. They said she was poorly but was sure to pull through. Marie left grapes and a letter for her, telling her of her love for her and eternal gratitude, and that she would visit her again as soon as she returned from France.

She then did some shopping in Edinburgh – underwear, swimsuits, party frocks and all, whether Mr Brickville approved of it or not – and bought a smart, dark-blue suitcase.

On her return home, she packed, took a last circuit of the castle and its grounds to remind herself of her youth and said goodbye to the cook and Mrs McGarrigle. She had an irrational feeling that she would see none of them again, and that a chapter of her life was closing. Next morning, the rat-faced factor, Bain, drove her to the airport in almost total silence (for which she was grateful), and she was finally off.

Apart from a visit to Paris and Bruges with the sixth form, she had never been abroad before. The Aunts had deplored travel. It was one of Aunt Bertha's favourite dictums that 'travelling narrows the mind'. No one quite knew what it meant, but Bertha thought it the height of acuity, and she refused to budge.

'We live in a beautiful home in a beautiful county in the most beautiful country in the world. You may keep your air-crashes and your controllers' strikes and your little plastic trays. I shall stay at home where peace and beauty flow. And so shall you, Claire and you, too, child. Time enough to gad about later. The most important discoveries lie within us. He that is tired of Fife is tired of life. Ha ha.'

Anyway, as Marie sat in her window seat, and sipped a glass of white wine, she reflected on poor Aunt Bertha's and Aunt Claire's wafting to Heaven in a situation rather like this, but the little plastic trays were made of pearl, and the surroundings were even more beautiful and congenial than the sight of the sparkling sea and the little fluffy clouds far below, and the air was full of angels, eternally crying 'Hosanna' and things.

Her thoughts turned to Nanny, too, hopefully still on earth. Marie had sent her flowers and a bottle of her favourite vintage-style port, 'the best is wasted on me, lovey', and promised to go and see her on her return; but she still felt worried about her, and a little dismayed to be leaving her in the lurch, waking up from her operation without a friendly face or a glint of glee.

A smooth voice interrupted her thoughts. 'We are approaching our final run-in to Nice Airport. Please extinguish your safety belts and fasten your cigarettes.'

The Captain, it seemed, was a joker. She hoped he was a better flier than humourist.

Suddenly they seemed to be flying very close to the sea and Marie braced herself for a watery grave, and an imminent confrontation with The Aunts, but they came down to earth with the mildest of bumps on a long promontory of a runaway built low over the water.

It looked exceedingly hot outside.

The man next to her winked. He had been trying to talk to her all through the flight. 'First time you been to Nice, is it? Nice by name and nice by nature. Know what I mean?'

She didn't know what he meant but it reminded her with a pang of Nanny, and how they'd laughed over her milk and Nice biscuits when she was little. 'But Nanny. A place can't be called Nice. It's silly. Is there another place called Horrid?'

'Oh yes, lovey. There's lots of Horrids. But I don't expect you'll ever go to them. Would you like a Horrid biscuit?'

Peals of laughter, and then, 'I hope I go to Nice one day. It sounds niece.'

And here she was. And there Nanny was. And one day she'd be in horrid hospital and somebody else would be in Nice. The man handed her a card as they got up.

'Harvey Ambrose, Multifab Sales Manager. I'm off to the Media Conference. Get in touch if you want to take in a show. Ooo la la! Nice? It takes the biscuit. But you've got to know where to go. I know a place … it'd make your hair stand on end. There's this negro … he sits and thinks about it, bollock naked he is, and after about five minutes he does the doo … you know … does the doo like a ruddy Niagara. That's what I call a show.'

She looked at the man with curiosity as though he were a recondite weevil but all through passport control he kept adding little extra titbits.

'He doesn't touch himself, mind. Nothing like that. It's very dignified, very tasteful. Philosophical almost. Then after five minutes … whoosh…'

She was afraid Mr Brickville might be there and she would have to explain her embarrassing companion, but fortunately she caught sight of a solitary chauffeur holding a board with her name on it, while Harvey Ambrose spotted some fellow delegates. She could hear him regaling his companions on his latest conquest as she walked off after the chauffeur.

'I was sitting next to this little cracker. You could see she was longing for it…'

People, she thought, were like dogs. They couldn't see a pathway without wanting to foul it. Even so, there had been something rather sad and touching about him.

* * *

Mr Brickville's villa was up in the hills above Cannes.

All around it were flowering hibiscus hedges of bright whites and reds, and in front, far below, was the yacht-dotted sea.

The car sent by Mr Brickville, after passing a number of discreet little driveways turned in at the most discreet one of all, crunching decorously on the gravel in front of a large white house, shuttered against hot sun. Marie got out, grateful to leave the ambient chill of the air conditioning for the faint blood-warm breeze charged with herbs and flowers that ruffled the curtains of the noonday heat.

Mr Brickville appeared at the front door and came down the steps to greet her. It was a shock to see him in white trousers and a short-sleeved, white shirt like a bowls player. There was not even a hint of a pin-stripe or indeed of a slightly pained expression.

'Welcome to Le Bavelot,' he said. 'I trust you had a not too taxing journey.'

She thanked him and assured him this was the case – or was it that this was not the case? The man was full of litotes. He could never say something outright. It always had to be the opposite of the appropriate sentiment, and then qualified with a negative, as if the full-on truth were too painful to bear. She had resolved to try and be pleasant to the man whom she thought she might have misjudged. It wasn't his fault that he was a dry old stick. She thought perhaps she could cheer him up a bit. It was certainly not difficult to feel cheered herself. Bright green lawns composed of that curiously coarse-textured continental grass sloped down to where she could see an azure swimming pool flanked by shaded tables. Far below, Cannes glittered, its traffic moving like jewelled beetles. A delicious aroma wafted suddenly from an unseen kitchen.

'Claudine will show you your room,' he indicated a uniformed middle-aged maid, dark of hair and eyes, 'and then perhaps you would like a swim after your travels. Lunch will be served at quarter to two.'

So began a holiday that was, to one brought up in the cloistered company of maiden aunts, a vision of another kind of paradise. There were days of lying in the sun beside the pool, eating delectable meals – Mr Brickville was particular about his food – and drinking the fresh and fruity wines of Provence.

Mr Brickville must have made some similar resolve to her own, for within his powers, he put himself out to be obliging, even attentive. It was true, he found it difficult to laugh – his laughing muscles had all dried up – and he would use expressions like 'I trust' when 'I hope' would do.

And there were days when he had to spend much of the time on the telephone, and when tidy men in short shirts would come to the house and talk about money. On these days she would sometimes go down to Cannes with Maximilien the chauffeur who would stay while she went down and lay on the *Plage Sportive* watching the antics of the oiled bodies and the little sailing boats that plied from the jetty and trying to ignore the attentions of the brilliant black Algerians who sold beads and rings and belts and bags and strange sugared nuts. The owner of the place was a hawk-eyed, leather-faced Frenchwoman called Marguerite who also paid her one or two discreet attentions.

Sometimes too, later, after a drink at seven on the villa's terrace, she would come down with Mr Brickville and they would eat at one of the restaurants on the Croisette in the smooth night under the stars, or they would drive into the hills and dine at Mougins or the Colombe d'Or at St Paul de Vence with its vine-covered terrace under the ancient walls where Picasso and Braque had stayed and painted, and the swimming pool where the rich showed off their costly, golden bodies.

'I'm afraid it must be boring for you, Marie,' said Mr Brickville on one of these occasions. 'Just an old stick like me for company.'

Eating good food in such a beautiful place didn't seem dull at all in spite of the old stick but she wondered momentarily how old the stick actually was. Probably something really old like fifty? It was difficult to tell. There was something about him you couldn't quantify with years. She assured him that she wasn't bored, and that he wasn't boring.

'Even so,' he said, 'I have some amusement for you. A colleague of mine from Los Angeles is coming over with his daughter next week. I think you will find them good company. She is about your age.'

Marie felt not altogether happy about this development. She was so used to being on her own that she found company something of a problem. One of the good things about Mr Brickville was that he was generally unobtrusive. However, she politely expressed pleasure at the prospect.

Next day, she went down to the *Plage Sportive* alone again, choosing her favourite vantage point, segmented between the two low windbreaks of woven lath, with her private beach umbrella and just one mattress, *merci*, Marguerite.

She had spent some time being amused by the action of two very tanned French boys throwing a ball at each other and leaping about in their exaggerated way to the annoyance of a very white English couple in the front row, when she saw him. He had been sailing one of the little boats and was just bringing it along the jetty. He climbed out, paid the little wizened peanut of a chap who looked after the flotilla and paused for a moment, surveying the beach, his red-brown hair ruffled by the strange Cannes breeze that always seemed to die on the stroke of midday.

It was unmistakably Mephistopheles.

Without thinking, she stood up and waved. Then she thought, why am I so pleased to see him? He let me down, the rat. The same variety of emotions seemed to be crossing his features as he gazed at her, with the added ingredient of initial puzzlement as to who should be signalling at him from a plage-ful of strangers.

Finally, advancing, he greeted her with modified rapture.

'Hello,' he said. 'It's my old friend Impervious.'

That was the name she had given when first she met him. Full marks to him for remembering.

'I am not entirely impervious,' she replied tartly, not waiting to go into all the ritual questions. 'Not to being left high and dry when I had arranged to meet someone. What are you doing here?'

It was clear what he was doing here. He was on holiday, sailing a skiff from the *Plage Sportive*. How dare he look so blameless and beautiful? He was a little puzzled by the heat of her retort. It obviously wasn't what he was expecting.

'Why…' they both began at once.

'You first.'

'No, you.'

They couldn't help smiling at each other, and felt better about it.

'Why didn't you turn up?' she asked at length.

'Why didn't you?' he replied.

'But … my great-aunt died and I had to go to her funeral. I left you a note asking you to come back on the Wednesday.'

'I never saw a note.'

'I left it on the tree with that big overhanging bough.'

'I thought you might have left something. I looked everywhere.'

'I'm sure you'd have seen it,' she said. 'Unless you're blind as a bat.'

'I'm not blind as a bat. I am noted for extreme beadiness of gaze.'

'In that case,' she said, suddenly having a disturbing thought, 'somebody must have taken it.'

'I thought you'd stood me up,' he said. 'I felt an absolute fool – and I missed my lunch.'

'Well, I wasted ours.'

'Tell you what, have lunch with me here and we'll talk. I've got to go and see my parents – we're staying at the Bleu Rivage – and then I'll come back.'

'Mind you do come back,' she told him. 'I won't forgive you a second time.'

* * *

As it happened, he did come back.

They had lunch in the shade of Marguerite's veranda, piling their plates from a long table of salads, Bayonne ham, salamis, pâtés, chicken, stuffed tomatoes, tuna, anchovies, salmon, *loup de mer*, couscous and selecting a *pichet* of Marguerite's waspish house rosé to wash it down.

As they tucked into the assorted delicacies – legendary for price as well as excellence – they exchanged histories.

His name was David Drummond. His parents lived in San Diego, just about as far away as it was possible to live from Castle Cowrie, but he had relations nearby – Perthshire was thick with Drummonds – and he had simply been taking a day out on his own, as it happened in the wrong wood. He had been looking for a small loch where some osprey were nesting in a forest a mile or two up the road, and had stupidly forgotten his map. He had got lost, and found her instead. He was now a Rhodes Scholar reading Economics at Oxford, though he had started as a chemist. Term had finished and his father and mother had suddenly decided to visit him and take him on a quick holiday in Cannes, and happily found rooms at the Bleu Rivage because frankly they couldn't afford the Carlton.

Marie in turn told him what little there was to tell of her life. The details were all fairly prosaic but there was no mistaking, for a chemist, the chemistry that was going on across the dapper pink tablecloth that Marguerite favoured.

The unshaded *plage* become hotter and hotter, scorching the feet of the unwary. Marguerite's little waitress started to take the dishes from the long table. Marguerite herself disappeared into her booth under the Croisette pavement. None but the diehards were left on the mattresses to fricassée themselves, but still the two of them talked on.

Finally, Marie looked at her watch and saw with horror it was four o'clock. Maximilien liked to be back home by half past three for his afternoon *devoirs* with his wife.

'I must go,' she said, 'dear David Drummond from San Diego, alias Mephistopheles.'

'What shall I call you? Couldn't-Care-Less?'

'Uh uh,' she shook her head, 'because I could care, you know.'

'I know.'

'But what are we going to do?'

'Meet here tomorrow?'

'I shall try. But if I can't, you mustn't fly into a fury, you know. My guardian can be tricky although he's being unaccountably good at the moment.'

'You have probably won his heart.'

The idea was ridiculous.

'*Tu plaisantes, Monsieur.*'

'*On ne badine pas avec l'amour.*'

He had done some French, it seemed.

'It would be awful. Like being kissed by a moth.'

'Moth doth corrupt.' He was serious for some reason.

'Don't be silly. Bit of luck, you being here.'

'Luck, nothing. I tracked you down.'

But she couldn't decide if he was serious.

* * *

She grovelled to Maximilien who didn't seem to be too distressed, sitting in his air conditioning looking out at a wilderness of pretty, ambulatory bottoms and thinking without enthusiasm of his sloe-eyed spouse's, though Marie was in such a state of joy she could have appeased raging Giant Polypheme himself.

She had always felt, in spite of her isolation and loneliness, that somewhere out there was someone who was her exact counterpart, who would make all the loneliness worthwhile. Perhaps there is someone like that for everyone, she thought, but the tragedy is that they never meet. Here, against all conceivable odds, she had found hers, lost him, and found him again. The very fact that he had reappeared so magically (whether or not he was telling the truth about the tracking) was proof that destiny, after so many quirks and cruelties, was at long last on her side.

As they drew up on the supertax gravel outside Le Bavolet, Mr Brickville appeared looking slightly pained. He hadn't looked like that for a week and Marie had thought she might have cured him of the habit, but no, it was back.

'I thought I made it clear, Marie,' he said, as Maximilien took the car round the back, 'I thought I made it abundantly clear that Maximilien should be back here for 3.30. I cannot expect him to be on duty to take us out in the evening if he has no time off in the afternoon. His wife Claudine is most emphatic about it. He must not become *enervé*. Really, I am most displeased.'

'I'm sorry, er, Hubert.' She hated calling him Hubert, but it was a sacrifice she was prepared to make. 'I'm sorry, Hubert, but I met a friend on the *plage*.'

'A friend? I did not know...' she thought he was going to say he did not know that she had any friends – but he went on, after a pause, 'any friends were here.'

'Nor did I. It was a friend from school.'

'I did not know you had any friends at school. You always seemed to be so ... aloof. That is what your report said.'

Why was he so keen for her not to have friends? Could David be right? Was he jealous?

'A friend from school and her brother.'

She had thought this out rather carefully in case Maximilien or someone reported that they had seen her with a young man. For some reason of self-protection or instinct of privacy, she didn't want to tell Hubert the truth about David.

* * *

By great good fortune, Hubert was suddenly taken up with a flurry of business.

'I'm sorry,' he told her at breakfast, looking up from the mail, the very morning after the fateful meeting on the *plage*. 'Something has come up and I have to go to Geneva for a day or two. Will you be able to amuse yourself? Your school friend, what is her name incidentally, is staying for a while?'

'Yes,' said Marie, giving the answer she had prepared. 'Teresa Sarle. She is staying at the Carlton with her family.'

It amused her to give the name of the arch enemy. She had specified the Carlton because she knew it would give off the right overtones of money. Hubert liked her to move within her class. It was one reason he would disapprove of Mephistopheles.

'My father's in oil,' David had told her.

'Like a sardine.'

'Like a sardine, but not as rich. Not everybody's a millionaire in oil.'

Her attention returned to the breakfast table as Hubert, fastidiously wiping the last vestige of croissant crumb from his lips with a blindingly white napkin, prepared to rise.

'Goodbye then, my, ah, dear. Maximilien and Claudine will look after you. Do not keep Maximilien from his afternoon siesta otherwise we will have a, ha, palace revolution. I trust that you will behave prudently. There are a lot of rascals in Cannes – as indeed there are everywhere.'

He brushed her cheek with crumbless lips, gathered up his papers, and was gone. She was surprised that, after his grave faces last night, he should so lightly have left her to her own devices but she guessed –

rightly – that Hubert, faced with the choice, would always put finance before family.

When he had left for the airport, driven by the *fatigable* Maximilien, she telephoned the Bleu Rivage from the drawing room.

'Hello, Mephistopheles,' she said. '*Ça va*? Things are looking up here. Guardian has gone to Geneva and the mice can play.'

'Wonderful,' he said. 'Meet you at the *plage* at eleven.'

She had the feeling as she put the phone down that someone might have been listening on another extension. There was just the faintest click of another receiver but she decided it must, after all, be funny French telephone noises and not significant.

Next she went to find Claudine and asked her how she might get a taxi.

'You wish to go somewhere, Mademoiselle?'

She had the feeling there was aversion in the black-olive eyes. Perhaps Maximilien had made a gallant reference to her bottom to the detriment of Claudine's own seating arrangements.

'I am going to the beach.'

'Mademoiselle does not like the swimming pool?'

'There is more company on the beach.'

'Ah. Company.'

She said it as though company might bite. But she came up with the number and time, yes, she was definitely listening when Marie gave the destination to the taxi switchboard.

However, once on the *Plage Sportive* again, in her favourite corner with two mattresses under the umbrella this time, all considerations apart from her joy at seeing David again were forgotten (though she did manage to write another quick postcard to Nanny telling her of his wondrous reappearance).

So began a sequence of the happiest days she had ever known. Life is, in emotional terms, a black and white affair, but love seems to flood it with colour – a colouring which is also in some strange way a drug. As Napoleon is said to have been inadvertently poisoned by his copper-arsenic green wallpaper in the damp climate of St Helena, so Marie was wafted to the garden of delight on the heady pigments of romance.

They swam, they lay in the sun, they sailed, they drank *citrons pressés* when they were thirsty, and cold wine when they weren't, they ate at Chantal's and at other little places along the Croisette. Sometimes, to Claudine's disapproval, she would take a taxi and drive out with him to mountain restaurants less grand than the Colombe d'Or but no less pleasurable.

And afterwards they would walk on battlements and kiss under the coming moon, sucking balm from each other's mouths for the bittersweet inflammations of the heart.

She met his parents after a day or two. They appeared pleasant, friendly, civilised people – the sort of Americans you rarely see portrayed on television drama series and who therefore come as a surprise to the European. They seemed pleased that their son, whom they clearly adored, had found such a decorous and charming companion, and because they were happy with each other's company, they didn't begrudge the time he spent with Marie.

Happily, her guardian was detained on business for the whole week. He had had to move on to Paris and then London. It seemed that he might be gone for ever and that she could go on living in heaven indefinitely. Then Claudine, with some satisfaction, dropped her bombshell.

'I have heard from Monsieur. He is coming back tomorrow.'

Marie told David about it on the beach. A shadow loomed over the day, dulling the sun and permeating every corner of the *plage*. The very *citron* lost its zest.

'What are we to do?'

'It's not the end of the world,' he told her. 'There's no reason why we shouldn't see each other.'

'He'll find a reason,' she said. 'He hates other people's pleasure.'

He thought she was over reacting, but the feeling of incipient doom started to communicate itself to him.

'Tell you what,' he said. 'I'll borrow my parents' hire car and we'll drive up to that place you liked for dinner tonight.'

The prospect cheered her. It was a little restaurant, high on the edge of a hill with a breath-catching view of the bay, where an old man and his wife bustled about among candles and chequered tablecloths, although for all their bustling there were – strangely, in view of the excellent if simple food – few customers. Perhaps it was too simple for these parts. Or up too wiggly a track. But whatever it was, it was the perfect place for the painful pleasure of the occasion.

They swore love for each other, they held hands, gazed into each other's eyes, vowed nothing could come between them except *salade niçoise*, and wood-grilled fresh daurade. And then, afterwards, between lone pine trees, lying on turf so aromatic it was the only garnish that could possibly improve each other's edibility, she felt her breasts blossom under his touch and her underwear (summer) being gently removed and something else, as she melted, replacing it, something that seemed to fill for ever all the emptiness and loneliness she had known in her life, and wasn't in the very slightest bit like the reflective and even philosophical activities of the negro in Nice.

'I want to marry you,' he said when it was over.

'You don't have to say that.'

'Yes, I do.'

'All right. Darling Mephistopheles. Why not? I am eighteen. I can do what I like.'

'I've one more year at Oxford. I'll get a job and we'll get married.'

'A whole year?'

'Eleven months.'

'I shall never want anyone but you.'

* * *

She didn't get back to Le Bavolet until three in the morning. She was aware that Claudine had spotted her coming in but she was too exhausted and happy to care, and she fell into a sleep of wonderful profundity as soon as she sank into bed.

The next thing she knew, there was an urgent knocking at the door, and a brilliant light in the room. She had forgotten to draw the curtains. It was morning, she discovered, but early: about seven o'clock. Couldn't they have let her sleep till nine as usual?

'What is it?'

'Mr Brickville is on the telephone. He wants to speak with you.'

It was Claudine.

'Can't it wait?'

'No, it cannot wait. He rang last night but I told him you were not in.'

Marie felt her heart sink. She knew there would be trouble. Yet, nonetheless, she felt buoyed up by the memories of last night and the wonderful sense of loving and being loved.

'All right. I'm coming.'

She huddled on her dressing-gown and shuffled along after Claudine to the drawing room.

'Hello?'

'Hello. Is that you, Marie? Marie, I am deeply displeased. I understand from Claudine that you did not return until three in the morning.'

Thank you for nothing, Claudine, thought Marie.

'Well?' said Mr Brickville, more than slightly pained, 'I am waiting.'

Really, thought Marie, this is absurd. I'm eighteen and I'm being treated like a child.

'I was with my friends,' said Marie. 'And do we have to talk about it at seven o'clock in the morning?'

'Do not be impertinent, we will talk about it at any hour of my choosing.'

'You are my guardian not my jailer.'

'We shall see about that,' said Mr Brickville with a menace that she had not heard before in his voice.

'Was that all you wanted to say?' she asked.

'No, it is not. I told you, I believe, that my American colleague, Tony Prelati, and his daughter Francesca will be coming to stay with us. Well, they are coming today and, alas, I shall not be back until this evening. I want you to receive them and to see that they are looked after. I imagine it would not be too much to ask you to desist from your hectic social whirl for one day, at least until I am back. Then we can perhaps discuss the whole matter and see if I cannot persuade you to adopt a rather more moderate course. I naturally only want what is best for you. Well?'

'Of course I'll receive them, Hubert. I'm not completely graceless. I won't leave them alone for a second if that's what you want. But I still have my own life to lead.'

'That is what we shall discuss. Meanwhile I have given instruction to Claudine for the day's refreshment, and Maximilien will collect our guests from the airport. They will be with you at 12.30.'

She had at least anticipated that today would be out as far as David was concerned, so she was able to feel calm about it; but the notion of further separation – which Hubert had more than hinted at – was deeply troubling. However, there was nothing she could do about it now.

'Very well, Hubert. And what time will you arrive?'

'I shall be with you for dinner.'

'Good,' she said, though her heart did not feel it. It was better to humour him.

'You do not have to say that,' he said in a grisly imitation of her own words to David yesterday.

'It sprang unbidden to my lips,' she replied, too glibly.

'We shall see,' he said again. 'Until tonight, then.'

'Until tonight. Goodbye.'

He could have said it all at nine o'clock, she thought as she put the telephone down; only that would have been far too amenable of him.

She wondered suddenly whether she should have told David that she wasn't on the pill. It wasn't the kind of thing you wanted to talk about when you were lying under such brilliant stars with the scent of all the herbs of Provence about you.

* * *

Tony Prelati was a great smiler which was a considerable relief. She had been afraid that he would turn out to be someone in the mould of Hubert. Indeed, you couldn't really imagine Hubert having such a smiling friend, but there it was, the evidence was large as life: deeply tanned, dark curly haired and doubtless lecherous as a sparrow. His daughter was another matter. She was, of course, a brunette, she had to be with a father like that, but in other respects she was an archetypal Californian: beautiful in a rather beefy way but ever so slightly sulky about the mouth, and very, very cool. You could see that she felt she was coming, and indeed had come, to a dump.

'Did you have a good flight?' Marie asked them as she met them on the steps.

'Fine, great, terrific,' said Mr Prelati.

'Lousy,' said Francesca.

It set the tone for the visit.

Funny that Hubert hadn't mentioned that Prelati was a Reverend.

She spoke to David on the telephone after lunch, and they confirmed their vows of dedication. Now that they had become so close, the parting seemed intolerable.

'Never mind, darling,' she said. 'I'll call you tonight after he gets back. We'll meet tomorrow.'

She was conscious again of the strange clickety noise on the telephone. Did they never stop watching, these people?

After a late afternoon round the pool with the Prelatis during which she covertly examined the smiling Reverend, wondering what made him smile so much, and whether it was the same thing that made his daughter frown, and what had happened to Mrs Prelati, they all wandered in to change and prepare themselves for dinner and Mr Brickville's return. She was missing David so much that it hurt. Every minute away from him seemed an age; a whole day was an unendurable epoch, a vast grey dreary pre-Cambrian landscape, featureless and fog-bound.

As if to echo her sentiments, the afternoon's imperceptible haze was turning into cloud. There were faint mutterings from far behind the villa, way up in the mountains where the clouds normally sat like fat white cottage loaves, but now seemed to be rolling down like porridge.

She took a shower and lay on her bed, trying to read the latest John le Carré. She got up, paced about, sat down and started to write a letter.

'Darlingest and far above the ordinarily wonderful David, since Mephistopheles sounds much too diabolical for such a good egg, and talking of good eggs, I suddenly wondered whether...'

She stopped. This was no time to voice anxieties about birth control, a subject upon which she knew very little anyway. It certainly hadn't been part of the convent's curriculum. She threw the letter into the waste paper basket, and started again. She had written no more than a line, however, when she heard the crunch of a car on the gravel outside. Mr Brickville had at last returned.

She dressed hurriedly, wishing she could get rid of that sense of dread when he was in the offing, and went to the drawing room. He was standing there talking to Claudine. He did not smile when he saw Marie, but merely acknowledged her presence with a slight bow. She waited while the muttered conversation continued and helped herself to a vodka and tonic from the tray by the window. Drops of rain as big as chaffinch's eggs started to fall very slowly upon the terrace outside. The muttered conversation ceased. Claudine withdrew. Marie could feel Mr Brickville watching her, but he said nothing. To break the silence, she asked some ritual questions about his flight.

'The journey was satisfactory, thank you,' he said at last.

'Would you like a drink?'

'I see you have got into the drinking habit.'

'It's not exactly a habit,' she said, biting back the irritation. 'I thought you might like some company.'

'I am used to my own company,' he remarked bleakly, 'but yes, I will have a small whisky since you are there.'

She poured him the whisky, and added water and no ice the way he liked it.

'Enough, enough,' he said, then more mildly, 'The Prelatis are comfortable, I hear.'

'Yes.'

'She is a charming girl, is she not?'

'She seemed somewhat … er, tired.'

'Of course, of course. I am sure that you will get along famously.'

She thought it most unlikely, but said nothing. He sipped his whisky as if it might be poisoned.

'Now,' he said. 'I must ask you to do something, or rather not to do something that may conflict considerably with your wishes.'

'What is that, Hubert?'

'I must ask you to see no more of your, ah, friends, at least for the few days the Prelatis are here.'

So that was it. She was to be denied the very oxygen of life. She swallowed hard, her heart pounding. 'May I ask why?'

'The Prelatis are very dear friends. It could be rude if you were always haring off on your own account.'

'I would not be always haring off.'

'Nonetheless, I wish you to do as I ask.'

'And if I refuse?'

'Then we shall have to take certain steps.'

She imagined him for a moment on the floor of Bettina Darby's Dancing Academy, above Bettina's stables, where she had been taught the rudiments of the foxtrot and the quickstep one summer holidays, gravely taking certain or indeed uncertain steps. Then she turned on her heel and left the room. As she hurried down the corridor towards her bedroom, she saw the smiling Prelati coming towards her, but she simply couldn't face him. She tore open her door, banged it shut and threw herself onto her bed, sobbing.

She lay there for half an hour, flattened by the situation and that narcotic effect of love which turns happiness into rapture and sorrow into desolation. Finally, she rose from the bed and looked at herself in the mirror. Her face was blotched and her eyes red and puffy. If David were to see her like this, she reflected wryly, it would solve the problem altogether. He would turn and run from this streaky monster.

Thinking about him made her feel better.

She washed her face, dabbed her eyes with cold water and put on a little lipstick. She would find an opportunity to telephone him after dinner. If things went on like this, she would just have to run away with him. She rejoined the others in the drawing room. They all looked up as she came in, as though they had been talking about her. Prelati gave her a particularly beaming grin, his teeth white as a row of war graves.

'I thought you were trying to dodge me there, uh, Marie. You'd make a great three-quarter with a swerve like that.' He laughed heartily to show he was making a joke.

'Sorry, Mr Prelati. I had a sudden attack of hayfever. Thunder sometimes brings it on.'

'Is that so? Well...'

'Thunder gives me the creeps,' said Francesca, shooting Marie a glance of – could it be? – sympathy.

Dinner was dreadful. Mr Prelati told anecdotes that seemed odd coming from a clergyman, though perhaps they ordered things differently in California. Hubert made little donnish jokes about international law on which he was an expert (Marie noticed he never made jokes about money). And Francesca tucked into her food with a kind of suspicious voraciousness.

'What d'you call this, Hubie?'

'That is a coulis of tomato.'

'Coulis? It's kind of thin for ketchup. And this?'

'That is a *rouille*.'

'Rooey phooey. Tell you what, it's giving me hot lips.'

After dinner, they all sat in the drawing room and drank coffee. The men had an Armagnac each and Francesca had a green Chartreuse, which she called chartrooze.

'You ought to have one, Marie,' she said. 'It's sticky like some kind of candy.'

She was becoming progressively more matey.

Finally the storm began. The fat raindrops had stopped, started again, held off, and now like some kind of celestial pee in the night after a party, the clouds could hold off no more. All heaven seemed to be emptying around the villa while peals of thunder bounced and banged about the house like a rackety lavatory seat.

Francesca got up and walked a little unsteadily to the door.

'I can't take this. I'm going off to bed. I'm going to climb right down under the covers and I'm going to stay there. Coming, honey?'

'Er no. I'll just sit up for a while. I can't sleep when there's a storm.'

'Suit yourself. Hope the thunderbugs don't bite.'

Marie thought maybe the two men would take the opportunity of calling it a day as well. Mr Prelati must be tired from his travels and so indeed must Hubert, but they were pulling their chairs closer together and starting to talk earnestly in low tones, while refilling their glasses with Armagnac.

'We're going to be talking shop, Marie,' said Hubert, pleasantly enough, but there was no mistaking what he meant. 'We wouldn't like to think we were boring you,' chimed in the Reverend.

She could see there was no point in waiting. There had to be some other way of getting in touch with David. Why were there so few telephones in Le Bavelot? There was, after all, a socket in the wall of her bedroom, but there was no receiver. She thought she knew what the reaction would be if she asked for one. Perhaps if she got up very early in the morning...

* * *

She woke at half past five to a morning of crystalline, pristine freshness – the storm's reward. She leapt from her bed, slipped on a frock, brushed her hair and, with feet of thistledown, crept from her room.

A floorboard creaked in the corridor. She paused, listened, and then went on – down the marble stairs and into the marble hall. The dining room door was shut. She advanced and very quietly turned the handle. It wouldn't move. She thought there must be some mistake and turned it harder – still nothing. The disagreeable truth hit her. The dining room was locked.

She stared about her. It had never struck her for one minute that she wouldn't be able to get to the telephone; and now she thought, overreacting again with love's adrenalin, I'll never be able to reach him. But, with an effort, she controlled herself and reflected upon the situation, realising something she should have thought about before – to telephone now, at this hour of the morning, would have raised the most awful problems at the Bleu Rivage. Of course, what she would have to do was write a note and deliver it by hand so that he would get it with his breakfast. She found notepaper and a pencil in a drawer of the marble-topped table by the wall and hastily scribbled a message.

'Darlingest David, I am held captive in durance vile while some Americans are here. If I can't get in touch it's not because I don't love you, in fact I love you all the more, and it grows like a pearl in my sadness at not seeing you. I will contact you again at my earliest convenience. Far more love than I can afford, M.'

She had just finished writing it and was pushing it into a little brown envelope when she heard a faint sound behind her and turned in terror of discovery, thinking it must be Hubert. Her feelings were modified but not entirely allayed by the sound of a female voice.

'Hello, honey. And what might you be up to so early in the morning?'

Francesca stood halfway down the stairs in a little-girl nightdress. 'That candy syrup was stronger than I reckoned,' she said. 'Drink always makes me wake too soon. What about you? A billet doux?'

She had seen the envelope.

'Oh no,' said Marie too quickly. 'A letter I've been meaning to write.'

'You can confide in me, honey. Don't worry. I won't let on to old dry-as-dust.'

The temptation to tell someone about her predicament was too great. They sat on the stairs while Marie explained something of the situation in a low voice. Francesca made appropriately soothing noises as she heard that she and her father had been the reason for the interdict on Marie's excursions. She did, however, demur at one point.

'But honey, marry him? Aren't you both a little young? Why not just enjoy yourselves and think of marriage later. There's always other boys. Have you ... You know ... been with him?' Francesca leaned forward earnestly, her fringed top lip slightly drawn up over her front teeth.

Marie was far too far into her confession to deny the truth.

'Well, then,' said Francesca, 'enjoy, enjoy. Is he a good fuck?'

'It's not like that.'

'Not like that? What is it like? Back to back? *Soixante-neuf*?'

'We love each other.'

'Ah, yes, love. I've heard of that. It's a gas.'

Marie remembered a hymn they used to sing at the convent and it didn't seem blasphemous to quote it now.

'If he is mine and I am his, What can I want or need?' she said. It wasn't a gas. It was a solid.

'Right, right,' said Francesca. 'Like it. Poetry always gets me in the gut.'

She patted her slightly protuberant stomach. Her bosoms also wobbled their literary sensitivity. Marie felt that ideally she would have preferred a more delicate confidante but there was no doubting the robustness of Francesca's attention.

'So what you going to do now?' demanded the American.

'Well. I thought I'd slip out now and find a taxi or get a lift, walk if I have to, down to the Croisette, and drop the note into the hotel. He might be up. I could see him and come back here without being missed.

'Good thinking,' said Francesca. 'It's worth a try. Shall I come with you?'

The idea of the strapping Californian lurking around while she was assuring David of her undying devotion did not strike Marie as being the ideal background for her message.

'No,' she said hastily. 'I don't want to get you into trouble.'

'Trouble nothing. I eat trouble.'

'Well … I think perhaps I'd better go alone. I mean you're not dressed.'

'I understand. You don't want to take a gooseberry. I'll cover for you while you're gone. Off you go.'

She put her hand on the latch and turned it obligingly for Marie. But the door did not open. Francesca looked dismayed.

'Oh my God,' she said, 'the son of a bitch is locked. Of course. The whole thing's on alarm. You know what he's like about security.'

Marie felt a surge of panic again. She was never going to get a message to David. It was going to be a replay of their earlier debacle. She felt the tears start to prick behind her eyes, and turned away miserably.

Francesca stepped forward.

'Look, honey, I know what it's like. I've been in love. Have I been in love? I had this guy called Hamilton. What a creep.'

She went on about how she'd loved Hamilton and how her father had disapproved and Marie, in spite of her dejection, started to grow a little bit impatient. After all, this was her misery. She didn't need reminiscences of back-seat bundling in Venice, California, to jolt her out of her sorrow here and now. Then Francesca redeemed everything.

'If I'd had you around then, honey, you'd have done the same for me. So I realise the least I can do is do it for you.'

'Do what?'

'Why, deliver the letter, dumbo.'

Of course. It would be much easier for Francesca. She didn't have Hubert's eye on her all the time. She could pretend to go shopping or something, and just slip the note into the hotel. Marie was so moved she kissed the American on her hairy top lip.

'That's really fantastic of you. Could you … would you do it today?'

'Sure. Nothing simpler. Just as soon as they open the goddam door. Well … after breakfast, anyway.'

Francesca liked her food. It was hardly fair to expect her to go on an empty stomach. Marie gave her the envelope.

'You'll just leave it, won't you? I mean, there's no need to wait for an answer,' she said.

She still didn't like the idea of David and Francesca meeting. It wasn't jealousy or anything – just a sort of instinctive prudence. Francesca seemed the kind of person who could be indiscreet.

'Don't worry, I'm not going to steal your beau.'

'I didn't mean that. I meant…'

'What's this? An early morning pyjama party?' It was Hubert's voice, jocularly disapproving.

'We were thinking of going out for a swim before breakfast,' said Francesca coolly. 'Only some bimbo locked us in.'

She had secreted the envelope somewhere among the little girl flounces of her nightdress, and looked every inch the Californian baulked of her bathe.

'I thought we might be having a problem,' said Hubert, 'so I came down with the keys. An unfortunate necessity, I'm afraid. They've had a number of break-ins around here. There we are.'

The door opened. A brilliant morning bounded into the hall.

'We'll just get our swimsuits,' said Francesca. 'You coming?'

'I won't join you,' he said. I've got to call Tokyo – But go ahead. I'll see you at breakfast.'

'He didn't notice anything,' whispered Marie in the corridor upstairs. 'Thank you more than I can say.'

'Think nothing of it. If you can't rely on your friends who can you trust?'

* * *

Good as her word, Francesca suggested a trip into town to her father over the breakfast table.

'I need some things. Like, would you believe, seems I only packed one swimsuit. A Californian with one swimsuit,' she included Marie in the conversation, 'is like a cat with one life.'

'Maximilien can take you down,' said Hubert, smarmily.

'I think I'll stay up here if you don't mind,' said her father, smiling away at everybody. 'It looks as if it's going to be real hot. I know what you're like when you go shopping, honey.'

'I'm sure Marie would keep you company,' said Hubert pointedly. 'She's a great one for trips to town.'

Marie almost felt tempted to accompany her – but on second thoughts she decided it might prompt Hubert to come and keep an eye on her, although he normally made a point of avoiding the town by day.

She was about to plead the excuse of a slight headache when Francesca forestalled her.

'To be honest, I prefer to be alone when I'm shopping. I don't know why. I guess I feel I can take my time. You don't mind, honey?'

'I don't mind.'

'That's settled then. I'll be back for a swim before lunch.'

She drove off with Maximilien after disposing of an *orange pressé*, two croissants and several cups of coffee.

'I realise I'm going to need a bigger size,' she said. 'These pastries really get to you.' She patted her stomach just above the point where poetry really got to her.

'Goodbye, honey,' she whispered as Marie saw her to the car. 'Don't worry about a thing.'

The morning passed in a gathering saturation of brilliant heat. Marie went down to the pool and swam, and lay in the sun, and moved to the shade of one of the umbrellas where she tried to read.

Tony changed into his trunks and came over to where she was lying, the gold bracelet on his wrist shining like a snake in the black grass of hairiness. She sensed he wanted to talk, but then Hubert walked down in his white ducks, and Tony and he sat at a table in the shade, apart, and spoke about money.

Marie thought she would go mad waiting for Francesca to come back. The sun itself seemed to have stopped in its tracks, stuck at noon in a liquefying firmament. At last, she heard the sound of a motor and the distant cornflake crackle of the gravel. She lay there, not liking to show too much interest or to betray, by expending too much energy in the heat, the stir of her emotions. Finally, Francesca appeared in a very pretty one-piece whose sides were cut almost up to the armpits.

'Very fetching,' she heard Hubert comment.

'Honey, if you were naked you'd be more decent,' said Tony, approvingly.

Francesca dived in, swam four lengths and, at long last, came and lay down beside Marie.

'It's OK,' she said. 'It's done. I gave it to the concierge.'

'Oh, thank you. Did you see him?'

'Honey, it's about a hundred in the shade down there. Everyone's on the beach. Anyway, I thought you didn't want me to see him.'

'I didn't and I did.'

'Love is a hallucinogen,' said Francesca. 'Frankly you're better off with dope.'

* * *

Marie wasn't expecting to hear from David immediately, but after two days she became nervous.

'What's happened to him?' she asked Francesca. 'You're sure you took the letter to the right place?'

'Relax, honey. Sure I'm sure.'

Two more days passed, a week, and still there was nothing. She would be going back to Scotland in hardly more than a fortnight. The situation was becoming impossible.

The more depressed she became, perversely, the more the atmosphere at the villa seemed to lighten. Hubert became positively jocular while the Prelatis seemed locked in a permanent rictus of mirth. Only Marie spoiled the party. Only Marie wandered about like a black cloud looking for a suitable place to precipitate. Was it her imagination or was Francesca becoming progressively less interested in her? Marie concluded it must be her fault; weep and you weep alone. But she couldn't stop weeping alone in her bedroom and in the solitary walks among the orderly French flowers at the top of the garden where the shadows of the cypress trees cut pools of blackness out of the overtended lawn.

'*Come away, come away, Death. And in sad cypress let me be laid,*' she thought, looking down on the boisterous group by the water's edge. The party had been joined by two new arrivals from America: a beefy merchant banker called Durstine and a small, smart art expert called Snell. Snell had Mrs Snell with him. Mrs Snell was also small. She wore a great deal of dark feathery hair and various ornaments of gold upon which her head seemed perched like a parrot's. She thought her husband the cleverest and funniest man in the world so long as he agreed with everything she said.

The additional guests did nothing to cheer Marie's state of mind. The villa was full of laughter but to her it was like the yelping of hyenas. Finally, she could stand it no more. She got up early one morning, pocketing her passport and money and resolved to go down to Cannes at any cost, even if she had to break her way out of a window. The front door, however, was only latched. Evidently the burglary risk had suddenly taken a dive. There was something slightly worrying about it – nothing was simple where Mr Brickville was concerned – but she did not let it hold her up. She was too intent on going to see David.

Normally the walk down to the Croisette would have taken the best part of half an hour. She did it in twenty minutes, hardly noticing the road beneath her. She was going to be with him again, that was enough. David would get her out of this horrible house, rescue her from these laughing strangers. His kindly parents would entirely see the point of them getting married at the earliest possible opportunity.

She ran down the Croisette, crossed the double lanes between two palm trees, narrowly missing a racing cyclist who swore at her in three languages, and leapt up the steps of the Bleu Rivage feeling that she had come home. If they had a room here, she could stay!

The policy of the reception desk at the Bleu Rivage in those days was to be as off-hand as possible to the British, without being actually rude. If you wanted servility, they seemed to be saying, you could pay for it at the Carlton next door. Marie didn't want servility but she did want some semblance of interest.

'*Oui.*' The man hardly bothered to put his paper down.

'Mr David Drummond.'

'*N'est pas ici.*'

'Mr Drummond? Mrs Drummond?'

'*Pas ici.*'

'What d'you mean, *n'est pas ici*? Are they having a swim?'

'*Non.*'

'Have they gone out?'

'*Non.*'

A horrid premonition started to cast its shadow, cypress-like, across her hopes.

'Where have they gone then?'

The man shrugged. '*Ils sont partis.*'

'*Partis?*'

David had said they were staying for at least ten more days.

'*Bien sur, Mademoiselle. Partis. Vous savez? Ils sont pas ici. Ils sont allés.*'

She steadied herself against the desk. She couldn't stop shaking.

'*Quand ils sont partis? Aujourd'hui?*'

'*Ils sont partis il y a deux jours.*'

'Where ... *ou est-ce qu'ils allaient?*'

''*Sait pas.*'

It was like a re-run of a nightmare. She muttered something at the concierge and stumbled out towards the street. Then, on a sudden thought, a flicker of a spark of possibility, she turned back and clutched at the desk again.

'*Oui?*'

'Mr David Drummond. *A-t-il laissé quelque chose?*'

'*Quelque chose?*'

'*Un message ... une lettre...*'

'*Moment.*'

Fish-face peered down at a cache of hotel jetsam hidden underneath the counter-top.

'*Non, non, non, non ... Alors, oui ... Mademoiselle Marie?*'

'*C'est moi.*' She tore the envelope from his hand and sat down in a corner of the lobby.

Dearest Marie, she read, and stopped. Since when had she been Dearest Marie? Darling Marie, perhaps, sweetest most Adorable Marie, certainly. Dearest Marie? What kind of talk was this?

Dearest Marie, I don't even know if you'll get this, but I felt it was the safest bet. My parents have asked me to promise not to get in touch with you, but I feel I must break my promise just this once. It is not your fault, you see...

The letter floated like a pantomime fairy in front of her eyes. The air seemed suddenly very thick and rich. Not being able to bear the thought of fainting in front of Fish-face, she managed to get up and walk outside. Steadying herself on one of the pillars beside the steps, she spotted a bench shaded by palms and facing the sea. After a restorative series of deep breaths, she felt able to cross the road, sit down and continue the worst half hour of her life.

* * *

It is not your fault, you see, she re-read, '*because I am sure that you did not know about this awful thing, this problem that there is. Of course my folks would not have found out if it weren't for some New York friends who were passing through. You know my folks are the most tolerant of people but they want the best for me, and this thing, well, they just could not live with it.*

Marie went over the paragraph half a dozen times. The message – that he was leaving her – was unmistakable. But it simply did not make sense. She was aware of some man sitting next to her, endeavouring to engage her in conversation, but he might have been occupying a completely different set of dimensions for all the notice she was able to take of him. She read on, hoping for and dreading whatever enlightenment there was to come.

And now it strikes me that, as you don't know, it might have been kept from you for good reasons: to protect you from the truth about your father. I feel that they should have told you since you are now of an age to know the truth – and because further evasions will only lead to more heartbreaks. It now falls to me to tell you things that will shock and pain you – and how I wish it could have been someone else. But no, perhaps it is better this way.

The truth, as I understand it, is this. Your father was a very rich man, half-American, quarter-British, quarter-French; heir to a union of two commercial banks with vast international interests. He had a distinguished Army record during his National Service and won the Military Cross in Korea. Afterwards, I'm told, he patronised the arts, and poured money into the development of the better kind of 'pop' in Britain and the US. (It was perhaps this that led him into drugs?) He seems to have taken little interest in the business side of his inherited empire. This also led to problems because the more he amused himself with music and the Californian way of life (he came over in the fifties and more or less settled), the more his business interests began to go wrong. He had some obsession with a particular period in French, and indeed English, history – the time of Joan of Arc and her dashing lieutenant, the Baron Montmorency-Laval, otherwise known as Gilles de

Rais, from who he claimed descent. He claimed to have discovered some literary work of this person and spent more and more time and money on this project to the neglect of his family and fortune.

They were years of tremendous change in the business world, according to my folk, and your father seemed unwilling or unable to come to grips with it. He continued to behave like a baron when he should have been a president. The cash (even his) started to run out, and the more it did, the more he engaged in crazy projects.

A voice – strangely familiar, though she could not remember from where – interrupted her concentration on the extraordinary story David was telling her.

'There's this black man. I went to see him at this place in Nice. Like to go along? He just sits and thinks about it and whoosh. You'd go a bundle on it. Weird and wonderful. Know what I mean?'

Marie turned her head. Her companion from the aeroplane was sitting beside her, gesturing and plucking at her sleeve. It only accentuated her sense of being in a bad dream.

'There you are. Harvey is the name. Thought you were in a trance. I was due for a break so I took a couple of weeks off after the conference. Great place if you know where to go. Got a little apartment up in the hills. Care to come along?'

Marie shook her head dimly as if talking to a shadow.

'Reading.' she said. 'Busy. Can't you see?'

'Stuck up tart.'

He said it without rancour.

She addressed herself again to the letter with its weird combination of David and Oxford essayism.

It was a strange time in California in the fifties, David told her. *'There was a growing population of drifters, beatniks and free-love enthusiasts. There were drugs, there was wine. Half of them didn't know where they were and half of them didn't care. Your father and his friends started to give parties. He had this castle – it was a real one transported stone by stone from the Loire by some madman years ago – in a remote valley up in the mountains. And word started to get around that some of the kids who went there never came back. As I say, it was difficult to know because no one really knew who was who or where they were at. Hash, LSD, amyl nitrate, coke – minds were blowing all over California. Anyway, some remains were discovered and pretty soon the police were called in, and your father hopped across to Mexico just before they got enough evidence to arrest him. It was said that he was up for no less than forty murder charges and a number of other counts that included rape and kidnap. I'm sorry to have to tell you all this, Marie, but you need to know.*

A couple of his friends were arrested and they testified that your father would take his victims up to a room in the castle, mainly boys around sixteen, seventeen, string them up, sexually assault them and then strangle them. I understand he went from Mexico to San Salvador where he started it up again. But this time they caught him and after a trial, where he first denied everything and then confessed, he was convicted and shot. There was a great deal of publicity about the whole affair. The name Lavell came to be little short of Eichmann as a symbol of evil in those days. It is still remembered.

My folks are the most liberal people, Marie. But they do not want me to be involved with, let alone marry, the daughter of a monster. They are afraid of bad blood. They will take me away from Oxford, stop their support for my research and disown me if I persist. I love them and I love you. I also love my work. That makes two against one, Marie darling, and I simply don't have the strength or, I guess, the guts to fight it at the moment. So I must say goodbye. I won't give you my address or ask for yours. It is better that we don't see or even write to each other any more. This has been the saddest, oddest letter I've ever had to write – and, I guess, that you've ever had to read. Please don't think too badly of me. Believe me, I shall never stop thinking of you and remembering our night under the stars. Your all-too Mephistophelian David.

The man beside her was babbling something. Words and sentences formed and dissolved in her head. '...*jeunesse dorée* all around. What can you be thinking of? Stood you up, has he?'

Marie nodded mutely as the tears poured down her face, too numb at the loss of David and the appalling contents of the letter to do anything but weep. She took out the letter and re-read it until her tears started splodging the blue ink and she had to put it away again. Her fragile world had shattered and she could hear the pieces pattering around her. She rose and hailed a passing cab. There was something she had to do. She had to be quite certain.

'Come on, Harvey,' she said to the man. 'Get in.'

* * *

They were all sitting round the pool as the taxi drew up. Then some of them rose to their feet. Only Francesca and Durstine still lay, laughing together. Francesca's big buttocks, divided by the tight shiny black one-piece, looked strangely metallic, like twin communication transmitters beaming into space. Perhaps it was they who had transmitted to David's parents the details of her father's life and death. It was a base enough act. Marie told the taxi to wait, whatever happened, got out of the car and stood fixedly gazing at the buttocks. She was conscious of Hubert and Prelati and the little man Snell advancing upon her. It seemed to take them an age to walk across the grass. Time seemed curiously disjointed, running in fits and starts as though it needed greasing. Hubert was trying to persuade the man and the taxi-driver to go but the man was not to be deflected. Hubert was leading her into the villa. Harvey followed as if he were a paying customer at a walk-in drama or a visitor to a lunatic asylum's annual pantomime.

'You look pale, my dear. You must have a Cognac.'

Prelati poured her brandy from the decanter and she tossed it back. There was a sudden false dawn in her throat and stomach.

'Can't beat a drop of the hard stuff,' said Snell in a false Irish accent.

'Is it true?' asked Marie, wildly, looking at them as if they were zookeepers.

'Is what true, my dear?' asked Hubert.

'Is it true about my father? That he tortured and murdered boys? He was a monster? They shot him? Is it true? IS IT TRUE?' she shouted.

The faces exchanged glances, looked grave. Harvey's eyes flicked between the speakers, Wimbledon-style.

'These are grave matters,' said Hubert, 'and perhaps should not be aired in public. I am only thinking of you.'

'Ask for me tomorrow and you shall find me a grave man,' she said.

'Who told you this?' asked Hubert at length.

'Hamlet,' she said.

'Come, come, my dear. Your father.'

'The king my father...'

'Who told you this about your father?'

'David,' she said, and burst into tears.

'Aw, c'mon, honey,' said Prelati, thinking better of proffering his handkerchief and finding a tissue.

'The young man? It was very wrong of him,' said Brickville.

She stopped blowing her nose. 'It was not wrong of him. He was the only one who would tell me the truth. It was right of him.'

'It was wrong of him to tell you, without warning, without … preparation, something your own family for good reason withheld. We didn't wish to upset you unnecessarily.'

'No one prepared him. If I'd known, I could have done. And you are not my family.'

'I see there is no reasoning with you,' said Brickville, pursing his lips.

'It is true, then,' said Marie.

'Yes, it is true,' agreed Hubert. 'But I could have wished it to be revealed to you more opportunely. After your eighteenth birthday, I should have told you. But that discussion will have to be postponed. Who were these wicked people who breached such a confidence, who spread such vile…' he was going to say lies but changed it to '…rumours?'

'It wasn't a rumour,' said Marie, crying again. 'It was true. Everybody knows now.'

'Perhaps you had better go and lie down, honey,' suggested Prelati.

For some reason the suggestion stung her. 'Lie down?' she said. 'I'm not going to lie down. I'm getting out of here. No…' as Hubert and Snell moved towards her '…leave me alone. I'll kill you.'

She grabbed a glass jug and swung it wildly.

'Now, now, my dear,' said Brickville. 'We don't want any more killings in the family.'

She put down the jug and looked at him, at all three of them. 'I'm going to pack now,' she said. 'Don't try to stop me. I'm going to pack and I'm leaving in that taxi. He'll hear me scream if you try to stop me.'

'Very well,' said Hubert, 'if that is what you wish. Doubtless your money will soon run out and you'll come back when you've had time to reflect. Remember, what I did was for the best. I carried out your aunt's wishes. Your father's … fate is not my fault. Meanwhile, may I urge prudence? Find a room by all means. Cannes is full of rooms. Have a good ponder. I believe you'll find you come around to our – to my – way of thinking. Above all, avoid compromising situations. Cannes is full of compromising situations. Remember there is a certain wildness in the blood.'

'Thank you, Hubert,' she said. 'I'm not likely to forget that, am I?'

While they exchanged glances once more, she left the room.

Packing took less than five minutes. She simply threw all the essentials and a couple of dresses into a single suitcase, and left the rest for the passionate housekeeper to squeeze into.

Everybody was lined up in the drive when she came out. Francesca came up to her and threw her arms around her in a Judas-like embrace, squeezing her with her shiny, buttock-like bosoms.

'So long, honey. Don't do anything I wouldn't do. See you soon, I guess.'

No one made any attempt to stop her. Harvey detached himself from the assembled company and joined her. She and Harvey climbed into the car while the taxi-driver put her case in the back.

'*Vous voulez?*' he asked.

''*Sais pas,*' she said. '*Autre part.*'

The taxi crunched the gravel. No one waved.

* * *

She had decided to ask the cab to drop her on the Croisette again so she could sit and think some more.

'Chin up, then,' said Harvey as they slowed down. 'Tell you what. I'll buy you a drink at a little place I know. Make you feel better.'

She allowed him to direct the driver down the road, past the palms and private *plages*, down towards the public beach and the more regrettable café-bars. She seemed to have no will, and was content to bob along after his whim like a listless dinghy. They turned off the main square and struck up into the old town.

'You'll love this,' he assured her as they alighted. 'Ethnic. You'll go a bundle on this one.'

It turned out to be a perfectly ordinary little bar in a tiny hidden square which held a single tree and five tables.

The man ordered pastis which she ordinarily disliked but she drained it without even adding water.

'Good girl,' he said. 'I can see you're a goer.'

She was still in a state of shock but after three more pastis she was beginning to feel some return of sensation, chiefly that of the man's hand on her thigh.

'I like you,' he said, 'I really do. Soon as I saw you on the plane, I said "Harvey," I said, "you're in luck and no mistakes". It's not often I'm moved. Very particular, I am.'

'Could I have another drink, please?'

'Certainly. *Garcon!*'

He failed to pronounce the C with a cedilla, and clicked his fingers in a ridiculous travesty of certainty. It seemed to work, for the patron came scurrying out, cocking an inquisitive black olive eye.

'*Encore les pastis,*' said Harvey.

'*Mais oui, M'sieu.*'

109

More pastis appeared, this time with a plate of patron's eyes in oil. Swimminess had now entirely superseded shock in Marie's sensations.

'But I haven't introduced myself,' said Harvey. 'Harvey Ambrose Sales Manager for the Multifab Organisation. We're heavily into household products and disposable wipes for kitchen surfaces.'

'Oh.'

'I don't suppose they mean much to you, eh? I expect you don't remember those years when rags were used instead of disposable wipes.'

'I expect so.'

All this talk of wipes and products was stirring something in her mind. Something rather important. What was it? Ah yes. She'd missed her period. Her period was two days late. She'd never missed her period, not once since the first time. She suddenly sat bolt upright. The import of the realisation scattering the mists of aniseed.

'I'm going to have a baby.'

'No. You never.'

'I am.'

'Well, you've come to the right man. I can keep you in hygienic surfaces for life.'

The offer was so ridiculous that Marie couldn't stop herself from laughing.

'There you go,' said Harvey. 'Overwhelmed, that's what you are. It was a generous offer. But there's no need to take on.'

'I'm not laughing, I'm crying. I mean, I'm…'

It made her laugh all the more until she found herself crying uncontrollably. She was dimly aware of being half-carried to a taxi – she knew it was a taxi because of the bobbly noise the engine made – and then she passed out.

* * *

She woke with a headache in somebody else's bed, in a room with drawn shutters and the smell of drains.

It was the worst awakening she had ever known; and as full awareness flooded back, she pushed (as the French say) a little cry of distress. Things couldn't be this bad. They simply couldn't. David must have made some mistake. She couldn't be the daughter of a monster – she with her gentle tendencies and her art – it simply wasn't possible. She would have to talk to Nanny. Nanny would say it wasn't true. David would come back as soon as he knew that there had been a mistake. Someone else with her father's name, that must have been the thing, simple as that. But the more she reassured herself, the more the black toad in her stomach gave her the lie. It is true, said the toad. You must suffer. Those poor children died in agony and shame because of something in you. You are guilty too.

It made it all the more imperative, if she were indeed pregnant, that she should not bear the toad. What she was thinking was unthinkable to herself as a Roman Catholic – but as a human, surely, she had a duty not to extend the bloodline? Meanwhile, the only good thing about pregnancy was that, whatever had passed in this bed, it would not end up with her having the appalling Harvey's baby.

What had passed in the bed though? She explored herself gingerly, finding that though her dress had been taken off, her bra and pants had been left apparently undisturbed. She didn't like the thought of the salesman peering at her underwear but it was better than a cold ravish any day.

She groaned again. Far from home, lost, quite possibly pregnant, short of money, no friends and – worst of all – condemned to remaining friendless. All those whispers about bad blood now came back to her; the Aunts in the garden, the Abbess, the nuns at school, the strange behaviour of Harriet's mother who wouldn't let her go to New York, Mrs McGarrigle, the Prelatis ... everyone had known except her. They had viewed her, all of them, as some kind of freak. It explained so much of her loneliness and puzzlement over her life. How dare she feel so condescending towards Harvey? She was lucky to have Harvey. If Harvey had ravished her until her fillings fell out, she could have no cause to feel anything other than gratitude for some human attention.

She groaned once more – a groan not so much of self-pity as of self-disgust. She got up and looked at herself in the mirror, stepped out of her pants, undid her bra, and examined herself minutely to locate the mark of the beast. The smell of drains was like incense to her. She was steeped in vileness.

At that moment, Harvey came in. If Harvey had dreams of delight – and it is not in a salesman's brief to have dreams of any kind – but if he had, it would have been to come into his bedroom and find a pretty girl looking at her naked body in the wardrobe mirror.

'Oh, it's you,' she said. 'Do you want to fuck?'

Harvey, as it happened, ridiculously, was rather a good lover, which was just as well because, apart from her night under the stars with David, her experience was strictly limited.

He drew her to him and ran his nails down her back, down between her buttocks and up again which made her suddenly shiver with ... no, not with pleasure, with – there was a word for it – lust. Lust was for the damned.

He stroke her breasts and ran his tongue like a little red Hoover up and down over her nipples. She could feel the dampness begin to gather in her loins. So this was what the girls at school snickered about! It was worth more than a giggle.

He knelt down in front of her, in front of the mirror and began to lick her as though she was the most delectable fountain of fruit, of ... what was that ridiculous fruit called? A kumquat! As though I were a kumquat, she thought. Monstrous, of course. A Monstrous Kumquat. Oh yes Harvey, happy salesman. I am not going to forgive you for this. You will be condemned to ... Oh yes.

She stood there looking down at him as he licked – she would draw him like this – she ran her hands over herself, over Harvey's mouth and over her own. She came with a great groan – it was groaning day – and Harvey looked up at her, smiling wetly like a pleased dog – and pushed her slowly back onto the bed.

* * *

The next few days passed in a bizarre fugue of drinking sessions and loving. They hardly went outside the apartment which was just as well because Harvey's little place up in the hills faced on to a corrugated workshop for tractors and industrial vehicles.

It was true, if you craned over to the right, that you could catch a glimpse of the distant sea, and over to the left a distant vision of a church atop a walled village, but mostly it was tractors. However, had it been a vision of the Celestial City itself, it would not have made the blindest bit of difference to her. In fact, quite the reverse; the Celestial City would have tormented her with its promise of benefits and peace. Hell's fire would have brought her out, because there she belonged.

Meanwhile, Harvey's bed and the bottle were the nearest fires she could find, and she stoked them with a will. If she was condemned, she had to accept the role and not shiver in the wings. It gave her a sense of wonder to see the effect she had on the man. They would put the negro out of business, she thought. She could practically make Harvey ejaculate just by looking at him.

On the fifth day, Harvey – who had been reduced by pleasure to a white-faced, red-eyed relic of his former bouncy self – a mere Hologram Man held together by his moustache – apologetically announced that he would have to be getting back home.

'What?' Momentarily shocked, she sat bolt upright in bed, her breasts still making him gasp with delight.

'I've got a job, you know,' he said.

Of course he had. The world was out there, forcing decisions again.

'O disposable man,' she said sadly.

'It's all very well for you but I've a wife and nappies to support.'

She was not surprised. 'You never told me.'

'I'm sorry, Marie. Honest. I didn't want to spoil things.'

It didn't make the slightest bit of difference as far as she was concerned. He could have wives and mistresses all over Pinner or wherever it was he lived. She deserved no better, but it would have been nice to have been told.

'Don't worry, Harvey. Can't be helped.'

'You're a good sort, Marie.'

'No I'm not. I'm a bad sort.'

'You're good in bed.'

'That's bad in my book.'

'It's been the best week of my life.'

Poor man, she thought. There have to be better things for him than drunken fornicating. The Abbess would say it is the devil's work, substituting the great uncleanness for the good, but she didn't argue with him; there were other practical problems which he never voiced.

'What will you do?'

'I don't know. Don't worry about me.'

She had never spoken about her background. It was the last thing she wanted to discuss. When Harvey had touched on the subject, she had deflected him with other touches. Similarly she had not questioned him about his own life though she suspected that there might be little of interest or improvement to be garnered from it. The pub, the wife, the sales target.

'Is there nothing I can do?' asked Harvey, putting on his trousers regretfully.

She looked at her bag and counted her money: 800 francs and £50. Whatever she did now, she was not going back to Le Bavolet.

'You could lend me enough for a ticket to Edinburgh,' she said.

The only tie she felt in the world was Nanny. She had to see her.

'I'll give it to you.'

'Lend,' she said. 'Not give.' She felt she wasn't worth a gift.

'Have it your own way. I'll call the airport now.'

* * *

She bought a few more clothes and some make-up in a Prix Unique at Cagnes-sur-Mer – she didn't want to go through Cannes itself again for fear of meeting Mr Brickville or some other member of the party – and she said goodbye to Harvey whose plane for London left first.

There were tears in his eyes as he kissed her. She had the guilty feeling that life would never be the same for him again.

'I shall never forget you,' he said.

'You must never forget I owe you £150,' she replied.

She had taken his business address so the money, when it arrived, wouldn't embarrass him in front of his wife.

'I've forgotten that already; it's you I can't get rid of. "And I shall love thee still, my girl, till all the seas run dry."'

What a change had come in the brash Harvey since first they'd met! Instead of the ejaculating negro, he was spouting Burns. What would the Abbess make of that?

'Forget me, Harvey. It was a good fuck, that's all.'

'Shhh.' He was almost prim. But the shock of the words had the desired effect. You couldn't harbour romance for a girl who said fuck so loudly in public. Home and the kitchen surfaces and Multifab were calling, to say nothing of the fractured syllables of the flight announcer.

He kissed her more restrainedly and was gone. Suddenly she felt terribly alone. She had little experience of travel, and the airport seemed large, noisy and frightening. She was hungry and thirsty but she didn't like to approach the forbidding-looking bars. Everyone seemed to know exactly who they were, what they were doing, where they were going. Only she, the outcast, was a drifter. And nowhere does the drifter feel more vulnerable than in a French airport.

She finally found a table and ate half a croissant that someone had left on a saucer, under the resentful eye of an Algerian cleaner. When her flight was finally called, she was feeling as low as it is humanly possible to feel without sinking through the earth like an out-of-control graphite reactor core. An inertia, a passivity, had settled over her again. It was not to be dispelled for many months.

She had done what she could, she had been what she might, but the forces of fate had been too strong for her. She was not what she had supposed herself to be. With one stroke, David's letter had accomplished what secret police interrogators and wise psychiatrists endeavour to undertake in days, weeks and years. It had taken her apart. The suppositions about herself, the limestone-like drippings and accretions which go to make up the stalagmites of personality, had been broken off at a stroke. She was nothing again, a fragment on the end of a drip of time; the child of a monster, blood not on her hands, but in her very veins. How many people had suffered as a result of that bad blood of hers!

And at 30,000 feet over the Massif Central, eating compressed *pâté aux pistaches* and drinking a large glass of Côtes du Rousillon, though the outcast felt better in herself, she only found her mind wandering more freely. She could not cry. The situation was too serious for that. Perhaps it would be better if she killed herself.

'Don't worry,' said a voice next to her. 'It may never happen. Scared of flying?'

She looked around at a fit-looking, donnish man in his early fifties. He had greying salt-and-pepper hair and amused, very pale, blue eyes that gazed steadily at her from behind gold-rimmed lenses, taking her in at his leisure.

She shook her head. She would be quite happy if the 727 nose-dived into the extinct volcanic cap of the Puy de Dôme far below, but she didn't like to say so.

'Trouble, then?' asked the man. 'Want to talk about it?' she shook her head again. He had a cultured American accent, pleasing after the boisterous Prelatis.

'Perhaps you would allow me to buy you some champagne? I have found it the only reliable antidote to trouble.'

In her passive state, she found this direct offer easier to accept. And it was true, the Piper-Heidsieck did lend a certain swirliness to her black cloud. She had feared the American might want to talk but he merely smiled, raised his glass and read his paper.

Just as they were nearing Edinburgh and the seat-belt sign had come on, he spoke to her again. 'In case you ever need help,' he said. 'Do call.'

She looked at the card he handed her. It said: Felix Middleburg, The Other Judas Inc., and gave addresses and telephone numbers both in London and New York. She put it in her bag and gave him a polite smile. The unaccustomed action of the facial muscles made her realise it was the first time she had smiled for some time.

'Thank you,' she said.

'I shall look forward to hearing from you. *Au revoir.*'

* * *

The hospital was deathly warm, and the sister was full of concern about Nanny whom she called Miss Henderson.

'Such a shame. Miss Henderson is heavily sedated. If only you'd come a couple of days sooner.'

'Will she ... wake up again?'

'I don't think so. Doctors say Miss Henderson only has a few hours.'

Poor Nanny, Marie thought. She must have felt lonely in this place.

'Did she have any other visitors?'

'There was an older man last week. Quite distinguished he was. Friend of the family. Very kind. He brought Miss Henderson such lovely Californian grapes. Pity she couldn't eat them but Mrs McIlwraith in the next room enjoyed them so much.'

'Oh good.'

'You must be very quiet when you go in.'

'Yes,' she said, 'mousy quiet.' That was what Nanny used to say.

'That's the spirit,' said Sister. 'You bought some flowers? What beauties! But she mustn't have flowers in her room. It's gone to the lungs, you see. But Mrs McIlwraith will be over the moon.'

Marie wanted to tell her that her father had killed thirty young boys after sexually abusing them. There was something about the Sister's comfortable white starch that invited such a shocking disclosure; but she'd probably take even that in her stride. Everything would have its pigeon-hole in Sister's scheme of things, each waiting for its inevitable docket.

Nanny was lying, looking as white as Sister's apron, on a narrow bed with various tubes stuck in her. Her eyes were closed. Even her face was shut up as if Nanny, tidy as ever, had put away all the pens and papers of thought and expression, folded neatly against Judgement Day.

'Nanny.'

There was no response, not a flicker of an eye or a stirring of a wrinkle. Marie advanced and took her by the hand.

'Careful,' adjured the Sister, leaving the room. 'I'll be just outside if you need me.'

'Thank you.'

Marie stood holding Nanny's hand while the tears rolled down her face. She was weeping, not for herself but for the quiet, good, lovely little life that was being extinguished in front of her, and for the bright cheerless public manner of its ending, with strange people pushing tubes up her nose and no one to visit her but a gentleman with grapes she couldn't eat, the purpose of whose visit she would be too polite even to enquire about.

'Sorry, Nanny,' she said. 'I'm so sorry.'

The fact that she had been with Harvey, in bed, surrounded by the smell of drains, while she could have been here giving comfort to the poor old thing did nothing to improve her feeling of guilt. Everywhere she turned these days, guilt and more guilt and still more guilt surrounded her, grimacing and louring and leering at her like the gargoyles of Notre Dame.

Suddenly she was aware of a tiny movement deep down in the wizened body; almost, as it seemed, a flicker inside the brain.

'Nanny. It's me ... Marie.'

The eyes opened. Sea-pool eyes, little red-rimmed wells of sadness and wisdom and pain that had looked on death and would do so again, presently.

'Ma…' She had so little breath in her wasted lungs that she couldn't manage the full name.

'Shh, Nanny. It's me. I love you, Nanny.'

A single tear, all that the desiccated frame could furnish, squeezed out and hung just below the corner of the eye. The lips formed, the throat strained to speak. The effort was too great and Nanny sank back. Marie felt a tiny answering pressure of her hand. She was thanking her for coming.

'I know, Nanny. I'm sorry I didn't come before. I was in France with Mr Brickville. I didn't realise you were ... like this ... I've been so selfish.'

'Not…' The old woman finally got the word out.

'Not? Not what, Nanny?'

The sister came in. 'Time's up I'm afraid. Miss Henderson is so tired.'

'She's awake.'

'What? She can't be.' The sister hurried over, saw the open eyes.

'Well, it's almost a miracle.'

'...guilty,' said Nanny with a little groan, squeezing her hand very tight and sinking back with her eyes open.

'That's it, I'm afraid,' said the sister, going through the rituals and finally closing the eyes. 'So glad you could make it. They like to go on their way with a loved one near.'

'How do you know?' asked Marie. 'How do you know, how could you possibly know how they feel?'

The Sister was astonished and displeased. 'It stands to reason, doesn't it? And now, if you don't mind, we have some tidying up to do.'

'You'll die one day,' sobbed Marie, tears streaming down, and well out of control, 'and then we'll see who likes it.'

'Now there's no need to talk like that. You'd better be on your way.'

'Yes,' said Marie, 'and no loved one near either.'

* * *

What had Nanny been trying to say? Did she feel guilty about keeping the father's crime secret from his daughter although she had done so for the best of reasons? Or was Marie not to feel guilty because her father had been a monster? It all amounted to the same thing, she thought, as she switched off the light of her cheap hotel bedroom – cheap because she had changed her French francs and now had only £120 in the world. There was now nothing for it but to lose herself somewhere, to go away where she was not known, anything rather than return to the castle and the chilly jurisdictions of Mr Brickville. She fell asleep and dreamt of being chased by Mr Brickville across every possible terrain and circumstance as he turned from wolf to snake to pterodactyl and back again into Brickville.

In the morning, looking out at Edinburgh's cheerless brown battlements, the urge to shed her associations with everything that she had known and everyone who knew her was stronger than ever. The notion of killing herself had subsided as a result of the previous evening. She felt that what Nanny was trying to say had made it impossible. She must live with her degradation.

The problem now was money. Even the lowest of the low needed up-keep. Had she no training for anything at all? In the lobby of the hotel, she asked the aged receptionist if there were any papers. She was handed the London *Evening Standard* of the day before.

'Someone left this,' the crone said. 'Ye can have it for free if it's any guid tae ye.'

She took it out with her to read over a coffee and, thumbing through the small ads, as she wondered what it cost to rent a flat in London, she came across a notice ringed by the previous owner in red ink: 'Personable girls wanted to train as croupiers and hostesses for London's most exclusive new casino.' She jotted down the number and rang it from a callbox.

'Merrymaid Agencies. Can I help you?'

'I should like to train as a hostess, please.'

'Hang on a minute. Vi, someone here to train as a hostess. Oh. Right. Hello, caller. What is your name?'

'Er. Marie er...Sinclair.'

No point in giving anything away.

'Right, Marie. Can you come on over?'

'I'm in Edinburgh.'

'Edinburgh? Goodness me.' There was a silence.

Marie sensed a hand over the phone. 'Hello?' she said.

The voice re-emerged. It was a London voice. 'D'you want to come in, then? Or what?'

'Tomorrow,' said Marie.

'Right, then, dear. Here's the address. Ask for Madeleine.'

Marie took the train and turned up next day in her best Prix Unique dress at Beauregard House, an undistinguished pudding-faced building near Victoria.

* * *

'Is this where the casino is?' she asked the purple-haired receptionist.

'Good gracious, no. That's in Mayfair. This is personnel, publicity and administration. Take a seat. Madeleine won't be a minute.'

Madeleine was half an hour, during which Marie had ample time to take stock of the drab street outside, the unprepossessing reception room with its uncomfortable purple-padded (purple, she learned, was the Merrymaid house colour) circular seats and curved white cubicles and the receptionist who surreptitiously ate her bogies when she felt you weren't looking,

Finally Madeleine arrived. She was a breathless redhead, majestically built, in a white blouse and green tartan skirt. 'Sorry to keep you,' she exhaled. 'Emily, isn't it?'

'Marie.'

'Ah yes. All at sixes and sevens today. We've got the Americans in.'

'The Americans?'

'Parent company.'

'Oh.'

'Would you like to come to the interview room?'

123

'Right.'

She followed the girl down a corridor to a small white room containing two white, purple-padded seats. The far wall was taken up by a single pane of mirrored glass.

As far as Marie could tell, the interview went satisfactorily. She gave her age and the address of the bedsit she had found that morning near the shabby hotel in King's Cross where she'd spent the night. Madeleine started asking questions about her health, her height, her measurements and her weight.

'All right,' she said at last. 'Now I always ask candidates if they mind taking their clothes off. It is part of our standard routine just to make sure everything's in order. We have bizarre cases. There was the one-legged lass, and of course there have been one or two sad instances of handicap. We can't afford to take chances. Our Merrymaid motto is, once you're in, you're on. We look after you very well, I think you'll find. So, Marie, I ask you now: would you mind stripping off for us as the final stage of your interview? An interview that I may say has been, so far, most satisfactory.'

Marie shrugged. If the woman wanted to check that she had two legs and two breasts that was all right with her. Who was she, Marie, to object to that? A blood test might have been something else. That was where her deformity was. Compared with the badness in her blood and in her bones, she couldn't help thinking that a breastless mono-ped would have passed the Merrymaid test with a rating of *summa cum laude*.

As Marie stepped out of her bra and pants, Madeleine looked at her expertly. 'Just walk up to the mirror, dear, and turn around. Oh, yes, very nice. Smile at the mirror. Head up. Let's see those breasts. Our Merrymaids are renowned for their generous charms. Thank you, dear. You may get dressed. That's more than satisfactory.'

'You mean I've passed?' asked Marie, covering her generous charms with Prix Unique synthetic lace.

'Just a formality now,' said Madeleine. 'Mr Ledbrow.'

There was a pause and a tall, heavy man with a serious expression entered the room followed by an even taller, heavier, more serious American – at least Marie judged him to be American from her acquaintance with Messrs Prelati, Durstine and Snell. When he spoke she was proved right.

'Say "hello Mr Merriman" to Mr Merriman. You're in luck. It's Mr Merriman himself.'

'Hello, Mr Merriman,' said Marie.

'Ve-ery nice,' he observed. 'I congratulate you, Marie. You have made Merrymaid. There are girls who'd give their eye-teeth for what you got. And men who'd give a lot of something else. Know what I mean, Madeleine?'

'Oh, Mr Merriman,' said Madeleine, archly, looking as if she might add a 'fie' at any moment.

'Give Marie ten days training, and send her down to Pilgrim's Piece for the weekend after next. All right, Marie?'

'You're a privileged person, you know that?' Madeleine whispered to her as she helped her into her coat.

'She can start on eight grand plus dress allowance and service. This one I like. I'm going to take a personal interest in you, Marie. You've got class.'

It was true, Marie thought, she had got class – only Mr Merriman didn't know what sort of class it was.

* * *

125

The normal course for a Merrymaid hostess was three weeks, but as Marie had many of the qualifications already – table manners, dress sense, social poise, aptitude, conversation, information, cleanliness 'above and below', these being the course mandatories – it was cut to ten days in her case.

'I have a rule,' said Madeleine, who turned out to be the course supervisor, 'never to ask my girls why they want to be a Merrymaid. I ask them everything else: boyfriends, sex life, religion, aversions, but the fact that they want to be a Merrymaid is enough. The course itself weeds out any unsuitables. But in this instance I am curious. Why have you, a girl with many options, settled on this particular career?'

Marie thought for a bit. They had just been through a particularly gruelling session of first-base croupiering. 'I just want to,' she said finally. 'Isn't that enough?'

'Of course it is. I stand reproved. Now, would you like to tell me about your sex life?'

Marie told her what she seemed to want to know, and Madeleine told her about Pilgrim's Piece.

'It's very old, you know,' she said, 'Jacobean at least. Set in the rolling Sussex countryside. I never know why countryside has to roll but there it is. I'd rather have my countryside standing still. I was caught in an earthquake once near LA. Talk about rolling countryside, it was jumping all over the place. You'll go to California if you play your cards right. Anyway, back to Pilgrim's Piece. Forty acres, parkland, tennis courts. You play tennis? Good. We can cut that lesson too. Heated swimming pool, sauna, jacuzzi, you name it. Own projection theatre, squash court. You play squash? Never mind. We've had three cardiacs on the squash court, so you're well out of it. What else? Fishing, Clay pigeon shooting, horseback riding … you like horseback riding? Good…'

'But what exactly do they do there?' asked Marie.

'I ride in the park with Mr Merriman sometimes,' said Madeleine. 'The new casino is going to make the others look like cheap paste and cardboard. I am in love with Mr Merriman.'

'Oh,' said Marie. 'Ah.'

'I know it's hopeless but what can I do?'

'Nothing, I suppose,' said Marie.

'You suppose right, Marie. I can do nothing. But I can dream. Would you like me to tell you about my sex life?'

'Er, well,' said Marie.

'You're right. It would overstep the delicate boundary between pupil and tutor. All I will tell you is that, in my fantasies, I am in his arms every night.'

'Ah,' said Marie. She was finding it a useful syllable.

'Where were we?' asked Madeleine, her red cheeks extra flushed.

'I was asking what exactly they do at Pilgrim's Piece. Who goes there apart from Mr Merriman?'

'Well,' said Madeleine, calming herself, 'there are business associates, VIPs…'

'VIPs?'

'It's sort of public relations, you know. We ask people we think may be helpful to the organisation. Peers, politicians, industrialists, top journalists, merchant bankers, academics…'

'And do they come?'

'Some of them.'

'And where do the hostesses come in?'

'We are there to see the guests have everything they want.'

'Everything?'

'What you do in the way of personal hospitality to the guests is entirely up to you. But, in the relaxed country atmosphere, Merrymaids have been known to lose their heads. Romance is in the air.'

'I see.'

'You'll love it. Everybody does. The cuisine is A1, and some of the people you meet, well, you'd never have thought it. We had a bishop last year. Had the party in stitches!'

'It does sound merry,' said Marie. It didn't sound the sort of place Mr Brickville would come to at any rate.

'Merry is the word,' said Madeleine. 'You'll see. Come, come. Time to learn our cocktails.'

Madeleine drove Marie down to Pilgrim's Piece in her new Mini Cooper. She was very proud of it.

'A company car,' she said. It had a Merrymaid sticker in the back. 'Come make Merry,' it said. Somebody had written 'Who's Merry?' on it.

She took her mini through the ranks of Mercs, Jags and Porsches, and parked it discreetly around the back near the kitchens. A van was unloading crates of champagne.

'Merrymaids use the back door unless accompanying guests,' she told Marie.

Inside she led her into a sort of servants' hall next door to the housekeeper's office. There were six other girls sitting there smoking and reading magazines. They looked up when Madeleine and Marie entered.

'This is Marie,' said Madeleine. 'And this is Wendy, Louise, Tracy, Stephanie, Julie and Margot.'

'Hi, Marie,' said Margot, a small girl with brown hair, sharp features, a Merrymaid bosom and quick blue eyes. 'You the new kid? Abandon hope all ye who enter here.'

'Now, Margot. What sort of talk is that?' said Madeleine. 'Margot's a great one for jest. We encourage a quick wit ... up to a point, don't we, Margot?'

'Oh, we do, we do,' said Margot.

All the girls were in their Merrymaid outfits already: a country wench effect in cream and purple with short skirt and exceedingly low-cut, though high-propped, bosom. The bosom was the hallmark of Merrymaids just as the leg or the buttock was the forte of some of the rival organisations. Merrymaid bosoms trembled on the edge of total revelation like golf balls on the tee in a very high wind.

'Better go and change now,' said Madeleine. 'Margot will show you your cubicle.'

Margot took Marie up some back stairs to a long, low room at the back of the building overlooking the rubbish bins. It was divided by thin wooden partitions into a dozen little sleeping booths. Each booth had a bed, a chest of drawers, a chair, a hanging-cupboard and a bible.

'It's no great shakes, I'm afraid,' said Margot, looking out at the bins. 'In fact, the great sheikhs have the best rooms. Doubtless you'll see them all in good time.'

'Ah,' said Marie.

'You're a funny kid. You don't seem to show anything.'

'Show?'

'No emotion. You just let it happen.'

'That's right.'

'Don't you mind? This place? All these silly old farts pretending to be important people, and just dirty old men when it comes down to it?'

'No,' said Marie. She didn't mind. It was no more than she deserved.

'Well, you're lucky. I mind. I was a dancer but I broke my ankle. It didn't heal properly – like I can't dance any more. So I dance attendance instead. Oh yes, Mr Ledbrow. Oh certainly, Mr Akropolis. Sit on your face, Sheikh Addad? The pleasure is mine.'

'Girls.' They could hear Madeleine calling nearby.

'Hurry up and get into the tart's costume, Marie,' said Margot imitating Madeleine. 'Best tit forward.'

Marie unpacked the two regulation Merrymaid uniforms she'd had fitted in London, and changed under the watchful eye of the other girl.

'You'll be very popular, dear. That's right, you won't need a bra. The words Merrymaid and brassière should never be used in the same sentence.' Margot was imitating again.

It was true, the Merrymaids costume made any other support unnecessary. Marie could feel herself wobbling precariously near the very limit of exposure.

'Mind how you lean forward,' Margot advised. 'It isn't done to lose a breast overboard. Suggestion is everything but it walks only a millimetre ahead of indignity.'

Marie had heard the phrase employed more than once back at the pudding-faced building in Victoria. She had learned to walk leaning slightly backwards, a couple of millimetres ahead of falling over.

'Ready? We've got to go now. We're to have a pep talk from Old Merriman himself.'

* * *

The girls piled into a study decorated in a free interpretation of the Victorian manner. The walls were lined with books, most of them leather-bound volumes that had not been opened for many years. In between the book were pictures, hunting prints on one side, Rowlandson scenes of huge-bottomed girls sitting upon old scholars' knees on the other. There was a log fire crackling in the grate with an intricate ornamental clock upon the chimneypiece surmounted by a gilt Cupid. There was a great globe, yellow with age, standing in a corner with little purple flags on it representing the spread of the Merrymaid empire. There was a purple leather pouffe and there was a table with a great book on it, bound in purple leather, open, with what looked like photographs of Merrymaids inside it. There were two huge leather armchairs with purple cushions. On one of them, asleep, was a large wolfhound with a purple leather collar. There was a great mahogany desk covered with tooled purple leather which held a purple leather blotter and silver milk churns, which served as purple pen-holders.

Behind the desk sat Mr Merriman. Mr Merriman was wearing a purple dinner jacket and a face the colour of thunder. He didn't waste any time on pleasantries or how d'you do's.

'Which one of you is Margot?' he barked.

Margot raised an arm carefully so as not to dislodge anything.

'You Margot?'

'Yes, Mr Merriman.'

'Get out.'

'What?'

'You heard me. You run down me. I'll run-down you.'

'R … run down?'

'Don't play the innocent with me. Get out.'

'Please, Mr Merriman. I don't understand.' Despite her previous bravado, Margot was obviously frightened and distressed. She needed the job, it seemed.

'You called my guests, what was it? Silly old farts pretending to be important people?'

'No, I...' She looked wildly at Marie, wondering how he could have known.

'No,' said Mr Merriman, 'she didn't tell me. It's no good looking at her. Come here.'

Margot hesitated, then advanced to the desk. She looked small and vulnerable beside the great purple symbol of authority.

'Here,' growled Mr Merriman, basso profundo, motioning her beside him.

She moved nearer. There was a pause. None of the girls moved. Marie stole a glance at Madeleine who was standing behind them with her eyes fixed devotedly on the master. The wolfhound woke up and gave two enormous barks as if echoing its master. Margot lifted an arm as she ducked involuntarily to protect herself and one of her breasts fell out.

Mr Merriman gazed on her with satisfaction as she struggled to replace it and then ran sobbing from the room.

'Now,' said Mr Merriman, suddenly in a good humour and addressing himself to the rest of them, 'it's my pleasure to welcome you all to another Pilgrim's Piece Weekend. Our guests include Hamish Tysoe, the broadcaster and celebrity; Sheikh Mustapha el Saba of the Emirates; Professor Ivan Presscott of Reading University; Lord Ettenwater; Bruce Kahn, the international stock exchange guru; one of the under-secretaries at the US Defence Department, over here on a visit, Josh Piecowicz and, last but not least, a very good friend of mine, Dicky Henshaw of the The Other Judas Charity Trust…'

Marie knew that name, though she couldn't remember why. Perhaps she should be careful with Tricky Dicky. Merriman, still speaking, his eye roving round his audience and his girls like a helicopter searching for low life, suddenly fixed his gaze on her as though his sensors had registered a misfit.

'…they are all very, very seriously wonderful people, and I want you to make them feel just very much at home. You will find your dinner partners on the table by the photographs. Marie…'

'Yes, Mr Merriman.'

'Since this is your first visit with us, I want you to use your eyes, take the place in, don't miss a trick and stay very close to Madeleine and me. You will be sitting on my right at dinner.'

Marie saw Madeleine go white and sway slightly at this last piece of information. She had doubtless been hoping for the place of honour herself, especially after her useful titbit about Margot's indiscretion.

'Oh, right.'

'She's a gas, that one,' said Mr Merriman. 'I tell her she's sitting next to me at dinner and she says "Oh right". Can you beat it? Can you beat that, Madeleine?'

From the look on her face, Madeleine would not simply have liked to beat it, she'd have liked to lash it within an inch of its life and then submerge it in salt water. But she said nothing. It was the only way with Mr Merriman.

* * *

Marie found Margot touching up her face in her cubicle. She was still in her Merrymaid dress.

'Aren't you going then?' she asked. 'I thought he'd told you to leave.'

'Good God, no. He loves that barking bit. He practically had an orgasm when I popped out. He'll do it to you one day. He does it to everyone. Just cry a bit and make sure the tit comes out, otherwise he's really cross. He must have caught a complex as a baby. You wait till I catch that bitch Madeleine. She heard me when I was talking to you. She's always creeping about.'

'Ah.'

'You're right. I'd better watch it. You can't play the party popper trick too often.'

Somewhere down in the house a gong sounded twice.

'That's the drinks gong. Come on, we're on parade.'

Margot led Marie down the corridor to a small door which opened on to one of the main landings of the house. As they descended the great staircase together, Marie was aware of the grey-haired man in the panelled hall peering attentively at their legs. He stepped forward as she approached ground level, and introduced himself with outstretched hand.

'Hello,' he said, smiling in a clenched sort of way and showing tobacco-browned teeth. 'I'm Ivan Presscott. And you are…?'

'Margot,' said Margot, stepping forward trimly. (The costume evoked adjectives likes 'trimly'. 'Pertly' was another favoured by the monthly Merrymaid magazine which was the flagship of the Merrymaid enterprise, featuring Merrymaid of the month amid other buxom undertakings.)

'Ah, Margot. I see,' said Presscott professionally, as if she had introduced a subject which prompted the greatest speculation, 'Margot. Yes. Very well. Mmmm. Margot.'

He 'mm'ed and 'Margot'ed a bit more and Marie was just about to pass on towards the half-open door through which emanated sounds of conversation interspersed with the chinking of glasses when the Professor spun round and stopped her with a yellow-fingered hand on her shoulder.

'Not so fast, girlie,' he said.

Marie turned. 'Yes?'

'I want to know your name.'

'Marie,' she said.

'Oh that's very nice. Marie. How very nice that sounds. But don't you think "Marie, Professor" would sound even nicer?'

'Marie, Professor,' said Marie.

'That's much better. That's ever so much better. Because that is my title. I am Professor of Applied Psychology ... you have heard of applied psychology? That is the subject in which I profess to be an authority. Professor Presscott from Reading. I am more psychotherapist than behaviourist but my door is always open. Reading is the city mainly built on biscuits — and which houses the university in which I pursue my chosen subject which happens to be...'

'Applied psychology,' said Margot. 'Sounds fascinating. Terrific.'

'You are a bright girl,' said the Professor as he led the way into the drawing-room. 'Your friend seems rather dull.'

The room was full of very important people trying not to look down the Merrymaids' dress-tops.

* * *

Margot went on with the Professor and joined a group near the fire, but Marie lingered behind, looking, for want of anything else, at the furnishing of the room. It seemed to be well done. There was no purple here: green brocade curtains, green-covered sofas and chairs, a huge Persian carpet lying on polished wood; paintings on the walls, good ones, probably of the Norwich School – yes, she was sure there was a Crome and on the far wall a couple of undoubted Boningtons. There was what looked like a Roubiliac bust on a plinth beside the window; a gilt framed looking glass; some famille rose vases; an Adam fireplace and a Steinway grand piano.

Her art teacher had been something of an authority on fine art and had taught her well. Marie was conscious that in happier times she would have examined all these treasures more closely. She now merely registered them without great pleasure or surprise. They were good things. They happened to be there. She knew that she should do something about her listless attitude – it couldn't be good to drift along like this – but try as she might she could find no energy, no hope. It was as if much of her mind had been shut up like a holiday house, with dustsheets, waiting for the moment, if it ever came, when someone would draw the blinds and let the sunlight in again. Perhaps, she thought to herself, perhaps this is what a breakdown's like after all. Someone at school, a girl called Loretta, had suddenly started screaming in chapel one day. The nuns had hustled her away, and told the girls later that she had had a breakdown. They had talked earnestly about it afterwards. Breakdown was such a dramatic word – as if you suddenly wouldn't work any more, like the school bus, with a piston sticking out through your head. This dullness of hers, Marie thought, this wasn't a bit dramatic. But then dullness couldn't be dramatic, could it, unless you were someone like Dryden or Pope: 'The midwife laid her hand on his thick skull, with this prophetic blessing: "Be thou dull"' – That was dramatic. And yes, indeed, that was what had happened to her. The blessing – like her father's disgrace – had simply got through to her rather late.

She felt a hand falling upon her now, not upon her skull, but upon her shoulder. It made her breasts wobble and she steadied herself apprehensively. 'A penny for them,' said a practised voice, mellow with the self-pleasure of a professional communicator. 'You are lost in thought. I had been hoping to attract your attention.'

'Oh,' said Marie. She looked up and saw a youngish-oldish man with that peculiar gloss on his face that comes from public exposure.

'You have probably seen me on television,' said the man. 'You watch *Who's the Chump?*'

'No,' said Marie.

'You must be the only person in this room who doesn't.'

'I'm sorry,' said Marie.

'Don't be sorry. It's rather refreshing. I'm Hamish Tysoe.' The man held out his hand.

Marie shook it. It was rather disingenuous making such a polite and formal gesture with one's breasts surging around like buoys in a swell. 'My name's Marie,' she replied.

'You're new here, aren't you?'

'Yes.'

'Thought so. What are you doing here? You somehow don't look the sort.'

'The sort of what?'

'The sort of Merrymaid one usually finds here.'

'Oh.'

'Not that it's not charming to find you here,' he added quickly, thinking that she might be offended. 'It's most particularly absolutely spiffingly charming.'

He used words like 'spiffingly' a great deal in his programme. It encouraged contestants to be even more chumpish than they were normally.

'Thank you,' said Marie. 'But it doesn't matter.'

'Doesn't matter?'

'I wasn't offended.'

'Ah.'

A footman dressed like a flunkey came up with champagne. Hamish Tysoe sipped thoughtfully.

'I'm in the Summoner's Room,' he said at length.

'Summoner's?'

'All the bedrooms here are named after characters from the Canterbury Tales. You mean you didn't know? Pilgrim's Piece you see.'

'I see.'

'Last time I was in the Nun's Priest's Room. But this time it's the Summoner.'

'He had a fyr-red cherubinne's face,' said Marie, dully.

'Capital,' said Hamish Tysoe. 'Absolutely ripping.'

He fell about, slapping himself on the thigh, as if she'd said the funniest thing in the world. One or two of the other guests looked over, curiously.

'Well, I must say,' he spluttered at last, wiping his eyes, 'I didn't expect to hear Chaucer tonight. Not from a Merrymaid. I expect you'd tell me the names of the two heroes in *The Knight's Tale* if I asked.'

'Arcite and Palamon,' said Marie, without enthusiasm.

English Literature had been taught religiously at the convent, although *The Miller's Tale* had been side-stepped.

Tysoe went into an ecstasy of thigh-slapping.

'What's up, Hamish?' enquired Mr Merriman.

'This girl of yours,' said Tysoe, wiping his eyes, 'this girl of yours actually has some frontal lobes.'

'I know that,' said Merriman, slightly testily. 'That's why she's a Merrymaid. We pick 'em for their frontal lobes.'

'*Lobes*, Merriman … brainbox lobes, not *globes*. Although the globes are great too.'

'Sure, sure,' said Merriman, smiling broadly now, 'that's the way we pick 'em. That's what sets Merrymaids apart. Personality, brains, lobes, globes … that's our pecking order. Isn't that so, Madeleine?'

'Oh definitely, Mr Merriman.'

The gong for dinner sounded.

'Would you like to take my arm, Marie?' said Mr Merriman as though bestowing the ultimate benefit.

'Oh, right,' said Marie.

'Doesn't that kill you?' said Mr Merriman to the company in general. 'I say to her would you like to take my arm, and she says "oh, right"!'

Everyone laughed except Madeleine who was half-pleased at her latest recruit's success, half-sick at being denied the longed-for favour.

'Remember,' said Tysoe in Marie's ear as they went in to dinner, 'Summoner. I'll summon ya.'

'Oh, right,' said Marie.

Tysoe doubled up with laughter. It was strange how the phrase seemed to have that effect on people. What she really wanted to do was identify Dicky Henshaw and find out what he and the charity were about, but so far, because of these strange media and banking baboons, she'd had no opportunity. Margot had told her 'the real fun' started after dinner. Perhaps her opportunity would come then.

* * *

The dining room was, in its way, as well-appointed as the drawing room. There was a Reynolds on the wall behind the Sheraton sideboard, flanked by a couple of Lawrences – each one a portrait of a lovely woman. There was a voluptuous Etty nude over the mantelpiece.

The table itself was long, enticingly caparisoned with white linen and sparkling silver, like a bride for her spouse, and adorned with a pair of exquisite Georgian candlesticks whose light was thrown back a thousand times by three different sizes of Waterford crystal beside each place.

'You sit here,' commanded Mr Merriman, 'beside my very good friend Dicky Henshaw.'

Now that was more like it, Marie thought. She turned to her right and was greeted by a thousand-watt smile. Dicky Henshaw was a sleek man in his late forties with dark hair, tanned face and very white teeth.

'Hi,' said a grizzled man inclining to portliness who was drawing out a chair opposite her. 'Josh Piecowicz.' He had a look both of cunning and authority about him that Marie had seen before on a portrait of a sixteenth century pope by Lorenzo Lotto.

'How do you do,' said Marie.

'Doesn't that fold you up?' said Josh Piecowicz.

'Sure does,' smiled Dicky Henshaw. 'I thought style had gone out the window till I came to Britain.'

'But in a Merrymaid, for chrissakes?'

'Why not in a Merrymaid?' rejoined Mr Merriman. 'I would have said you would expect it in a Merrymaid.'

'Yeah, I reckon you would say that,' observed Mr Piecowicz, wryly.

'Oh really, Mr Merriman, this is awfully nice wine,' said

Merrymaid Trisha, a stunningly pretty redhead from Chelmsford, with a 40B bust and a brain the size of a mustard-spoon, who was sitting next to Piecowicz. She would show the little newcomer that she wasn't the only one with a bit of style. She crooked her little finger round the Waterford stem and sipped her Corton-Charlmagne, pouting with what she considered ladylike refinement. You could see Piecowicz wishing he had a Waterford penis. He turned to her, transparent with lust.

Henshaw, however, was made of suaver stuff. Marie had noticed that, almost alone among the men, he didn't seem interested in bosoms.

'I understand you're from Scotland,' he said to her.

Merriman shot him a glance that Marie intercepted. Who had told him that? She was sure she hadn't mentioned to anyone where she came from. It was the kind of question Merrymaids (UK) Ltd did not ask. But there was no point in denying it. She did not have the energy.

'Och aye,' she said.

'Beautiful country,' he said. 'We have offices in Glasgow and Aberdeen, of course.'

'Of course,' said Marie. Smoked salmon had arrived and she pushed it listlessly around her plate.

'Sometimes our chairman goes there. He says it's business but I reckon it's the fishing.'

'Fish?'

'What you're eating now.'

'Oh. Salmon.'

'King of fish, Marie. You can't say "oh, salmon". Not of salmon out of the Spey.'

'Oh. Right.'

'I like your attitude, Marie. You're really relaxed.'

'Oh?'

'I'm sleeping in the Pardoner's Room. I hope you'll come round later for a chat.'

'Ah. Well…'

'If you ever felt like moving on…' he lowered his voice so that Merriman, who was being buttonholed by Madeleine, couldn't hear. 'If you ever felt like moving on from here, we could maybe find you a job.'

'In Glasgow?'

'If you like.'

'I don't think so, thank you.'

'In the States, then.'

'Ah.'

Even in apathy, she could see there might be some advantage in going to America. It would be a fresh start. With the Aunts' name, her old name, of Sinclair, no one would connect her with her father and the taint of Lavell. She leant towards the man with renewed attention

'Think about it,' said Henshaw.

'Oh, I will. Right. Certainly. I should like that.'

He seemed surprised. 'You would?'

'Tell me about The Other Judas,' she asked.

'Well…' the man looked at her again with a puzzled interest, almost like the dawning of perception.

'It started life as a charity, a family trust actually, but it became more commercially involved: finance, property, building, banking, funds – though there is still a charitable arm. It is run, of course, from the US of A. California, actually.'

The American on the plane. Marie felt she was on to something here. She was curious to know more.

'What was the original charity?' she asked. 'The family trust, you said?'

Henshaw frowned. All this was slightly outside his area, which was real estate. 'It was a foreign name...' he started to say. 'Wait a minute ... You say your name is Marie?'

But Merriman, who watched the conversation at table like a Wimbledon umpire, now stepped in. 'Say, Dicky, property building, banking, trust funds – that sounds dangerously like shop. You know the rules. No shop talk at table or you have to drink a sconce.'

Merriman had discovered the possibilities of 'sconcing' from a Professor of Theology at Trinity, Oxford, where the sconces were quart-sized silver bowls or chalices, which sat on each long table. If anyone at dinner in Hall spoke of sex, religion or politics, or the portraits on the wall, the sconce could be called for and filled with beer. The unfortunate defaulter then had to drink the contents in a couple of minutes. It all appealed to Merriman's well-developed sense of the potentials of humiliation.

Dicky, for all his suntan, paled. Sconcing was not to be taken lightly, scrubbed you out for much of the evening if not all of it, and there was something about this girl that he wanted to explore – well, two things actually.

'The girl asked me, Sam. You can't call that a sconceable offence.'

'You were talking shop, Dicky. Don't try and wriggle out of it. Or do you want her to be sconced too?'

The idea seemed to appeal to some of the diners. They wanted to see a Merrymaid paralytic with drink – and it wouldn't be the first time. But others demurred.

'Over my dead body,' cried Tysoe, who did not wish the Summoner's Room to be a lonely place that night.

'And mine.'

'And mine.'

Marie felt quite the mediaeval lady as knights sprang to her support while Madeleine looked daggers at her.

Merriman now called the table to order. 'I propose a sconce for Dicky Henshaw. Does anyone want to second that?'

There was a pause while the men considered their positions. At length, the Professor from Reading raised a hand. He reckoned he was in academe not finance, and Henshaw couldn't touch him.

'Professor,' called Merriman, 'you out for blood too? You wanna second me?'

'I reckon so, pardner,' said the Professor, in an ugly imitation of a Western, which offended Merriman though he hardly showed it.

'Fill the sconce,' commanded Merriman, and the butler stepped forward with two pints of foaming ale (it was always at the ready) which he tipped into the chalice.

Henshaw shot a look of venom at the Professor – bang went Reading's funding for King Henry's Chair of Mediaeval History – grasped the silver sconce and managed to down its contents in the desiderated time, before sitting down unsteadily and remaining rather quiet for a while. Marie was relieved. It had seemed to her that Henshaw had been on the verge of putting two and two together. She had learned enough about The Other Judas for the moment. At any rate, that was one awkward invitation for the night that she would not have to find an excuse for. The game show host, Tysoe, however, was still looking at her hungrily. In the quiz game *Who's the Chump?* they apparently never took no for an answer. He had turned away momentarily to talk to Margot who was sitting on his other side, and who was in turn next to the Professor.

Merriman leaned over while Tysoe was otherwise engaged.

'How's it going, Marie?'

'Fine, thank you,'

'No problems?'

'None.'

'I'm very pleased with you, Marie. You can come to my room later. That's the Host's Room. Like he ran the show. Know what I mean?'

'Sure.' She could sense Madeleine gazing at them anxiously.

'I've not read the Chaucer piece,' he continued, 'but I understand it's spoken of well. You didn't tell me you were into culture. I like that. I really do. I'm going to make you our education person. First thing you do, make me a reading list for my bedside table. Can't promise I'll read it but it'll sure look good.'

After the salmon came the duckling a l'orange. A pale garnet coloured Clos de Vougeot was dispensed into the second of the Waterfords, and conversation became more and more animated. Trisha from Chelmsford was now rather drunk. The edge of her left nipple had started to peep out of her costume, scuttling in again like a rabbit every time she put her fork down.

Marie thought, if I wasn't so depressed, I'd be depressed. This thing is going to go on for hours. I don't like any of them. The conversation's ridiculous. The only good thing about it is the food and that's no good because I can't enjoy it. I can't enjoy anything. If I'd been brought up a protestant, I'd kill myself – tonight – in the Pardoner's, the Summoner's, the Nun's Priest's, the Reeve's, the Knight's, the Squire's, the Manciple's or even the Host's Room. But I can't. I don't believe in God any more, but I just can't kill myself.

The duckling gave way to cheese. Cheese was succeeded by summer pudding and clotted cream. An exquisite Château d'Yquem was served, transmuting the chaste crystal to tones of Silurian resin.

A Merrymaid called Martha was doing something unseen to the Sheikh which was causing him the utmost entertainment. Trisha's tit was scampering all over the place as she showed Josh how to work an imaginary pair of castanets. Margot was telling Tysoe a succession of dirty stories much to the distress of Professor Presscott who was being ignored, and Madeleine was telling Mr Merriman how great and good he was – a subject of which he only intermittently seemed to tire.

Finally, coffee was announced, and they all trooped back to the drawing room. A very old Denis-Mounié Cognac was distributed to some. Others opted for the 1938 Warre port.

Margot went to the piano and played some Cole Porter songs, singing in a small, high voice. Trisha succeeded her on the Steinway and played chopsticks hideously.

'Come on,' said a voice in Marie's ear. 'You can do better than that, surely?'

It was Dicky Henshaw again, raised somewhat from the dead. There was something knowing about the man, almost as though he were reading her thoughts. She got up. Madeleine was leading Trisha away, urging moderation.

'But I want to play,' Trisha was saying. 'Let me play. I want to play.'

'Mr Merriman says…'

'I don't care what Mr Merriman says.'

'You'll be playing another tune tomorrow.'

Marie sat down at the piano. There was something very soothing about the piano and the touch of its cool white keys. She hadn't played for years but she remembered a tune that Miss McKenzie, who had taught her up to Grade 5, used to make her play because of the B flat key. She tried a few chords and then started to sing:

'A North country maid
Up to London and strayed,
Although with her nature it did not agree.
And she wept and she cried and bitterly she sighed.
And she wished once again in the North she could be.
O the oak and the ash and bonny ivy tree,
They flourish at home in the North Country.'

There was a moment's silence when she stopped, and then they started to clap.

'Bravo,' shouted Dicky Henshaw.

'I like it, I like it,' bellowed Mr Merriman.

'Can I play now? Why can't I play now?' shrieked Trisha.

Marie thought of something else: a song from *The Yeoman of the Guard* that Nanny used to like. And what was the song called? She knew it was appropriate in some way. She could sing it now. Was it 'Strange Adventure'? That was another song, though appropriate in its way. It was called … yes … 'A Merryman and his Maid'. What could be better? It was a duet – Nanny used to sing it with her – but she'd have to do the best she could.

'A Merryman and his Maid,' she announced.

Everybody fell about.

'A cabaret,' they cried. 'I like it.'

Mr Merriman was convulsed, almost speechless, with surprise and pleasure.

'*I have a song to sing-o,*' she started.

'*Sing me your song-o,*' another voiced chimed in. She recognised its owner as Bruce Kahn, the stock exchange guru she had seen at the end of the table. It was nightmarish to sing these nursery songs in this awful place.

'It's the song of a Merrymaid nobly born
Who held up her noble nose in scorn,
At the song of a Merryman moping mum
Whose heart was full and whose mouth was dumb,
Who sipped no sup and who craved no crumb
And who sighed for the love of a lady.'

'Hey-dee, lady…' Kahn joined in where Nanny used to,

'Misery me, lack-a-day-dee,
He sipped no sup and craved no crumb
But who sighed for the love of a lady.'

Mr Merriman sat gasping like a stranded haddock before he could find his voice. 'Why did nobody sing me that before? You guys should've told me,' he turned on Madeleine.

'We didn't know it, Mr Merriman,' she confessed.

'It's Gilbert & Sullivan,' said Marie. 'We used to sing it at school.'

'We didn't know it,' repeated Madeleine, almost in tears at her dereliction.

'Not know it. Not know what's going to be our Merrymaid anthem. Why, goddammit, that's just terrific. Get the agency to rewrite that moping mum bit – I never hired a moping mum in my life – but the rest will do just fine. Who is this Gilbert Sullivan jerk?'

'I'll get it sent up from Town tomorrow, Mr Merriman.'

'You do that.' He turned to Marie. 'Hey, kid, that was great. You write that down for me sometime, huh?'

'Oh. Right.'

'Hear that? Oh, right. Hear that, Lord Ettenwater? English style.'

'Oh, right,' said Lord Ettenwater, an ageing sex-obsessive of impeccable lineage. On the pretext of congratulating her on her style, he happened to mention that he was sleeping in the Nun's Room.

Later, they all had to play sardines. Marie got into a broom cupboard she could have sworn was empty, only to find it full of Bruce Kahn.

'Well, well, well. Two songbirds in the nest,' he said, catching at her bosoms as though they were a bull market, and knocking the points he had scored with 'The Yeoman of the Guard' right off his rights issue.

She managed to put a hoover between herself and the financial guru, and started fending him off with a dustpan. It was sheer instinct. She didn't really care whether she fended him off or they fucked against a squeezed-mop, two brooms and some floor-polisher. It was all one to her.

'Ow. Silly little bitch,' he said. 'Come here. I can make you rich.'

'I am rich,' she said, and immediately regretted it.

He lowered his hands. 'Well, well, well. I wonder who you are and what you're doing here. Rich girls don't come here unless they're very weird. Like to come and tell me about it. I'm in the Wife of Bath Room. Not the wife of bathroom, you understand. The Wife of Bath Room. Subtle difference. It has a bathroom, of course. The Wife of Bath bathroom.'

He was clearly rather drunk.

'I'm sorry,' she said instinctively, 'I'm having my period.'

'Oh fuck off,' said the financial guru.

It was an accurate forecast as far as he was concerned..

However, it was not an excuse she could field the next weekend, for it was reported to Mr Merriman and Madeleine kept notes on these things.

Marie stayed with the Merrymaid Organisation for three more weeks and then decided that was enough.

* * *

In those days, abortions were still hard to come by unless you had a doctor's certificate, and Marie didn't even have a doctor. The day after the party, she had asked Margot what she should do.

'Oh God,' said Margot. 'That's tough. Merriman will have a seizure. He hates girls getting pregnant. It's bad for his image. Sex is good clean fun. It's not for procreation.'

'I was pregnant when I joined,' said Marie.

'That's against the rules too.'

'I'm not worried about Merriman. I'm leaving anyway.'

'That'll give him a cardiac. You're his little star,' said Margot.

'I don't want to be anyone's little star. Not even Merriman's. I'm not star material.'

'That's what you think. Still, if you want out, I don't blame you. He'll lay into poor old Madeleine for bad recruiting.'

'I'm sorry,' said Marie.

'I'm not. What will you do?'

'I don't know. I'll have the abortion and then I'll think of something.'

'I thought you were a Catholic.'

'I was a Catholic.'

Margot jotted something down on a scrap of paper and passed it to her. 'You could try this place. I don't guarantee anything,' she went on. 'The guy I knew might have moved on. He was all right. It could be someone else now.'

'You had an abortion?' Marie asked.

'Oh. Yeah. Two as a matter of fact.'

'What's it like?'

'You feel bad afterwards. I did, anyway. Bad in the head, you know, depressed.'

'I know.'

* * *

Marie simply climbed out of a downstairs window at Pilgrim's Piece with her suitcase early one morning, walked two miles to the station and caught the early train to London. She bought a newspaper, made a cup of coffee last for two hours in a café and went to the address Margot had given her. It was a grim-looking house in an old terrace near King's Cross. She knocked at the door and after some time it was opened by an Asian woman in a dirty white apron.

'Yes?'

'Dr Janes?'

'He not live here now, What you want?'

'I want Dr Janes.'

'He not live here now. What you want?'

The conversation was becoming circular. Marie tried a new tack. 'I wanted to see him about a baby.'

'You want baby?'

Marie got the feeling that, with the instinct of a true trader, the woman would negotiate anything.

'I don't want a baby.'

'Ah. Then you come to right place. Please to step inside.'

Marie hesitated but she had screwed up her courage. Catholic or no Catholic, she felt she had to go through with it.

The hall smelt vaguely of curry and disinfectant.

'Sit in waiting room, please. Doctor will see you soon.'

She waited half an hour in the dingy partitioning of what had once been a classic rectangular Georgian drawing room. The walls were peeling, the net curtains yellowing and the reading matter two years out of date – sold no doubt as a job lot to Dr Janes. She was just about to get up and walk out when the Asian woman re-entered.

'Doctor will see you now.'

She was ushered up the stairs to a room where a small Asian man crouched behind a desk. This seemed strange until she realised he was tying his shoelace up. Upon seeing her, he straightened himself and smiled expansively.

'Come in, come in. I am Dr Patel. Push off, you old cow.' This last was addressed to the woman who seemed to want to linger. She shut the door behind her and Dr Patel pointed to a chair.

'Sit down, please. Now, what can I do for you?'

'I'm enquiring about an abortion.'

'Abortion, abortion. Let me see. That will be one hundred pounds. Cash on the button.'

'That's all right,' said Marie.

'I should like to see it, please. In cash. We have some terrible disappointment. Terrible.'

'I will bring it with me,' said Marie, thinking it might be wise not to lay the money out on the desk just yet.

'As you wish. But no song, no supper. That is house rules.'

'I understand.'

'Now I should like to examine you. Take off your clothes and lie on the couch.'

152

Dr Patel did not bother to turn his back while she slipped off her dress, rolled down her tights and took off her bra.

'Yes, yes. Nickies too,' he flapped at her panties.

She stood there holding her hands in front of her wondering what on earth she was doing, but Dr Patel had no such doubts.

'Onto the couch, please. Knees up.'

Marie lay there, exposing her most secret places – those which the cream of international society had so coveted – to this seedy little man who burrowed about like a mongoose. All she saw of him was a greasy scalp revealed by thinning hair.

Finally, he put some kind of oil on a pair of rubber gloves – she hoped to God they were new; he certainly hadn't washed his hands – and reached up into her so sharply it made her gasp.

'Ahh.'

'Quiet, please.' He withdrew his hands and stood over her. She put her legs down feeling slightly sick. She reminded herself that there was no indignity that she did not deserve.

'You are two months pregnant? We must not wait too long. Bring the money. Would tomorrow be suitable?'

'Yes. I suppose so.'

'Suppose, suppose?' he lectured her as she dressed. 'You should have supposed when you got up to your tricks. You should have supposed the time-honoured consequences. Yes? What is it now, old cow? Can't you see I am busy with this young lady?'

The Asian woman had come in with a slip of paper. 'Mrs Shamir wants some pills for the dog,' she said, smiling broadly in explanation to Marie, 'he got worms.'

* * *

153

Marie booked into a cheap hotel and lay on the curve-shaped bed looking at the ceiling. Outside, the autumn evening was squeezing dull tear-like rain from a brooding sky. All around her, in the little cheap rooms of the cheap hotel; in the shoddy bed-sits and the squalid flatlets; in the hopeless bed-and-breakfast establishments where homeless families waited eternally for housing; in the council estates where children screamed, muggers mugged and fear and apathy stalked the graffiti-ridden walkways like the smell of fried 'convenience' individual dinners and urine; in the sodden squats; in the lodgings; in the hostels; in the Council Care Centres; in a hundred thousand pokey little flats and houses, the inhabitants of that particularly despondent part of North London waited for whatever deliverance from pain, hunger, boredom or despair the evening would bring. The human engines throbbed like clapped-out taxis and the massage parlours did their best to cope with the traffic.

For Marie, as the light declined, the darkness brought no relief. She thought, if I am not prepared to kill myself, I cannot kill the child. All right then, I must kill myself and have done with us both. But that would be two deaths and I should be twice damned. Not that I believe such things. I am damned anyway by blood. And if I believe that, should I not then kill the child who is heir to it too? The child will be quarter monster?

She fell into a restless sleep racked with dreams in which she pleaded for her father's life who also turned out to be her bloodstained child.

She woke up early, horribly hungry, to a brilliant sunrise, determined not to go back to Mr Patel. She would have the child and leave it safely somewhere as soon as it was born. The question now was, what should she do for the next seven months? Winter was coming. She had saved, from her Merrymaid pay, about three hundred pounds. It wasn't going to get her or the little bastard far.

She went out and had breakfast in a Kwality Bar. The predictable breakfast platter – bacon, egg, sausage and tomato – accompanied by toast and coffee confirmed her feeling of determination. The menu said 'please ask your waitress if there is anything further you require', so she asked her. The waitress's bosom – she would have done well as a Merrymaid – projected the name Elise on a plastic rectangle.

'Yes?' said Elise, halted in her clackety course across the 'farmhouse' tiles.

'I need somewhere to live and I need a job.'

'You and who else, luvvy?'

'Just me.'

'I mean the whole world's looking for 'em, ducky.'

'Oh.'

'Sorry.'

'It does say ask on the menu, I mean if there's anything further you required.'

'It doesn't mean accommodation.'

'I know.'

Elise was momentarily interested. Her real name was Tessa. She thought it boring but she was much more of a Tessa than an Elise. And Tessas – as opposed to Theresas – are usually rather nice people. Who was this girl who was playing games with management's carefully researched menu board? A thought struck her.

'Are you pregnant or something?'

'Yes.'

'You poor thing.'

'My fault.'

155

'You want to get rid of it quick.'

'No.'

'You're soft in the head. Look, I must get on.' Someone was shouting 'Elise' from an edifice that looked like a brick-kiln in the centre of the restaurant.

'Don't worry,' said Marie. 'Thank you anyway.'

'Come back tomorrow at four. I'll see what I can think of.'

'Elise,' shouted the chef.

'What's the matter? Caught your dick in the microwave?' She shouted back.

One or two of the other regulars joined in. Insults were part of the early morning feast at the Kwality Bar.

* * *

Marie bought a street map and spent the rest of the day wandering round the neighbourhood. It had struck her that perhaps she might have gone to somewhere more wholesome than King's Cross. It might have been better for the child. But somewhere wholesome could contain people who might have heard of her – Brickville, putting the word out, alerting the police. Somewhere wholesome could even have people who knew her. Girls from her school came from all over the wholesome place. And somewhere wholesome would have been expensive.

Besides there was something suitable about this part of town. It was, she discovered as she walked, a sort of down at heel no man's land between the classical elegance of Bloomsbury and the ordered gentility of Islington. There were Georgian houses, but they had come down in the world.

The shops themselves were indications. Food was cheaper here: a hundred little Asian establishments stayed open till all hours undercutting the big supermarkets. There were strange junk shops crammed with spindly chairs and derelict nests of tables. There were Indian restaurants and Chinese takeaways; laundromats; pawnbrokers; a little low shop which mended watches, called Time Out of Mind: Antique and Ridiculous.

She passed in front of this and finally went in. She had in her bag an old fob watch given to her by her aunts on her sixteenth birthday, which she'd been told had belonged to her grandfather, and which she thought she might be able to sell if it could be made to work.

Inside, the shop was filled to the roof with timepieces of every description. There was a constant irregular noise of time at work, a whole choir of ticks and tocks from the slow basses of a couple of grandfathers (one with a moon, the other with a ship sailing across its face), on to the tenors of the hunters and half-hunters and the half-heard descants of the wristwatches, which lay in a glass case jumbled under the counter.

An ancient spring-bell, which had sounded as she entered, seemed to have no effect on whoever ran the establishment. She waited patiently for she was in no hurry. She closed her eyes and listened to the time.

'Chronos, Chronos, mend thy pace,' said a soft Fife voice, a little way behind her. 'You are perhaps the still unravished bride of quietness, close friend of silence and slow time that I have been waiting to meet.'

She opened her eyes and saw a man in his late thirties, of medium height, slight build, dusty brown hair and pale blue watchmaker's eyes.

'You have a watchful manner,' she said.

For the first time in two months she had made a joke. She started to cry.

Instead of being embarrassed, the man came round the counter and held her comfortably against his shoulder.

'I'm sorry,' she said, after a while, 'it was the joke.'

'People normally laugh at jokes,' said the man, proffering a handkerchief. 'Especially their own.'

'You come from Fife,' she said, blowing her nose.

'That is true. How did you know?'

She hesitated. She did not want to give any hints to anyone, not even to the nice watchmaker.

'I had a friend once who came from Fife,' she said, 'from Pittenweem.' It was where Nanny had come from, a fishing village.

'I know Pittenweem,' he said. 'We came from nearer Edinburgh.'

'It's a long way from Fife,' she said, gesturing round.

'I've been here twelve years.'

'Will you go back? Will ye no' go back again?'

'Maybe. In time.'

It made her feel good to hear the soft Scottish voice. She wanted to keep him talking.

'Time is the operative word everywhere,' he said.

She dug around in her bag. 'Could you mend this watch?' she asked.

He examined it, opened its glass, prised up the back, inspected the little, still engine inside. He put a round watchmaker's magnifier in his eye and peered at the cogs and wheels. It made him look both quizzical and expert.

'It's very dusty,' he said. 'It needs cleaning, and the winding shaft is broken. I'll have to make a new one. Can you leave it three weeks?'

'It's no good to me like that. What would you say it's worth mended?'

The man looked at her curiously. 'You wouldn't want to sell it, would you?'

'Maybe.'

'I'd give you fifty pounds for it now.'

'Done,' she said.

'No, no,' he said. 'Let's see how you feel about it when it's going. I won't charge you if you still want to sell.'

She tried to make him change his mind but he was adamant.

'You're a funny sort of businessman,' she said.

'I'm not a businessman at all,' he replied.

She suddenly had an idea. It was silly, of course, but there was no harm in asking.

'You wouldn't be needing an assistant, would you? Someone to clean up and ... help with the business ... deal with the customers while you're working?'

The man scratched his head. 'Well, now,' he said. 'That of course is exactly what I need. There's only one problem.'

'What's that?'

'No money.'

'I wouldn't need much.'

'How much is not much?'

'Well...'

'I couldn't afford more than forty pounds a week,' he said.

'That's enough...' she replied.

'You can hardly get a room round here for forty pounds a week. Do you have somewhere to live?'

'I'll manage,' she told him.

She suddenly knew that this was where she wanted to be until she'd had the baby: in this house of hours and minutes, with the strange watchmaker who spoke with tones of home.

All at once, as if to confirm her certainty, all the clocks in the place started striking twelve.

'If I'm employing you, I'd better know your name,' he said.

'Sinclair,' she told him, the name coming easily to her again. 'Marie Sinclair.'

It was only a half-untruth.

* * *

Elise, whose real name was Tessa, had changed her white apron for a navy-blue coat and met Marie outside the Kwality Bar, taking her across the road to the Anacapri where they had a cappuccino each.

'I've got something for you,' she said 'but I don't know as you'll like it. It's a squat.'

'A squat?'

'Yeah. My boyfriend lives there but he says there's a room going.'

'What would it cost?'

'A squat costs nothing. Mind you, you have to pay for the electricity and things. I should think a tenner a week would see you through. Then there's food and things. You contribute as and when. I always try to smuggle a bit out of the Kwality if dickhead's not looking. Anyway, what d'you think?'

'It sounds good.'

'Come and see anyway.'

They took a bus north towards Archway, and walked up Filkins Street, a little road lined with mid-Victorian houses terraced up the side of a low hill. On one side, some of the houses had been boarded up, and here

Tessa stopped, ducked round behind a shrub that was growing in a derelict front garden and knocked twice, then three times at a boarded window. Marie was aware of an eye being applied to a knothole in the wood. There was a pause. She looked around her with some misgiving. It didn't look exactly the sort of place where one would prepare a layette.

'Hiya, Tess, love.'

A young man with a ponytail and an earring was approaching from around the side of the house. He put his arm round Tessa and they kissed each other.

'This is Will,' Tessa told her. 'Will, meet Marie.'

'Hiya, Marie.'

'Hiya,' she said.

Will let them round behind the house to a pitted yard half-full of ruined prams and bits of bicycle. There was a door open through what had once been a small French window.

'Come in,' he said. 'Mind your skull.'

Inside, there was a slight smell of damp mingled with a whiff of gas, but the room she entered was reasonably clean, if sparsely furnished. A long-haired girl was sitting on a sagging chaise-longue knitting a baby's pullover and listening to the radio. There was a pram beside her in which a baby was sleeping.

'Chrissie,' said Will.

'Hiya,' said Chrissie.

'Hiya,' said Marie.

'Chrissie is Will's wife,' explained Tessa. 'She's also my sister.'

Marie paused for a moment to digest the relationship between the three of them. It all seemed perfectly natural.

'Family of drop-outs,' said Chrissie. 'Father was a beatnik before beatniks were invented and never grew up.'

'Is he here too?'

'Somewhere. He bust his brains on acid so he's a bit vague. Mother's here somewhere too.'

'I didn't expect a family house,' said Marie to Tessa. 'It's very nice.'

'You must be joking,' said Chrissie. 'I'll show you the room.' She put down the knitting and led the way upstairs. Tessa and Will stayed behind with the baby. 'Mind the third one up,' she continued. 'Dad put his foot through it.'

They arrived at a half-landing where there was a bathroom. Chrissie opened the door.

'That's an old gas boiler thing. It works most days. It'll kill you if you don't open the window. Gets a bit nippy but it's better than being dead. At least that's the general view.'

They climbed to the top of the house and Chrissie threw open a door at the end of the landing. The room inside was lit by a gable window which looked out on to the yard and beyond to a little park. The light, already beginning to fade, was sufficient to show a white chair, a white tallboy, a white table with a cracked mirror on it and a cast-iron bedstead on which a very large man in a Kaftan was asleep.

'Oh God,' said Chrissie, and shook him.

'Ugh,' said the large man, and turned over.

'Dad,' said Chrissie resignedly, then suddenly shouted 'Pigs.'

The monosyllable had an electrifying effect. The large man sat bolt upright with a look of terror on his face, swung his legs off the bed, dashed out of the room and clattered down the stairs without a word. Somewhere below they heard a door slam; then silence.

'I know it's cruel,' said Chrissie, 'but it's the only thing that seems to work. He's got a room of his own. This is the spare. Like it? Sorry about the carpet. Still, it is the Torygraph. You can walk over the Establishment.'

Marie saw that the floorboards were covered with back issues of the *Daily Telegraph*.

'I like it very much,' she said. 'Can I move in tonight?'

'Sure. Why not? Tessa tell you about the money? If you want to eat with us, it's twenty quid a week.'

'Fine.'

'That's settled then. You can meet Mum later but she's tanning at the moment.'

'Tanning?'

'Sure. She's got a sunbed in her room. It's her hobby.'

'Tanning?' repeated Marie.

'Travel magazines,' said Chrissie.

'Ah. Right,' said Marie, falling back on Pilgrim's Piece talk.

'Like it?' asked Tessa when they returned to the living room.

'It's great. Thank you very much.'

'You're a funny one,' said Chrissie. 'You talk posh. Don't suppose you want to tell us who you are?'

* * *

There followed, for Marie, a long interval of respite. She could not call it happiness because happiness is impossible when you have lost certain habits of self-esteem. A monster's blood … she had to be always on her guard, always conscious of the guilt that she carried in her veins. It robbed her of any satisfaction that she might have had at her own beauty or the growth of the child within her, for its blood too was tainted.

She sometimes thought of David – it was a line of conjecture she tried to avoid because it brought with it so much pain – but when she thought of him it was still with love. It had not been his fault, or his parents'. The fault was hers. There was nothing anyone could do about it.

It was such an irony that she should be carrying the child of the man she adored, who did not even know that she was pregnant; a child that half of her still believed she should do away with now, while there was still time. But she was instinctively protective of the child and incapable of killing it. She knew that it would have to be abandoned as soon as it was born – a little Spartan to be left on a bare doorstep.

These thoughts preoccupied her. The Duckett family, that was the name of her hosts, could see that there was something that weighed on her, but they were too tactful to mention it. At least Chrissie and Will and even the bronzed Mrs Duckett could see. As far as Mr Duckett was concerned it didn't really matter. He confined himself mostly to observations like 'Oh, man' and 'Too much' whatever the subject of the conversation, smiling with ineffable peacefulness upon all and sundry – except, of course, when those animals that live in sties were mentioned.

As for Ivo McVitie – 'no relation to the biscuits' – he kept his watchful observations to himself. There were plenty of them but he did not like to disturb so excellent an assistant nor evoke a repeat performance of the tears of their first meeting.

October gave way to November, and all around the little shops started to put their decorations up.

'Shall we have decorations?' Marie asked.

'Our customers don't expect decorations,' he smiled.

'All the more reason to have them.'

'Nothing too expensive, now.'

She bought some coloured tinsel and some snow spray and contrived to make Time out of Mind look both festive and mysterious. The grandfather clocks were decked with white beards which gave them a ludicrous but not unsatisfactory appearance. 'After all,' said Marie, 'they are grandfathers.'

Whether because of the decorations or a sudden surge of interest in old clocks, business started to pick up. People had always come from far afield to have their antique timepieces repaired, but now there was a positive queue of expensive cars disgorging pin-stripe-suited men from the West End who would never normally have set foot in the windy streets around King's Cross.

'Business is booming, Marie. If this goes on, you can have another five pounds a week.'

It was welcome news. She had decided to save as much as she could so that there might be a little money to put in the baby's carry-cot when she left it. And indeed, at the end of the month, Ivo included the extra £20 in her pay packet. She was so pleased, she gave him a kiss. She thought nothing of it, but she noticed he'd gone a little red.

He tried to make a little joke about it. 'What would I have got for an extra £10?' he asked. 'No, don't tell me.'

She liked their days together. They evolved a satisfactory pattern that soon became a ritual. She would arrive at five to nine, open the shutters, and Ivo would come down from his little flat upstairs and start winding the clocks. She would put on the kettle and bring out the biscuits and they would have a cup of coffee and a chocolate McVitie – 'damn good chaps, these McVitie's' – while she opened the mail. Next, they would go through the books to see what bills were getting paid, who needed invoicing and who was ready for a reminder. There were only a few of these. Most of the business was done in cash. Finally they would look at the log to make sure they were up to date with their repairs.

At nine-thirty she would unlock the door and the first customer or two would drift in.

Around eleven, she would bring Ivo a cup of coffee and another McVitie's at his desk.

'Not another McVitie?' he would say in his best Kelvinside manner. 'We're just running away with the profits there, Marie.'

For lunch they would have a cup of soup and a sandwich upstairs in his little living room. Sometimes, he would get out a bottle of malt and pour himself a dram. 'Just one, mind,' he would say. 'Two's no good for the eye. Will you not have one?'

But Marie didn't like the taste of Scotch. Besides, she thought it might not be good for the baby. There was still little sign of it to any but the most discerning eye, and Ivo's eyes seemed fully focussed on the tiny intricate matters of his trade. She would, sooner or later, have to tell him what was going on, but somehow she wanted to put it off. She sensed it might affect him in some way.

Ivo lived sparely in his two little rooms. His one indulgence, apart from the dram, was music. He would play her opera through the lunch hour: *The Magic Flute*, *Cosi Fan Tutti*, *Il Trovatore*, *Cavelleria Rusticana*.

Sitting there with her sandwiches, listening to the music, watching Ivo rapt in his chair with his dram cupped in his hands, she thought: this is what marriage must be like. I could have married Ivo if things had been different. And then she thought: if things had been different, I should never have met him.

At two o'clock, the concert would come to an end. Ivo would collect the plates and Marie, trailing clouds of Mozart, would go down to unlock the shop door. The morning's pattern would be repeated until four, she would put the shutters up, lock the door again and check the takings with Ivo. By six, she would be on the bus back to Archway.

Their customers were extraordinarily varied. Sometimes it would be a local housewife with her hair in curlers, a cigarette in her face and slippers on her feet who wanted her Westclox mended; or a boy who had broken the glass on his stopwatch. At other times it would be antique dealers and even noted collectors with things that need special parts to be made by hand.

'There is nobody else in London like you, Mr McVitie,' said an old man who had arrived in a Bentley. 'Indeed, I doubt if there is anyone else in the country. What would we do without you?'

'That was Sir Walter Duchesse,' said Ivo when the man had gone. 'And that is part of the movement of a Tompion.' He indicated a small brass wheel that lay on the counter with two of its cogs missing.

'A Tompion?'

'Tompion was one of the greatest clockmakers who ever lived. That wheel was made in 1694. The clock which Sir Walter owns, and which that belongs to, is probably worth £100,000.'

Marie was beginning to see Ivo with new eyes – not just as an original and entertaining employer, but as a craftsman, an artist even, in his own right.

'Why do you bother with the little local stuff?' she asked.

'We always have to bother with the little local stuff,' he replied. 'The world is not just made of Tompions, or Sir Walters for that matter. Local stuff is the grass that holds the hill of society together.'

'Who said that?'

'McVitie said that. Hear the words of McVitie.'

She smiled at his self-mockery. 'Hear the words of McVitie,' she quoted, 'who present, past and future sees. I think you are a time-traveller.'

'Not a traveller,' he said. 'Oh no. I am a servant of time. I am time's slave.'

'What does that make me?'

'You are time's slave's slave. Or, if you like, time's fool. When are you going to have the baby?'

She gasped. 'How long have you known?'

'Some weeks.'

'Who told you?'

He put his watchmaker's finger to his nose. 'I nose,' he said.

'Well, you're very clever,' she said. 'I thought it didn't show.'

'I come from a large family,' he said. 'I was the youngest of eight. My sisters were always having babies. What shall we say? June?'

It was indeed the month when it was due.

'That's the time,' she said.

'I suppose there is a father, Marie? You're not one of the virgin Maries?'

'There is a father. But he's not around.'

'Ah. I shall ask no more questions.'

'I'm sorry.'

'Don't be sorry. I imagine you have a doctor. Ask me if you need anything. And tell me when you want to stop work.'

'Oh,' she cried. 'But I don't. Don't send me away.'

'I won't send you away. But when the child arrives, you'll need to spend some time with it. Babies are rather demanding, I seem to recall.'

'It's all right,' she said. 'I'm going to make arrangements.'

Ivo gave her a long look. 'I'm sure you are,' he said. 'Come, we will talk no more of it until you wish to. It is five to one. Let us close the shop and listen to some Handel. You know his "Triumph of Time and of Truth"? "Bright quirks of music, jagged and uneven, make the soul dance upon a jig to Heaven".'

He held the door to the stairs open for her. She turned and smiled at him.

'Thank you, Ivo.'

'Careful now. No jigging.'

* * *

The Duckett family, though unusual in many ways, was an undemanding one. Mr Duckett spent most of his time sleeping wherever he could, but Chrissie had given Marie a key to her room so he couldn't get at her comfortable pillow. He did not in the least resent it. There were many other corners in the house where, as he put it, 'a cat could nap'. His other favourite dictum was 'there's a quack in the old duck yet as long as you know where to squeeze it'. There were not many candidates for squeezing but it didn't seem to bother him.

Mother Duckett travelled extensively in her room and would occasionally invite Marie in for a trip to Ceylon or California. Her method of travel was very simple. She had a number of props – Chrissie said she'd been a wardrobe mistress in a travelling theatre group once – and her way was to dress the room with a stage palm or cactus, lie on the sunbed for a while, and then come out and drink rum, or tequila or rice wine while playing suitable music on her wind-up gramophone. She would smoke and posture and utter scraps of languages. She always knew, wherever she was, the name of the best hotels. Marie tended to refuse the drink but enjoyed the records which were old and scratched and irreplaceable.

Probably because the parents were so weird, Chrissie and Will were both resolutely normal. Chrissie ran the house and Will provided the money. He was a runner for one of the commercial film companies down in Soho and earned a substantial income, as is the way with commercial people. Chrissie also helped by knitting genuine ethnic sweaters from all over the world which sold for large sums in the West End.

'How long can you stay in a squat?' Marie asked her once.

'As long as you like, until they serve an Order.'

'What's that?'

'A dangerous structure order. If they can prove it's dangerous they can save us from ourselves.'

'What about the owners?'

'If they can prove they need to live here themselves they can get us out. But the owners here are the Council. All they want to do, eventually, is pull the lot down and enlarge the park. But they've run out of money for the foreseeable future, so we're safe for at least three years.'

'Why doesn't everyone do it?'

'A lot of people do. But there are disadvantages. You've got to find the right building in reasonable condition with a landlord that doesn't really mind. Otherwise you're always moving and that's a drag. I don't think Dad could take another move.'

Marie looked across at Chrissie. They were sitting outside in the sun with Chrissie's child in the pram shaded by a plane tree, which grew, secure perhaps in its dendroid intuition – standing against the brick wall at the end of the area – that it would be spared for the eventual park. It was a benign November day, one of those days

170

which, in London, could be any time of the year: almost warm enough to lure Mrs Duckett, with her palm and fire-water, down from her sunbed.

'What's it like having a baby?' Marie asked.

'Bloody painful,' said Chrissie. 'I wouldn't do it again if I could help it.'

'Oh,' said Marie. She had rather hoped Chrissie would say she'd sailed through it. 'What happens?'

Chrissie turned and looked at her. 'Don't you have a doctor?'

Marie swallowed. 'Yes, of course, but…'

'What happens is you go into labour, you go to the hospital, you get into a white gown, you get shaved, you go into a labour ward, the pains are coming every minute, the nurses lie you back and the doctor tells you to push. You ask for some gas and the doctor says not till you need it, so you push a bit more and now it's nearly killing you, so you get some gas, which doesn't help much, and you push and push till you think you're going to crack like a blasted oak and suddenly, when you think you can't take any more, you feel this thing coming out of you, splosh, and they drag the whole lot out and you give a great groan of relief and they say it's a boy or it's a girl according to choice, and then you hear the little bugger crying, and suddenly it's in your arms and you feel weak and wonderful and it really and truly actually does all seem worthwhile for a day or two. That's if everything goes all right.'

'What about the cord?' asked Marie.

'Oh, they cut that when it comes out.'

'Is it difficult?'

'They just get a scalpel, cut it and tie it. What d'you want to know that for? You won't have to do it.'

'I just felt I should know. Sort of, if I got caught short somewhere.'

'You won't get caught short. They're dead keen round here on whipping you in in good time. And by the ninth you don't feel like moving very far afield. Who did you say your doctor was? We've got a good one round here.'

'Oh. It's … all right. I've got one where I work. He's very good. It's easier, really. I can get time off, you see.'

Chrissie looked at her, and shrugged her shoulders. 'I expect you know best. No business of mine.'

Marie put her hand on the girl's arm. 'Thank you, Chrissie. It's really kind of you to let me stay. I don't deserve it.'

'Course you deserve it. Will's crazy about you, or haven't you noticed? Just as well you're pregnant or Tessa'd be dead jealous.'

'Don't you mind about Will and Tessa?' she asked.

'Mind? I'm happy for them. No point in finding trouble where there's none. We didn't suit each other, Will and I. But he's a nice boy. We're all fine.'

A leaf fluttered down from the plane tree and, puffed by a little breeze, dropped at their feet. Chrissie picked it up. 'Funny thing about a plane tree,' she said. 'You can take all the leaves of all the trees and use them for your compost, but if a single plane leaf gets in amongst them, it ruins the lot. An old gardener told me that.'

Marie shivered. A premonition of something unnameable flew over her heart like a cloud's shadow.

* * *

Just before Christmas, a man came into the shop who caused Marie a considerable amount of unease. It wasn't that she recognised him, but she thought he recognised her.

He brought an old fob half-hunter with him which Ivo said would take a month to mend, it being nearly Christmas. The man seemed unperturbed. Marie surveyed him during the exchange. He was medium height, expensively dressed, with one of those dark coats with a black velvet collar which she had seen Mr Brickville wear when he had come up to the castle. His hair was dark and sleeked back. He had little black eyes, white teeth and a sleek manner. He reminded her of Dicky Henshaw. He was, she guessed, in his early forties. He had just the faintest ghost of an accent. French? Italian?

He turned to her when he had finished his discussion with Ivo, putting his little receipt slip into his wallet and buttoning up his velvet-collared coat.

'Happy Christmas to you both – and no doubt I shall see you again before the happy birthday.'

'Happy Christmas,' said Ivo, and then, 'say Happy Christmas, Marie.'

'Happy Christmas,' she smiled, but she was troubled.

When the man had left, she turned to Ivo. 'Surely I don't look so obviously…'

'What's wrong with being pregnant?'

'There's a lot wrong with being pregnant,' she said

It was the first time she had ever complained. Ivo looked at her quizzically. 'You are a strange girl,' he said. 'You and your nanny from Pittenweem. I hope that I may be able to help you one day.'

'You help me already,' she said. 'You shouldn't help me more. I'm the plane leaf in the compost.' She told him more about the disastrous effects of the plane leaf.

'You are a self-dramatist,' he said. 'You should write a libretto, I shall set it to music, and then we could sing it at lunchtime. We will call it 'Lament of a Plane Girl'.

They both laughed. When Marie turned she thought she saw the corner of a velvet-collared coat flicking out of sight to the right of the window.

'I didn't trust that man,' she told Ivo.

'Then we shall keep his valuable watch until he pays. There is only money,' said Ivo. 'Time and money. They both meet here on equal terms.'

He was given to gnomic utterances when he felt like teasing her. For once, she was cross with him.

'It's all very well for you...' And then she stopped. How could he know? How could he be expected to know?

'I know more than you think, young lady.'

'What? What do you know?'

'I know that you are hiding from someone. You have run away from someone.'

'I'm over eighteen,' she said.

'I know you are. But you are still hiding. And I am not sure that you aren't hiding from something inside you too. No, not the baby. Something that is in yourself, that makes hiding impossible.'

She was suddenly angry. The truth of what he was saying stung her too much. 'You...' she stammered in her rage, 'Wh ... what gives you the right to ... what do you know? Who do you think you are?'

'I think I am in love with you,' he said. 'Will you marry me?'

Her rage all at once abated. She started to laugh. Ivo looked hurt.

'That's a fine reaction to a good Scots proposal,' he said.

'It's not ... it's not you I'm laughing at,' she told him, collecting herself. 'It's just ... life.'

'Life is very droll,' he said, 'as I have heard it said, to the man who thinks. But to the man who feels it is a pain in the testicle.'

Marie slowly stopped laughing. She looked at Ivo. 'You don't know what you're asking,' she said.

'I think I do.'

'It's worse than this.'

'Tell me.'

'I can't.'

She saw the hurt look on his face, and was instantly remorseful. He was a rare friend, but she could not possibly marry him. The fact that she did not love him wasn't so important, or that she was still so young. Her strange upbringing had left her, she knew, immature. To have found a home and a good, kind, interesting husband would have been more than enough. Even the fact that she still loved David didn't matter: that was impossible anyway. No, the real barrier was that dark, inexorable, inescapable mass blocking the tunnel both of her past and her future. She was trapped here in the tick-tocking present. There was no way out.

'I would like to marry you, Ivo, but it's not possible. I'd like to tell you why. One day perhaps. Can't we just go on for a while?' She knew it was a stupid and impossible thing to ask even as she said it.

'Of course we can,' he lied.

'I'm so grateful to you,' she said.

'Gratitude is the most difficult emotion,' he told her. 'Don't be grateful. Gratitude is first cousin to resentment. I have noticed it when I have sometimes excused what you call the local stuff from paying a bill.'

'I won't ever resent you,' she said.

'The other thing is,' he said, 'I should really tell the Revenue that I am employing you. Do you know your national insurance number? It doesn't matter if you don't. We can leave it for a while. Say you are self-employed.'

She looked at him.

'I'm afraid I don't know my number,' she said. 'They seem to have missed me out.'

He smiled. 'Like the base Indian, they threw away a pearl,'

She wanted to give him something but she had nothing but herself. She almost asked him if he would like to sleep with her, but she knew instinctively that he would be mortally offended – and he was right. Like so many things around here, it was all a matter of time. The idea of them going upstairs for a quick screw was absurd. It would destroy everything.

* * *

Christmas at Number 19 Filkins Street was a wonderful affair.

On Christmas Eve, they had all (except Chrissie who was baby-sitting) gone to the local church for midnight mass. Even Ivo, who stoutly maintained his agnosticism, came along. It was generally accepted in the Duckett family that he was her boyfriend and neither of them felt like correcting the assumption.

The church was high Anglican and the service practically Roman Catholic, so Marie felt suitably at home, and the Vicar followed the form of the old prayer book which relieved Ivo.

'I was afraid we might be asked to kiss our neighbours,' he whispered.

'Thank you very much,' she whispered back.

'I don't mind kissing you at all,' he told her. 'My problem is with the gentleman on my right.'

She looked and saw a bristly drunk sleeping on his further side. There were a number of drunks in the church but they seemed soothed by the service.

As the tale of the birth unfolded and the familiar words and music sounded once more across the years to her, Marie – who had given up faith and hope – felt a surge of the greatest charity for that other Mary. She herself was going to need a cattle shed, or the North London equivalent, for her baby. She knew she could not have it with the Ducketts. Chrissie would want to bring in a doctor and the whole story would be out. She would, at some point, have to leave. She looked across at Ivo. He too was watching her.

'Solemn things of mystic meaning: Incense doth the God disclose…'

Ivo had a fine, light tenor voice. Beside him, the drunk had stirred and was singing bass in perfect harmony. Everyone seemed transformed by the splendour and oddness of it all.

'Gold a royal child proclaimeth, Myrrh a future tomb foreshows.'

She felt a shiver of apprehension again at the words – fear for the Christ, for everyone. Wasn't a future tomb lying somewhere down there in the tunnel for her, for all of them?

The priest was starting his sermon now. '…And the Lord hath laid on Him the iniquity of us all.'

Perhaps it was indeed true that Christ's shoulders could carry even a monster's guilt, but it seemed too much to ask of a baby. Marie had the strangest sensation that she was looking in at the rest of the world, like a hungry child through a window.

After the service, they went back to the Duckett house for mince pies and mulled wine, which Chrissie had been preparing for their return. Old Duckett rolled himself a particularly fat joint and subsided onto the sofa singing 'Remember, O thou Man' in a soft undertone over and over again while his wife regaled them with details of where they would be spending Christmas tomorrow.

'The Brabazon in Perth,' she said, 'that's where we're going. They have the most wonderful white beach with every possible convenience. And I may say that their champagne, at its best, is a match for anything from Rheims or Epernay.'

'The only thing I know about Perth,' said Ivo, 'is that no gentleman wears a kilt south of the railway station.'

'Perth, Australia, dear. Silly boy. Look out for the sharks, now.'

Chrissie yawned. 'I'm knackered,' she said.

'Me too,' said Will.

'Me too,' said Tessa.

'Goodnight, everybody.'

The two of them started off towards his bedroom.

'You'll be staying, won't you, Ivo?' said Chrissie.

For some reason, neither Ivo nor Marie had thought of this possibility. He blushed.

'Oh no, I've got the van…'

'Of course he will,' said Marie, suddenly.

Ivo looked at her and smiled in a manner that completely transformed the careful, attentive features. 'It's Christmas already,' he said.

* * *

'My love, my fair one,' he said. 'Are you sure it's all right?'

He made love to her with a sort of abandoned consideration for he was frightened of squashing the baby, but his watchmaker's delicacy saw them through without mishap.

She lay and tried to respond and loved him for being so gentle and so passionate. Her breasts, growing larger now, filled his delight.

'I could float out to sea on them,' he said, 'and never be heard of again.'

'Don't do that,' she laughed. 'I know someone who might need them.' But even as she said it, she knew that she was wrong. He could float out to sea as far as he liked. The child would be fed by someone else.

'Don't sigh,' he said.

'It wasn't a sigh,' she told him. 'That was a gasp.'

In the morning, there was a stocking hanging at the end of the bed for her.

'Happy Christmas,' he said.

'How on earth did you get it there?'

'Ah.'

'You're a magician.'

It was true. There was something of the magus about him. She started opening the packages – all neatly wrapped with watchmaker's precision.

'A gold watch! You're mad. It must have cost you a year's profit.'

It was the most beautiful little Edwardian wristwatch with an enamelled face and classically delicate hands. It felt as light as a wren's egg and was hardly bigger. Its back opened revealing her initials, MS.

'I believe it is a genuine Fabergé,' he said. 'It came into my hands some years ago. I have been looking for a suitable recipient, so it was really convenient when you came along.'

He helped her put it on and she kissed him.

'That's not all,' he said, pushing the stocking nearer. 'There's more.'

There was a frankincense candle. There was a jar of Bain de Mer crystals.

'The nearest I could get to myrrh, I'm afraid. I asked the girl in the shop for myrrh and that's what she gave me. Mer.'

'Quite near enough,' she said. 'I wouldn't want to be nearer. A sea-bath's jollier than embalming fluid. Weren't you talking of floating out to sea last night?'

'We shall float out together in a sea-bath.'

She opened the rest of her presents. All of them, including the little musical box that played 'Scotland the Brave', betokened his consideration and love for her. It both touched and worried her that he should care about her so much. She judged that he had not had many girlfriends, had probably never been in love. Whatever happened, she felt he was going to be hurt.

The last present she opened was a lump of coal. It touched her almost more than anything, for Nanny had always put a piece in her stocking.

'Ugh, Nanny. Why did Father Christmas give me coal?'

'It's for good luck,' Nanny would say. 'We always used to find coal in our socks in Pittenween.'

It became a kind of joke between them. Whenever Nanny went on about the way things were when she was a girl, Marie would say, 'And we always used to find coal in our socks in Pittenween.'

'So we did,' said Nanny, 'so we did.'

To stop herself thinking about Nanny, Marie went to her cupboard and got out the present she had bought for Ivo. She had been going to give it later, after lunch, but this seemed an appropriate moment. It had involved considerable research and great expense – money she had put aside for the baby – but Ivo was undoubtedly a good cause. She had enjoyed tracking the books down. It had involved a Saturday trip to the Charing Cross Road and many disappointments before she located Iolo Williams' definitive two-volume opus, published 1868, with lithographic illustrations on *The Life and Works of Thomas Tompion, Clockmaker.*

Ivo opened it carefully, looking at her the while. He seemed to have an instinct that he was going to be surprised – but it still didn't prevent him from being totally astonished. Almost too much so, it seemed, for his eyes filled with tears as he turned the pages.

'This is too much, dear Marie. I have only seen it in the British Museum. I never could find it in a shop and, if I had done, I knew it would be far too expensive to afford. Of all the things I can possibly think of, you have chosen the one that's … I can't express it. If I am a magician, you are a witch – a white witch, of course, as befits the season.'

They smiled at each other and she let him make love to her again for it was Christmas and soon there would be no more opportunity, even for a careful clockmaker.

Finally they got dressed and went down to coffee and toast. Will and Tessa hadn't surfaced but Chrissie was doing energetic things with brandy butter in the kitchen.

'Can I help?' said Marie.

'Everything's under control. We're not eating till seven. Why don't you go out? It's a lovely day. Lunch when you like.'

Outside, Nature itself seemed to be celebrating the feast: the sun brilliant in a pale blue sky; ground and trees lightly dusted with icing; cold air making breath come away in great clouds like cigar smoke.

'Where shall we go?' asked Ivo. 'Church?'

'Not church, I think. I know we should but…' But it made her melancholy. It invited thoughts that she didn't want to face again so soon after last night.

'Sorry, Jesus,' she said.

'I think he'll forgive you. Forgiveness is his speciality.'

'You don't believe in him.'

'Oh, I believe there was somebody called Jesus who lived two thousand years or so ago. He was a remarkable man, no doubt. I just don't know that he was the son of God.'

They began walking.

'Do you believe in God?'

'Have you heard of a book called *Shakespeare's Monkey*?'

'No'

'It's only recently out. But the author argues against the existence of God, saying that the ordering of Nature, the rules of physics if you like, could have evolved by evolutionary trial and error.'

'Like the monkey on the typewriter writing Shakespeare if you gave him long enough?'

'That is his analogy – with a little help from the typewriter, he says, like prodding the monkey when he makes a mistake. But I disagree. I would say God set the fuse and let it spread. In that sense I believe there is a God. But what he is and whether he has the faintest interest in humanity and, if he has, whether he would be mad enough to let his son – and what could we mean by 'his son'? – come to Earth and take on human form in order to be sacrificed for our sins is another matter.'

He suddenly broke into a snatch of Handel's *Messiah*, echoing the text of the vicar last night.

'"And the Lord hath laid, hath laid on him the iniquity of us all".'

A couple coming the other way smiled at them. 'Happy Christmas.'

'Happy Christmas.'

'So you believe in evil, then?' She asked.

'Certainly I do.'

'And in sin?'

'Sin is evil but is evil sin?' he asked.

'How d'you mean?'

'Sin is like getting your whites dirty. But evil can't be white because, if it were, it wouldn't be evil.'

'But *do* you?' she persisted, 'Do you believe in it?' It was important that he gave her an answer.

'I believe that we have the choice – to keep our whites white or to splash about in the mire. Most people these days wouldn't agree with that. Their notion of good and evil has become confused with legality.'

'Do you think that you can inherit sin?'

'According to the Christians we have all inherited sin.'

'Yes, but some people more than others.'

'I suppose there may be a genetic tendency as well as an environmental one. Bad blood and all that.'

There it was. He had said it. They walked on in silence.

'I'm not as blind as you think, you know, Marie. Is there something eating you? There is, isn't there?'

She was tempted to tell him everything there and then while she had the chance. A fleeting notion crossed her mind that the whole course of her life might change if she took it. But the enormity of the thing – on Christmas Day, on Parliament Hill Fields – talking about a massacre not of the innocents but of the defiled, perpetrated by her own father … it was too much.

'It's nothing,' she said. 'Just the old Catholic upbringing.'

'Ah,' he said, knowing she was lying. 'What you need is some good Calvinist hell and damnation.'

* * *

When they returned, the house reeked of the bonfire smell of hashish. They found the family gathered in the living room eating Christmas cake in a unconvinced, anticipatory sort of way and listening to Mr Duckett reminiscing, as he smoked, about his experiences in the early fifties with hippies and motorbikes in California.

'Compared with this so-called swinging city,' he said, 'it was paradise in those days. Oh, man … the light up in the mountains … and that ocean … and the climate. Talk about milk and honey…'

'I shall go there presently,' said Mrs Duckett, clasping her glass fervently in anticipation.

'Only it wasn't milk and honey,' said Mr Duckett, warming to his theme. 'It was wine and pot … and sex, of course, whenever you wanted it. It was like picking fruit.'

'I shall go there presently,' repeated Mrs Duckett.

'Steady on, Dad,' said his daughter. 'It's only five. You don't want to get too high before dinner. Not in front of our guests.'

Ivo waved a deprecating hand. 'Don't worry about me,' he said.

'You'd like a joint?' asked Mr Duckett.

'It doesn't agree with me,' said Ivo. 'I just fall asleep. I wouldn't want to miss the goose. But don't mind me. Please go on.'

'Where was I?' asked Mr Duckett.

'California,' said Ivo.

'Ah yes.' Mr Duckett took a long pull on his joint and was silent for a minute or two as his mind bowled faraway on sandy dirt tracks.

Marie had tensed at the mention of the land that had been the scene of her father's disgrace. She listened with a curious premonitory dread.

'It was like paradise but with the Devil in it,' he said at last. 'That was what made it interesting. Just the milk and honey would have been boring after a bit. Sun and wine ... those golden bodies ... we were very relaxed. Weren't we relaxed?'

'We were very relaxed,' his wife agreed.

'We will be relaxed again,' said Mr Duckett.

'Not as relaxed,' his wife suggested. 'Not as relaxed as we were. We can never be that relaxed again.'

Her husband disagreed. 'We shall see,' he said.

He returned to his reverie. 'It was all going to be different,' he mused. 'It was a new start. The young were going to cut out all the dead wood, all the crap, all the laws that hung around us like spiders' webs. We were free spirits. It was like the rule of the saints. But, oh yes, there was danger.'

He took another long pull at his joint and fell silent again.

'What sort of danger?' Marie asked him at last.

'There was danger from without and within. Like the preacher man said. He was crazy of course, and no advertisement for religion after what he did with a girl we called Two Hats.'

'Two Hats?' said Ivo. 'Just the two?'

'She never wore much else. That was all she had. Two Hats. And what the preacher gave her. The danger within was some filly who didn't know where to stop. It was part of the rules of the time. There was no stopping. Do what you like 'cos if you wanted to do it, it had to be natural. But no stopping got some of them into trouble. In the end, the rules are made by your own golden body. That's what they couldn't figure out. There were golden boys who went blind looking at the sun, high as a sputnik on LSD. There were golden addicts with hepatitis and syphilis and funny diseases no one ever heard of. And there were winds that just blew out like candles on stuff even I never got to know about. Oh, man...'

Here he fell silent once more, waiting for speech and thought to catch up with one another.

Marie forced herself to ask the question. 'What about the dangers from outside?'

'Outside?'

'Outside.'

He half rose to his feet, imagining that she was referring to something in the street.

'You said there were dangers within and without,' she explained.

'Ah.' He sank back onto the springless sofa and took another drag.

'Dangers from without. Well ... where the innocent gather, you can be sure there'll be wolves. Oh, some of them were just crazy. I knew of one guy who used to have a thing about women. He used to rape girls and then circumcise them. You wouldn't believe it, would you? But it happened. Circumcise.'

'Dad,' protested Chrissie, coming in from the kitchen.

'She asked,' he replied mildly, 'I'm telling. One should always beware of people with fixed beliefs. Then, of course, there were anarchists who thought that any outrage – bombing, murdering the innocent, corrupting the youth – was OK so long as it rocked society. Then there were the racketeers. They didn't want to change society. They just liked to make money. Drugs, mainly. Music ... prostitution ... organs ... There was danger all right. The police could run you in, beat the shit out of you – even top you in your cell. There were funny religions that would take you over, turn you inside out, brainwash you and spit you out again. There were group orgies, group killings ... and then of course, there was Castle Perilous. That's what they called it. The end of the road.'

Ah, thought Marie, here it is, this is the one.

'I never went up to that part of the Sierras. You didn't if you knew what was good for you. There were rumours of alchemy, black magic. It turned us on. We heard the stories. It was said to be a beautiful place. But it didn't do to go up there. Funny thing was, that was a genuine old French Château some millionaire way back had brought over, stone by stone. It was supposed to have been owned by the original Bluebeard. Talk about history repeating itself. People were saying there was another one. Oh man ... the tales that went around. People disappearing ... boys and girls...'

Marie listened with growing unease. At any moment he was going to mention what for her was unmentionable.

'How did he get away with it?' asked Ivo.

'There was just this drifting population. Nobody knew where anyone was.'

'It's nearly time for dinner,' said his daughter, finally. 'At least I know where you are. Let's open some champagne and talk about something else. You've frightened Marie with all that rubbish. She's gone quite pale. Sure you're OK, love?'

'I'm all right, thank you,' said Marie.

She wanted desperately to tell them the truth but she couldn't. The daughter of the monster would hardly be welcome at their feast. Ivo smiled at her and gave her a glass of champagne. She took a despairing sip, trying to ignore thoughts of the baby inside her. The choir of King's College, Cambridge warbled on from Chrissie's cassette player:

Herod the King, in his raging,
Charged he hath this day,
His men of might in his own right,
All young children to slay.'

The goose was carved, the sprouts were served with chestnuts, the roast potatoes had just the optimum quality of golden crackliness, the glasses twinkled in the candlelight, even the crackers provided an unexpected bonus of trinkets you might actually want and bad jokes you hadn't heard before: Q *Who do the mermaids get to look after their pianos? A The tuna fish*… The Christmas pudding with its sprig of holly flamed merrily instead of the usual blue spatter and yielded to each one of them a little silver sixpence.

Everyone talked at once, and Marie joined in as best she could. They thought she was being quiet only because her baby made her feel that way, but afterwards – after the final joke had been cracked and the last garnet bead of Burgundy had been drained – in bed with Ivo, she suddenly gave way to tears.

'What is it, Marie?' he said to her in the half-darkness. 'Is it the baby? Why don't you let me marry you?'

She clung to him but she could say nothing. Slowly the sobs subsided and at length Ivo drifted into sleep as she lay staring at a patch of stained ceiling that assumed strange enigmatic expressions in the light from the street, wobbled by the curtains in the Christmas wind.

* * *

Two weeks later, coming back to the house from Time Out of Mind on a rainy Tuesday night, she was surprised to see, as she negotiated the boards blocking the passageway beside the house, that there was no welcome light shining from the Duckett living room. And when she tried to put the key in the door, she found that it had been blocked up. It was odd. They hadn't said anything to her about going out or changing the lock.

'Chrissie,' she said softly, then called it out loud, banging at the door. There was no reply.

She began to get worried. Chrissie's baby would normally have been in bed by now. What could have happened to them all?

A sound from the shadows in the yard made her heart and hand fly to her mouth.

'Who's there?' She called. 'Is anybody there?'

'It's not pissy Chrissie,' said a man's voice, unpleasantly.

'Who are you? What do you want?'

'Police.'

'Oh.' It was as unwelcome to her as if it had been a mugger.

'Perhaps you'd like to return the compliment? Who are you?'

'I live here,' said Marie, fear making her squeaky. 'My things are in there.'

'I beg your pardon,' said the voice, 'but you are wrong. You don't live there. Nobody lives there. That house is owned by the Council and it is scheduled for demolition. QED, you do not live there. You *did* live there perhaps, but no longer. In any case, you were trespassing. You are trespassing now. So if you would kindly accompany us, we will escort you down to the station.'

Two large men in grey trousers and tweed jackets now emerged from the shadows. Marie started to scream.

'There's no call for that,' said the spokesman of the two. 'You can raise the roof off for all I care. You can lift the very clouds from the firmament, but bugger all good it'll do you. This your case with your belongings? I should hate it to burst open in the mud.'

Marie stopped screaming and made as if to follow the two men round to the road, but just as the second one was negotiating the boards, she doubled back and crept through the Duckett's emergency exit – a hole in the wall behind the broken-down shed, which led out on to the little park.

'Oi,' she could hear behind her. 'You, come 'ere!'

She let them go charging away into the darkness while she sneaked back into the yard and made her way towards the front of the house again. Halfway there, she discovered an added bonus. They had left her case on the ground in the eagerness of their pursuit, so she picked it up and ran down to the Archway Road where she took a bus back to the shop. She could feel the baby, excited by the chase, bundling around inside her like a Russian doll.

All the way to Time Out of Mind, she had been praying that Ivo would be in. She knew he sometimes made late collections or deliveries if clocks were old or delicate. He hadn't said anything about it tonight but there was always the chance. However, her luck was in. There was a light shining in the flat above the shop and, when she rang, she heard footsteps flying down the stairs.

'Oh, it's you,' he said with some relief. 'Come in, come in. There've been some funny people around. The telephone's rung but there's no one there when I answer it, and once or twice the doorbell's gone. There have been shadows at the window, whispers … I was beginning to think I was incubating paranoia. What brings you? You are, as you know, welcome. You have brought your case, I see. Excuse me while I master my delight.'

In spite of his jokey way of talking – he always did that when he was trying to show he was not too ridiculously pleased to see her – she could tell that something had bothered him. He led the way upstairs, carrying her case, pushed up a chair for her and put the kettle on for tea.

'The Ducketts have gone,' she told him. 'They didn't even leave a note. Or maybe they did, and the policemen took it. Will the police know I'm here? I think I resisted arrest.'

'They won't know if the Ducketts don't tell them. They'll have looked in your case, of course, so they'll know your name. But they won't know where you are.'

'They didn't seem to like me very much.'

'The police don't like anyone very much. They can't help it. It's part of their vocation. I'm so glad you're staying. It's time you thought about where you're going to have the child. You should've seen a doctor long ago. Long, long ago.'

'I'll go tomorrow,' she lied; she couldn't bear the thought of another doctor poking her about. You read about schoolgirls having babies in the toilet. Why couldn't she just slip it out somewhere quietly? She didn't want the world involving itself in her own private affairs or finding out that the baby had Bluebeard as its grandfather. They might not love it as it should be loved, poor thing.

'Will you marry me?' Ivo asked presently.

She thought about it again. He was kind; perhaps she could grow to love him. But would she have to tell him who she was? 'Not now,' she said. 'Perhaps later.'

She smiled at him to show she was pleased he had asked.

* * *

The next few days were happy ones for Ivo.

He spent some time discreetly searching for the new whereabouts of the Ducketts – it was decided that Marie should not return to the house in case the police were still interested in it – but there was no sign either of the Ducketts or the Law. On his third visit, he saw demolition equipment parked in the road. On his fourth, the room where he had slept with Marie was shockingly exposed to the street with a hole through its side. On his fifth, the place was a heap of rubble.

'It's as if the Ducketts had been uncreated,' he told Marie. 'Are you sure we ever slept there? Did we know them? Who are the Ducketts? They are figments.'

'They would have left a message if they could.'

'They were gypsies. They are not like other people. Their home is a punctuation between movements. Remember what he said? A drifting population? He's still doing it.'

'But they were so ... there. Chrissie and the baby. Mrs Duckett with her sunlamp ... I feel as if I've lost ... myself. I must find them again.'

Ivo began to sing a ballad Nanny had sung long ago in her castle room before lights out, and for a moment Marie was back in the old place.

'Three gypsies came to the castle gate,
They sang so high, they sang so low.
The lady sat in her chamber late,
Her heart it melted away like snow...'

'Do you think the gypsies will come for me, Nanny?'

'Not while I'm around.'

'I'd like my heart to melt away like snow.'

She was suddenly homesick and wished she could be a child again. Ivo sang her the rest of the 'Raggle-taggle Gypsy', but she was not easily consoled. There had been a homely quality about the Duckett establishment and now it was a heap of stones and smoking timbers. It seemed to her now like an image of her whole life – one minute substantial, safe and orderly; the next dust and shards of broken mirrors.

* * *

The shop was not busy in the after-Christmas weeks. It allowed Ivo to go out and collect some of the clocks that had been waiting for this slacker season. While he was away, Marie busied herself upstairs in the little flat making some order out of the bachelor chaos. It was going to be a squeeze for two. As for three – there seemed nowhere for a cot to go except in the clothes cupboard.

She was just assessing whether the clothes might not, after all, be kept downstairs at the back, when she heard the doorbell go. Walking to the front of the shop, she saw the muffled figure of a man standing at the counter.

'Can I help you?' she asked.

'Do you have the time?' said the figure.

It was a cold day. His scarf was tight up against his face almost to his mouth and his hat was pulled down over his eyes, but she would have recognised Brickville's voice anywhere.

'Do you have the time?' he said again.

She had almost managed to put him from her mind, consigning him to the smoke along with the rest of her memories, but his tones woke the old fear in her.

'Go ... go away,' she said to him. 'Now. Go away.'

'Come, come, Marie. That's not very nice. I've come to take you home.'

'No ... no.' A panic seized her. She retreated back into the shop, pushing the fear away with her hands. 'No ... no!'

'Come, come, Marie,' he kept repeating and started to advance towards her.

She stumbled back down the passage. If only Ivo were here. Why couldn't he come back now, just open the door and walk in?

'Just a little of your time,' said Brickville, stepping past the counter.

She backed into the workroom where Ivo kept his instruments – a hallowed place. She upset a tray of cogs and winders, which went spinning along the floor, crunching under her feet as she retreated.

'Go away,' she mumbled. 'Private here. Not allowed. Over eighteen.'

'I'm coming for you, Marie. We have lots of legal business to discuss. I've come to take you home.'

Behind her she suddenly felt her hands close on a long round object, Ivo's glass paperweight for his invoices. There was nowhere for her to retreat to now; her back was pressed against the desk.

'Don't be silly now, Marie. We've got your room ready for you. You'll be much more comfortable there.'

'Don't come any nearer,' she said.

'I don't want to have to use force,' he said. 'But I shan't hesitate. You know it makes sense to come with me.'

He crouched a little as he approached – his arms out, his face still muffled, his hat firmly down over his eyes, his greatcoat buttoned to the top like a scarecrow's. There was a moment's doubt in her mind as to whether this nightmarish figure could really be the dry-stick guardian she remembered, but of course it was he; she'd know that dry-as-brick voice anywhere. How had he found her?

'Come along, now. Don't keep me waiting. I don't have all the time in the world, you know.'

He was almost on her now. Once he grabbed her, she knew she'd be lost. He made one more step towards her.

'Come, Marie. There's…'

She held the paperweight firmly and hit him very hard on the head as he learnt forward. He went down with a look of the greatest surprise on his face, the words still coming out of him like blood.

'…no time … to be … lost…' He slumped sideways, his eyes still staring up at her, his hat knocked askew, still on his head.

She wanted to scream but she could not. She had the dreadful feeling that, though he was dead, he would get up and follow her.

'Do you have the time…?'

Running back into the passageway, she grabbed her coat and fled out into the street. There was no one around. In the distance, she saw a bus coming, ran up the road to the bus stop and climbed on board. As the bus pulled away, she looked back towards the shop. No one came out. She found herself shivering violently.

* * *

When Ivo returned, he found his shop open but no sign of Marie. Hurrying inside, he took a quick look over the tall pine cupboard, which acted as a screen to the back of the shop, saw nothing, dashed upstairs, ran down again, closed the shop and sat for some time by the counter with his head in his hands. Something told him that she had gone for good.

The thought of Marie's absence, life without her, overwhelmed him. There was something terribly final about the way she had left the shop open. She had been frightened, of course. She had always seemed to be dreading that something would catch up with her. What was he to do? Call the police? She had always been so reluctant to have dealings with the Law. Perhaps he should wait a little to see what happened.

He sat for ten minutes, half an hour, then could bear it no longer. Standing up, he hurried out and made a round of all the possible places she might be, even going to the burger bar and the little hotel where she had spent her first night in London, but he found nothing.

He hailed a taxi and took it back to the Duckett's street. The pile of rubble offered no suggestions.

An old watchman tending a fire of door frames and timbers, greeted him. 'Looking for something, Mister?'

'Someone who used to live here. A girl.'

The smoke from the fire billowed for a moment, eddied and vanished.

'Ah, girls. We search for them all our lives. On our deathbeds we're still patting their bottoms as they take our temperature. And where does it get us? Clinkers … ashes. Don't look for her here. It's a dead end, this is, Mister.'

Ivo mumbled something and turned back to the cab.

'Where to?'

There was nowhere to go but Time Out of Mind, while the taxi driver told him about his holiday in Bolivia.

He entered the shop with the faint and (he knew) unreasonable hope that, in his absence, she might have returned; but nothing had changed. A curious enervation possessed him. He felt he couldn't move, couldn't think. He dragged himself once more around the shop, though again doing no more than looking cursorily over the cupboard at the back. Finally, he went upstairs and lay on the sofa, his mind filled with heavy shapes and wordless clouds, and presently he fell asleep.

At around two in the morning, a fire started downstairs in the workroom. It was said later to have been caused by faulty wiring. The building was old and the fire burnt merrily. There were few neighbours to raise the alarm so it took some time for the fire brigade to arrive and it was too late to save anything but the adjacent shops.

Among the casualties were scores of watches and clocks, a number of barometers which were also a speciality and the proprietor. No other body was located.

Time Out of Mind had many mourners among the horologists of London, but it soon found its place in the disused lumber-room of memory.

* * *

Marie sat on the bus, oblivious of its stops and starts, careless of its destination. Her mind was in tumult; she had killed a man. No, not just a man, she had killed her guardian. There had to be a legal term for such a crime, common or guardian murder wouldn't be enough.

It would be impossible to prove it was self-defence. Why would she wish to defend herself against a man who was an old family friend? If it had been an intruder, it would have been a different matter. But this was a – what did they call it? – an open and shut case. She was glaringly guilty; her father's daughter. How could she kill a man? She'd had no training. It had to be in the blood. She thought about Ivo. He would return and find the body. He would look for her but in the end he would be bound to tell the police. There would be a search. Everywhere would be watched. Her face would be in the newspapers, on television: MONSTER'S DAUGHTER SLAYS GUARDIAN. She thought about giving herself up but she could not bear the thought of having her baby in prison, midwifed by iron-faced wardresses, shackles round her legs while she laboured.

She felt a hand on her shoulder. Out of the corner of her eye, she saw that it emerged from a dark uniformed arm and she started, but sank back when she realised it was the ticket collector again, a man with a ferrety face and a twitch in his eye to whom she had given all the change she had in her pocket.

'Sorry to disturb,' he winked, 'but we've come to the end of the road.'

It seemed an appropriate location. 'I'll get off, then,' she said.

'I thought you was going to fly up to 20,000 feet just then,' he said, 'you was so startled. Nervous disposition? Or carrying a dark secret?'

'Both,' she replied, winking back in spite of herself.

'Ho, ho, ho.'

'Where are we, please?'

'You're in Barnet,' he said. 'Barnet depot. Live round here?'

'No.'

'Where are you going, then?'

'I…'

She was going to say she didn't know, but it would look too suspicious. 'I'm going to my aunt's.'

'Oh yes? Where does she live, this auntie of yours?'

'Barnet.'

There used to be a butterfly called a Barnet, she thought, long ago when such things as butterflies had their place in her life. It cheered her momentarily until she remembered it was a Burnet.

'Whereabouts in Barnet?'

She thought quickly. 'Burnet – I mean Barnet – High Street.'

'I didn't know anyone lived in the High Street. It's all shops.'

'She has a flat.'

She wanted the man to leave her alone now and got up in a gesture of departure.

'What number in the High Street?'

'None of your business.'

'Oh, it is my business. You see, you haven't paid your full fare. I'm just establishing where you're going in case of default. Because I happened to see, when you give me that money, you didn't have no more in your coat. Remember? You were shuffling it around. And as you don't have a bag, I say to myself "Oh, oh".'

'"Oh, oh" or "owe, owe".'

'Sorry?'

'How much do I owe, owe?' The stupid joke made her feel hysterical. She pressed the top of her head down. She thought she was going to cry uncontrollably.

'Ten shillings.'

'I haven't got ten shillings.'

'I thought not. What number the High Street?'

'A hundred and thirty-one.'

'Liar.'

'It is.'

This was mad. It was like school. The man leaned forward. She could smell his bad breath: metallic, cheesy.

'How do I know? 'Cause there isn't no High Street in Barnet.'

Was he telling the truth or bluffing? She felt like a trapped animal.

'You'd better come with me to the inspector,' he said.

Her experiences at Merrymaids came at last to her rescue.

'You can feel my breasts,' she said, 'for ten shillings.'

'That's more like it,' the man said, looking up and down to see no one was coming. 'Hand up your skirt as well.'

'I'm pregnant,' she said. 'For God's sake.'

'I don't mind,' he said. 'You're young. I haven't felt a young girl for years. I probably won't again.'

'That'll be a pound extra,' she said. God knew she needed the money. The bus throbbed away. Steam covered the windows. Five minutes later she stumbled off the bus and was sick in a hedge.

It was dark now. The bus depot was situated in a distant corner of the town. Marie started walking away from it. In the intermittent, edge-of-the world street lights she saw a truck coming towards her. She stuck out her thumb and jumped about in the road. The lorry stopped.

'Did your mither no' tell ye not tae take lifts from strangers?' asked a Scots voice, from Glasgow this time.

'I'm past caring,' she said in her best Fifeshire, 'and that's the truth of it.'

'A Scottish lassie, eh? Well, ye'd better hop up. I'm away to Harwich.'

It was a three-hour drive. On the way, she told him a carefully edited version of her story. He gave her some tea and, when he put her off, he pressed a five pound note into her hand.

'I don't believe a word o' it,' he said, 'but it passed the time well enough. Good luck tae ye.'

It was ten o'clock at night. A light rain was falling irregularly, flicked and whisked about by the chilly wind that blew across the harbour. Somewhere a liner hooted, a door clanged, a tarpaulin flapped and rigging tapped its crazy, insistent Morse. She was nearly five months pregnant. She had six pounds in the world. She was hungry and tired. She wanted to die.

* * *

Marie woke in the darkness to the chink-chink-chink of metal on mast. She huddled her coat about her in a vain attempt to generate warmth but the wind was everywhere, touching and tweaking her with fingers so cold she'd almost (but not quite) have opted for the old ferret's paws in the bus.

She remembered now where she was. She had found a little hut that stood obscurely in a fold of the ground, hidden on every side by great warehouses. It was not a very comfortable little hut. It smelt of bitumen and fish and urine, but it was better than lying out on the dock. She hadn't bothered to look around it beyond assuring herself it was empty. She had just cast herself on a pile of canvas on the floor and slept.

Now, however, something had woken her: a faint noise. There it was again: footsteps, and now low voices. They were coming towards her. She shrank back into the darkness. There was a fumbling at the door, the sound of a latch being raised, a swirl of cold wind and a brilliant flashlight beam which held her transfixed as a rabbit.

'Well, well, well,' said a man's voice. 'What have we here?'

Is there anything more loathsome than a man's voice saying 'Well, well, well', she wondered. She felt like Caliban being discovered on Prospero's island.

'Looks like a girl, Mr Tarber,' said another voice, in mealy tones.

The first man sniffed ostentatiously. 'Pretty kettle of fish,' he said.

They had said the same of Caliban.

'Name?'

'I … I'm not doing anything.'

'You're right you're not doing anything. But what were you thinking of doing?'

They started to rummage about among the rolls of old canvas.

'I was trying to sleep. Who … who are you?'

It couldn't be the police again, bounding out of the dark. They would have said so, wouldn't they?

'Security,' said the mealy one called Izzard.

'Oh. I'm not doing anything.'

'You shouldn't be here. There's a lot of funny folks think they can come and go on the docks, but they can't and that's a fact.'

'Not while we're around,' said Mealy-mouth.

'We're employed to sniff out vagrants, vandals, riff-raff, smugglers, scrubbers, drug-runners and the like. Which category do you come into?'

'Oh,' she said bravely, 'I'm a vandal. Anyone can see that.'

The man Tarber advanced on her and showed her a ham-like fist. 'Don't,' he said, 'don't ever try and be clever with me. See that? What is it?'

'It's a fist,' she said.

'You're right, it's a fist. Tell her about my fist, Mr Izzard.'

'It's a fist I wouldn't tangle with. It's a fist I've seen split a face, like a pumpkin. It's an 'orrible fist, miss. Better avoided.' He looked at the fist as if it were a prize boar.

'Right, then. Where's the package?' said Tarber.

'What package?'

'I said "don't".' He raised the fist again, surveying it, then nuzzling it against her cheek, where it pricked her with its boarish bristles.

'I don't know about any package,' she said. 'I'm pregnant.'

'Pregnancy is not innocence,' said Izzard, apothegmatically.

'Quite the reverse,' said Mealy. 'Pregnancy is experience.'

However, they seemed a shade less suspicious of her. The fist was withdrawn.

'Running away, is you, then?' asked Izzard.

'Yes.'

'I've seen them come, I've seen them go,' he sighed.

'Here it is.' Tarber had located a brown paper parcel about the size of a brick hidden in the corner under a pile of staves.

'Right, you,' said Tarber to her. 'Don't breathe a word of this. Top security, understand? We're after the big one.'

Marie had no idea what they were talking about.

'She can't stop here, though,' said Mealy.

'Too right she can't stay here. She'd compromise the whole operation.'

'I've nowhere else to go,' said Marie, sensing an opening.

'Mr Tarber, I been thinking,' said Mealy.

'Steady, Mr Izzard.'

'No, seriously, she's pregnant … nowhere to go. There's a bed at our house. And she could take the package back for Mrs Izzard to deal with. It could be convenient. Mrs Izzard loves a mother-to-be.'

'I think you've got something there, Mr Izzard. It would solve many problems. But can she be trusted?'

'Show her your fist again, Mr Izzard.'

Marie was shivering so much she found it difficult to express any more alarm, but she managed an 'ugh', or the equivalent, at the proximity of the enormous knuckle. It seemed to satisfy her captors. She was given strict instructions where to find the house – and lurid details about what they would do if she failed to deliver – and was then directed on what the men described as a 'security route' through a little gap in the wires and down a path that wound behind the great sheds out onto an industrial estate. From there it was but a step to number 4 Buddleia Close.

She had the feeling that she was followed all the way.

* * *

Mrs Izzard was expecting her.

'Simmy rang,' she said. 'He told me to watch out for you. Poor you. You must be all in. I'll look after the parcel, shall I? There we are.'

Mrs Izzard was small and plump and fluffy with large blue-tinted spectacles. They made her look like a predatory dormouse. She took Marie's coat and ushered her into the living room. It was as if she regularly entertained dishevelled mothers-to-be at midnight.

'Sit you down. Put your feet up on the pouffe. You must be all in. Cocoa? I knew you'd like cocoa. Here's a shawl for your shoulders. That's better. We don't want you losing that baby now. Sandwich? I expect you're famished. Cheese and pickles? Beef and gherkin? Tomato, lettuce and crispy bacon? Good. I knew you'd like a sandwich.'

Even though Marie was grateful for the warmth and the refreshment, there was something a little oppressive about the softness and comfort of the place; but she was too numbed by her experiences to be able to do more than submit to it.

She wolfed down her sandwiches (her hostess made her one of each), gulped her hot chocolate and followed meekly as Mrs Izzard led her up to a bedroom. As bedrooms went, it was a boudoir.

'Pretty, isn't it?' said Mrs Izzard. 'So pretty. Pink for a girl, blue for a boy. Call me prejudiced but I think pink's prettier. The toilet's just through there and the bathroom's opposite. You've got your individual kettle and teabags and a tin of biscuits in case you get peckish. I know you have these little fads when you're a mother-to-be.'

'I killed my guardian,' Marie said, suddenly. She had to tell someone.

'I expect so, dear. Never read it myself. Better to cancel. Don't worry about a thing. You just get a good night's sleep. It'll all be better in the morning.'

Marie slept till ten o'clock and woke feeling wonderful. Then, as memory returned, her optimism clouded over. She would have to go to the police. It was no good. She couldn't run away. Now Brickville was no longer around she felt better about coming out into the open – even if it just meant being locked up. But was he no longer around? She must have dreamt it, but she was sure he had nightmarishly risen up. *Have you got the time?* She could sense those spiderish hands clawing at her, the gelid eyes staring, and she burrowed back under the bedclothes with a shudder.

Mrs Izzard tippety-tapped at the door. 'It's only me. Are we awake? Would we like a nice cooked brekky? We have grapefruit, muesli, scrambled eggs, sausage and kippers. Coffee or tea? Brown or white toast? Come down in your dressing-gown. There's one on the door. I took your things away for a wash and brush-up.'

Marie followed the smell of cooking down to the kitchen.

'Sit you down,' said Mrs Izzard. 'Simmy's still asleep. Late shift. How's baby feeling this morning? Who's a lovely boy, then?' She made as if to pat Marie's stomach.

'Fine, thank you,' said Marie, edging backwards.

'Mumma says fine but what does baby say? Baby says he's hungry. Here you are, Mumma. Florida grapefruit, nice and pink. Wolf it down and then let's see what you can do to a Loch Fyne kipper.'

'Can I have a boiled egg, please?'

'Scrambled eggs and a Loch Fyne kipper. Mustn't be selfish must we? We have two to feed, you know.'

Marie tried to protest but it was useless. She pushed the food down with growing impatience. She didn't want to be rude but the woman was ridiculous. She kept plying Marie with toast and marmalade ('Rose's Lime or Dorothy Carter's Glorious Thick-Cut?') long after it was perfectly obvious she'd had enough.

Finally, Marie stood up. 'Could I have my clothes, please? I really think I ought to go now.' She wanted to get in touch with Ivo to tell him not to worry, that she was going to the police.

'Go now?' Mrs Izzard looked dumbfounded.

'Yes.'

'But you've only just arrived.'

'I didn't come here to stay.'

'Oh? What did you come here for, then?'

'I came to ... deliver a parcel.'

'What? What parcel? Where?' Mrs Izzard's softness, it seemed, had teeth. Her glasses glinted angrily. Her mouth curved down, her nose beaked. 'Simmy,' she shouted.

'Yes,' came an answering, yawning shout.

'Come on down here.'

Mealy Izzard came slowly down the stairs, pulling a Chinese dressing-gown with a yin and yang sign over his spotted pyjamas.

'What's cooking?' he asked. 'Kippers?'

'Never mind that. This young lady ... this ungrateful girl ... this viper in our nest, Simmy ... she says she brought us a parcel last night and I say what parcel? What do you say?'

Izzard rolled his eyes. 'Let's get this straight. I heard the word parcel?'

'You did.'

'Is she saying we have, in some manner, made away with a wrapped object that she transported to these four walls?'

'She is.'

'Then I say to her one word.'

'What's that, Simmy? What is your one word?'

'Fist.'

'Oh, that's a terrible word. I hope you won't have cause to use it in this house again.'

She turned to Marie, suddenly all smiles once more. 'You see, dear? You must have been mistaken. There was no parcel. You must have dreamt it. You were ever so tired. Why not go and have another little rest? You must be gentle with yourself.'

'I'd like my clothes, please.'

'Now come along, dear. Your clothes are dirty. I'm putting them in the wash. Rub-a-dub-dub.'

Strangely enough, though Marie was almost crying with frustration she was also conscious of a sense of pleasant fatigue beginning to steal over her, like a child at bedtime. She allowed herself to be led upstairs.

'Fist,' she kept saying, 'fist.' It was a silly word. It made her laugh.

'Where were you thinking of going in your clothes?' asked Mrs Izzard as she tucked her up.

'The police,' smiled Marie, and fell asleep.

* * *

Marie was once more a captive: not in the same manner as her previous captivity under the watchful eye of Brickville and his minions, in the luxury of a millionaire's playground, but in the sense that she was a prisoner of her own body. Of course, that is what we all are, she thought, but she was not just locked in by her normal frame; she was shackled by the womb. The extra bump of her shape, let alone whatever sedative it was that Mrs Izzard kept giving her, made it hard to contemplate the necessary exertions for escape. Stealth and speed were becoming impossible.

Yes, she thought sleepily, looking at her ballooning belly in the mirror the next day, ponderous was the word. Just one day of food and rest seemed to have blown her beyond any memory of yesterday's body.

In the days that followed, eerie days of dreams and food shot through with occasional glimpses of lucidity, she wondered whether she would have been able to escape anyway. Mrs Izzard watched her minutely, keeping her dressed only in the most ridiculously fluffy maternity nightwear which made her look like an ostrich, a big body on top of two spindles.

'Why are you keeping me here?' asked Marie one day, as Mrs Izzard brought her breakfast in bed. 'I want my clothes. I want to go now.'

'Keeping you here? Whatever next? You can go this minute if you like. I won't ask where you propose to have our poor baby.' Mrs Izzard had taken to calling the child 'our'.

'I … I have friends…'

'And money? You got money?'

She had six pounds.

'I didn't find any money in your things,' said Mrs Izzard. 'Still if you want to go, you'd better be off. The only thing is, I burnt your clothes.'

'Burnt?'

'Well, I didn't know where you'd been, did I? I didn't want lice. They smelt of old fish. We don't like the smell of old fish, baby and I. Mr Izzard doesn't like the smell of old fish, do you, Simmy?'

Izzard was passing on the way to the bathroom in his dressing-gown.

'I can't abide the smell of old fish, and that's a fact. I won't have it in the house. When Mother cooks a kipper, we wrap the leftovers in foil.'

'Costly,' interjected Mrs Izzard.

'Very costly. But that's how strongly we feel about it. How did we get on to old fish?'

'Her clothes. They smelt, remember?'

'To high heaven. You must have been sleeping on a haddock in that hut.'

'We burnt them. It was the only thing to do.'

'The only thing. Does she want clothes, then?'

'She wants to leave us, Father.'

'I say,' said Mr Izzard. 'Oh dear me, bit sudden, isn't it?'

'You could borrow mine,' said Mrs Izzard. 'But I think you'd find them too small. Bust size we might do a match on? Fancy trying one of my bras?'

It was the last thing Marie fancied trying. There was, beneath all the prettiness and fluffiness, something faintly fusty about Mrs Izzard.

'She wouldn't get far in a bra,' observed Mr Izzard. 'Not in those peekaboos you favour.'

'Oh, Simmy,' giggled Mrs Izzard. 'Take no notice, dear. Now I can see you're feeling tired. You just relax and don't worry your head about clothes. Time enough for clothes when Baby's born. What we should be worrying about is baby clothes. I've already started a layette.'

* * *

One afternoon, Marie woke up early from her after-lunch sleep and more alert than usual. She could hear voices out in the front garden. Drawing her frilly nightie around her, she wandered over to the window.

Mr and Mrs Izzard were talking to a man in a Mercedes who had parked in the road by their driveway. They seemed to be engaged in some intricate discussion. Marie had by now almost forgotten who she was, what her life had been, and any future seemed totally unfathomable; but her instinct for escape was still strong.

Now, she thought, this is my chance. She pushed on the ridiculous fluffy slippers, slipped on the frilly dressing-gown and crept down the front stairs, peeping out of the little round window on the landing to see that they were still talking. Reassured, she continued on her way.

She had prepared herself for the back door in the kitchen being locked but, by some carelessness of the Izzards, today it was open. Outside it was very cold and a light drizzle, half-sleet, was falling. There was a gate in the yard leading on to a small passage that served the little group of semi-detached houses for the removal of dustbins.

Marie had never heard much from the house next door, but she knew it was inhabited and now she could see through the steamed-up windows of its kitchen someone in blue moving about at the sink.

She was so cold in her pathetic little frilliness that she could imagine the baby nuzzling up inside her. Her feet were almost as blue as the slippers. Cautiously, she raised the gate latch and moved into the yard. She could hear a radio playing inside the house. She launched herself at the door and beat it urgently.

'Coming, coming,' said a voice.

The door opened. Marie was so cold that she couldn't even look up. All she could do was hunch and shiver. 'You've got to help me,' she said. 'Please. I'm being kept against my will ... next door ... police...'

Sensing a silence, she forced herself out of her rictus of shivering and opened her eyes.

An enormous knuckle was almost blotting out the light, the hairs on its fingers pricking her skin as it slowly advanced.

'F-f-fist,' she said.

'You remember me, I see,' said the fist.

'Yes,' she whispered.

The first struck her three times, very softly, on the forehead. It hurt.

'Get back where you crawled out of,' said the fist.

She turned and ran back, into the kitchen, up the stairs and into her bedroom. The Izzards were still talking to the man in the Mercedes. She saw the man Tarber go out to join them. They all turned and looked up at her window as she ducked.

'What do you want of me?' she asked Mrs Izzard when she came up.

'Naughty Mummy, she'll catch her death.' The woman fussed and fluttered, tucking her up and bringing her biscuits.

'What do you want?' Marie asked again.

'We want our baby,' Mrs Izzard said at last.

'No.' Marie's reaction was instinctive. Though she knew she could not possibly keep the child herself, she couldn't bear to think of it being brought up in Buddleia Close by the Izzards.

'You don't want us to keep the child?'

'No.'

'Don't worry, Mummy. We won't.'

'Oh. Thank God.'

'We sell children here.'

'Sell?' Marie wanted to be sick.

'There's a very good price for babies. People all over the world want a nice British baby. You'd be surprised. What you casually got yourself into is a very popular concept.'

'Oh my God…'

'So just tuck up nicely, lots of rest and you'll be out of here in a trice, carrying on with your life. No one will be any the wiser.'

'I'll be the wiser. My baby will be the wiser. It's in the blood, isn't it? You can't change that. It'll be mine. Always.'

'Baby will be oblivious, dear. Baby will find a new mummy. Blood doesn't matter. It's upbringing that counts.'

Suddenly Marie wanted to tell the woman exactly who she was, exactly what was in the blood, but she was afraid she might harm the baby, even kill it if she knew. So Marie kept quiet and took her tea, which tasted just faintly bitter, and chewed her ginger biscuit while slowly the seeds of something hard and unforgiving and monumental – a redwood among emotions – started to grow within her. She would remember this day, confused, frightened, humiliated though she was, as being the one where she began to see the essential strangeness of her situation as though she were somehow picked out by fate, the game of life's Snakes and Ladders unfairly slanted against her… Much was still to happen to her, she thought. There would be many mischances, dejections, fallings from fortune, cruelties, hurts, even desolations, but she would meet them as a combatant not a victim. It was the least she could do for that last surviving blood relation inside her.

Meanwhile she lay and endured the hard softness, the cruel kindness, the oxymoron that was life at Buddleia Close. It was like being a prize cow, or a Strasbourg goose. All she had to do was lie there and fatten.

* * *

The baby was born, appropriately enough, on the first of June, 1964, just short of Marie's nineteenth birthday. It was a girl and she was the most beautiful thing in the world. She was fair as is the rose in May. It was not a difficult birth, but it was made unusual by the fact that Mrs Izzard had declined to call a doctor.

'I've midwived a dozen babies in this house,' she'd said, 'and never lost one. What do we need a doctor for? Men! If we do need one – I'm not saying we will, but if we do – we'll get old Dr Gaythorne who owes us a favour.'

'What about the birth certificate and things like that?' asked Marie in between contractions.

'Never you mind about them. Mr Tarber has friends in the right places. Documentations is the least of our worries. Now just you lie up here like a chicken. Open your legs and only press when I tell you.'

The baby popped out in due course. Mrs Izzard cut the cord and bustled round professionally.

'May I hold my baby?' asked Marie, later. She felt very weak and happy and tearful. The baby had something of David's look even though she was a girl.

'You may hold our baby. You have done well enough. But don't get too attached. If you persist in having babies outside wedlock – babies that Mr Izzard and I have not yet allowed ourselves – if you persist and you have no means of supporting the said baby ... why then! You must not get attached to it. This baby ... who does not have a name ... Baby Buddleia 14 we shall call her ... her naming will be the privilege of the proud new parents. They will be coming in six weeks to take her away. Before then, you will have gone.'

'Gone? But what about Lily?'

'Lily?'

'The baby.'

'You mean Baby Buddleia 14.'

'I mean Lily.'

'I advise you not to persist in your churlishness. The matter is out of your hands. You do not now have your condition to protect you. I hope I may not have to call Mr Tarber and tell him to bring the word which begins with an F over next week.'

It was strange how Mrs Izzard's fluffiness had fallen away from her once the child was born. Now she seemed what indeed she always had been: a corrupt midwife with a pulse for a heart.

'A tiny baby needs looking after. I need to feed her.'

'Feed her you shall for seven days. Then she must be weaned. Modern milks are excellent for baby. Some say even better than mother's.'

It was a sweet and bitter pain for Marie to suckle the child. The fact that she looked a little like David brought back to her how much she had loved him in that other world under the herb-scented stars. On the other hand, the child carried in its veins the reason why the affair had been doomed from the start. It made it an almost impossible contradiction for her. She had schooled herself not to want the child; just to have it born, as her (albeit lapsed) faith demanded, and then to bestow it safely was enough. She was too young to be a serious mother. She had only just grown up herself. Apart from anything else, family history didn't cut her out for motherhood. To give the infant its upbringing as well as its blood would be tilting the balance too much. Take it away from her and the child might learn gentleness and normality, shake off her diluted monsterhood under some benign, untainted roof.

But now, with the baby in her arms, the idea of parting was intolerable. A thought struck her.

'These people who are coming?'

'Yes'

'What sort of people?'

'What sort? People who want a baby, of course. Whatever next?'

'Are they good people?'

'Good? What sort of question is that? They are rich people that's for sure.'

'Where do they come from?'

'All over. Not from this country, of course. There would be complications. But ... America ... South America ... Canada ... Australia ... France – I've had one or two from France – even Turkey...'

'I don't want her to go to Turkey.' It sounded too foreign.

'It's not up to you, but I can set your mind at rest. Baby Buddleia 14 is going to California.'

* * *

The pain of parting from little Lily was too much for her. She cried all night and was up at cock-crow, red-eyed as the dawn. She cried not simply at the prospect of parting with her little friend but at the sheer pointless, futureless vista before her. She suddenly understood the old-boot-toughness of older generations of Aunt Bertha's. They were brought up to put feelings far down in their priorities. It didn't do to complain or feel sorry for yourself. Life was bloody but you had to get on with it. Society did not ask mopers out to dinner.

Perhaps, thought Marie, I too will grow into an old boot; I thought I was tough but I'm just a soft slipper at the moment. Of course, it was true that the Aunt Berthas often had big houses and long traditions behind them, which gave them a sense beyond themselves – of duty, service and words like that which the nuns at school had been so fond of.

But she, Marie, had been dispossessed. She was an exile, on the run, freed perhaps from Brickville, but condemned by her own hand. Somewhere out there the Law would still be looking for her. What had she done to deserve all this? She felt like Job: *'Lord, lord, why persecute thou me?'*

She had been born, that was where the mistake lay. If the mother she had never known had been alive, she would have chided her about it. Her other mistake looked up at her and made the little 'ooo' shape with her mouth that meant she was hungry.

She smiled and cried and fed her. It was the sweetness of things that made life's bitterness so hard to take.

Later they came and took her away. Marie spent the rest of the day in bed under sedation. Mrs Izzard was good at sedation.

Next day, still slightly drugged, she was given some shapeless clothes and her old coat (so they hadn't burnt everything) and escorted from the house by Mr Tarber with Mrs Izzard waving them on. Marie didn't bother to ask where her Fabergé watch might be. She knew the answer: what watch? Which watch? There was no watch. Did you see a watch, Mr Tarber?

'For those who have nowhere to go,' Mrs Izzard told her on the doorstep, 'we have a nice quiet place where our guests can recuperate. It is all part of the service.'

'What about my baby? Where's my baby?' Marie demanded. She had been saying it all morning.

'What baby?' asked Mrs Izzard, wide-eyed. 'She keeps talking about a baby, Mr Tarber.'

'I think she'll find that a fist in the face adjusts everything, Mrs Izzard. Wonderful what it can do to a wandering mind.'

'I'm sure she won't need that, Mr Tarber. Why, it makes me quite nervous to have it in the house.'

She shooed the fist out as if it were a wild animal.

Marie followed Tarber down the drive, across the arterial road, through the industrial estate and into the wilderness of the docks. It was a damp, cold June day – summer was late that year – and she shivered as she went. Threading their way past warehouses, they came at last to a little creek near the entrance to the harbour mouth. Here Tarber took her aboard an ancient hulk which they sometimes used, he said, as an office. They climbed down a hatchway into a small, dim, draughty cabin furnished with a table, two chairs and an old stove.

'Bed – in there,' said the man Tarber. He pointed to a door in the bows.

It was little more than a cupboard and unnaturally cold. It smelt of fish, river, mud, tar and fish again, or worse. There was a bunk against the bulkhead with some old horsehair blankets and a striped pillow with a large yellow stain. She looked at it and looked back at Mr Tarber. What was she supposed to do now?

'Right,' he said, 'this is your home for a while.'

'But…'

'Food and drink,' he told her, unloading the bag he carried, 'will be provided. This is not just a bed and breakfast job. This is all in. For starters, here's bread, two litres of water and an orange. I had to lure the orange from Mrs Tarber. Think yourself lucky. There's a slop pail in the cupboard for your necessaries and a rainwater tank above for you to wash with.'

'But…'

'If you don't like it, you don't have to stay. There's your six pounds back and twenty for expenses. Suit yourself. People normally stay for a week. When they feel refreshed, they tell me, off they go. I visit every day. There's no charge. Folk would pay a fortune for a location like this.' He waved his fist at the porthole.

Marie looked out on a vista of purulent marsh and distant chimneys. Chink-chink-chink went the rigging.

'Right then,' said Mr Tarber. 'I'll be off now. Just one piece of advice. If anyone comes by – not that they will but if they do – keep your mouth shut. You're having a holiday in a friend's boat you met in a pub ... the friend, not the boat. You know what happens round here to blabbermouths, don't you?'

She could imagine.

'They get to be blubbermouths,' he said, unnecessarily.

You could see it was a joke he had used before. She watched him go, without emotion, and just as emotionlessly she sat down at the table, pulling her coat about her and shivering. She sat at the table for an hour and then went into the cupboard, shivering, and lay down among the fishy army blankets.

Time passed. Night came. She started coughing. It was morning again. She drank some water, used the bucket, tried to eat some bread, lay down. It was night; she was coughing.

Faces, Brickville, coughing, hot, cold, day, night, dark, dark ... nothing...

* * *

She woke to see the face of a gentle middle-aged grey-haired man looking down at her intently. When he saw her open her eyes, he smiled. She thought she recognised him. A hymn they used to sing at school came to her mind.

'"And in the dawn",' she said, '"those angel faces smile, which we have loved long since, and lost awhile."'

'Thank you,' said the man.

'Not,' she corrected him, 'that I have loved you long since. But I suppose you may be an angel and I think I know you from somewhere.'

There was a sound from beside the man. A woman in white appeared. 'Shh,' she said.

'Another angel?'

You have been ill.

'I have been ternimal,' she said. She was so weak her mouth wouldn't work properly.

'She is still very ill,' said the white angel. 'She must not talk too much.'

'I am Felix Middleburg,' said the grey angel. 'We met on an airplane. You had my card in your pocket. It was your only identification. You are not in heaven ... or the other place ... you are in the Abbotsbury Clinic in London.'

'Oh.' The import of what he'd said slowly sank in.

She suddenly struggled, trying to get up. 'My baby ... I...'

'You must go now,' the nurse said to Middleburg, hurrying up again.

She gave Marie something cloudy to drink in a little beaker.

'Don't worry about it,' said the grey angel, 'it's all taken care of. Rest now.'

* * *

The room smelt of polished furniture, hyacinths and applewood smoke from the fire. A pale sunlight woke richness from the Persian carpet that lay across the parquet floor.

Marie, feeling rather precarious on her first day downstairs, wobbled towards the chair by the fire that Mr Middleburg indicated for her. She sank down gratefully.

'Now,' said he, 'it is time we had a little talk.'

'I'd like that,' said Marie. 'I still don't understand…'

'I will explain what I can. First of all, you have had both a breakdown and pneumonia. Either of them is bad enough. Together, of course, they could have been fatal. Luckily you were spotted by an alert security guard who found my number on you.'

'But…'

'No buts … I'm telling you what I know. The loss of your baby obviously precipitated the crisis, but I'll say it had been building up for some time.'

'But I didn't lose my baby. I didn't.'

'That's what the doctors told me you'd say. Think about it. Are you sure you had a baby, a baby that lived?'

'She cried. She made an 'ooo' face. When we are born, we cry that we are come to this great stage of fools.'

'Oh dear,' he said. 'This may take longer than we thought. Try to remember.'

'I remember being so sad.'

'Because the baby was dead?'

'Because they took her away.'

'Who took her away?'

'Mrs Izzard. The man with the fist.'

'We can trace none of these people.'

She was beginning to think that she really had been mad.

'What about the Time Shop? Time Out of Mind?'

'Gone, I'm afraid.'

'Gone?' What could he mean? There was no sanity anywhere.

'It burned down. The owner was killed. I'm sorry.'

'Ohhh.' She put her head in her hands and shuddered.

'Please,' he said, 'you mustn't disturb yourself. They think it was the fire that was the trigger – distorted things in your mind – made you run off. Perhaps you felt guilty, even.'

'Guilty?'

'About leaving him. Guilt is a great distorter.'

She didn't know any more.

'Poor Ivo.'

Mr Middleburg put his arm around her comfortingly. It was a long time since anyone had shown her so much kindness. She turned and held on to his hand, confused at finding such openness and security at last. He was like the father she'd never had.

'And what about the ... other man?' she asked presently.

'You kept talking about that,' he said. 'What other man?'

'Mr Brickville, my guardian,' she told him. 'He came to the shop. He was going to take me away.'

'I know of a Brickville, of course,' he said. 'He's quite a well-known name in the City. Dry old stick. Saw him last week.'

'You ... can't have done. I struck him. He fell down. I ran away.'

'I'm afraid it's all part of this problem of yours.'

'I did. I hit him.'

'Please,' he said. 'I'm not saying you're wrong. Life is, after all, an illusion in itself. Maybe what you say happened; maybe it didn't happen. Whatever the truth is, it was real to you. The important thing

221

now is for you to get better. I will talk to Brickville. I will tell him you need rest and that you appear to have a deep-seated aversion to him.'

'I don't appear to have. I have. I don't want to see him,' she said. 'Please don't bring him here.'

'Don't worry about it,' he told her. 'I shall look after everything. You are to stay here with me until you are completely recovered. And now I think it is time you went upstairs again. We don't want to overdo things on your first day.'

As he helped her up from her chair, she gave him a little kiss of gratitude.

'What was that for?' he asked.

'Saving my life, I think,' she said and then, remembering the burden that she carried and knowing that Brickville was bound to tell him who she was, 'for what it's worth.'

'It's worth a very great deal,' he told her, putting a finger to her lips.

'One more thing,' she said. 'Just one.'

'What is that?'

'My name.'

A look of concern crossed his face. 'Have you lost your memory?'

She shook her head. 'I am Marie Sinclair, but I have another name … my father's name.'

'And what is that?'

She could hardly bring herself to say it. At the same time, she felt she was emerging as something fragile and new. To shed a name is to shed oneself. It was butterfly time.

'Lavell. I am Marie … Marie Lavell.'

* * *

Felix, as she soon started to call him, was a charming and cultivated host. He was, it was clear, a man of immense wealth, and he carried his fortune elegantly.

The weather was warmer now, and though he did not try to make her do anything more than her strength would allow, he began to take her with him on little visits to places of interest: Glynde, Bodiam Castle, the Brighton Pavilion.

The house where she had been taken by him was called Hocking Hall. It was in Sussex, near the ancient town of Lewes. It incorporated a mediaeval building, situated in a pleasant spot between the Downs and a small river which had been dammed to make a lake. Hocking Lake trout were widely praised. Earlier, he had been obliged to leave for a couple of weeks to fly to New York but now his business affairs had been settled for the summer and he could – as he said – devote himself to pleasure. His pleasure, it seemed, was to be in her company.

It turned out that he had a ready wit. He was always smiling, making little jokes, telling stories to entertain her. The difference between her surroundings and her previous experience was so great that she sometimes thought it had indeed been a terrible black dream before, a land of shadows which, by some miracle, she had now escaped. Time slid by as smoothly as Sussex butter melting over mushrooms.

To test her luck, she ran away one day, though to say run would be putting it too limberly. She was still weak and had passing fits of confusion as to who she was, where she was, what she was meant to be doing; though these occurred at rarer intervals. Anyway, she walked away and made for the village of Hocking and then took a bus to Lewes without telling anyone. As it happened she grew quickly tired and, happening to see Mrs Beckwith the housekeeper coming out of the butchers, she hitched a lift back to the house with her.

No one seemed to have noticed that she had gone, or minded in the least, except that Felix, who had been doing complicated business things with his private telex machine and his secretary, fussed about her overdoing things. Thereafter she never even thought about escape. Twice she went to London with him in the Bentley to see her specialist. Each time, the doctor told her that she was slowly improving, that she must concentrate on the future and forget the past.

It had soon become obvious that Felix knew about her background: her father, her whole life – if not all the events after Time Out of Mind, which everyone seemed to agree were unknowable.

'I had a long talk with Brickville,' he'd told her. 'The old stick was quite upset when I told him what a dreadful guardian he had been. Imagine giving those dry old bones the job of looking after a young girl! Your aunts must have been out of their minds.'

'It wasn't them, I think,' said Marie. 'There was something about a Trust.'

'Oh, we'll get to the bottom of that,' said Felix, 'never fear. You're of age now. You have a right to know what the situation is.'

She walked over to the window and looked out at the clouds building up over the Downs.

'Are you sure you don't mind my...' she started to say it but couldn't finish.

'Mind? Mind what?'

'Me being the daughter of...'

'Your father? I wouldn't mind if you were Hitler's child,' he said.

She kissed him on the cheek. 'I'd like to know about the Trust,' she told him, knowing it would please him.

Felix rubbed his cheek thoughtfully as she left the room. Yes, she was mending fast.

* * *

The months passed slowly in the manor house which was the way Marie liked it. Sometimes Felix was there, sometimes he flew off to America, Japan, Italy, Australia.

Autumn came and a cold winter followed, although it was snug and warm in the house. A somewhat muted but charming little Christmas led into the new year. Here, too, there was a well-stocked library and Marie read a great deal – almost everything of Dickens, most of Jane Austen, Wilkie Collins, Somerset Maugham, Evelyn Waugh, Patrick Hamilton, Daphne du Maurier, George Orwell – and slept and slowly recovered. The cold lasted into March but then it was daffodil time and the gardens were full of them, lighting the old house with flowershine. Marie started to take walks, first in the garden with its lawn and arbours, and then into the woods and fields on unfrequented footpaths. When Felix was absent, Mr and Mrs Beckwith looked after her discreetly, kindly. By the time summer came, it was considered that she was completely better, though she still preferred not to go too far from the place she had started to know, and she felt no inclination to discover new people.

For her twentieth birthday in June, Felix planned a small dinner party in her honour. To her horror, he suggested inviting Mr Brickville.

'I couldn't see him,' she said. 'I couldn't.'

'We have to lay this ghost to rest sometime, you know.'

'Yes, but...'

'I shall be there. It is important that we have a meeting with him. We must talk about your future. He cannot do anything to you now.'

'I don't need a future. Can't I stay here?'

'Everyone needs a future. Even the future has a future.'

She thought he might have given in, but he was not to be turned. In due course, Brickville arrived. She saw him step out of the Bentley that had been sent to fetch him from the station in Lewes. It was the same man, the same slightly crouched bearing, even the same hat.

She had, in a perverse way, been hoping that she really had obliterated him in London, that there was some imposter masquerading as him, but here he was – unmistakably Brickville. She really had gone mad. They'd called it a breakdown but there was madness in the family, wasn't there? There were many ways it could break out; my father's house has many mansions…

She stayed in her room until the first guests began to arrive. Felix came up to fetch her down.

'The truth is that really everyone is mad,' she said. 'It's just that some people are better at hiding it than others.'

'No one frightening is coming,' Felix had told her. 'Just some neighbours who want to meet you.'

She put on a red dress and some pearls Felix said had belonged to his mother. Her hair shone in the lamplight as she came down the stairs. Everyone turned. She looked very pale, very beautiful.

'Well,' said one of the men, a jolly red-faced fellow who did something prosperous in Brighton, 'I wish I'd met you before. I wouldn't have got married to this old cow.'

His wife kicked him and smiled at Marie. 'Happy Birthday,' she said.

Marie smiled back. They gave her presents. She thanked them. Her eyes kept turning towards Brickville who stood by the fire talking to a woman in blue. At length Felix led her over.

'Say hello to your old guardian then, Marie.'

Marie walked over, trembling. She held out her hand without looking. 'Hello,' she said.

Brickville took her hand in his dry paws. 'Well, well, well,' he said. 'How time flies! I remember you when you were just a slip of a thing. Injurious time, I think Shakespeare called it.'

It was unmistakeable. He had not forgotten the clock shop. She mumbled something back.

'I gather we're going to have a little talk tomorrow.'

'I think so.'

'Well, I'll say no more – except to give you what after all is rightfully yours.'

He handed over a small, dispiriting looking parcel wrapped in dun-coloured paper. 'Open it, my dear.'

'Perhaps later.'

'Now.' He put his skinny hand on hers and she shrank back. Felix looked up and started to walk over.

'What is it, Marie?'

'A present from…'

'Don't you want to open it?'

'Now. Open it now,' repeated Brickville. 'Just a little keepsake. It'll go with your dress.'

Everybody was looking. Slowly Marie unwrapped the parcel. Inside was a small jewel box. She knew that whatever was inside was going to be bad but she had to open it. There was no drawing back. Slowly, she lifted the lid. Inside, on a little bed of red velvet, was a signet ring, its ruby flashing opulently in the firelight.

'What is it?' asked the jolly red-faced man.

Brickville picked out the ring and waved it at them, before turning back to her, smiling.

'This is the signet of Lavell. The serpent on a field of gules. Your father's ring.'

They could all remember the device. It was said to have been carved by Lavell with a dagger on each of his dead victims. Though it had been many years ago now, it was still vividly recalled to their minds, reproduced as it had been in countless newspapers and television programmes.

'You mean...' said the red-faced man, paling, 'she's...?'

'Yes,' said Brickville. 'A proud house.'

'You fool,' said Felix, catching Marie as she fell to the floor.

Dinner was a sombre affair, the pensive guests attended by visions of snakes carved in blood on young golden skin. The red-faced man's wife could not eat and started to cry. The party broke up in disarray.

Marie was already upstairs in bed.

*   *   *

Marie's relapse was dramatic and complete. She was confined to her bed. She did not wish to leave it. Her psychiatrist was sent for and presented an armoury of drugs and a complete change.

'She seems to have no wish to survive,' he told Felix. 'I advise you to get her out of England. There are too many associations here. I fear we may have the beginning of schizophrenia. She could be suicidal.'

'I will take her to America,' said Felix. 'Somewhere in the sun.'

At first Marie would not hear of it. She felt insecure out of her bed, let alone out of her room. But slowly, over the days, Felix persuaded her.

'I don't know why you put up with me,' she told him.

'Because I care about you,' he replied. 'There, I've said it. I'm sorry I should not have done. I was so upset. That imbecile Brickville. He thought he was acting for the best. He lives in another world.'

She looked at him wonderingly. 'Care about me? But…'

She had been going to say he was old enough to be her father, but she knew the word 'father' would catch in her throat.

'I know,' he said. 'I'm almost old enough to be your grandfather. But I happen to … like you.'

She admired the tactful way he got round the father problem.

'From the first moment you saw me?' It was the first time she had smiled since that dreadful evening.

'Precisely from that moment.'

She thought for a little. She didn't love Felix, she loved David. But as that was hopeless, and she had to do something with her life – at least everyone said so – she tried to smile again and used a phrase from games she used to play with the Man in the Wall all those years ago when he was being her knightly suitor.

'You may live in hope.'

Felix bowed.

'Now, where would you like to live? Of course you will be chaperoned. I have an apartment in New York, a villa near Florence – it used to belong to the Medici – a house in Beverly Hills … I think this place is out for the moment…'

'Florence,' she said.

But he shook his head regretfully. 'Great idea. Nothing I'd like better. Tuscany in the fall. Trouble is, I've got some important business coming up and I need to be in the States for a month or so.'

Where did he come from, she wondered? He didn't seem to be

American but on the other hand he didn't seem to be English. He had the ghost of an accent.

'New York, then?' she suggested.

'Fine.' He made smoothing motions with his hands.

'What does that mean?' she asked.

'We could pass through New York, stay a week or so, but really I have to be in LA, and that means Beverly Hills for us.'

'You ask me where I want to go and then tell me where I'm going?'

'I guess so.'

'But … wait a minute … California?'

'Yes–'

'I couldn't go there … my name … no…' She sank back and turned her face to the pillow in panic. Felix leant over and touched her. She looked up at him questioningly.

'I've thought about that,' he said. 'It's a big state. It all happened miles away and a long time ago. Anyway, I thought maybe you'd find it easier if you used my name.'

'Change my name, you mean? I could be Sinclair again – my aunt's name. That's what I was at school. I didn't know I was Lavell until Aunt Bertha died. But I can hardly get rid of it. It's on my back. I cannot keep changing my name. I won't know who I am any more.'

She felt feverish, finding it as hard to say Lavell as it would be to say Father. Felix smiled and shook his head gently.

'That wasn't what I meant at all. Not at all. What I meant was, perhaps we should get married.'

It was the last thing she had been expecting.

'Married? You mean us? Married?' she asked incredulously.

He laughed. 'No need to sound so shocked. Some would even be pleased.'

She was contrite. 'I'm sorry. I didn't mean…'

'Of course you didn't.'

'But…' she had to be honest, 'I don't love you. I like you … very much. I'm so grateful to you. But don't you have to love someone to get married?'

'That isn't my problem,' he said. 'I'm in love already. But love sometimes grows, you know. Sometimes like a weed. Sometimes like a rose.'

'May I think about it?' she asked. 'I don't want to be ungrateful. I can't think very well at the moment. I have to imagine what Nanny would say.'

'Nanny?'

'She was full of good advice. I don't know where she got it from. I never asked her about her life before she came to the castle. I never thought she'd had one.'

'What would she say?'

'Tuck up warm. Get the potatoes out of your ears. Least said, soonest mended.'

'It all points to a "yes", if you ask me.'

He was right. In a curious way it did. But had Nanny ever been in love? Had she ever married, had she ever – nasty potato-y thought – slept with a man?

'May I think about it?' she said. 'But can we stay here for some time. I like it so much here. I'm not ready to go yet. Next year perhaps?'

She felt strangely optimistic, and wondered whether some of the pills they were giving her were happy ones.

'Next year.' He bent over and kissed her. Her mouth opened to his, not with passion. She felt in a curious way that he was sucking out her resistance, her essence. It was not unpleasant. Ivo's little song came again to her mind.

Three gypsies came to the castle gate,
They sang so high, they sang so low,
The lady sat in her chamber late,
Her heart it melted away like snow.

PART TWO

PART TWO

The lawn seemed to have been applied with a trowel, it was so perfectly smooth and green. She looked out upon it with a sense of calm perplexity. What was she doing at this window? Whose lawn was it? How long had it been there? It presented to her a symbol of eternity. It was God's lawn. Epochs rolled over it.

Endless broth. And sleep, and more sleep. Where had she been? Was someone feeding her thoughts through a straw? Someone brought her a wheeled chair to fall asleep in. It had a stiff hood to keep off the sun, with adjustable knobs.

More broth. Someone washed her.

She fell asleep again, for how long this time she did not know but it seemed to her as not so long … and once more she was gazing at the lawn. Not a single dandelion or daisy disturbed its sleek contours. A thick green hedge marked the boundary to the right and left, and a tall wire fence, threaded with creepers, marked the forward boundary with the road.

It was not a lawn for playing on, that was certain. Even the birds seemed to pause before laying diffident feet upon it, and quickly flying on. It was doubtful whether any worms or grubs wiggled beneath. a. Nothing was dead under the grass and nothing was alive. She understood exactly how it felt.

A man's face peered at her, right in her face, attentively, and an angel in white stood at his shoulder. A bright light shone in her eyes so she knew she was in heaven.

'Is she ready?' the angel asked in an American voice.

'She is ready. Just five milligrams now of Solution D each day.'

It was a man's voice that was familiar to her.

She was back in the garden, and slowly, very slowly she became part of the landscape. Every day now they took her out in the

235

wheelchair with the stiff hood, and parked on the terrace looking out on the greenness.

The truth was of course, thought Marie as she gazed at it, the truth was that it wasn't a real lawn at all but texture-woven stuff like artificial hair. It was a lawn transplant. It only seemed to grow. Every week the taciturn gardener came as if to cut it, but it was all illusory. The grass wouldn't ever really take because the nuclear shelter underneath was too close to the surface. She was never actually shown the shelter, but she was convinced there was one. She sometimes wondered, though, how she would find her way down there when the nuclear war actually came and how she would get out afterwards if the exit was jammed.

Sounds of chatter, the clink of glasses and energetic splashing told her it was a lawn for well-toned bottoms to sit upon around the pool at the back of the house, as sometimes they did, though she could not tell who their owners were. It was a lawn like a fitted carpet at an international hotel.

She'd asked the woman about it when she came in with soup: 'Is it a lawn or a toupée?'

The woman looked at her and went to find the man. They told her that their name was Holdsworth, and they were like the Beckwiths in Sussex, only this was Beverly Hills. They were not rosy-cheeked and genial like the Beckwiths; they were altogether more formal as befitted the American idea of the butler. They inclined stiffly. They regretted. They followed orders. They told her that Mr Felix was away but had left instructions.

'You wished to ask me about the lawn?' said Mr Holdsworth.

'Did I?' She suddenly felt so tired again. The lawn didn't matter any more. It was just like a thousand other lawns she had seen when she had been someone else. 'I don't care about the lawn,' she said.

'Ah.' He turned to go away.

'Why are there no daisies on it?' she asked.

He turned back expressionlessly. 'You wish to have daisies, Miss?'

'It doesn't matter.'

'Daisies can be specified.'

'Please. It doesn't matter.'

Next day or week or month when she looked out, the lawn was covered with daisies in neatly ordered rows.

'How do you like the daisies, Miss?' asked Mr Holdsworth.

'I hate the daisies.' She wished she had never mentioned the daisies. All she wanted to do was to sleep, but when she slept she merely wanted to sleep some more.

Felix moved in and out of the house like a shadow.

'How are you, my dear. I understand you are improving. I am afraid it is a long haul.'

'Where are you?' she asked him. 'You keep changing shape.'

'Don't be silly, my dear. I am here by your side.'

'What is the solution?' she asked him.

'There is no solution. No easy solution. Rest and nourishment are the solutions. The building up of strength.'

'You said there was a solution. Solution D.'

'There is no solution D. Or A or Zee. You have been hearing voices inside your head. It can happen in cases like yours. Nothing to worry about … too much.'

'Is it the final solution?'

Where did that come from? Middleburg cocked an eyebrow. 'We will have to see, my dear, won't we?'

Was it her imagination or had California altered him? He didn't seem quite so sweet and gentle here; he was more business-like, more impatient.

'Did you order the daisies?' she asked.

'Of course. Holdsworth was greatly offended. The garden is his pride and joy.'

'Why am I so tired?'

'You have had a breakdown.'

'With a rod coming out of my head?' A memory came back to her from schooldays when she had been talking about someone having a breakdown with a little smiling dark-haired girl. 'Do you think it's like a car with a rod sticking out of the engine?' the dark-haired girl was saying…

'No rods. Just strain,' said Felix. 'You are on medication as you know. You will be better one day.'

'Why are you always going away?'

'I am busy, my dear. I have much business to attend to. The Other Judas is a hard taskmaster.'

'The Other Judas?'

'It was originally a charitable trust named after St Jude, patron saint of the impossible. Much of our profit still goes to charity. Our brand name is TOJI, as in The Other Judas, Incorporated. It is the fourth most loved brand name in the country, if not the world. The Japanese think it is Japanese. That is the just one of our companies. Then there are TOJI Pharmaceuticals…'

Her head swam. She was drowning in words.

'Don't leave me,' she said suddenly. 'You are all I have.'

Well, that was not entirely true. Somewhere there was a little girl, though Marie wasn't going to talk to him about her. Where are you, my baby? What have they done with you?

'Even when I am away,' he said. 'I am with you. The Holdsworths are my eyes and ears. They are caring people. You know that.'

He gave her a well-tended smile. Next day the daisies had gone again. Some new bottoms came to swim. She kept looking at them. Was she supposed to recognise them? One of them looked like someone she remembered. She would find her baby in the end.

'Who are these bottoms?' Marie asked.

'Here is your medicine,' said Mrs Holdsworth.

'How old am I, Mrs Holdsworth?'

'I believe you are twenty-three.'

'Where did I come from? How long have I been here?'

'You will have to ask Mr Felix.'

And so the days passed.

She sometimes wondered whether she needed all the medicaments they gave her. Not that she minded. She had nothing to be lively about. Being drugged was a very good reason for saying nothing, doing nothing, feeling nothing. Being drugged was a very good way of passing the time.

She did, however, discern with renewed attention through the foggy cloud of the months that passed, something that she had already suspected. Whereas in England Felix had been all attention and concern, in California his tender loving care had indeed become very much more of an abstraction. There was less emphasis on her wellbeing and more on security issues. An extra foot was added to the front fence and a burglar alarm was introduced that seemed to pay more attention to people breaking out than to burglars breaking in.

Marie overheard the Holdsworths discussing this very issue.

Felix remained on ostensibly friendly terms with her, but was Felix the same man at all? When he was at home, they did not kiss or cuddle. Although he had declared himself as good as in love with her, he had postponed any physical contact until she was well again. He discussed it with her the night after their engagement (a quiet ceremony, the exchanging of rings, witnessed – and purchased – by the Holdsworths). It would be unfair to her, he said. She was grateful to him for that. He did not seem to have any carnal feelings for her. He had smooth white hands and face; she loved him as she might an anaesthetist.

Sometimes, looking out of her window at the back of the house, she would hear the distant sounds of people enjoying themselves; the splash of a pool, the pling of a tennis racket; laughter; music; the pop of a cork. Once or twice she had shouted out: 'Wait for me. WAIT FOR ME!'

There was no reply. The world was going to a party to which she had not been invited. They were playing tricks with her. Her mind was full of the memories, the bee-murmur of words. Mrs Holdsworth came in with a cordial.

Marie had tiptoed out onto the landing many times, and tried one of the doors leading to the front rooms. They were always locked. One day, however, one had swung open. It gave on to a short passage which ended in another door. She was in luck again. She stepped into what seemed like a guest bedroom with windows that overlooked the front drive. Even as she watched, a small truck swept up the drive and a young man got out to unload some crates. She studied his actions as closely as if he had been performing a ballet. When he drove away, she returned to her room, pocketing the key. That night she dreamed that the young man was making love to her on the plastic grass where they were observed by Felix and the Holdsworths who kept shouting 'Ugh! What a mess!' at them.

She returned often to the front room but the young man didn't come again. One day when she was in the front room, a car drove up with a young couple in it. They got out of their car and rang the bell. It was answered by Mr Holdsworth.

'Good afternoon,' the young man said.

'Good afternoon, sir.'

'We are your neighbours – just moving in. Thought we'd come and introduce ourselves.'

'That is most kind, sir. Unfortunately Mr Felix is not at home.'

'Is there no Mrs Felix?'

There was an impenetrable pause before Holdsworth answered. 'There is but … she has not been well.'

'Say, that's too bad. Would she like to come and have a quiet drink with us? Or lunch or something?'

'I'm sorry, sir, but that's out of the question.'

Marie liked the look of the young man. He reminded her slightly of the young man with the truck. She started to rap at the window. Holdsworth looked up and his face went an unpleasant mottled colour. He turned the young couple round and got them into their car in two shakes of a lamb's tail.

When Felix returned he gave her a long lecture. The Holdsworths were her friends as well as caretakers of the house. She must not embarrass them. He took the key away. He hoped it was not going to be necessary to send her to a home. There was a very good one, he believed, in Santa Monica.

'Full of film stars,' he said.

'But I am in a home.'

'This is your home. The home I am talking about is rather less home-like. But it may be necessary to accelerate your care.'

This finally brought her up short. 'But you said you loved me. You said this was my home. I don't want another home.'

'It would be for your own good, darling. You are becoming uncontrollable. I heard you thrashing about the other night and groaning.'

That must have been the young man in the truck, thought Marie. He was making his way in rather regularly.

'I will be better,' she promised. 'See if I'm not.'

She wanted to do what would make him happy. He had done so much for her. She quietened down so considerably that they stopped giving her many of her medicaments and let her out into the garden where she wandered vaguely about.

'She has stabilised,' she heard them say.

It made her sound like a land-yacht. Yes, she was a skimmer now, no deep thought, no port of departure or destination, just an endless stable trundle around this sea of plastic green. It was better this way.

She watched old films on the television a great deal. She swam, lay in the sun, ate what she liked and grew quite fat. It was like being a superior kind of battery hen only there were no eggs. Not a day passed without the thought of her child crossing her mind, but there was nothing she could do. She rather thought Felix had not believed her when she said she'd had a baby. He regarded it as a phantom, part of her sickness.

As for her father – the architect of her misfortunes; monster and failure – she wished she could cut him out of her, that she could have all her blood changed. She asked the Holdsworths.

'Can I have all my blood changed?'

They looked at her askance.

'Blood is not oil as in an engine,' said Mrs Holdsworth. 'One does not change blood. Ugh! What a mess!'

'Not unless there is a very good reason,' said Mr Holdsworth.

'I have a very good reason,' said Marie.

'What is your good reason?'

But she could not bring herself to say. They reported her aberration to Felix.

* * *

Her twenty-fourth birthday on the old Midsummer's Day, June the twenty-fourth, the most magical day in the year, was celebrated with champagne for Felix and the Holdsworths, but not for her, as it would have interacted adversely with her medication. Felix gave her some diamond earrings.

As a special treat, they took her, wearing her earrings, for a drive in the Bentley Corniche. Holdsworth took the wheel. What fun it was. How they rolled along! People in the suburbs waved when they saw the old Bentley and the earrings.

'A change of scene is good,' said Felix.

They trundled sedately down avenues fringed with well-heeled grass where similar houses nestled amid recommended foliage.

'I bet they don't have pleached walks,' said Marie, with a sudden memory of a castle.

'They don't even know what a pleach is,' said Felix

'I don't suppose they even know the meaning of quincunx?'

'What is the meaning of quincunx?'

'It is a group of five trees arranged as four in each corner of a square with another tree in the middle.'

'We shall have some in the garden. Holdsworth!'

'Yes, Mr Felix?'

'Order a quincunx.'

'Very good, Mr Felix.'

'There you are, my dear. You only have to ask.'

Holdsworth asked to make sure she had got the name right, and would she write it down. She did so, specifying medlars. Next day fifteen medlar trees arrived. It struck her as being the definitive symbol of the absurdity of her life in the house in Beverly Hills where time and indeed life itself seemed to have no meaning.

* * *

And so the months passed, sliding like care-home trolleys, one into the other, carefully stacked, summer into autumn, autumn into winter – Christmas was celebrated in the minor key, champagne was opened and she was allowed a thimbleful – winter into spring. Her carers were slowly reducing the medication, they told her, but she still felt as though she were living behind Perspex. The idea of escape gradually formed in her mind. Her predicament was not dissimilar to her stay with the Izzards, at least there was no fist; but in a way what there was, was worse. She wandered about the garden, hatching vague plans and taking in the terrain.

The front gate, which gave on to a discreetly winding tree-lined avenue was electrically operated, very high and shut. It opened and closed, with two halves meeting in the middle, like the mouth of a crocodile, which welcomed little fishes in with gently smiling jaws. There was a camera, mounted to monitor who came and went, and there was wiring across the bars of the gates, which looked as if it could provide a nasty shock if the monitor didn't like the sight of you.

Marie looked at the gate. The monitor looked at her. 'Open sesame,' she said.

Mr Holdsworth appeared as if by magic, asking if there was anything wrong.

'Nothing wrong. Where does the road lead?'

'To Beverly Hills, Miss.'

The name seemed familiar. 'Where's that? Is that a person?'

Mr Holdsworth permitted himself a slight smile. 'You must be the only person in America who doesn't know where Beverly Hills is.'

'Or are.'

'I beg your pardon, Miss Marie?'

'Beverly Hills plural. Where Beverly Hills are.'

'Oh,' he said. 'I see. It doesn't work like that.'

'Why?' she asked.

'Well,' he said, fractionally losing patience as well as grammar, 'it just don't that's all.'

'Oh.'

'Beverly Hills,' he began again carefully, as if ashamed of his lapse, 'is – or are – a place in California outside the city of Los Angeles.'

'Why am I here?'

'You must ask Mr Felix that. You have been unwell. The climate here is very good. May I suggest the garden might provide a pleasanter outlook for you if the gardener were to put in a pleached walk at the back.'

Later she asked Felix the same question. 'Why am I here?'

Images, more and more, kept coming and going in her mind. It was as if she were surrounded by all manner of things she might know but that were hidden from her in a cloud of debris, or 'debree' as the Americans said.

'You are here because you have been unwell, my dear. The climate here is very good. Besides, I have work in Los Angeles. The Other

Judas – TOJI – owns a great deal of real estate in Television City. Have you seen the pleached walk the gardener has put in?'

Suddenly there was something coming out of the debree that she recognised. A pleached walk! A pleached walk at … a castle. She held on to it. Felix noticed the change in her expression. It made him look sharply at her.

'Are you all right, my dear?'

Something stopped her telling him. It was too vague. She didn't want to raise his hopes.

'I'm fine.'

'We don't want you overdoing things.'

'I'm all right. Really. Better every day. I shall walk in the pleached walk gathering pleaches.'

'That's great, honey. But you've still got to take it easy. You have all your life ahead of you. You've had a tough time. Relax.'

She could spend the rest of her life taking it easy, relaxing. She thought about it for a moment. It had not been easy so far.

'Why is the gate so high?'

'So people won't get in.'

'Why shouldn't they get in?'

'Because they might want to do us harm … steal things … We are very rich, honey. There are seriously envious people out there.'

'*J'ai envie de toi*,' she said.

'What was that?'

'Something the French say. It means "I want you", not "I envy you".'

He seemed pleased with her progress. 'If only more people would like and not envy,' he said.

She was fortunate to be with such a kind, rich man, Mrs Holdsworth said.

* * *

Another day when she was in the garden, strolling, doing nothing in particular, waiting for the end of the morning – waiting for the end of the world – when there would be lunch and then a sleep which would take her well towards evening and another day would bite the dust, she saw Mr Holdsworth instructing a workman, a tree surgeon with a motorised saw. He was showing him where to cut the yard-thick, unnaturally green natural hedge, which bordered the property, separating the garden from the next house's immaculate lawn.

'What sort of hedge is that, Mr Holdsworth?' she asked, approaching the two men.

She knew Mr Holdsworth liked questions about his garden.

'It is a wax-leaf privet,' he replied, giving her a wintry glance. 'We can remember its name because it gives us privetcy.' It was the nearest she had ever heard him get to a joke, but still he did not smile. Felix paid him not to smile. Felix was allergic to smiles.

Instructions to the garden operative complete, Holdsworth retired to the house to continue his gloomy offices. These consisted of attending to the fax machine which now and then spewed out instructions and information; running errands for Mrs Holdsworth who was, for a woman who favoured a put-upon expression, errand-heavy; and doing small repair and upkeep jobs around the property. None of these were as much fun for him as monitoring Marie, which was hardly a full day-job since she slept through much of it – but it was this supervisory activity which loomed large in his regime, only exceeded by his duties at the fax machine. It gave him a challenge and a purpose to see what she was up to and also, she had begun to think, it provided him with some kind of voyeuristic satisfaction. She sometimes had the feeling that he came into her room while she was sleeping and monitored her there, monitoring her underwear, although she locked the door.

It was a measure of her fiancé's new confidence in her recuperation that she was allowed now to be in the garden at the same time as an outsider like a tree surgeon, but it seemed to make Holdsworth nervous. He moved in and out of the house like a Mr Noah on a day of April showers. The fact that instructions had apparently been issued by Felix to be less obtrusive made him more nervous still.

He let his feelings be known to Marie, talking to her as if she were a wall.

'I can be obtrusive or I can be unobtrusive, there is no middle way,' he said.

The middle way left him on edge. A telephone started to ring inside the house and a shrill voice pushed a cry, summoning him indoors.

The arborist started the motor on his saw, as if in acoustic sympathy, and began to nibble up the wax-leaf privet. It made quite a racket, but Marie approached the fellow – he was on the elderly side, stubbly, with a peaked hat and sad eyes – and she smiled at him. The hedge reminded her of a dream long ago when she had played a game of hiding from the grown-ups. The operative showed interest in her approach.

It turned out the operative was deaf, but she managed to persuade him with hand signals that she wanted him to cut a niche in the hedge, by the fence, which, when she squeezed into it, would make her invisible to the ever-seeing eye that swept the lawn, while allowing her to see through the fence to the outside. Not that she had any particular outsider she especially wanted to talk to, apart from the elusive boy with the truck, but it was good to know she could if the opportunity arose.

She had played like this when she was a little girl, hide and seek with the grown-ups – although they usually didn't know they were playing – and now they had made her a child again. The man, evidently an artist in his way, caught on immediately; perhaps he had been asked to do the same thing many times in other predicaments. Anyway, he carved the most unnoticeable little cubby-hole you could imagine. It was simply asking for her to slip into it, though she realised that it must not be a regular retreat or it would be discovered.

Perhaps the young man with boxes might come by again, or a star like Kirk Douglas, or someone like Roman Polanski. This was Hollywood, wasn't it? Though it had shown few signs of its celebrity-quotient so far. Not so much as a bit part in *Ben Hur* had come by, so far as she knew. Of course, they might have come by and she hadn't seen them, in which case they might as well not have come by at all.

She slipped into the niche now, just to try it, and found it would do very well indeed – but then she heard Holdsworth calling. Luckily he was looking in the wrong direction when she emerged, and when he looked back she was lying on the grass behind the operative's hand-cart.

'Let's go to hell on your hand-cart,' she said to the operative, but he was dumb and could not speak, although he twirled his hands like the Lady Jingly Jones.

'Ah. There you are,' said Holdsworth.

'I do so love this garden,' she told him, 'and the smell of the grass and the cuttings of the wax-leaf privet.'

He allowed himself a thin opening of the mouth, the nearest he ever got to a smile – the garden was his pride, but not his joy, since joy was not on the Holdsworth menu of emotions. He didn't spot the niche at all. He went back into the house again. Marie renewed her conversation with the operative and motioned to him that she wanted him to cut a tunnel through the vegetation that would emerge at the other end of the hedge, nearer the house, but right up against the fence the property shared with its neighbour. That way, she thought, I can puzzle the Holdsworths all the more: sometimes here and sometimes there, tripping hither, tripping thither, nobody knows why or whither. Just a little bit of fun, which was in short supply. She had had tunnels in the laurel hedges in the castle gardens back at home, all the way down to the lumpy tennis court – a good place to eavesdrop on the grown-ups when there were any around.

The man received the idea with enthusiasm. She motioned to him that it should not be observable. It was a game. It could be their little secret. She smiled at him again, and he made the most perfect little tunnel you could imagine. She had expressly gestured to him that it should not be visible from the outside. It was just the sort of tunnel Alice's White Rabbit would run down. So before the man packed up and went his way, she gave him a little kiss which made his arboreal day, although he too tried to look up her frock which was not part of the arboreal plan.

'I don't like you looking out on to the road too much,' Holdsworth said, when he came out. 'It gives people the wrong idea.'

What would be the right idea, she wondered.

'It's good for me to see a little life,' she told him. 'Mr Middelburg wants me to find more energy. I draw energy from life. The passing cars, the trees, the breeze, the people, the animals…'

'Watch them but do not talk to them. We do not want to have to turn people away.'

He spoke about her as if she were an attraction at a fair.

'I am not the fattest lady in the world,' she told him.

It was as if she had never spoken.

She came out onto the lawn near the fence quite regularly now, sketching and pretending to be sketching. She had asked for pencils, crayons, watercolours, art paper. They had even bought her an easel. Sometimes she turned around and painted the house and sometimes she painted the houses across the road, and at odd moments she hid in the wax-leaf privet hedge and enjoyed the moment of power it gave her to be invisible.

Sometimes she drew the young man who came to her in the night, but she took care to hide the drawings in the wax-leaf privet.

* * *

One day when Holdsworth was tending a flurry of paper from the fax machine and Marie was leaning her elbows on the fence, well hidden from the house and looking out across the road to the opposite neighbour's garden beside it, she was reflecting – not for the first time – how everything in LA looked too perfect. Even the grass, like the hedge, looked artificial, and wasn't.

'Too blue, too tender was the sky,
The air too soft, too green the sea.
Always I fear, I know not why,
Some lamentable flight from thee,' she said.

The words floated into her mind like pollen. It was a translation of a Verlaine poem by Dowson. The English mistress at school had been one of the better nuns. She'd said Verlaine was somewhat regrettable. Marie found she was talking and quoting to herself quite often these days. The advantages of talking to yourself, she thought, was that you could always be sure of a sympathetic ear.

251

'Wine and woman and song,
Three things garnish our way,
Yet is day over long.'

'Gee, that's really pretty,' said a spotty boy on a bicycle, suddenly apparent but shadowy behind the thick mesh of the fence. 'Did you make that up?'

Marie though he must be the only spotty boy in California.

'No.'

'You like to come out some time?'

'No.'

'Why not?'

'I can't.'

'You married or something?'

'Yes. And my husband is insanely jealous. He makes Othello look like Percy the Pussycat. He doesn't shoot to kill, he shoots to maim. And do you know what he especially likes to shoot at?'

'Maybe we'd better make it some other time…'

'Uh oh, there he is now.'

The spotty boy got on his bicycle, did a wheelie, and shot off down the road. Marie carried on looking at the distant ocean. She thought: this is going to go on for the rest of my life. How boring my life would be if they didn't give me something to make me not unhappy. I don't want to remember the old days; it makes me sad. I like to be not unhappy. Everyone tells me so. It's a good place to be.

'Pssst.'

She reacted very slowly to anything surprising.

'Pssst.'

There it was again. She moved her head very slowly as if she were carrying a huge gourd on top of it. That was the effect of whatever it was the Holdsworths were still giving her. Not unpleasant, but slow.

A man was standing there. Where had he come from? He was holding a large envelope.

'Are you Marie?' he asked.

She was not surprised. Nothing surprised her these days. She looked at the man. He was, she guessed, about sixty years old. His eyes were very blue and seemed to have seen a great deal and his hair was silver grey. In spite of his blue eyes, he might have been Spanish or Mexican. He was spare in figure, almost gaunt. His face looked weatherbeaten or perhaps not beaten by weather but by life. He looked like a survivor who has survived a great deal. He had asked a question. Was she Marie?

'Not the one I was,' she told him.

The man looked puzzled.

'Would you mind asking me again?' she said.

'Are you Marie?'

'Yes.'

'I have something for you.'

He threw the heavy envelope over the fence, since he could not pass it through or under the wire, and it landed on the ground beside her.

'Take it,' he said. 'It will change your life for ever. Show it to no one. I will come back in one week's time. One week exactly, same time, same place. Be here.'

He seemed very intense. She looked at her watch. It was exactly twelve noon.

'Marie…' a voice was calling from the direction of the house.

'Don't let him see you, stay behind the hedge until I go in,' she said. 'Next time bring a ladder. A nice light one.' She surprised herself

253

by saying the bit about the ladder. It was as if someone else were saying it for her. Where would he get a ladder? He would have ways and means.

'Coming,' she shouted at the house. 'I am a prisoner,' she said to the man.

The man nodded. He understood. Perhaps he too had been a prisoner. He scuttled sideways under cover of the hedge. The letter would be read and confiscated if she took it into the house, so she hid the envelope in a thicket of the hedge, deep in the tunnel where it would be safe. There were no wild things to nibble or tear paper with rodent teeth in the perfect gardens of Beverly Hills. She now hurried to the upper end of the hedge where the tunnel stopped. Here she stepped out. Holdsworth was looking in the wrong direction again.

'Cooee,' she said.

He turned round.

'Here I am,' she said.

'Mr Middleburg will be coming back for a few days,' he told her. 'He has things to attend to.'

'When is he going to be here?'

'Tomorrow afternoon.'

Upstairs in her room, she confirmed that tomorrow would be Friday. Somebody had given her a diary last Christmas when she complained that all days were much the same.

'Make the days different,' someone had said, 'set down your thoughts.'

But her thoughts had been heavy as clouds that lour and do not rain, and the diary had not been used. But today it came into its own with seven more days of usefulness, seven more days before the man with the ladder came back. She started to write. Then she stopped.

Everything she did was under supervision. What was she thinking of? She tore up the page she had written into small strips, and flushed them down the lavatory for the alligators to read.

She would go to the tunnel and read the letter after her afternoon rest, otherwise it would make the Holdsworths suspicious, but she had to read it today, before Felix's arrival. If she waited until he came, he would be solicitous and demanding, watching her all the time, endlessly on the *qui vive*. These people had an instinct for subterfuge, perhaps because the layer of grease that oiled their money engine was paper-thin and they lived on lies.

Holdsworth was different, he had only the instincts of a lackey.

What could the letter be? Who could it be from? Even in her foggy cloud where the debree was particulated, the importance of this sudden communication woke excitement in her, tinged with some alarm. It was as if the sun had hit a fragment of glass in the darkness of her forest. She had become used to a state of no hope. Where there is no hope there is no disappointment, but still she could not but feel the lighting of a spark of possibility; and now the spark caught fire. The more she thought about it as she prepared for lunch – washed her hands and ran a comb through her hair, put on a little lipstick which she seldom did these days – the more she burned to read the letter. Of course she knew any undue interest would quicken Holdsworth's suspicions, especially with Felix in the offing, so she forced herself to eat mouthfuls of fried chicken, fries and salad, before putting her knife and fork down conclusively on her plate.

'I hope you are not sickening,' said Mrs Holdsworth.

She could hardly say she had been toiling over the preparations of the meal, since she and Mr Holdsworth knew that all the elements of the feast had been bought ready-prepared. Even so she managed to convey the impression of toil without actually putting it into words. She was good at conveying impressions.

'Perhaps we should curtail your time in the garden,' suggested Mr Holdsworth. 'The Californian sun is deceptive.'

'It is not the sun,' said Marie, instinctively defensive. She was almost unsustainably curious to know what was waiting for her in the tunnel. The rise in adrenaline fought with the drug and made her feel quite strange, but the result was a sharpness of mind along with a feeling of giddiness. She knew that she must behave as if everything were as usual, if not more so, so she forced herself to eat more of the strangely coloured, piquant-coated chicken that Mrs Holdsworth had so carefully fried. Why was it always chicken – and chicken so large as to be threatening?

'Mmm. Delicious,' she said

'You've changed your tune,' said Mrs Holdsworth, balefully. 'Eat more slowly.'

'So many tunes,' observed Marie. 'Don't you sometimes wonder how they can get so many tunes out of boring old doh re me?'

'It never enters my head for a moment,' said Mrs Holdsworth.

'I must get the garden shears sharpened,' said Mr Holdsworth. 'Somebody has been using them for a purpose for which they are not designed.'

'I hope you are not referring to me as somebody,' said Mrs Holdsworth, competitively.

'No, my dear, but you are not a nobody.'

Marie breathed a silent sigh of relief. Her excitement had not been noticed. Everything was proceeding as normal. 'I have done a new watercolour of the house,' she told the Holdsworths. 'Would you like to see it later?'

'I am no judge,' said Mrs Holdsworth. She didn't hold with art.

'I am sure Mr Middleburg will want to see it,' said Holdsworth, 'though I hope you are not taxing yourself. He is, after all, sadly delayed, but will be here in a few days.'

After a slippery pudding, Marie excused herself. 'I need to put the finishing touches to my picture,' she said.

'You must have your rest,' observed Mrs Holdsworth. 'Mr Middleburg is quite clear on that point.'

Marie folded her napkin and went up to her room. There was no point in alerting them to the ferment in her mind. However, after her statutory hour of siesta, she came down again. Mrs Holdsworth was in her room watching television and Holdsworth himself was tending the fax machine which she could hear chattering away. Now was her chance. She walked lightly across the lawn, sat herself in her artist's chair just to allay any suspicious glance that might be cast in her direction from the house, then after a few minutes, she stood up and walked to the top of the garden, which the camera could not quite reach, and crept into the upper end of the tunnel in the wax-leaf privet.

It was the work of a minute to locate and open the envelope. Inside, was a sequence of pages written in a flowing hand that spoke of education and yet lack of practice. The ink was mainly black, sometimes brown. The pages themselves seemed to have been gathered from various sources. Some were ruled, some on mathematical paper, others from old diaries, or menu lists; paper that had been hard won, and spoke of desperation. She settled herself back against the wax-leaf privet, shut her eyes for a moment as if to summon all her powers, and started to read.

* * *

The writing seemed to fly up at her, and for a while she could not make sense of the words, so powerful were the emotions that the sight of them evoked. This was her father's writing, the man whom all her life she had been without. It was like the presence of an evil ghost. It had seemed impossible that the endless submerged causeway of her life would ever change, but somehow out of the mists and the confusion, the suggestion of a path could be discerned, even if it lead nowhere, through a minefield. The words settled back onto the page, and she began to read.

To whom it may concern and damn you if it doesn't, this is the last testament of Giles Lavell, written in Chinchona Prison, Mexico, during the month of February in the year of Our Lord 1965, with no certain hope that it will ever see the outside of this accursed place or survive to tell the true account of the circumstances leading to my false arrest, rigged trial and unjust imprisonment.

To be honest, I write this first and foremost for myself since I do not expect anyone else to be allowed to read it. It will probably die with me. The gaoler is, as gaolers go, a civil fellow, and I daresay he would carry it out of prison for me; but he too is watched and it would be a shame, after his small kindnesses, to get him into trouble; so I shall have to think of some other recourse.

Regrettably, there is not much time. I have a troubling cough and an ulcer in my leg. The food is insufficient and the water foul, the mosquitoes remorseless; but all that is mere inconvenience. They will come for me but I do not know when. I have the feeling that it will be soon. I try not to sleep so that I may be awake for every second of the time remaining. I am as avid for life as those mosquito nymphs that hang upon the surface of the water. I suck at it, d'you see? Not that I want you to get the impression that I am afraid of death in normal circumstances, or in the course of action, but I am afraid of dying and having nobody know what has happened to me. I want my daughter to know for she has been the true victim in all this.'

Here the first few pages, clipped together, seemed to come to an end or, at least, to denote some kind of punctuation. The next instalment featured the writer – if it were the same writer – in a different mode. It was in French but of an antique kind and, although she spoke French well – her great-aunts had been very particular on that score – the ancient spelling and crabbed hand made it hard to understand.

To whom it may concern, and damn you if it doesn't, this is the last Testament of Gilles Laval, Baron de Rais, Marshal of France. It is written in the dungeon of Nantes Castle during the month of February in the Year of Our lord 1440, with no certain hope that it will ever see the outside of this accursed place or survive to tell the true account of my life and the circumstances leading up to my false arrest.

Indeed, now I think of it, I will bribe the gaoler to give it to one of my loyal servants with instructions to hide it in the fabric of my castles of Machecoul and Tiffauges so that, in future days, someone may find it and tell the true story of the monster, Gilles de Rais. The gaoler is, as gaolers go, a civil fellow and I daresay he would carry it out of prison for me himself, but he too is watched.

Regrettably, there is not much time. The shortness of it weighs on me. I try not to sleep so that I may live every second of the time remaining, for sleep is a kind of death. Not that I want to give the impression that I am afraid of death in normal circumstances or in the course of action.

If she were here, Joan, Saviour of France, my lovely Pucelle, she would tell you that I was at her side when we drove the English back – Talbot and the lot of them – to their ship at La Rochelle, scuttling like schoolboys. But the feats of arms, the glory, the trumpets, the martial airs, the cheering crowds, the spoils of victory, they are all cold now – cold as the ashes of the fire she roasted in. Yes, they cooked her as a witch, just as they will broil me too later – after they have half-strangled me, cut off my testicles, stuffed them in my mouth (I never cared for 'rognons blancs', particularly my own), and cut my belly four ways to let the bowels spill out like a pig's. That is the way they treat their heroes in France.

Of course, if I agree not to retract my confession, they will simply hang me without any of the trimmings. It is this that is giving me cause to reflect at the moment. As I say, I am no faintheart, but the prospect of my own balls in my mouth and my stomach split open for the general edification of the groundlings gives me, I must say, more than an ordinary twinge of distaste. It's not the pain, it is the exposure. Well, let's be fair, it is the pain as well.

I must stop writing for a space; I hear the gaoler coming with my supper. He knows I am writing this and he shuts an eye when his wife brings me vellum and ink, but we have an understanding that I shall at least pretend to conceal my labours. It's just in case one of the Bishop's men should pay us a surprise visit.

There was a gap here, and then the narrative continued.

The supper was good, though I confess I had little stomach for it – nor would you if you had had even as lenient a taste of the water treatment as they gave me – but more of that later. I might just add, in case you are ever down for it, that it's the cloth they stuff down your throat to make sure the water goes through properly, which really hurts.

After the torture, I believe it is customary for the prize prisoners to be fed and rested so that they can better appreciate the full drama and – yes, it has to be admitted – the horror of their end.

Beef stew, white bread, cheese and a pint of Chinon wine, better than balls in the mouth, a repast fit for a king or at least for Gilles, Baron de Rais and lord of Mortemer, Tiffauges, Machecoul, and Champtocé, who was in his day as rich and powerful as a king, richer indeed than that bumbling Valois Charles who would sell his own sister for a couple of castles and, as the word goes, did.

Where was I? Ah yes, I was about to launch into an explanation as to how I came to be in my present low state – truckle bed, rickety table, damp walls, dank floor – reduced from the grandeurs of my former establishment. Confess: you are interested? My tale is instructive and full of love, blood, treachery, chicanery and pain – especially pain – with not a little mirth and sorrow thrown in for good measure. What else makes a good romance?

My trouble, I believe, started with a quest for perfection. It has always been with me, right from my cradle. I always expected more of myself than I could reasonably fulfil – an uncomfortable sort of itch. I had to be the one who climbed the highest tree, rode the wildest pony, made the most noise, endured the stiffest beating. Perhaps if my mother and father had lived they would have seen to it that this excess of mine was curbed or deflected at an early age but my father died in an accident when I was ten years old and my mother soon after. I was thereupon brought up by my grandfather who had never been less than sixty ever since he was born. Yes, he was born an old miser, though he was indulgent to me so long as I did not impinge on his studies which were of a wealth-building nature – brigandage, chicanerie and coercion and all that sort of thing. If that happened, retribution was swift.

I was a trial to my nurse and a pestilence to Jehan, the man my father set to watch over me when I was five.

'Master Gilles, Master Gilles,' I can hear him now, shouting for me as I hid among the battlements of the castle or scudded away among the pine trees of our own little island of Rez, pounding after me doggedly in his riding boots.

'Margill, Margill,' he would cry, too short of breath for the extra syllable.

He was a good man and he died taking a blow that was meant for me as we fought in Normandy in the meadows above the river. So I grew up selfish, indulged, rarely disciplined, alienated, as you might say, from most of the world by birth but, even more by temperament. I was not a bad child, I believe. I was not cruel; I was amiable to visiting cousins and to the occasional other children who came my way. I even sheltered a poor boy who had run away from his master. The woods were full of stirring in those days as indeed they are now – waifs, brigands, displaced people, poor men hiding from the soldiers of either side, refugees, the out of work and the out of mind. I brought him food, lodged him in a hunting hut and commended him to one of the scullions whose mother took him in on the estate at Mortemer.

So my boyhood continued. When I was seven, my father hired tutors to teach me Latin, logic, poetry and music. At ten, he added Greek and medicine. Every fighting man should know a little medicine, he said; it has served me well. At eleven, I took my first ride at the quintain, and I believe I acquitted myself well with my little lance.

At thirteen – or was it fourteen? – I discovered a new sport. My penis, which had lain dormant for more than a dozen years suddenly found a life of its own. This, I understand, is not a unique experience but, rather like birth or death or torture, it seems entirely personal at the time. So my small serpent and I began to enjoy a … relationship, which, though it has brought me trouble, has given rise (the pun will not escape you) to no end of personal satisfaction.

If, at the end of my life, which seems to be next week, it comes to me and says "I trust I have given satisfaction, Master Giles," I shall be able to give it a heartfelt affirmative and you cannot say that of everything in these troubled times.

Here the sheets of yellowed, crumpled paper and the Old French came to an end. There were four further pages in the contemporary hand. The first two were matter of fact – an account of the writer's interest and growing obsession with the life of Gilles de Rais, a monster of part history, part legend. It then continued:

Our family, the Lavells – directly descended from the Laval-Lohéacs, first cousins of Gilles – have come a long way from the days of shame and disgrace of the mid 1400s when de Rais was a by-word for the most loathsome and profligate depravity, of devil-raising and child abduction. If they were true, the things he was said to have done, then I would not have done more than open the history books, peer into the darkness and then quickly shut them. But what I found led me to think that the abuser was himself abused. He might have been weak, he might have suffered from a kind of madness, but he was certainly framed by those around him who wanted his wealth and who wanted his castles and lands. He was plied with drink and almost certainly drugged by wormwood, the hallucinogenic ingredient in absinthe, and at the same time he was victim to every kind of quackery and deception. There was a recrudescence of witchcraft at the time of which the most famous instance was Joan of Arc herself. I will write down for you the facts as I know them, for I have set out to find out the truth, to clear a family, to remove the blot on our reputation; yes, the stain on the escutcheon. This seems a worthy aim if, like me, you bear an ancient name. Was Gilles's conviction in 1440 fair or corrupt, tainted by jealousy, envy, greed and the strength of little men? I steeped myself in his life and it became mine. I began to be obsessed – I surrounded myself with ancient documents, buried myself in old books, shut myself up in dark places. So much so that, as you will see, history began to do what it likes best. It repeated itself.

The next pages were written in a far more orderly manner as though they were almost part of a life her father had had before the darkness fell upon him.

I write this for you, Marie, so that you can see what it was that at first fascinated and then began, truly, to obsess me. It seems more than possible that we are descended from this gilded, spoilt, yet wretched and ultimately tragic fellow, deceived by those around him and persecuted, vilified, then robbed by his peers. I have told the man who brought you this letter to locate a document of Gilles's – no forgery – that I have stored in a secret place, so that you may better appreciate our history.

The story of Gilles de Rais, or Bluebeard as he became known, is fairly common knowledge in France and Britain and even here in America, not just to scholars of the French fifteenth century scene but to the informed layman. The problem is that people generally know only half the story. A brief summary will suffice for the moment, but even this will show that there is more to Barbe Bleu than meets the eye. For a start, in the context of a Baron like Gilles (who was, incidentally, reddish haired), Barbe Bleu does not mean blue beard. None of his contemporaries in the days of his former glory refer to him as having such a distinctive appendage. No – but they do tell us that Gilles had a great liking for his famous half-wild 'blue' Barbary horses. The steed more defined a powerful nobleman than did his facial hair.

Gilles de Laval-Montmorency, then, with his Barbary horses, came to inherit or acquire, while still young, not one, not two, but three great fortunes. The first was his father's, the second was his grandfather's, the third was his wife's, a young woman called Catherine who had large neighbouring estates, the match organised for him by his grandfather, de Craon, a fixer and a ruffian, almost a brigand. And it was he who engineered the acquisition and further building of Gilles's vast fortune until Gilles became the richest man in France, even richer than the king.

Gilles's father and mother both died when he was young. His grandfather either indulged the child or ignored him. The lad grew up handsome, brave and accomplished. His first military escapades were skirmishes against the

English with his own soldiery, but he soon made a name for himself as a military leader and became a Marshal of France, marching against the English foe with none other than Joan of Arc. It was said that they became lovers, but it is certain that she considered him a brave and worthy comrade in arms. He was signally helpful in raising the siege of Orléans with her and subsequently in their triumphal progress. He even assisted at the coronation of the King in Reims.

Then Joan was captured, tried and burned by the Burgundians, in league with the English, and everything started to go downhill. His grandfather, de Craon, who'd kept a jealous eye on the fortunes he had so painstakingly accrued for his grandson, died. Gilles began to spend prodigiously on his chapel and its choir and the concomitant clothes, treasures, art and jewellery. He poured energy into writing a monumental play re-enacting the glories of the Orléans siege. It was composed of twenty thousand lines, had a cast of hundreds, richly clad, with each day's production requiring a new change of clothing, and it consumed money like a Leviathan gorging on herring.

He now began to be surrounded by sinister people – a couple of cousins, de Briqueville and de Sillé and a strange youth known as Poitou, who caroused with him and drank massive quantities of heavy red wine and spices, known as hippocras, cut with wormwood, the hallucinogenic ingredient of absinthe. The two cousins seemed to have gained control of Gilles's exchequer, but there was trouble in that direction. The ready money was starting to run out. Most noblemen's wealth lay in land and property. So property, in this case castles, had to be sold, and it still wasn't enough. Various relatives tried to petition the king to forbid Gilles to sell any more of his fortune, but it was no good. He resorted to superstition to try and conjure money out of sorcery, and a priest was found who could raise a demon called Barron. The money was still not forthcoming. Worse, rumours started to circulate. It was said that children were starting to disappear from surrounding villages.

Just as she was learning the whole story, Marie was disappointed to find there were only three more torn and crumpled scraps of paper now, these looking as if they had been hidden in someone's shirt, so creased and distressed were they.

They tell of boys, sometimes girls, strung like capons or dancing on the end of a noose while I buggered them or spent myself upon their flanks; of the orgies of spiced wine and drugged sweetmeats; of the black arts and raised spirits and a demon called Barron; of the missing children in the villages and the huge heap of bones in the bastion wall ... These and others too loathsome to number are among the vile accusations levelled at me, for which they have not a shred of evidence and only the hearsay ramblings of my former associates who were too busy taking money from me to write down dates and times, or even to plant a corpse or two. My accusers have never found so much as a single body to bear out their tales. Where is the corpse, gentlemen? Or were you the murderers? I am guilty, it is true, of having spent too much on my play, but the lifting of the Siege of Orléans must be celebrated along with the feat of arms of my dear friend and comrade Jeanne d'Arc without whom we would still be ruled by the English. The costumes must befit such a production with cloth of gold where necessary and siege engines and gunfire and a cast of thousands obligatory. You cannot recreate a siege with less. My other decision, to remove the castle of Tiffauges to the Californian Sierras, stone by stone, might be questioned by some, but it was all part of the plan ... I must mount my defence on my own ground...

She turned the scrap of paper over but there was no more. The writer was evidently confused, veering from the distant past to the present and back again. She reached for the second sheet. The last letter was shorter, and the paper of better quality.

My dearest daughter,

I shall never see you again or be able to say sorry to you a thousand times for deserting you and for the weakness that overtook me. Alas, our weaknesses are stronger than our strengths. Your mother died and I was bereft. I was rich beyond reason and yet I felt that I had done nothing to deserve it. I did not feel able to bring up a little girl but I knew I had to keep you in safety, safely away from the kidnappers and the money-snatchers, and soon I was plunged into my work which led to darkness, but the work was important. I had always been fascinated by history, especially the history of our family. I had studied history at university, but now certain documents fell into my hands which lit the fire of obsession.

They seemed to prove that the Duke of Brittany, a de Montfort of course – a curse on the lot of them – had indeed been instrumental in framing our ancestor, casting the vilest of rumours about him, poisoning his mind, arranging evidence and planting false witnesses. I visited the land of the shadow of death and, like him, fell in with thieves who called themselves cousins. They plied me with pleasures and assailed me with pain, they poisoned me with wormwood and found me powders and potions to take away the agony. I lurched from pain to pleasure sunrise to nightfall and from week's start to month's end. There were séances and invocations of demons. I knew not where I was or who I was with, I only knew that I had to finish the work that I had started – the rescuing of our ancestor from calumny and shame. It had started as a sort of game with me, a sort of puzzle, a detective story and then it got out of hand. They played along with me but it soon became as if I was the man himself, accused and alone. And indeed I now realise that they were playing the same tricks on me that Gilles himself had endured. And I, obsessed with the man, went along with it as in a dream.

I met a man who was evil, Marie. My cousins Mittelberg and Brickville – they said they were cousins and in my hubris I never bothered to check – but I should call them my cozens since they cozened me out of mind and money – made dreams out of his pharmacopeia, and finally they brought the

Professor to me. He understood the poisons intricately and knew what each one could do. And then he delighted in exercising his ingenuity on me, in feeding me the ideas like twigs for the fire of unreason and fantasy to burn. It was exciting in a dreadful way, Marie. They called him the Professor.

He unmade me, my child, and then he made me up again until I did not recognise myself. And when they said I had done these vile things, I did not know but I could only feel that I had not. And all the while, the money was being spent. This sounds like a litany of self-pity as I read it, for it is you that should be the subject of this letter, you whom I abandoned and have allowed to suffer through the wrongs I have inflicted on myself. I could not be more sorry, and I am sorry for myself (again) that I could not get to know you. But, listen, Marie, this is important. They do not know that I am writing this. It may never get to you which is a nightmare in itself. But if it does, there is a way you can destroy them and get the money back for it is in a Trust. They took it from me and made the Trust before I could spend it all; to save it for my daughter, they said. And then they took control of it and used the false story of my evil to make you ashamed and wish to distance yourself from your inheritance. I can read them like the Book of Darkness.

You have been the victim of a monstrous canard and plot. Your future has been blackened, your family defamed. Every year they hold a Meeting with the Trustees, not all of whom are bad but, like many men of business, they are busy with other matters and they leave it to the executive directors to do the work. That is what the bad men will always try to prevent – your coming to the meeting. You have to go there and show your face. These men need you alive but always absent. That is what they will work on. You must make Brickville and Middleburg no longer executors. And do not marry, especially not marry one of them, until you have attended the meeting. That is the start of your new life. I hear the gaoler coming for me now. It is time to say I love you and will always be with you, for that is the gift of a father, I am part of you and they cannot take that away. Always your father, Giles Lavell.

The last note was brief, a précis of past troubles, composed after the others, a snatch of communication written in stolen minutes and ending with a fearful injunction.

They have deceived me. Brickville and his master Mittelberg have taken advantage of my sorrow and my passion of scholarship to build a castle of lies around me. They have abused my friendship, cheated me out of money, drugged my drink, poisoned my food and – if that were not in itself sufficient – now they tell me I have committed crimes of the vilest kind against young men and women, crimes about which they can tell the police unless I provide more money. Well, they can whistle up the devil's arse for that. There is no doubt, however, that they will do it – and take the money too.

I am caught in a trap of my own making for I have been stupid, blind, obsessed with my own studies and with the sorrows that have become a way of life for me unless I lose myself in the past. Please forgive me, Marie, if you ever come to read this letter – but never, I beseech you – forgive the authors of my ruin.

Your ever-loving father.

* * *

'Marie … Marie…'

She hardly had time to wipe her eyes. It was Holdsworth calling, and her hiding place must not be found. She started up and hastily thrust the papers back into the envelope. They must not fall into the hands of her guardians whatever happened. It would be a disaster. She pushed the envelope back into the recesses of the privet and peered through the leaves. All she could see were Holdsworth's boots, very close to her now.

'Marie…? Where is the girl?'

She gathered up her dress and scuttled like a little bird to the other end of the tunnel. She could see Holdsworth moving to the back of the house where the pool was.

'Here I am,' she called, waving her sketch book. 'I was the other side of the tree.'

He came down the slope towards her, looking vexed.

'I looked behind the tree,' he said.

She giggled, archly. I am not sick, she thought. I am not tainted or to be pitied. I can hold my head as high as these people – no, higher for I am not set on holding them prisoner against their will. Not yet, at any rate. She felt quite giddy as the shadows that had been around her mind for so long started to recede.

'I was teasing you,' she said. 'I just moved round to the other side. Like a fairy.'

'It is very wrong of you,' he said, 'to play your games and cause us worry. I shall have to tell your fiancé. It is becoming tiresome. The medication should be increased. You are becoming highly strung and troublesome. I cannot guarantee your safety if this goes on.'

She could see the beads of sweat on his forehead. He was what Aunt Bertha would have called *agitato*.

'I am so sorry, Mr Holdsworth. It was just a game.'

'That is as maybe. Mrs Holdsworth will be vexed, that is for sure. She was just baking a cake with her own hands for your tea.'

It would be a Mary Baker Cake mix, *that* was for sure.

'Ooh, my favourite,' she said. There was joy and power in deceiving them, but she must not let it go to her head. She must be calm.

'Well, that will have to be called off for a start,' he said. 'There will be no cake today.'

He was in a huff. She felt like one of the little kittens who would have no pie. But she was only going to be around for another seven days so what did anything really matter?

'We may also have to declare the garden out of bounds.'

'You know I love your garden.'

'We will have to wait and see when I tell Mr Middleburg. He'll be here by the end of the week, he says.'

'Oh, Mr Holdsworth, please don't tell him about my little game!'

He loved it when she did that. Poor Mr Holdsworth, little did he know that the gypsies had come to the castle gate and, as far as she could see, they were definitely of the raggle-taggle variety.

* * *

The next week was a torment for Marie, especially so since Middleburg's imminent appearance was anticipated by the Holdsworths with a mixture of pride and awe. Both Holdsworth and his wife worked themselves into little whorls and curlicues of fluster preparing for his arrival. Nothing must be out of place or random. The car was polished, the lawn was mowed and the wax-leaf privet was clipped and clipped again. If they could have re-waxed it, they would have done so with gusto.

Middleburg telephoned at the last minute to say he was arriving late for dinner and that threw Mrs Holdsworth into a panic: the Lady Hostess filet de boeuf en croute would turn to charcoal if kept in the oven too long and it was already done the way Mr Middleburg liked it. It must be taken out for a while but, at the same time, Mrs Holdsworth wanted him to have it piping hot, the way he liked it. What to do, what to do?

When Felix finally arrived, full of apology, the beef had the consistency of tennis shoes but it was hot and he praised it fulsomely when he finally came down to table. He seemed in good appetite and high humour and appeared almost uxorious to Marie as they sat in the drawing-room after dinner. He insisted on giving her a green Chartreuse which, at first sip and on top of her medication, made her feel swimmy. Then, when he had poured himself a second Rémy, he came and sat down next to her on the sofa.

'Well, my little fiancée, how have you been keeping?' he asked.

She could smell the brandy on his breath and feel his eyes on her bosom. She shifted as imperceptibly as she could to her side of the sofa. What had happened to the man?

'Better than a Lady Hostess filet de boeuf en croute which has been sitting too long in the oven,' she said.

'Ha ha,' he laughed. 'I can tell you are feeling better.'

'Some days better than others,' she said.

'But you are glad to see me,' he persisted.

Her poor father! He had been weak but he had not deserved what they had done to him. Of course, it had crossed her mind to wonder how much of what he had written was true and how much he had dreamt up as in a vision? It was all so disordered and nightmarish. Even the name of the castle was Cauchemar. She had heard from Mr Duckett what drugs can do – and hadn't Coleridge created 'Kubla Khan' from the same inspiration? Even so, no matter what anyone might say, her duty was to not trust Middleburg and to go along with much, if not all, of what her father had written. That was why she was going to escape.

'I cannot feel anything very strongly,' she told him, 'as you know.'

It was a good answer.

'Of course, of course.' He leaned a little closer. 'But don't you ever want to be ... a wife?' he asked.

'A wife? But I am not a wife.'

'But you will be. And some say one should ... practise a little.'

'I cannot practise being a wife until I am a wife,' she said. 'I cannot think of being a wife until I know what has happened to my daughter.'

'Your daughter, as I have told you, Marie, is no longer with us.'

'I know that. I want her to be with us.'

'I meant, my dear, that your daughter did not survive. She was born dead. I believe the phrase is still-born.'

'That cannot be right. I remember her little face. I called it her oo-face: her little lips were all puckered into that shape.'

'It is a memory induced by your condition at the time. You were ill, Marie, and your memory is serving you up what you wanted there to be, but it was not. Let us hope you may be able to have a child when we are married.'

She was not going to have this conversation. There was a word for it. What was it? 'It is otiose to speak of it now,' she said at last. 'The wedding must be at some future time, if it happens at all.'

'Quite so, quite so. Well, that is a matter I was coming to. I have made arrangements at the Registry Office here. We can be married next week.'

'Next week?' Oh God, she thought. Not before I have gone across the fence? I must not be married before then.

'I suggest tomorrow week. That is, Saturday.'

She was momentarily flooded with relief.

'The ceremony will be held in the house on Saturday and some of our friends will be able to come. We will have a party. Mrs Holdsworth will order a dress for you ...'

There was a limit to what Marie could stand in this charade. 'No, she won't,' she said. 'I will order a dress.'

'Very well. Mrs Holdsworth will help you order a dress.'

They left it at that. Marie surreptitiously poured the rest of the Chartreuse into a huge silver tureen of lilies which Mr Holdsworth watered every morning. She did not believe little Lily was dead. She could see the oo-face quite clearly.

'I need to go to bed now,' she told him.

'A wise move,' he agreed judiciously. 'You need to get your rest. It's going to be a busy week. It's going to be a busy life.'

She could see he couldn't wait to start playing husbands and wives. The amorous touch of those sugar-white hands would be like being stroked, very softly, by a mortician with a taste for Turkish delight. Soon she would be rid of all of them for she was now washed free from sin. Her blood was untainted. Her whole life had been wasted. What she had thought she was she had not been at all. She was like other people now.

* * *

She woke in a panic in the night.

What if the stranger didn't come on Friday? She would be married and her father's warning would come to nothing. Marriage would in some way give Mr Middleburg power over her and those mortician hands would be tying a cat's cradle all around her – across her breasts, across her stomach – tying her down. There would be no more pretence of 'would you like to?', only 'you will'. It would be a walking dungeon.

She felt dispirited next day, and slow. They must have slipped an

274

extra dose of Lethe into her bedside water. Felix was out all day for a meeting downtown. She got out her easel and sat in the garden painting Felix in his meeting with a number of faceless men. Holdsworth came round and looked at the picture over her shoulder – a thing she always hated.

'Why have the other people round the table with Mr Middleburg not got any faces?' he asked at length.

At least he had recognised Mr Middleburg.

'They are faceless men,' she told him. 'They do what is expected of them, they say what is expected of them. There is no health in them.'

'I hardly think Mr Middleburg would approve of your delineation of his colleagues.'

'That is how he likes them,' Marie told him.

Holdsworth would have continued the conversation but there was a loud buzzing from the bell indicating Fax Message Pending and he hurried away inside. The fax machine was a god that required his constant attention in case its sudden outpourings, like the ravings of the sibyl, might at any moment be cut short and lost.

'The faceless men are the ones who do what Mr Middleburg tells them to do without knowing what it is that they are doing,' Marie said out loud, as though the words had been put into her mouth like dabs of paint on a landscape.

She took the opportunity provided by the fax machine to dive back into the wax-leaf privet and read her father's papers again. They gave her the strength she needed. Felix came back late from his meeting, which had turned into dinner in town, and put Mrs Holdsworth – who had cooked a special Lady Hostess venison roast for him – into a dreadful state of tension between ill-humour and subservience. She took the ill-humour out on Marie and Holdsworth and saved the subservience for the master. She served him a Rémy Martin with an eerie, almost ominous, degree of obsequiousness and summoned Marie to attend the master. Felix, after his dinner, seemed keen to practise husbands and wives again, but after some embarrassments, Marie escaped to her room pleading a headache.

His eyes rested on her as she left the room, his expression dark and pensive.

*   *   *

The choosing of the wedding dress meant a great deal to Mrs Holdsworth, strange for such a sour woman but perhaps, Marie concluded, her sourness concealed a longing for something more; perhaps it was Holdsworth who held her back, or possibly Felix himself, who seemed to have a hold over everyone. Marie allowed these thoughts to cross her mind as she stood in her bra and knickers waiting for the various helpings of silk and tulle and froth to be poured over her.

Mrs Holdsworth did not allow Felix to come and join them, saying it was bad luck, although the thought of Marie in her underwear was making him eager to have an undress rehearsal of some kind. It was not her that he wanted, she knew that; it was the power he poured over her like tulle.

A small, rugged assistant from Bridal Reverie had arrived with box after box of textile froufrou which she now proceeded to unleash with small, encouraging gushing sounds. Marie tried them all on obligingly, since she knew she was not going to be married at all on Saturday, and Mrs Holdsworth positively twittered with pre-nuptial girliness, tweaking the dresses and running her hands over Marie as though she were going to marry her herself. Perhaps that was what she wanted, thought Marie. In which case she too was going to be out of luck. Finally a dress with sewn-on roses was selected, which made Marie look like a cherry trying to get out of a knickerbocker glory, but it seemed to make everyone happy.

When it was all finally over, champagne and a cold collation were served. A hot luncheon was out of the question since Mrs Holdsworth had been otherwise engaged, but the Holdsworths were invited to join Mr Middleburg and his fiancée. Felix was back in high humour and listened to the Holdsworths' suggestions for a list of guests that she had never heard of.

'We will have to invite Helmut,' he said. 'And the Garfisches.'

'The Garfisches?' Holdsworth murmured. 'Is that absolutely wise, Mr Middleburg? You know what happened last time they came over.'

'Indeed I do. They quarrelled and she threw him into the rose pond,' replied Felix, eyeing Marie. 'Maybe she can teach you a thing or two, my dear.' It was meant to be seen as a joke, but nothing Felix did or said was totally innocent.

'And what about the Pfizers and the Stumpfs?'

'A lovely man, Mr Stumpf, sir,' said Holdsworth. 'So caring to his old mother.'

'A shame he got into that trouble with his talks at the children's home.'

'I'm sure if he did anything, he meant it kindly,' said Mrs Holdsworth. The champagne, coupled with the earlier bridal dressing, seemed to have evoked something very much like the milk of human kindness in her bosom, though it would no doubt curdle when she returned to the Holdsworths' quarters.

'Then I suppose I should invite some of the other directors,' Felix said, casting a sidelong glance at Marie.

That did indeed interest her. But why the glance? Marie felt sure it meant something. Who were the directors? And directors of what?

'They're sure to come if you ask them, sir,' said Holdsworth. 'After all, you hold the strings.'

Had Felix always been like that, Marie wondered? Playing with his marionettes as a child? Playing cat's-cradle as a baby?

'They're not a bad lot – loyal enough, though Grindlay's a chancer. Goes to the Merrymaids Club, I hear.'

Marie's ears pricked up. This at least was something she knew about. Of course, there was bound to be one in LA. The information was useful. Mrs Holdsworth made a sour prune-sucking noise at the mention of Merrymaids; it was clear she didn't hold with such things. Or perhaps she secretly yearned to be one of their number...

'Why men have to go to such places I do not know,' she said to Marie in a horribly sisterly way.

'Oh come, Mrs H. The female form is a lovely thing. It has inspired artists down the ages,' said Middleburg.

'And dirty old men down the corridor.'

That stopped them in their tracks. Mrs Holdsworth had made a joke. It seemed to Marie a good moment to retire. 'I think I'll take my rest now,' she said. 'The morning has been quite taxing.'

'Of course, it has,' said Felix. 'You go up and I'll look in later.'

'No really,' protested Marie. 'I cannot rest if people look in.'

'Not even your fiancé?' asked Felix, archly. 'Surely he's not "people".'

Mrs Holdsworth looked at her like a mediaeval villager crowding into a bedchamber to celebrate a marital deflowering.

'Not a fiancé,' repeated Mrs Holdsworth, simpering. '*He's* not "people".'

'Not even a fiancé,' Marie told them, and left them to it.

Felix's left eyebrow raised very slightly which was the nearest he ever got to incredulity, but Mrs Holdsworth was having none of it.

'First night nerves,' she said. 'I well remember how I felt when Holdsworth swept me off my feet.'

* * *

Next morning, the day before her planned departure, Marie started to feel almost guilty as the food, drink and chairs began to roll in and preparations for the party took shape on every side. Too bad she was going to spoil the fun. She felt sorry for all the people wasting their time: the girl wreathing foliage so prettily, so pensively, around the entrance to the marquee; the pastry chef, wherever he was, piping out his choux; the violin section polishing their medleys from *The Merry Widow*.

Marie loitered at the fence watching vans and trucks arrive and the electric gates that led on to the road slowly opening and closing like a sea-monster's mouth, accepting and regurgitating marquees and long trestle tables, damask tablecloths and silverware, bowls for the roses, champagne flutes, great silver buckets for the bottles, chairs in gold with rococo mouldings, napery and drapery, ashtrays and cuspidors, music stands and chairs for the band, a baby grand piano all in white, sound equipment, cherubs with trumpets, cherubs without trumpets, cornucopia of every kind and silver-plated finger bowls, while in and around them all, with a long list in her hand like a chatelaine, floated the strangely affable form of Mrs Holdsworth, transmuted from the bitter woman who nursed a viper in her bosom, into something approaching an attendant of the goddess Hymen.

True, a certain waspishness emerged when it was discovered the caterer had sent the wrong napkins, but this was just a dash of vinegar to offset the general balm. Whenever she glimpsed Marie, she would smile knowingly and give little laughs and *oeillades* as if to indicate her knowledge of what was to go on ere long between the sheets. Marie wondered whether she was mad – whether all of them were mad – and were keeping her prisoner not because Felix and his cronies were stealing her money but to stop the world learning of their difficulty.

Marie drifted about, looking at all the activity which was ostensibly just for her, remembering a man who cared for clocks whom she would have married happily, a boy by the sea whom she would have married deliciously. Did they really think they could replace them with a grey man who had stolen her father's money? And yet, there was a strange feeling in her stomach as though the life she had known, that she had accepted along with any number of relaxing Quaaludes, or whatever it was they were giving her, was going to be substituted for something altogether more precarious.

And here was Mrs Holdsworth again, walking beside her, coquettishly, her angular frame ill-suited to the playful role of best friend and confidante.

'You know,' she said, 'I really liked your painting. I wanted to say that. We have been instructed not to enthuse. Mr Middleburg says it is bad for you to become excited about your talents for they will lead to nothing and only disappoint you.'

Marie nearly burst out laughing but contained herself. Was it possible, she wondered, that Mr Holdsworth had never made love to Mrs Holdsworth, or penetrated her in the way of men? Did he even have such an organ? It might explain her swings of mood and the excitement she displayed at the prospect of matrimony in the house. How would Mrs Holdsworth fare when she learnt of her protegée's defection? To have softened from her hardness and have to grow hard again would undo her. Still, Marie thought, Mrs Holdsworth hadn't been brought up from her earliest years with the sense of shame and self-worthlessness she herself had. Someone would have coaxed her and stroked her and told her that she was a lovely little Martha (for that was Mrs Holdsworth's name) with not an apothecary's scruple of bad blood throughout her infant frame. Besides, thought Marie, she has been a willing collaborator in my systematic incarceration, though I am someone who has never done her any harm. Sorry, Mrs Holdsworth, got to go. Over the fence and far way.

That evening she excused herself after dinner, pleading nerves and exhaustion again, which was in fact not far from the truth. The excitement of escape was upon her. She could hardly imagine that she could actually do it, or what it would be like when she did. Her apology was reluctantly accepted by Felix who would have liked some conversation about money and signatures and the responsibilities that come with marriage.

'Could we not delay that until we actually *are* married?' she asked him. 'There will be time enough. My head aches.'

'Of course, my dear. Time and money. The two most important currencies in the world. And law, of course. Time and money and law. Good night.'

'Time and money and law, Three things garnish our way...'

'What was that?' he asked.

'Oh, nothing,' she said. 'Your three currencies reminded me of something.'

Marie's dreams that night were full of steps, secret doors, soaring ladders, nameless possibilities fringed with alarm and someone chanting secrets.

Time and money and law,
Nothing is stronger than they,
Until death closes the door.

* * *

The next day dawned bright and fair as mornings always do in Beverly Hills, which rather robs them of their wonderfulness. Marie woke up in the bed in which she'd spent so many unprofitable nights, wondering what on earth she could take with her as she fled across the fence from safety into danger. She needed both hands free and no encumbrance for, if there were a ladder, she would have to climb it fast. Felix liked her to wear frocks but today she needed something that lent itself to climbing ladders. She chose some navy shorts and a light blue shirt. She came to the conclusion that if she wore two pairs of knickers it would give her a spare. She would have to wrap the envelope with her father's letters around her stomach or even put it down the back of her knickers, even if it gave her a flat bottom. She would have to do that in the wax-leaf privet tunnel. That was all the luggage she could afford and it pleased her to think that she was leaving the old life behind; that not even a shirt or a scarf would remind her of the comfortable profitless past. It did cross her mind that she had no money, but that was something that could be resolved. Escape was the order of the day.

This morning she did not drink the steaming cup of English tea that Mrs Holdsworth brought every morning to her bedside, but poured it down the basin instead. It was, or could be, one of the ways they induced the listless euphoria which had characterised her stay in Beverly Hills. There was to be no more of that.

After breakfast, everyone had something to attend to. The fax machine pattered away as ever while Mr Middleburg was in residence, but now it seemed to have overdrive attached and Holdsworth had to be in constant attendance, with furrowed brow and hovering finger. Felix wandered in and out to deal with whatever the matter in question might be: now shuffling digits, shifting money around – cooking a cash omelette as Mrs Holdsworth put it – and now answering questions from suppliers about parking facilities and vegetarian alternatives to the menu. He was a tower of strength; the driver of this whole machine.

'I am a cousin of your father's,' he had confided, 'not so close as to be consanguinous but near enough to understand the family and what it has gone through. It was one of the great families once. On a par with the Courtneys and the Cavendishes but French, you understand. The Laval-Lohéacs were Marcher lords, originally, with lands on the border of Anjou and Brittany.'

'So how did you come to be a Middleburg?' she had asked him.

'My mother married Antoine Middelbourg of Alsace. He was an Alsatian.'

Marie had barely stifled a laugh. She imagined Middleburg being suckled like Romulus and Remus by a wolf. And then she thought of the full moon. Did he prowl the corridors to see if he could look in sometime? There was, in spite of all the smoothness and the gloss of wealth, something feral about the man, something of Pan perhaps or, more likely, old Silenus.

'I made the family my passion and my goal,' he told her. 'I could not stand aside and see its fortune wasted and its name traduced.'

And so, she thought, you decided to take it from my father and from me – but by marrying me, Middleburg, wolf-man of Alsace, you are not paying back your dues, you are making your position perfect.

Marie made her way among the many people who were coming and going across the lawn, some for the house and kitchen, others straight to the marquee, which stretched across almost the entire length of the garden, almost up the to the wax-leaf privet hedge. The electronic gates were slowly opening and shutting, and she might have escaped there and then if anyone had been waiting to collect her. It gave her a notion about the electric gates as an alternative to the ladder. The interesting thing about the gates as they closed was that – if something like a truck wanted to come in – they paused awhile as if in contemplation before they opened again, giving several minutes' opportunity for escape before pursuit could be undertaken. Her ladder idea seemed precarious to her now, especially climbed at speed … and then what? A swallow dive into the arms of the ill-nourished, Spanish-looking man? She could see herself lying concussed on the tarmac with the Spanish-looking man unconscious beneath her.

Her rescuer would not be there until noon so there was no point in making an immediate, unplanned dash. Some would say it was crazy to trust a stranger but he was, after all, her father's messenger. He would at least arrive. He would not let her down. She went in to the wax-leaf privet tunnel, found her plastic bag and distributed the contents around her person. She knew she looked a little ungainly, maybe lumpen, but in all the throng and press, no one was really going to notice.

She walked up to the verandah and found a seat where she perched, looking down at the general activity. Felix appeared and stood at her shoulder.

'You looked flushed,' he said. 'I hope you have been taking your medication. There is something different about you today.'

'I only feel strange when people ask me how I am feeling,' she said.

A tall, lean, hard man was standing just behind Felix. He had long, bony fingers with hair on them, hard as a nutcracker.

'This is Crosbee,' he said. 'I have asked him to keep an eye on you.'

'Hello, Crosbee,' she said.

It wasn't Crosbee at all. It was Fist, she was sure of it. She said nothing. Where is my daughter, Fist?

'Hi, Marie.'

It was Fist, with an American accent and a crew cut. She decided to let him think she had not recognised him and to keep calling him Crosbee to his face.

'Why?' she asked Middleburg in alarm. 'Why Crosbee?'

'You know how dizzy you can be. I am busy today and Holdsworth is tied up, we all are, so I thought it would be good to have another all-seeing eye.'

'I don't want an all-seeing eye. He frightens me.'

Felix did not have a saving measure of absurdity like the Holdsworths.

'Don't excite yourself, dear. I know you better than you know yourself.'

Had he noticed the pages of foolscap tucked around her stomach and lodged around her kidneys? He moved away but he kept glancing at her as he hovered about, checking the arrangements. It was quarter to twelve. How was she going to approach the fence and leap to freedom if Fist were watching her all the time and Holdsworth was on her tail? At thirteen minutes to twelve the fax alarm went and Holdsworth had to go in. At eight to twelve he came out. At four minutes to twelve, the fax blinked its red light of warning and in he went again. Marie saw an opportunity to evade Fist and darted into the wax-leaf privet tunnel at the top end. She ran down to the bottom where the garden's front fence started and peered out to see Fist looking around, perplexed, and moving into the house. At twelve, the man who had known her father in prison arrived with a ladder. She called him. She had a new plan. Wait till the gates were in the first stages of being about to close then climb the ladder, concussion or no concussion.

'I have borrowed some wheels,' he told her. 'It's over there.'

He seemed to be waving towards an ancient Chevrolet, its colour and number plate almost obscured by dust, parked next to a large, blue van.

'Put the ladder over the fence,' she said. 'I hope it's not heavy.'

He pushed it up and over. It was very light aluminium and had a rope attached to it.

'We must wait,' she told him, 'until the next truck comes in the gates and they close. Then they won't be able to get out and chase us.'

'You think good,' he said. 'Like Papa.'

'Great,' she said.

After a few minutes, a truck arrived and passed through. The gates began to close.

'Now! I'm going to climb to the top and jump over.'

He looked nervous. 'Throw the rope over first,' he said. 'Then I pull it over when you've jumped.'

'You have to catch me.'

'I'm no good at catching. They drop me from the prison team.'

'I'm coming,' she said. She wobbled at the top of the fence, seven and a half feet up, spread out her arms and flew. 'Catch,' she called.

She landed in a heap on top of him and they both fell onto the road, laughing.

'Ow.'

'Are you hurt?' she asked him.

'Only my dignity. Now I introduce. I am Felipe.' He offered his hand, which she took.

'Well, come on then, Felipe.'

There were cries from the garden as Fist spotted what had happened. Felix appeared as if summoned by fax.

'Quick,' she said. 'Grab that ladder.'

There was just time to snatch it back before Crosbee arrived. He leapt at the fence, trying to climb it, but it was a good fence. It had been built just for the purpose of keeping someone in. n.

Marie was making for the Chevy's door, but Felipe indicated a pair of bicycles standing against railings on its further side.

'Wheels?' she asked

'All I could do,' he said. 'Follow me.'

They leapt on the bikes and peddled away furiously, Felipe leading them down a pedestrian-only path which he had previously reconnoitred. 'No car can follow,' he cried.

Behind them she heard the gates clang shut behind the van that had entered the grounds, restricting all other egress for a few precious moments. Even so, she could see Felix's Bentley speeding down from the garage, hooting its horn. Too bad it couldn't get out just yet.

'Won't they catch us up?' she panted.

'We are using the paths,' said Felipe. 'I was in prison with a getaway driver. He teach me these tricks.'

'Do you know where we're going?' she asked.

'I think so.'

The path ended suddenly and they had to cross a road to get to a further path on the other side. As they emerged to cycle across the road, they were almost run over by the same delivery van that had bought them their moments of time. Fist had managed to get the keys for the parked van and, as soon as the gates reopened, had driven after them.

'Look out!' Felipe called out as Fist crammed on the brakes, stalling the engine, and leapt from the cab. He spread his arms wide and Marie was barely able to swerve and evade the bony fingers.

Coming up from the bottom of the hill was Felix and the Bentley, driving straight at the bicycles, but Felipe and Marie were away down the other path. There was no way Felix or Fist could follow them in their vehicles. Felix pummelled the Bentley's horn in an ecstasy of frustration.

Felipe and Marie, pedalling strongly, took the scenic route for home down the walkways, grassy places and gated roads Felipe had recced over the previous weeks. Only when they neared home, which turned out to be not far geographically, but seemingly light years away from downtown LA, did they venture onto streets that the visitor never sees. There were a number of people hanging around, most of them Latino like Felipe, with an admixture of black.

'Welcome to Echo Park,' said Felipe. 'Not the best address in LA, but it has a good lake.'

They reached Felipe's place in five minutes, parked the bikes in a friendly garage run by a Mexican friend of Felipe's and walked through passageways and alleys for a further five minutes to throw off any further pursuit. There was an ugly moment when Marie thought she saw the big, black Bentley saloon nosing round a corner and they shrank into an alleyway, but there was still no sign of Fist.

'LA is full of big black saloons,' said Felipe, and so it seemed.

Marie had escaped. She was appalled and exhilarated at what she had done – had she really managed to outwit the man who had taken her father for all he had and punished him for letting him do it? How great his rage would be now under that smooth, grey surface, how that vein of his would throb at his temple! What would he do next? He wouldn't let it go; he was that kind of person – always plotting the next move. But this time he would not be one step ahead.

* * *

There were certain practical problems to think of that Marie had not yet raised with Felipe. Where, for instance, was she going to spend the night? Felipe's room was not so much a room as a long cupboard. There was just about enough space for a single bed against the wall by the window. There was a sink and a gas ring where Felipe made coffee. There was a shower and toilet room, which was a cupboard within a cupboard.

Marie looked round with some dismay. She felt exhausted by the efforts of the day and could not face looking for lodgings that evening, but equally she wasn't going to share a room with Felipe, however much he had done for her. Luckily he had thought of that.

'I ask my landlord if he had another room, and he say yes.'

'But I have no money.'

'We will think of something.'

'I could pawn my ring,' she said, looking at the ruby with the insignia of Laval which she had come to love, 'if there were a pawn shop around.' It would be a wrench but she needed money, at least in the short term before she thought of some other course.

'There is one,' said Felipe, 'just down the alley. I show you later. Come, now I show you your room.'

He took her upstairs to a slightly larger place than his own with its own kitchenette and shower room. A small, dark man appeared, Jaime the Mexican, friend of Felipe, owner of the house. Introductions were made. She looked around. The tap in the kitchen dripped. There were sheets on the bed. The place didn't smell too bad. There was a window looking out on a yard and a dusty tree.

'You like?' asked the Mexican.

'It's fine,' she said. At least it looked clean. She was in no position to be choosy.

'You fix details with Felipe,' said Jaime. 'I go now.' He smiled, and scuttled down the stairs.

'Jaime always busy,' Felipe told her, 'he run shop, he run house, he run taxi. He run for Congress soon.'

'He seems very nice. He even made the bed.'

'I make the bed for you,' Felipe corrected her. 'One small thing I do for my friend's daughter.'

'Thank you, Felipe. And for everything.'

'It is no more than he do for me. Indeed, it is much less.'

'What is Jaime going to charge for the room?'

'For a friend, not much, and he can wait for money for a day or two. Now, maybe you move in here now, the shower works, the water is good and later we find a diner and get something to eat. You must be tired. Tomorrow we talk and I show you a little more of your father's writing; nothing much, but it will add to your understanding.'

'I need to buy clothes,' she told him, 'when I have raised some money at the pawnshop. All I have is what I wear. And also, I need to pay you back for all your time and research and expenses.'

'What I have done needs nothing,' he told her earnestly. 'I do it for your father who help me when I am down and teach me English and many things and books to read.'

'You are very kind, Felipe, but I must pay you for any outlay, like the bicycles, and food tonight if we go out. I have known what it is like to be not rich.'

She did not like to call him poor but he was very evidently short of funds.

'That is good of you,' he said. 'We can talk about it tomorrow too. I will come and tap at your door in forty minutes.'

He left her alone in her new home with a packet of tea, milk, sugar, a towel, a bottle of shampoo, a bar of soap, even a hairbrush which he had bought the day before in preparation for her arrival. She was touched by his consideration and the generosity of such a poor man and she kissed him on the cheek as he left. Then she shut the door and sat in the saggy excuse for a chair (quite comfortable, actually) and let the day's events filter through her mind. In the space of a few hours, her life had changed completely. It gave her a wonderful sensation, the old feeling of freedom. Even though she was physically exhausted, she felt transfused as if the old, tired, drugged blood had been taken out and filled with the altogether good stuff. Anything was possible now. She sat like this for half an hour until she looked at her watch and sprang up. Felipe would be here in ten minutes.

The shower actually worked – it had looked as though it wouldn't – and the water was approaching hot. She felt much better as she stepped out, towelled herself dry and put on clean pants before stepping back into her shorts. Still, this was an adventure. She had had comfort without hope for too long.

Felipe tactfully gave her ten minutes longer than he had said and then he knocked, poking his head round the door.

'We go to a diner just round the block,' he told her. 'I think we have enough exercise for one day.'

On the way, he showed her where the pawnshop was, just across the street.

'He's not bad man, old Pfeffer,' he told her. 'He can seem mean at first. You just have to work your magic on him.'

The diner was a far cry from Mrs Holdsworth's dining room, but the food was homemade and home-cooked. They ordered beer and meatloaf and fries. It all rather reminded her of the days in King's Cross and the occasional extravagances she had enjoyed in the poverty of the squat. The meatloaf was excellent and so was the beer.

'How do you live?' she asked him.

'Very little,' was his reply.

'But how?'

He scraped a living out of running errands and walking dogs. He had even taken up baby-sitting but it really wasn't for him. Sometimes Jaime would let him drive a taxi. Sometimes he was employed to drop fliers through letter boxes. Employment was difficult for an ex-convict. He seemed such a nice man, the mystery was, why had he ended up in prison? In the end, as they spoke of this and that, and he descanted on the life of the poor in LA, which you don't hear much about, Marie asked him.

'I killed a man who was beating a woman in the street. I didn't mean to kill him. It was an accident. But his friends didn't like it.'

'Did you know the woman?'

'Yes.'

'And that was in Mexico?'

'Yes.'

'How long were you in prison?'

'Ten years.'

'And why was my father in prison in Mexico?'

'He escape from California over the border. The Mexicans arrested him. The police here ask for him back, but the Mexicans say one of the victims is Mexican, so they keep him in Mexico. He was a prize, you know, your father, although he never hurt anyone. They were proud to have him though they treat him like shit. Tomorrow I show you more letter.'

Tomorrow, she thought, that was when reality would kick in. Tomorrow she would find money at the pawnshop and, once she had some decent clothes to wear, she would find work. And then, having solved the pressing problem of survival, she would find an answer to the overriding problem of her life: her father, and the mystery of her upbringing. For the moment, the food and the beer had made her sleepy. Even Felipe was yawning. He paid for the meal out of a clutter of small change in his pocket and they were soon back at the flat. He left her at her door and said good night.

'Thanks so much for everything,' she told Felipe. 'Tomorrow I pay you back.'

'I won't…'

'No protesting. I will.'

She gave him a good night kiss on the cheek which made him blush. She slept very well that night in the room looking out on to the dusty tree, even though the curtain didn't quite fit.

* * *

Seeing Fist masquerading as the bony Crosbee at Middleburg's house had brought her up short. Could it really be him, so far from Harwich and the kipper-smelling docks? It seemed entirely unlikely, but she had learned nothing was impossible with Middleburg. At least it gave her renewed hope of finding little Lily, though she shuddered at the thought of the man and his hammy fist. Of course, Middleburg would have him in his web. He could be outside the building even now.

It was Middleburg who himself had come to claim her, no doubt liaising with Fist when she was lying sick nearby in the old hulk on the marshes. Fist's presence in LA now added a physical dimension of fear, but she comforted herself with the thought that it would only be on a temporary basis. He would not want to be long removed from the house with the ruched curtains and oppressive central heating. He and his barley sugar neighbour surely could not long be parted?

Meanwhile, what was she to do about her immediate survival in LA? Wherever Lily was, there was nothing she could do for her without some kind of centre to operate from and money to carry the project forward. She only had one thing that she could possibly pawn and it was not something she cared to part with. However, the more she thought about it, the less she could avoid doing what had to be done.

Next morning, she woke late in her strange bed, and after an initial sense of dislocation tinged with excitement, moderated by alarm, she rose, washed under a cold tap and visited her teeth using the brush and toothpaste Felipe had kindly provided the night before. In the kitchenette, she boiled a kettle and made a cup of supermarket instant coffee which she found abandoned in a cupboard, then hurried downstairs and peered cautiously outside the front door. On seeing no Fist and, plucking up courage, she ventured out and hurried round the corner to find the pawnshop. She entered guiltily, as one does at pawnshops, feeling the ancient ring on her finger, pressing the door open wide under the swinging sign of the three golden balls and the legend 'Pfeffer & Volkers, Pawnbrokers' in faded gold type.

This ring was the only tangible connection with the family she was heir to. It had caused her pain in the past and she was half glad to be rid of it now, though she knew that she shouldn't be. It was her only possession, but there was nothing else for it. After all, she told herself – and all her ancestors if they were listening – she was only pawning, not selling, it.

Mr Pfeffer was not easily impressed, nor was he known for his generosity – certainly not by Mr Volkers who had died ten years before – but even Pfeffer was blown away by the ring with the blood-red crest of Laval upon it as it lay on the counter behind the window of Pfeffer & Volkers at 127 Caraway Street. He expressed his interest in a rich soup of sound that mixed American with what was left of the ghettoes of Middle Europe.

'How did you come by this?' he asked her. 'It is the design, what they call the device, of an old family. I have not seen a ruby like this in all my born days, and they are long and hairy. But something about it mystifies me. It is a very, very good stone.'

Did he really say hairy? She rather doubted it but decided not to comment.

'It was given to me by my great-aunt,' she said. 'We are supposedly descended from the Lavals whose crest it is.'

'Then why are you getting rid of it?' he hectored her. 'Of course you will say it is not my business, but our ancestors are all we have.

We carry them around in our blood and in our face, in our bone and in our belly, in our voices and in our hair if we have it.'

'I am not getting rid of it,' she corrected him. 'I am pawning it because I need the money. How much will you give me, Herr Pfeffer?'

'I will give you five hundred dollars,' he told her. 'Jewellery like this is not fashionable. The young girls will not wear him.'

'History is always fashionable,' she told him. 'What other stone has such a history? Make it two thousand dollars. Did you know it once belonged to Bluebeard himself?'

'You make that up. Foolish girl. You cannot pull the wool over old Pfeffer.'

'Bluebeard was my father.'

'You don't even joke about such things.'

'That is my family crest. It is five hundred years old.'

Mr Pfeffer paled and made some kind of mid-European cabbalistic sign.

'It is a cursed stone? You are a witch? I give you one thousand.'

'It'll curse you if you mess me around, but your customers will love a cursed stone. There are twenty different witches and earth magic societies in my street alone. Tell your clients it's cursed and you'll double the price.'

The old man looked at her half-admiringly. 'You want a job,' he said. 'You come and work for me here.'

'I might at that,' she joked.

'I give you two thousand for the ring but you come back for it within a month or I sell him for five thousand.'

'It is not worth five thousand dollars,' she told him. 'It is worth fifty thousand. It is priceless.'

Marie tried to take the ring off her finger but found it curiously resistant. She had to go to the old man's sink and put some soap on her skin before she could get it off. And when she put the ring on the counter, it fell on its side and rolled towards her. She thought she was imagining it, it was probably just silly, but she felt an immediate lightening of her spirit when it was gone as if it were a rune that had been cast against her. Perhaps, she thought, there is evil in it. She almost felt sorry for the old man as he counted out the fifty dollar bills. Would he be walking home, glancing over his shoulder at the thing that could be felt but not seen? Would it come leaping after him, impossibly fast, as he ran hopelessly over the sand and fell? Or would a hand like a spider come crawling towards him over his bedside table, wearing the very ring that he was now placing in the display window on its finger?

'How much would you pay me if I worked for you?' she asked, although she knew the old man was joking.

'Don't take the job,' he advised. 'You can do better.'

* * *

The first thing she did was to return to Felipe's studio. She found him drinking coffee and talking to Jaime, and she give him a hundred dollars. He looked at her as though she were a miraculous witch. There was definitely magic around today. But he shook his head and pressed the money back.

'Keep it,' she said. 'You have done more for me than ever I could reward.'

'You need to live in this wicked city,' he told her. 'Money goes fast.'

'I owe it to you,' she said to Felipe. 'If it hadn't been for you I would be married soon to that terrible man.'

297

'I promise your father I look after you.'

'And you have done a great job of it. You have been a tower of strength,' she said, and kissed him again. 'You are an obelisk.'

'That is the third time you kiss me. You make me blush,' he said, happily.

'And now,' she told him, 'I have to buy some clothes. I am going to try and find a job as a Merrymaid.'

He looked profoundly shocked. 'You cannot do that. Your father would not allow it. You show your titties to these sad old men?'

'It's not great but it's all right. They pay good money and it makes them happy.'

'And then they sleep you afterwards.'

'No they don't.'

'Well, you know best. But as your father's friend I am not happy.'

'You will be happy if I bring you some vino and a nice big steak.'

'It turn to ashes in my mouth. Maybe.' He smiled at her, a sad little smile. She realised then that he was at the end of his strength. His time in prison and yesterday's activities had squeezed the life out of him. He had been through too much.

'I will find information there at Merrymaids. A man they spoke of, called Grindlay, is a director of the company and a member of the club,' she told him. 'If I can win him over and talk to him, if I can trust him, I may learn more about my father's money and what they have done with it, and about the company they have built.'

'Well, that is different. But there are too many ifs. You go and bring back the nice big steak. But...' and here his face clouded '...do not take lightly what I have told you. These people are not just very dangerous, they have the cunning of the devil – literally.'

Marie could see he believed what he was saying, but she could not quite bring herself to agree. Middleburg and Brickville were essentially grey men. They exuded power and money – but she doubted they would have the appetite to encourage a man into savage and murderous debauchery in order to steal his fortune. There were easier ways than that to make money and rest in your bed. Was she being too highly strung – as Aunt Bertha used to say, too much of a taut Maxply – looking for more trouble than there was? There might be a perfectly reasonable explanation for everything that had happened. But of course that had been the downfall of her father: not believing the worst.

'You may be right,' she told Felipe at last, 'but the game demands a move and my move must be to Merrymaids. I worked with these people once before when I had nothing, so I know what I'm letting myself in for. There is something I need to find out. Meanwhile, could you ask if anyone knows of a French castle up in the Sierra? I know it sounds unlikely but I heard of such a place at my last address.'

'Nothing is unlikely in California.'

'First of all, I am going shopping. I need clothes.'

'Keep your eyes open. There will be people looking for you.'

'I promise.'

'And when you come back I will show you the last of the letters. The others were all destroyed by the guards as I escape. I tore my pockets on the wire and they fell out.'

'Too bad but at least we have something. I will be some time, but back this afternoon and then we will talk.'

'Be careful.'

* * *

She bought the clothes she wanted at a little store she found in Melrose Avenue where the prices were half those in the big stores and the clothes looked better. She guessed the regulation dress for LA was much the same as Pilgrim's Piece, smart but sexy, and why not? She liked what she had chosen; even so there was a considerable dent in the two thousand dollars she had extracted from Mr Pfeffer.

On her return to her apartment, she found a large envelope had been pushed under the door. There was no sign of Felipe. She poured herself a glass of water, threw her shopping bags on the bed and sat down to read.

My dear daughter,

If only I could undo those things that I have done to your detriment, but I cannot. It is useless to wish for favours from time, the most implacable of the gods. All I can do now is explain to you, whom I never met except when you were a tiny baby.

I was brought up spoilt in circumstances of wealth, for we were – and are – a great family. The money came from my great grandfather who built railways (he was a sometime colleague of Brunel) and also from my American grandmother whose family owned coal mines and made steel. The Lavells, I believe, are descended from a Norman family who once owned a string of castles on the borders of Brittany. The name is thought to be an anglicised version of the French Laval. Forgive me if you know something of this already. I will come back to it later.

I never had to bother about money. We were supposed to be above all that sort of thing. It was considered déclassé even to talk about it. A gentleman was either a sportsman or a scholar. I chose the latter pursuit, fool that I was. If only I had raced a great yacht or followed the hounds and bagged the grouse and stalked the red deer…

I went up to Oxford in 1934, as young men were encouraged to do in those days. I wasted much of my time but I did become interested in my subject of History. I was especially intrigued by the fifteenth century which, along with the sixteenth, seems a sort of no man's land buffer zone between the high Middle Ages and the New Age of art, politics and enlightenment; a time where magic and science intermingle, where Joan of Arc met and admired our supposed ancestor Gilles de Rais.

I didn't do enough work at university but my interest in the subject kept me from being too abject a failure. I achieved a reasonable Second. After taking my degree, I still had no idea of what I really wanted to do. It was summer, I drove down to the Riviera in my Bentley with a friend from Oxford, and we fooled around for a month or two, generally having a good time.

And then I met this lovely girl. You know, occasionally, if you're lucky, you meet someone you seem to have known before, someone who seems to know you inside out. It was like that with Amélie. Her family came from near Rouen, but she was on holiday. She was French, of course, and looked like a dark angel, caramelised by the sun and made all of good things. She was adorable. We could not be parted from each other. I asked her to marry me.

Normally, I would have taken her home to meet my parents, but I had hardly seen them since I was at school. They were divorced. My mother lived in Rome and my father ran the family businesses in London and New York. I had more than enough money, I was with the girl of my dreams and there seemed no hurry to go home. We had a year or so of happiness together. We moved back to England, married, and bought a house near Henley, and then the war started.

I was a young officer in the Light Infantry during the war. I went to France, narrowly escaped at Dunkirk, snatched a little leave, and then I was off to Africa, saw action at Tobruk. Got blown up in Alamein, was off duty for a while and then I found myself, towards the end of 1944, home on leave.

That is when Amélie and I made you. Then I went back to France. We fought our way into Germany. Saw some things as we advanced that I will not tell you about. They stay with me to this day. Then at last I was home again and Amélie and I picked up where we left off.

Of course it wasn't the same old England. Austerity was round the corner, but in 1945 everyone was happy that the war was over and won. There were dances, dinners, parties and shows in London. Amélie was visibly pregnant but she didn't let it stop her. She gave birth to you halfway through the year You were the best thing that ever happened, and we quietened down a lot... We found a wonderful nanny for you. I even started to do a little research with a view to a book on the English in France in the fifteenth century, but the call of leisure was still strong. And then, coming home from dinner one evening with some friends – I was driving – a car came round a corner on the wrong side of the road, we crashed and Amélie was killed. We were laughing at something – she died laughing. The other driver was convicted of manslaughter and sent to prison.

For six months, I was in despair. I took to drink. And I started an affair with drugs that led me down to hell. Facilis descensus averno: *the road to hell has a gentle slope. I will come to that later.*

I missed her terribly, every moment of every day. I woke missing her and I missed her still as the waters of sleep closed over me. My dreams were full of her and sometimes I dreamt that she was still alive and I woke to a desolate morning. Sometimes I thought I could hear her voice talking to me just out of earshot. I neglected you shamefully; yes, I almost blamed you for the accident – we could have stayed the night but she wanted to come home to you. Your nanny was wonderful, but the truth was, I could not bear to see you. I am so sorry to have to tell you that, but I feel it might help to explain my hurt and despair. Tiny though you were, you reminded me too much of your mother.

I went to hell on a succession of handcarts. Drink, drugs, low life, low company, mountebanks, gambling and spongers. And then at last one day, waking up in a strange bed with no idea where I was, I made a decision; it had to stop. I would become a recluse and a scholar and I would devote myself to the period of history that interested me.

I plunged into it with the same addictive devotion that I had shown for debauch. You and Nanny were sent up to a small castle our family had in Scotland, with instructions that I was not to be interrupted in Oxfordshire. Meanwhile, I had come across a distant cousin of mine called Middleburg (God knows where he came from – the Burgundian or Alsace side, I think he said) in some casino or bar who made himself obliging to me, a necessary man and excellent researcher. We worked together well for several years which is why I trusted him. He helped me with research into this Gilles de Rais who, it seemed to me, might have suffered a gross injustice at the hands of his enemies and of history itself. As I looked deeper and deeper into the past, this Middleburg, my cousin, became indispensable at tedious things like admin; he paid bills for me, signed cheques, stood in for me at board meetings, I really didn't have time for all that sort of thing. In the end, he made the suggestion that I should move to the United States and, most especially to California, since my previous low life, followed by my present bookish ways, had engendered a lung infection that refused to clear up. The desert air, he said, would prove remedial. We were concerned that I might become consumptive – even in the forties, it was an inconvenient disease. I embraced the idea since California in those days still had a certain promise about it, a promise bleached by the sun, uncluttered by memory.

Once ensconced in Los Angeles, we set about looking for a suitable base where I could carry on with my studies undisturbed. I had accumulated a small library of reference into the early fifteenth century and I needed space, somewhere congenial to my pursuit, big spaces where I could pace and think and take myself back in time to this poor forebear of ours, hemmed about with enemies and vicious people. Middleburg, in conjunction with another cousin of ours – so-called since I could not verify it nor did I even want to, a man called Brickville, whom he had found at some gathering in London and persuaded to come over and help him attend to my requirements – bought a lease on what was supposed to be a French castle up in the foothills of the Sierra, built by some eccentric millionaire who had gone bust. At any rate, this place, the Château de Cauchemar as it came to be called, fitted the bill exactly. It had silence, it had space, it was well protected from unwanted visitors. The air was good. It seemed ideal and we moved in.

It was here that the nightmare began. It was necessary for me to go to New York – which I did with Middleburg – where I had to sign certain documents which appointed Middleburg as my deputy and signatory. The lawyers raised their eyebrows but, because I was so rich, they didn't like to cross me. I just wanted to get back to my library and poor old Gilles de Rais and his enemies. He too was a man obsessed.

When I returned, the castle seemed to have acquired a few new guests. It did not matter to me so long as they kept out of my way. They were friends of Middleburg and his crew. These too stayed away much of the time, working away at making money for my company, they told me, and I was foolishly and gullibly satisfied. A young friend of theirs, a fellow called Prelati, stayed and became a kind of surrogate host, which suited me well. People stayed and ate and drank a great deal as they do in English country houses, but they left me alone. There was music and dancing, some of the guests were women, there was song and even theatricals of a kind. There were people who called themselves the Merry Pranksters. One particular fellow called Eliphas was a magician, rather a good one, as I recall. A good man – he tried to warn me about Prelati and even Middleburg, but I would not listen.

She stopped reading for a moment. Prelati, she thought. I know that name.

I had started to take a little cocaine to keep me awake, there was a great deal of marijuana smoked – no good to me for it made me fall asleep – and one of the people who came was a professor of psychology who advocated a substance called LSD, which has the effect of heightened perception. He also advocated a magic mushroom called psilocybin. And mescaline too. I had come to something of an impasse with my studies for much of the evidence seemed to suggest that Gilles was guilty even though I found that hard to accept. In despair, I asked the Professor if I could try his pharmacopeia and he gave me some to take. An extraordinary perception overtook me with far-reaching intuitions about the object of my studies, of consciousness, myself and the universe. I travelled down vast abysses and merged with a giant flower. It seemed to me that my hero was guilty and not guilty. He could be both the same, at once.

In this manner, weeks passed and I was tightly wound into the nightmare surrounding poor Gilles until it seemed I was in the cauchemar *myself and becoming the very man I wrote about. My consciousness, my sense of reality had become obscured; shadows passed, terrible visions assailed but I was powerless to act. A wicca, a tall man with staring eyes and a mane of blond hair, a very devil, said he could raise the spirit of Gilles de Rais for me and made me watch while the nightmare happened and kept happening, a true* cauchemar, *and I could not move. There was darkness and blood and the thudding of a drum. There were girls, boys and children too young to be there. I saw them but where did they go, what did they do? Figures moved in procession, someone screamed. Malestroit, Bishop of Nantes, the Duke's brother, came to protest, but he was sent packing. Someone gave me papers to sign of which I knew nothing…*

Morning again. The mist clears. They tell me they have found the bodies of 39 children and there may be more. How did they get there? How did they go?

As it happened, I had been signing my wealth away, but one thing I did not sign, nor could have done, was a paper for my heir – the little girl Marie whom I had left alone with her nanny in the Castle of Fairlie – to sign herself when she was old enough. In the strange back and forth of my life, I had dreamt of Amélie and she'd told me to be alone with the old lawyers. And so it happened, and I asked them to do this. The paper I signed stated that, come what may, when you were twenty-five all that I had would be yours. I thought it might be considerably diminished, little realising that Middleburg and Brickville were turning my huge estate into something enormous for themselves. They have the devil's own luck.

A special paper was drawn up returning all of my share to you. And that is where you find yourself now, my darling girl. They have accused me of terrible crimes which I have not knowingly committed. They have done it to blacken my name and to make their takeover of my affairs seem to be in the family's, in the public's, interest. The police are coming for me but Middleburg and Brickville talk of sending me over the border to Mexico so that I can escape. I am sure it is for their sake rather than mine. I am less trouble in Mexico, the prisons are harder, and the death penalty more certain.

If I should not see you again – which seems likely since Eliphas, my loyal servant here, tells me to make ready – I can only leave you my story and beg you to forgive me. Had your mother not died, your life and mine would have been different. Think of that. Perhaps the good times are happening somewhere else and what we have here is just the reverse, the negative of that life. Somewhere we are strong and happy. Meanwhile here, in this place that we know as life, remember that your adversary the devil walketh about, seeking whom he may devour…

They are coming for me now, they will take me over the border and the Mexican police will pick me up. There is no extradition treaty with the USA. I will be a prize exhibit like a Fat Lady, the Most Evil Man in American

History, a monster, a legend. They will keep me alive for that reason and treat me abominably. They will scourge me. And when the excitement has died down, they will kill me. I am not afraid, but I fear for you.

Pray for me.

Your loving father,

Giles Lavell

* * *

Marie put down the last sheet of paper and found that she was shaking. She had not expected to be so moved. She had thought that she knew about pain, but reading her father's account, she realised that she only knew one piece of the giant jigsaw that says Human Suffering on the cover. A phrase from her childhood English lessons came to mind: 'thoughts that do lie too deep for tears'. Yes, that is what they were. Her powers of response seemed to have dried up. It was like seeing Fate at work; a moment of weakness followed by that implacable turning of the screw. She wanted to feel sorry for him, but she also wanted to blame him. She wanted to blame him – but could not, because she felt sorry for him.

And the tragedy of it all was that it was so unnecessary, so frustrating. It could so easily all have been different. She turned at last to Felipe who had crept in and was sitting quietly beside her, saying nothing.

'What do you think? You have read all this?'

'He ask me to read. He teach me to read.'

'What do you think?'

'I think he was unlucky, but I am sure he is not wicked man. He did not do those things that they accuse him of. How could he? The wicked ones were the ones you have met. They knew there were many new people come to California in those days after the war, displaced, nowhere to go. Murders, rapes, gang fights, suicides … people were glad to get rid of the bodies and they were all sent round or collected by someone, or some people, at the castle.'

'Where did they keep them?'

'Oh, they were buried in a pit nearby. Convenient for evidence against your father.'

'How do you know all this?'

'I tell you. I had to kill a bad man once. The word got around I was a killer. I know things.'

She was silent for a moment. There was still all the other stuff that Felipe did not know about her childhood and upbringing.

'You must forgive him,' Felipe said as if reading her thoughts.

Could she do that? Forgive him for those days of loneliness and shame in the cold castle? The dread of bad blood? The cold shoulder of the girls at school? The rejection by her own boyfriend's parents? The oppression and cruelty of Brickville, the menacing caringness of Middleburg, the loss of her baby to the Izzards and Fist. Hard to forgive. Of course, there are always excuses. Her father's own upbringing was responsible. He had been encouraged from an early age to think only of himself, heir to a kingdom of gold. That was why his love for Amélie was so shocking for him, she thought. When she was gone, all he'd had left was ruin and a broken idea of himself.

But having a bad time yourself doesn't excuse giving a bad time to somebody else, especially when it's your own child. And hadn't she just done that to her own child? That was another thing she couldn't get away from. She turned to Felipe again. 'Did he believe he had done those terrible things?' she asked him.

'I do not really know. We were both in prison in bad circumstance. He was weak and sometimes hardly conscious. He taught me English and I taught him to survive. I am afraid he was the more successful. His mind had been torture with drugs. He hardly knew who he was any more.'

'But did he do these things they accuse him of?'

Felipe shook his head. 'I am sure he did not.'

'And is he still there in that dreadful place?' A sudden wild hope filled her that perhaps, after all, she was not alone in the world, that she had a father – not a monster, but a man much-abused. 'I was told long ago that he was dead. I must go and see him.'

'No. I am told they move him – somewhere more terrible still. He died there. No one survive. It is for enemies of government.'

'Are you certain he is dead?'

'For sure. I make enquiries. I know a man who know…' he corrected himself, 'who *knew* one of the guards. He catch fever and die.'

Hope vanished as quickly as it had grown. 'How did you get out?' she asked.

It was a question she had been anxious to ask but somehow it had seemed embarrassing to do so. She looked round at the wretched apartment and realised that Felipe was literally starving. She must buy him more food. Even with what she had given him, he was still paying off his debts. He couldn't afford to feed himself, let alone feed her, but she was so happy to be free of Middleburg and the poison they were giving her that she felt quite undaunted. She smiled and the older man seemed quite warmed by it. He answered quietly but honestly. He too was weak – it cost him much to speak at all.

'I understand why you ask,' he said. 'Of course I can. It is a question we all ask in prison about every kind of privilege or privation. Why me and not him? There was change of government and my accusers had been discredited. But his so-called crimes were so enormous that there was no chance he would ever be release. It would be a crime against humanity to let him out. Imagine in a place like that! A crime against humanity! It was a crime against humanity to keep anyone inside that prison.'

She knew what her father had been accused of – accused and found guilty. She was silent for a moment. 'How did you find me?' she asked.

He smiled. 'Not so much how as why. I promised your father before they take him away that I would find you, no matter where you were or what it cost. It is possible to find anyone with a little patience and some criminal friend.'

'What made you think I would still be alive?'

'He says they need you alive to sign the documents. He told me he had signed them himself when he was under the drugs, but they would need you to sign them when you were of age. They would know how to try and make you sign them.'

She shivered. She knew very well that what he said was true. There seemed no end to their power or capabilities.

Felipe passed his hand over his face. Was he unwell, Marie wondered. His colour was up, she noticed, as he sank back a little in his chair. He saw her looking at him with concern.

'I caught malaria in prison,' he told her. 'It come back a little now and then.'

'Can I get you anything?' she asked.

'A cold beer from my fridge,' he said. 'And one for you. I get them.'

He started to rise but she pushed him back. 'No,' she said. 'Leave it to me.'

'Take the keys.' He smiled gratefully and tossed them over.

She returned in a couple of minutes with the beer. They drank in silence for a moment.

'You must have spent ages looking for me all that time,' she told Felipe. 'Few people would do so much for a stranger they had met in jail.'

He thought about it, brows furrowed. 'He was a great man,' he said. 'Your father was a scholar, a saint. He rescue me when I had nothing to live for. I would not break my word to him. He ask me to find his daughter and tell her the truth.'

'Tell me about him,' she asked. 'What sort of man was he?'

'He was a gentle man and a gentleman. He seemed to carry a great *dolor*, how you say … sorrow when I knew him but he was not without laughter. He was like a professor, a scholar. It was his passion.'

'What did he look like?'

'He was tall, thin, dark hair with high forehead and bright pale eyes like yours, forever studying and reading. His obsession was to put right the wrongs done to your ancestor Gilles de Rais. He bought this old castle someone had brought over from France. He called it Cauchemar. Your father's error was the folly of a very rich man who does not pay attention to his business affairs. He left the running of his fortune to his cousins. This was mistake in two ways. They were not just on the make, not to be trusted, they were evil. And when certain envious people told them of his interest for Gilles de Rais – your father say that Joan of Arc introduce Gilles to the old religion, the witches – they make him ill with drugs and keep him prisoner, feeding him lies, fantasies, drugs and poison. When I meet him he is man broken by poor food and ill health but even then he has not lost his kindness or his scholar interest. He teach me English and even some Latin.'

He thought about it for a while.

'And the other thing that never leave him is his love for you, his daughter,' he told her.

They sat in silence as she tried to imagine her parents – her mother who would never be old, and her stricken father whose hand had written these words and touched these pages; riches to rags and dust to dust.

'So here we are,' she said. 'Now what is to be done? How am I going to punish the people who have done this?'

* * *

It is hard, when you are twenty-four years of age, to feel laden with the sins of your father, or burdened by the obscurity and uncertainty of his fate. However, a sleep, a bacon sandwich and a good cup of coffee from the diner around the corner conspired to encourage optimism.

Marie put on a summer frock, said goodbye to Felipe and took a bus to downtown LA where the richer shops were and the richer people looked important. Wilshire Boulevard started here on its course northwest across town. A bit further on it became a more relaxed sort of street, but here it bristled with shops and offices. Well, actually, it didn't bristle. It didn't even flaunt. It stated.

Further out, there were gardens, white houses where people lived and more leisurely businesses, but here, there were department stores, office buildings, an upmarket gentleman's club called the St James's, a theatre, a sprinkling of fine restaurants and trattorias whose fragrant offerings – bakery and cakery, patisserie and rotisserie, wine and roses and specials of the day – wafted across the pavements, lending a certain relish to the business of the day.

And just round the corner from the Los Angeles Athletic Club on Figueroa Street was the LA version of Merrymaids, lending a certain frivolity and forbidden fruitishness to the muscles and Mammonry of the area. Outside the establishment, lit up decorously on one flank of the building, was a gargantuan Merrymaid picked out in neon lights.

Marie, remembering her days at the establishment, was adjusting her expression into one of wise innocence – an oxymoronic cut of jib much favoured by the management of Merrymaids – when heels behind her on the pavement stopped their clickety-clacking, and a voice said, 'It can't be.'

It was Margot, whom she had last met at Pilgrim's Piece, still unmistakably the same but in a more prosperous mode. 'What are you doing here, Marie?' she asked.

'I want to be doing what you're doing. Making money, I hope. I thought you might be here, don't know why.'

'You must be crazy. The LA version of Merrymaids is just like Sussex only worse, though the men are even richer.'

'Have you got time for a coffee before you go in?' Marie asked.

'Just about. There's a place round the corner.'

They found a table and ordered a couple of coffees with milk, the English way.

'How did you end up here?' Margot asked. 'I was worried about you. You disappeared. Did you have the baby?'

'It's a long story.'

'I bet it is.'

'Too long for now. I'll tell you all about it later. I just wanted to ask about Merrymaids. Do you ever get any customers from a company called The Other Judas – TOJI?'

'We sure do. They're based some way outside town but have an office here. They seem to own everything, They probably own Merrymaids now. They certainly own this coffee we're drinking and this chain of cafés.'

Margot pronounced it caf*ays* – she had picked up more than a smattering of Americanisms during her stay.

'Have you met a bloke called Grindlay?'

Margot's eyes widened. 'As a matter of fact, I have. How do you know that name?'

'I heard someone talking about him. He said he's not as bad as most of them.'

'I want to hear everything,' Margot said.

'You will.'

'Meanwhile, it seems your ear is close to the ground. What's the game?'

'I'll tell you about it later, I promise. But first of all I have to get myself a job.'

Margot glanced at her watch. 'And I've got to go,' she said. 'And you come with me. Wait, you're not pregnant again…?'

'Good heavens, no!'

'You'd be amazed the records they keep. They'll have your name down somewhere. Let's go get 'em.'

Merrymaids LA was very much modelled on Pilgrim's Piece, only larger and even more lavishly 'British'. A butler greeted them, and, when Margot explained Marie's mission, directed them to a door that said PRIVATE with two chairs and a small sofa outside it. They sat and waited.

'I'll go in first,' said Margot, 'so I can tell her a bit about you. The personal introduction is a good thing at Merrymaids.'

The PRIVATE door opened ten minutes later, and a secretary dressed in a white blouse and purple skirt beckoned impatiently.

Margot got up and went inside. After a short interval, she appeared again, and Marie followed her back into an office remarkable for its austerity considering the lavishness of the entrance and the vestibular largesse. Inside the room was a big wooden desk and two spindly chairs. The hatchet-faced woman at the desk couldn't smile because her face would have cracked if she had. But it didn't matter because she wasn't given to smiling. On the wall hung prints of what looked like Victorian penal establishments.

'Who are you?' she asked Marie, and then to Margot. 'I know who you are. Trouble.'

'Why, thank you, Miss Leon. You say the nicest things. And here am I introducing a girl who has already worked for Merrymaids in England – where she would have been Maid of Honour if she hadn't left,' said Margot.

Miss Leon fixed Marie with a basilisk eye. 'Why did you leave? Don't tell me. Let me guess. You were pregnant.'

'Yes. How did you know?'

'It's always the prettiest ones.'

'Thank you.'

'So you want a job again, Miss…?'

Marie hardly hesitated about the name to give? There was nothing against reverting to Sinclair for Merrymaid purposes. Margot said everyone here went under aliases. The management might want to know for tax purposes and things, but there was time to sort that out with someone Margot said she knew. 'Marie Sinclair. Yes, I would like to work here, please.'

'What about the child? This is not a job for a mother.'

'I lost it.'

'Tough. So don't go getting pregnant again. Margot here says you

315

had good ideas for the company. So keep having them. But not too many. You have card, a passport?'

Marie thought quickly.

'Yes, but not with me.'

A card? Middleburg would have it, whatever it was. And he wasn't going to let it go, nor her passport. She had it when she travelled to and from Nice. She would have to sort it out with Margot.

'Drop it in sometime. OK, Margot, you can show her round. Marie, you can start tomorrow.'

'Thank you, Miss Leon.'

Margot led the way out and gave her a hug in the hallway under the eye of the butler who batted not an eyelid, then she took Marie into the full exorbitance of the Los Angeles Merrymaid experience. There were drawing-rooms for smoking and drinking and even taking tea, there were billiard and snooker rooms, there were bars glitzy and bars pubby, there were great dining-rooms for eating and speaking, there was a cabaret room, an intimate night club, a casino and a ballroom, which sparkled like a Fabergé tiara (if he ever made such a thing). There was a games room, a gym, a bathroom with Turkish amenities, a sauna and, of course, an Olympic-size swimming pool. Then there were the bedrooms with beds so large and inviting that Marie found it quite difficult to refrain from leaping into them on the spot, though she had slept soundly last night at Felipe's – more from the nervous exhaustion of the last few days than the homely qualities of the apartment. It was hard, as she explained to Margot, to share your sleeping space with a hoover.

'Oh, but you must come and stay with me!' cried Margot.

'Better we stay friends. I have got a room to myself and a shower. And now we've got all this.'

'But it's not for us. Any more than it is for the goldfish in the morning-room,' said Margot.

'At least Felipe's cupboard of a bedroom is mine and it's private.'

'Meanwhile, you will have this lovely golden cage to disport yourself in.'

'And I will disport,' said Marie. 'All this,' she put her hand to head and shook her hair like a screen goddess. 'What more could the man about town want?'

'Compliant goddesses.'

The Merrymaid costumes were a little more sophisticated than the Pilgrims Piece variety, better tailored and sexier, and that included the swimwear. The house rules were more or less identical. You could show as much bosom as you liked but not the whole job. You could go as far with the guests as they wanted, but it was not obligatory. Everyone must be clean, presentable, well-mannered and merry as the night was long.

* * *

That evening, Marie met up with Margot and, over dinner at a trattoria, they filled in the gaps.

'What's it like here, I mean compared with Pilgrim's Piece?' asked Marie.

'It's a little more relaxed but it's rather more dangerous. It's like the police over here. They carry guns while the British bobby doesn't. Things can go seriously wrong. One of the girls was killed a year ago. The management keeps quite a close eye on you, for your own good, they say. Everyone's a bit jumpy after the murders last year and now the trial...

317

'What murders?'

'You *have* been out of the scene. Some guy called Manson and his girls. It seems they crept about people's houses, stabbing them.

'I'm glad I was out of the scene if that's what the scene's been about.'

Marie shivered.

'Air conditioning too cold?' asked Margot. 'I asked them to turn it down, but they say the customers like it.'

A waiter hovered. They ordered *insalate tricolore, escalope Milanese* with zucchini and a bottle of Californian pinot noir. Marie realised she had not eaten since yesterday breakfast.

'Tell me what's happened since we last met,' said Margot. 'You know, I've thought about you a lot. What really happened to the baby?'

Marie told her as much of the story as she felt was repeatable.

'What? They took your baby and you did nothing?' exclaimed Margot who wanted one of her own.

Marie felt defensive. 'There was nothing I could do. I was drugged and there was Fist who was seriously dangerous. I think of her all the time.'

'I'm sorry. I didn't mean to be tactless. They're bastards. They've probably got her somewhere. They know where she is.'

'That at least gives me hope.'

'What about this Middleburg?'

'He saved my life. I thought he was just a kind stranger ... someone I met on a plane.'

'But it turns out he was a step in front of you.'

'They always have been, at every turn.'

'That's some organisation. And then this Middleburg turned out to be not such a kind old silver-haired gentleman. He was the chief jerk.'

'He kept me prisoner. The worst of it was, I accepted it. I was so tired. I just couldn't be bothered.'

'They wanted you to marry him? Why would they want that?'

'I guess it's money. I'll be coming up for my twenty-fifth birthday in June. Middleburg says that's when I can take my share of the business. Or maybe they need my signature for me to resign my interest in the company. To be honest, I'm tired of it all already. I shouldn't be here. I should be out of the country, thousands of miles away. Let them get on with it. But then I think, how can I harm them? How can I bring them down?'

'This is where they are. This is where you have to hurt them.'

'I know. And I'm scared.'

'They can't kill you, they need you alive.'

'They need me half-alive. That's what frightens me.'

'We could go to the police.' Margot hesitated. 'But not in LA.'

'Or a judge or someone?'

'Do you have a visa?'

'No. I don't think so.'

'That's no good.'

'How do I get one?'

'Do you have a passport?'

'No. But I need one for Merrymaids. And something called a card.'

'A green card. That's important but it can be arranged. At least, something good enough to satisfy them.'

'I need something really good if I'm to complain officially. I can't complain about Middleburg to anyone if I'm officially not here.'

It was an impasse. The girls looked at each other. Margot shared the last of the bottle between them.

'We can put the passport off for a while. Let's see what Grindlay has to say about Middleburg,' she suggested. 'Grindlay's not a bad sort.'

'He mustn't know who I am. I don't want him to connect me with my father.'

'No one uses real names here at Merrymaids. I'm Immie. You can be Katie.'

'I'm pretty sure Middleburg would never come to the club. He's not the sort. But they're like that fungus that grows underground. They're everywhere. They grow on money. You have to keep washing your hands.'

Margot laughed. 'They've really got to you, haven't they?' she said.

'Are you surprised?'

'Not one little bit.'

* * *

Thursday was the big evening at Merrymaids and tonight a group called The Beach Boys was playing. Bob Merriman usually turned up if he was in town, and all the staff were expected to be there. He liked to run his eyes over the girls before the big money arrived. Margot had told her that the man, Grindlay, was expected – maybe she could engineer it so that Marie sat next to him at dinner.

Bob Merriman stopped when he came to Marie in the line and his eyes narrowed.

'Wait a minute,' he said. 'I never forget a face. Haven't I seen you somewhere before?'

'Yes, sir,' she said. 'At Pilgrim's Piece.'

'Hey, you were the Maid of Honour who left to have a baby, right?'

'Right.'

'And you told me about that song, the "Merry man and his Maid"? That was really cool. I loved that song. Gilbert and Sullivan, right?'

'Right.'

He started singing in a surprisingly good baritone.

It's the song that is sung by a lovelorn loon,
Who sang to the light of the moon-o,
It's the song of a Merry man nobly born...'

He stopped singing as suddenly as he had started. There was a round of applause from the girls. And then he started again.

'Heydee lady,
Misery me,
Lackaday dee,
He sipped no sup and he craved no crumb,
But he sighed for the love of a lady!'

'Go on, Mr Merriman,' they giggled. 'Bet you've never had to sigh for the love of a laydee.'

But he shook his head. There were shadows in Mr Merriman's life too secret to mention.

'What happened to the baby? Do you have her at home?'

Marie thought it prudent to lie. 'She's back in England with her father. We are separated.'

'Too bad,' he said, without condolence.

'Yes,' she said. 'The chapter is closed.'

He clapped his hands. 'To business,' he said. 'We have a full house tonight. And you,' to Marie, 'no more babies or you'll be out on the street again. Nothing personal but Merrymaids is for maids not mothers. Hear that, girls. You're to be maids not mothers.'

'Yes, Mr Merriman.'

'He's in a good mood,' whispered Margot.

And so the evening began.

Jack Grindlay turned out to be a tall, fair, good-looking man in his forties. Athletic once, he was just developing a little bit of a spread around his middle. He was one of those men who genuinely enjoy the company of women. Margot and Marie sidled up to him in the drawing room as the guests stood drinking champagne before dinner. Just at that moment, Merriman clapped his hands again and the conversation stopped.

'Just wanted to welcome you all to our Thursday Special, our favourite night of the week. Other nights are great but Thursday is Special. Champagne's on the house and the night's all before us. Dinner first and then a cabaret. We have a very special guest, raconteur and singer Jack Fieldfinger from Princeton where he lectures on something so clever I can't even pronounce it.'

Pause for dutiful laughter.

'And then, well, a little dancing, a little gambling, some more wine and conversation and happiness ahead. Do what thou wilt, that is our motto, but don't frighten the horses.

'Welcome once again to Merrymaids – oh and a special welcome tonight to our newest Merrymaid, Ma...'

Here he paused for a dreadful second while Marie thought he was going to say her name, which would have meant an immediate retreat from the place as far as she was concerned, but he corrected himself so fluently she decided people would have thought they hadn't heard him properly.

'...my special favourite, Katie from England.'

There was a polite burst of applause and Marie curtseyed prettily. Curtseying was much favoured in the Merrymaid ménage.

'Dinner will be served in ten minutes. So if you want to adjust your dress, or your expressions, now is the moment to do it. Thank you.'

There was more polite applause before the sound of a typical British country house gong resonated in the hall. People started to move, most of them towards the dining room. Margot gave Marie a look and they tagged along with Grindlay who chatted easily about some motor race he had attended and the winery he had invested in and the film star who had bought a house next door to his home in Beverly Hills. He was evidently, as employees go, a close follower of the company ethos: good at his job, whatever it was, a likeable man, but not a driver; the sort of successful man that very successful men get to do their bidding. As Hospitality and Entertainment Vice President, his job took him up to the company castle to supervise the cellars and the wine and cigar merchant's more important deliveries.

'Whereabouts in Beverly Hills?' Margot asked with a glance at Marie.

'Oh, just beyond the Boulevard.'

Not far from where she had enjoyed the hospitality of Middleburg and the Holdsworths.

'Do you know Beverly Hills at all?' he asked Marie.

'Oh no. I've only recently arrived. I used to work with Merrymaids in Pilgrim's Piece.'

'I just love that place.'

They found themselves places at the long table, which sat a hundred guests. It was customary at Merrymaids for all guests on formal occasions to sit together. You spoke to your neighbour and he or she spoke to you. It was a quirk of the place. Very St James's, as Merriman liked to say, though the London clubmen's eyes would pop to see what went on under the table.

'What is it you do, Mr Grindlay?' asked Marie, with innocent curiosity (or what looked like it) as a waiter poured them all a glass of something good. 'My friend Immie said you worked in a castle. Is that right? It must be wonderful to work in a castle.'

Better to work in a castle than to be brought up in one with two maiden great-aunts.

'Call me Jack,' said Grindlay, 'and you are Katie, right? And you are going to tell me what Katie didn't do?'

'Really, Jack. Immie told me you were a nice man for a businessman and that you were intelligent and full of wit. That is why I asked to sit next to you. I don't know what you were saying to her last time, but you are really going to have to work harder than what Katie didn't do.' She smiled very sweetly at him to show she was hoping he would fall in love with her.

'I didn't know we were going to be smartasses tonight, Immie,' said Grindlay, smiling. 'Your friend here says she expected me to be little short of Einstein.'

'She is full of surprises is our Katie. Sharp as a surgical lance.'

'Ouch. Yes. And as therapeutic no doubt … Well, Katie, to answer your question. Sometimes I'm up at the castle where our research company and our labs are, but mostly I'm at head office here in town.'

Katie was about to make some reply about wanting to see the castle, but was interrupted by waiters dishing out hot bread rolls and dishes of butter. The table was filling up fast. Someone came and sat down next to Marie but she didn't immediately take him in. She gave a polite half-glance and looked back at Grindlay. He offered a bread roll.

'This is the bit I always like most,' said Marie, tucking into the butter. 'Somehow the rest of the meal never quite matches up to the first bite of bread.'

'The sauce is called appetite,' said Grindlay. 'Doesn't Shakespeare saying something about it?'

'Let good digestion wait on it,' said Margot.

'Whew! You girls. You're too damn quick for me,' he laughed.

Her new companion, the one she hadn't taken in, turned to Marie. He was not white nor was he exactly brown. He did not look like an Arab. His face was hawk-like, *accipitrine*, a word she had saved against a rainy day.

'"You are neither white nor brown but as the heavens fair,"' she said.

'I'm Joe,' he told her. 'I am a guest.'

'We are all guests at the banquet of life,' she said, she really didn't know why. It was either absurdly pretentious or unsuitably deep, she could not decide which. Maybe the man could not either. He glanced at her, amused.

'You're not the usual sort of guest here,' she said.

'How do you know? It's your first night here.'

She laughed. 'I just know,' she said.

'And you're right. It is my first time too. Good food…'

The beef Wellington had arrived, perfectly rare but delicate, like cutting a Christmas pudding, with new potatoes suspiciously like Jersey royals (flown in) and fresh-minted garden peas. Merriman liked to keep the English flavour. It gave the occasion a certain cachet, no matter what people got up to later.

'Who invited you?'

He indicated Grindlay.

'You work with him?'

'Oh no. I supply their wine. I am a wine merchant.'

'This is yours?' she asked. It was a gorgeous wine, deep red but very clear, with not a hint of inkiness.

'No, but I wish it was. It comes from a vineyard very close to Romanée-Conti. You know about wine?'

'Not as much as I should.'

'I should be very happy to instruct you sometime,' he said. 'Wine and woman ... all we need is song.'

'Wine and woman and song, three things garnish our way, yet is day over long,' she said.

'I am sure it would not be,' he said. 'What is that anyway?'

'It is a villanelle. It consists of a series of verses in which the first and third line of the poem keep repeating alternately. It is a French form but the poet is English in this case.'

'How does it go?' he asked.

'Wine and woman and song,
Three things garnish our way:
Yet is day over long.

Lest we do our youth wrong,
Gather them while we may:
Wine and woman and song.

Three things render us strong,
Vine leaves, kisses and bay;
Yet is day over long ... And so on,' she said.

'Well, I didn't expect a poetry lesson this evening. Hey, Jack. This girl has been giving me an education,' he shouted above the general hubbub.

Grindlay turned. 'You know, Joe, I think she has a lot of surprises up her sleeve,' he said.

Marie had a sudden frisson. Did he mean just that or was there another meaning hidden underneath like pepper under a strawberry, something only a sensitive palate could discern? Margot shot her a glance. Did she think so too? Were all these people here in on a secret that was hidden

326

from her? It was easy for her after all she had been through, after all they had put her through, to develop a certain paranoia in strange surroundings. All these people, all these events, might be connected and every new strand could lead back to the one single inescapable one.

The pudding came and went – it was indeed a strawberry confection with the lightest of orange cake and cream to set off the sweet sharpness of the fruit.

'Only the English really understand a strawberry,' she said to no one in particular.

'Can strawberries speak? What language do they use? Strawberry talk? Let us talk strawberry,' said Grindlay.

'As I was going to Strawberry Fair, ri-fol ri-fol, buttercups and daisies,' sang Margot, and that was the end of that.

There was coffee, taken at the table, with *petits fours* of the most delectable kind, strange fruits half-known and naughty biscuits and cakes that sent a shiver through your mind. The lights grew dimmer and the music changed to a darker note.

'What is it they do up there?' she asked the man called Joe.

'I am a Red Indian,' he said, as if she had not spoken. 'Did you ever meet a Red Indian wine merchant?'

'No, I am afraid not.'

'Don't be afraid.'

'I am afraid,'

'And I think you are right to be. Life is full of latency. The … isn't over yet.'

The Beach Boys seemed to become all at once very loud. Someone was shrieking with laughter. She lost one of the Indian wine merchant's words.

'What did you say?'

She thought he had said that the game was not over yet, but she could not be sure. Grindlay was shouting something at him now. The moment had passed. She thought fleetingly of her father alone, in a noisy place, with people shouting, trying to make sense of where he was, what he was doing, the mystery that he was trying to uncover, taking upon himself the plight of his distant ancestor beset by men stealing his land and his money, killing his people, covering his ears, shutting his eyes, trying to think but disturbed by witches.

People were leaving the table now, some to listen to the cabaret and dance a little, some to go to the casino and some already making their way upstairs.

'Hey,' said Grindlay to Margot and Marie, 'like to play?'

'Sure,' said Margot.

But Marie wanted to see the cabaret.

'Me too,' said Joe the Red Indian. 'Let's go along.'

'Meet up later,' said Margot, giving Marie a little wave.

Marie and Joe walked over to the cabaret room which was set out like a lounge bar with separate tables and comfortable chairs facing a small nightclub-type dance floor at the edge of which, facing them, sat a lean, rangy man at a piano. She didn't catch his name at that point. He wore an amused grin and he was playing, expertly and with a kind of sprung energy that reflected his expression, a selection of melodies as a kind of overture to his act. She had the feeling that this was going to be good. She felt Joe's hand steal round her shoulders and made no attempt to remove it. It was the first time she had had any sexual overture, apart from Middleburg's if you could call that an overture, since her London days and she felt good about it. When everyone had settled down, the man started singing in an amused, springy and sardonic voice which was curiously satisfying.

'Would you like your soul grilled or fried?'
That was the question they asked me when I died.
I can tell you I was quite astonished
And I asked for the waiter to be admonished.

'For my soul is not a fish like a sole or a sprat.
A soul, I said, is more valuable than that,
It is a precious and eternal item.
A soul, I said, lasts ad infinitum.

'It is not to be fried or devilled or grilled
And served on a plate like a cutlet, frilled.
That's what you think, they chortled to me,
But a soul to us is a delicacy,

'It tastes like a crisp, with a touch of pancetta,
Or Italian flat bread only very much better,
It tastes of smoked salmon, a hint there of fish,
But no way does it spoil this exquisite dish…

'There's a soupçon of foie gras, *a little burnt toast,*
And a tweak of slipped sanctity – that we love most.
That's all very well, I said to the creature.
But you're not having mine, whatever your nature.

'Down here, they said, that is not to your choice.
What to do, then? I asked, with tremulous voice.
Too late, they replied, your soul is our food.
They gave me a piece – and it was rather good!'

The elastic-fingered man at the piano had a wonderfully sardonic face. You felt he knew the absurdity of the world and was pained, but at the same time amused and even moved, by it. The words were fine but the music was extraordinarily plangent: tuneful, gay, wistful.

'I tried dinners, I tried diamonds, I did everything to please. I gave her all my love and she gave me ... herpes...'

That was how it seemed at the time, the cleverest thing in the world, though she spotted Merriman looking thoughtful at the words. No Merrymaid ever had such a thing as the dreaded HSV-2, at least not officially, and the company doctor worked overtime to keep it that way. Any suggestion of a blister or weeping sore and you were out – at least temporarily.

'Oh for a robot, a robot lover
Once you've got one, you'll never want another.
A silent companion most of the time
She don't need champagne or mescal and lime

Just sits around with a goofy grin
But on the job she goes like sin
And you don't have to say
After each screw:

'How was it, how was it, how was it,
How was it, darling, for you?'

He put tremendous verve and stretch and sinew into his *how was it*. It brought the house down and everyone joined in. And then there was 'The Girl Called Flo'.

'That day we ran away all the way to Santa Fe,
And the train broke down and we made merry –
We drank the bar dry, mostly she, partly I,
And then she started on Mexican sherry!

'Oh no, no, no, that girl called Flo,
She's the pick of all the crop!
She looks so cute but she's full of guile,
Give her an inch and she'll take a mile,

'She says she's a virgin but she's in denial,
And she don't know when to stop!'

By the time it was over, Marie discovered that she hadn't laughed for far too long and that laughter made her feel smoochy. She took the Red Indian away to dance and it was like copulation with clothes on.

'You want to come upstairs?' she asked.

He shook his head. 'Never on a first date,' he laughed.

'I thought I was meant to say that.'

'Let's have a coffee,' he suggested. 'Anything else to drink?'

She shook her head. She needed to be more clear-headed than she was. Around them, couples in varying stages of affection (disaffection was not allowed at Merrymaids but there was just room for disinclination) jostled, seethed and clung.

They sat on a sofa and he ordered from a waiter.

'You want to see the castle?' he asked.

She was sober again, lust subsiding as quickly as it arrived. She was on her guard now.

'Which castle?'

'Where I deliver my wine.'

'What is its name?'

'Château Cauchemar they call it.'

She was interested now. 'Do you know what that means?' she asked.

'It's a name, isn't it?'

'It means Nightmare Castle. I believe it was modelled on one in France. Some mad millionaire. Its original name was Tiffauges. I don't know why they changed its name.'

'So you know the place?' he asked, surprised.

'I bought a book called *All around LA* this morning. I was reading something. Castles in California. That sort of thing.'

'Don't you want to go? It's only a little more than half an hour away.'

'I'm fine. It just gave me a shiver. Not a bad shiver. You gave me a shiver.'

'I like you, Katie. You don't seem like ordinary Merrymaid material, not that I'm a member. But I can tell you're different. That's why I don't want to go upstairs with you. It's like a rich man's knocking shop.'

'Oh. Thank you.'

'Why are you here at all?'

'I need to earn money.'

'Good reason.'

'What sort of Red Indian are you?'

'The Chumash Tribe. We were coastal people, out on the Channel Islands, San Clemente. But I have to say my mother was from Norway and my father was only half Chumash. So I am a mongrel.'

'I like to think of you as Red Indian. It's very exotic. Do you mind?'

'Not at all.'

'I have never met a Red Indian before. Come to that I've not met many people at all.'

'Come on. Let's go to the castle. It looks good and spooky at night. Don't worry. I have a driver. In fact I even have some brandy in the car.'

She thought: it's not the first time he's visited Cauchemar by night, but she dismissed it as inconsequential. The castle of which she'd heard so much was about to be revealed; a place of ill omen for her father – and what for herself? Considerations of Joe's past, or indeed his future, liaisons were scarcely relevant at this point. Indeed, Mr Merriman himself would have been proud of her since the prevailing ethos at Merrymaids was that only the present mattered.

'OK,' she said. 'Let's go.'

'The car is at the door.'

* * *

It was a Roller. It was warm. They were separated from the driver (who really did look like a Red Indian) by a glass partition. As soon as the car glided away, Joe brought out some Armagnac and poured her a glass. She sipped it cautiously. She glimpsed the label on the bottle. The Armagnac was older than both their ages put together.

'Very good,' she said. 'But why a Rolls, not a Buick?'

'When you're in the wine business you need to travel first class.'

'Fair enough.'

She had said goodbye to Margot who wondered whether she should come too, but Grindlay had assured her that the Red Indian was a good guy.

'Best of luck,' she had said. 'He's all right. See you tomorrow.'

Margot knew why the castle held a fascination for Marie. There was a secret in it, as in most castles, but this was a bigger one than most and had to be uncovered.

The car rolled on, through the long streets and out into the darkness, the brandy warming her as they left the streets behind. She held Joe's hand and he put his arm round her shoulders. They were moving up into the hills now, through wooded valleys and past rocky outcrops. It struck her again that she should feel nervous. Somewhere out there Middleburg was searching for her and she was, even now, going to his lair, the very nerve-centre of the company's operation. The hills on either side rose higher. The car and its occupants seemed alone in an increasing hostile world.

'What happens out here?' she asked Joe.

'Very little. The badlands means the land is bad: little water, just rocks. They used to do some mining and some farming, but nothing much now. If anything, they mine for water.'

'So why did they plant a castle out here?'

'It's owned by a company called Messinger's. I think they wanted to be quiet and undisturbed. No one much comes here, though it's not so far from LA.'

'Who lives in the castle?'

'Only a few keepers and estate guards most of the time, but just now and then it becomes active like a volcano. The AGM, for instance, is a house party. Big shareholders and vice-presidents. Quite a hooley, it is, and a lot of wine goes down, I'm glad to say. Up beyond the castle are the labs and workforce houses but they mostly keep themselves to themselves.'

'When is the next AGM? Can I come?'

She had spoken without thinking but Joe looked at her curiously.

'I shouldn't think so,' he said slowly. 'Security is very tight. I'm not invited. I am sometimes allowed to give a little talk about the wine they're drinking. Perhaps you could be my assistant.'

'Like a magician's? Spangled tights? I could do that.'

'There is a funny feeling about the castle if you ask me. Call it my Indian blood, but there is definitely an atmosphere. Some say there are parts of it still undiscovered. They say it was brought over stone by stone, sometimes room by room. Something came over with it. The nobleman who lived in it was said to have raised demons. Look. Up ahead to the right. There is it now.'

The hairs on the back of her neck rose as she gazed. The huge edifice frowned down upon them as if they were naughty children who had strayed into the wrong place. It perched over, or perhaps straddled was the better word, a dip between two peaks, looking like something out of Grimm. She gasped.

'It looks friendlier by day,' he said. 'But not much.'

'Why on earth did they buy it?'

'For some reason they thought it was intrinsic to Messinger's and TOJI as well. One of them owns the other. There's some history in it that they thought would add public relations appeal. And besides, what child or grown-up can resist a genuine mediaeval castle? There's a visitor centre. Also it's a good place to have Messinger's high-security laboratories – sited unobtrusively, of course.'

'What do they do in those?'

'Research for the Government, and other stuff for TOJI which is a kind of front, I suppose. Nobody really knows and it's better not to ask.'

'I'm surprised they were allowed to pluck the castle up and take it away.'

'It was done long ago by some millionaire in about 1880 when the French were at a low ebb. Now we're getting a little closer you can see the full … what adjective would you use to describe it? … majesty of the place.'

'Power,' she said.

'Yes,' he agreed, 'power is the word. They do like power even though they describe the origins of the company as charitable. And the holding company is still a charity though I don't know how much charity they actually do. It opens doors for them.'

They were now a couple of hundred feet below the castle. Joe rapped on the dividing glass, and the chauffeur stopped the car at a place where others had evidently done the same, a pull-in where the road narrowed. She craned up to gaze at the turrets and battlements. The sheer enormity of it was impressive; what must it have taken in effort and money to move so many stones of this colossal bulk?

'Worth coming?' Joe asked.

At that moment a light came on in one of the highest towers and a spidery figure could be observed looking down upon them.

'Look,' she said, pointing at the lighted window. But just as she said it, the car was enfolded in a light so dazzling they could see nothing, not even each other.

'I had heard they had invested in a searchlight,' Joe said, 'but my normal visits here are by day. I didn't realise that they were quite so sensitive to visitors. I hope they turn it off or we'll be stuck here all night.'

'Who was the man in the tower, d'you think?' she asked.

'No idea. The permanent staff live in accommodation at the back somewhere.'

She thought, with a wild hope: perhaps it is my father…

There was the sound of something whirring overhead, followed by a report from the direction of the castle.

'Duck,' shouted Joe, pushing her down.

'What was that?' she asked.

'That was someone shooting at us.'

The searchlight continued to cover them for a minute or two, then, as suddenly as it had arrived, the light went out.

'We'd better get out of here,' said Joe, 'or I'll have to start shooting some arrows.'

'They weren't firing at us?'

'Not *at* us. They were firing near us, or over us.'

'Warning us to get out?'

'Yes.' He tapped on the window at the driver. 'Drive on,' he said.

The Rolls glided forward.

'What's going on in there?' she asked.

He shook his head. 'New product development? Testing new drugs? Maybe better not to know. There's a whole complex of new buildings behind the castle.'

'Suppose we drive round the back and see what's stirring?'

A gap had appeared in the trees and a driveway showed amongst them, leading to a gatehouse. Joe tapped on the glass, and the Rolls stopped where the road widened.

'I think perhaps not tonight. The worst scenario is we get shot. The second worst is that someone with a gun corners us and keep us in the castle.'

'For how long?'

'As long as they like. No one knows where we are.'

'The driver would tell people.'

'The driver would be here, with us.'

'They can't do that.'

'Oh, they do what they want. If they can bring a castle from France, don't you think they might be capable of locking up a few unwanted visitors?'

She wasn't ready to be locked up again. It seemed an age since she had been freed, but it was only a week. Her moment would come.

'Very well,' she said. 'Let's go home.'

When they finally reached her disreputable building in Echo Park, the faint first watercolours of dawn were dabbing away at the night. She turned up her face to kiss Joe as the Rolls drew sedately to the side of the street.

'You live here?' he asked, trying to play down his initial incredulity.

'I live here. Not your usual dropping off point?'

'No. But I can work on it.'

She gave him another kiss and got out of the car.

'See you again,' he said.

It wasn't a question.

'See you again.'

The car oozed sedately on its way again as she opened the front door of the little block. On her way upstairs, she tried rapping at Felipe's door to show him the wonderful sunrise but he had maybe seen too many through a prison window, she thought. As she had a copy of his key, she opened the door to check that he was all right – he had told her he was normally an early riser – and stepped inside.

'Felipe,' she called, softly.

No answer.

She stepped over and touched his shoulder. She shook him gently, then harder. There was no response. She turned the light on and felt his pulse, his head. The head was clammy and cold. The pulse was very weak. The faithful servant of a father she had never met was going the way of his master.

She rushed out onto the stairway to look for Jaime, located him in the All-Nite bar round the corner which she knew was a favourite (Jaime led a strange nocturnal life which was something to do with drugs) and dragged him by the hand to Felipe's bedside. Jaime too felt his pulse and forehead.

'He very sick. Fetch ambulance,' he said. 'Call 911.'

The ambulance arrived with remarkable promptness, wailing its path through the pristine light of dawn, and soon Felipe was gathered up and taken away. She wanted to ride with him but Jaime was his nominated next of kin and there was only room for one.

'I bring you news straightaway,' Jaime said.

She went to bed and fell into a deep, uneasy sleep. Jaime came back when the roaring light of noon was banging at the blanket that passed for a curtain in her bedroom.

'Felipe is gone,' he told her. 'He say goodbye.'

She was desolated: for herself at having lost her first friend in LA, and for Felipe that he'd died without her when he had done so much on her behalf. There was a small collection for a gravestone, organised by Jaime, though he seemed vague as to where the grave was going to be. It was to be decided. She dipped rather too generously into her savings, but Felipe had been her friend.

* * *

That evening she was back at Merrymaids punctually, if unwillingly, at seven o'clock. It was Friday and the punters were in weekend mode. Margot greeted her excitedly.

'How did it go?' she asked.

'Joe was good.'

'Did you … you know?'

'No. He's sexy. But he's all right. Interesting.'

'I told you he was all right.'

'How was Grindlay?' Marie asked.

'Not so bad. He was a bit funny about you going up to the castle.'

'Funny with you? It wasn't you who put us up to it.'

'No, he was just … funny. There something confidential going on up there, he said.'

'Well, someone shot at us.'

'Shot? Like bang bang you're almost dead?' Margot had been there, done everything, but she was impressed.

'Yes. It went fizzing past. I think it was just to warn us off.'

'And it did.'

'What is it that's up there? I feel I should try and get in,' Marie told her.

'Even though it's shooting at you?'

'It wasn't shooting at us. It was just making a point.'

'Not a very hospitable one. Maybe if you get closer it'll turn out to be a pussycat?'

She paused, scrutinising Marie. 'Are you all right? You look a bit down.'

'My friend died. He had malaria.'

'Oh God. What a bummer. I'm so sorry.'

'I don't have so many friends I can afford to lose one. But I have to move on. Cancel out and pass on, so the man said.'

'What man?'

'I don't know, but it's in a play somewhere.'

* * *

So began the pattern for a number of weeks. Days full of the flutter of perfume and alcohol, food, pretty girls and affluent men who, if they were not themselves rich, wielded impressive expense accounts. Nights of low lights, lots of cleavage, drinking, snorting and snogging. The girls took Quaaludes, which were a fashionable relaxant, and everyone was happy. No Merrymaid ever looked melancholy. It was a contradiction in terms.

Marie was certainly among the prettiest of the Maids, though not necessarily the most popular because she would not go to bed with anyone, but she was very much prized as a dinner companion, and would, on occasion, give a cabaret. It started one night when the regular artist had laryngitis and the management was caught short. A call went out to anyone who had a turn or an act. She must have been drunk because she put her hand up. She had started to write songs, funny songs based on the place and the people who frequented it, and now she rendered them in a voice that was both demure and on-turning. She teamed up with the pianist who was something of a composer and the result seemed to go down a bomb. Mr Merriman actually gave her more money for doing them. She even got Margot to join her on occasion.

Things went on like this, and then, one evening, after she had given her little show, a voice behind her said: 'Hello, Marie.'

It was David.

He looked older, a little sleeker. Not quite as she remembered him. She was interested to find her heart hardly missed a beat, but there was still the moment of memory, of shared physical intimacy, and of embarrassment, that had to be sealed off like a police tent over a corpse.

'What are you doing in a place like this?' she asked.

'I was going to ask the same thing of you.'

'Where have you been? What have you been doing?'

'I got married,' he said.

'Oh.'

There must have been a momentary interruption in the power supply. Or was it someone fiddling with the dimmer switch?

'And divorced,' he said. 'It was a terrible mistake.'

It was definitely the dimmer switch because the place seemed to brighten up again no end. It was almost too coincidental that he would turn up now, here, but she could not disguise her happiness at seeing him.

'Oh,' she said. 'That's a shame. But what are you doing here?'

'I am in the oil business, like my father. I was working in San Diego but we have just opened an office here. A friend of mine who works in LA said this place was fun.'

'And he's right. Look how much fun it is.'

'Never had such fun,' he said, seriously. 'Can you forgive me for deserting you?'

'Can you forgive me for having a cloud over my name?'

'For having a crazy dad?'

'It turns out he was framed. I'll tell you about it. But that's not why you have to forgive me.'

'Why do I have to forgive you?'

And then she thought: I'm not going to blurt it out like this; I am not going to tell him about the baby now. This is not the time or place. I am going to find out if he's still the same person first.

'For not getting in touch. You told me you lived in San Diego and I did nothing to find you when I came over to LA. I guess I was too ashamed. Yes – and angry,' she said.

'But at least we've met now. I know we can't just pick up where we left off, not just like that, and there's a party of us here, but can I take you out to dinner and we can catch up?'

'Sure,' she said. 'Monday is my night off.'

Joe would have to suffer, which was unfair and, yes, not what she wanted.

'Monday it is. Let's go to Gianni's. Eight o'clock.'

It was an Italian place she knew – quiet, not too Chanel and champagne.

'Great. But not next Monday. Monday fortnight.'

There was a particular reason for that.

'Sure. And … what are you doing here – in all this?' He gestured at her Merrymaid costume. 'Nice though it is,' he added.

'Money,' she told him. 'Simple as that.'

'Oh. Cute.'

'I'm seeing someone else,' she said.

'I would expect nothing less.'

She reminded herself how much had happened since last they'd met. Maybe she hadn't known him that well – they had both been almost children. And how did she know he wasn't another decoy or tease set in front of her by Brickville and Middleburg? How did she know that everyone she met and everything that happened to her was not part of the game? This David seemed subtly different from the one she had known, less Oxford, more California. She supposed that was to be expected. She wondered for a moment whether he was in fact the same man at all, but that was ridiculous.

'I have to go back to my party,' he said.

'By the way,' she told him, 'for obvious reasons I'm not Marie Lavell over here, I'm Marie Sinclair. Although in the club I'm Katie. And sometimes I don't know who I am.'

'Join the club,' he said.

She kissed his cheek demurely – she still hadn't made up her mind about him; something was there, but that was in another country – and they said goodbye.

* * *

Next day she called Joe to tell him about the change of plan – no dinner on Monday fortnight. Mondays had become a regular engagement. She thought he might be in love with her, but he was waiting, being a wise Red Indian, to see if she was in love with him. She imagined him, bent over the tracks of the evening, reading the undergrowth of the conversation, seeing where the twigs were leading.

'I wouldn't change it for anyone else,' she said, 'but this is a friend from way back.'

'A good friend?'

'Yes. But that was then.'

'Let's hope then does not become now.'

'I sort of hope that too.'

'We'll meet again on Monday? Or at the club this week?'

'Yes to Monday. I don't really like seeing you in there. I'm rather on duty, so I can't give you the time I'd like. I have to share it out on the rest of them.'

'So long as you only give them time, I don't mind,' he said, smiling. 'Don't give them anything else.'

It was a difficult course to steer at Merrymaids for the Maids were requested, though not ordered, to bestow at least cuddles and kisses if called upon to do so. Luckily, she was popular enough to get away with flirting without fornicating. There had been a couple of near squeaks, one of them when Joe had been present, and he had almost become involved in a fight which would have done both of them no good with the management.

'I need that job,' she told him, reminding him of the scene.

'I could get you a job in wine.'

She imagined herself telling people she was in wine, like a prune.

'You could call me Prunella,' she said.

'I would like to do that.'

'I don't think it would be a good idea for us to work together. It would alter the balance of power.'

'Ah, you English.'

'Or whatever I am.'

She hadn't meant to go into all that with him – not yet at any rate.

'What does that mean?'

'Oh, my father died long ago, but I believe he was partly French. And I was brought up in Scotland.'

'And what does your mother say?'

'She died too, when I was still a baby.'

'You poor thing. So you are an orphan?'

'And a survivor,' she said, firmly. 'See you Monday.'

* * *

It was hard for her these days to know whom to trust. She was almost sure she had trusted Felipe; his story rang true but there was just a suspicion that his finding her had been more than the result of hard work – how had he supported himself while he was looking for her? – he had spoken of a little money that her father had told him about, in a hidden place, but it seemed to stretch credulity a little. Had someone else funded him? Why should she not trust him when he had rescued her from Middleburg and the Holdsworths? And why should he have died like that? Of course, she wasn't blaming him, but at the same time it was rather odd. She had asked at the hospital if they'd kept anything of his, but all they'd said was that it had been collected. By whom? Not by Jaime – according to Jaime. And then she thought: maybe death is always rather odd; no one you meet has been through it before. But still there was a small question mark over Felipe.

She was sure she trusted Joe.

As for David, there was something about him that alerted a tiny part of her mind. Why would he turn up like that? Paranoia was an easy step from where she was now, and the people in the street seemed indeed to look at her strangely, but she told herself they looked at each other strangely too. Though there could be no doubt that Middleburg's spies were out there somewhere.

She didn't have that feeling at Merrymaids. The other Merrymaids were friendly, perhaps because to be a Merrymaid you had to be a bit of an outsider, and they recognised her as such. If there was any supervision by the management, it was purely professional, just like the routine medical check-up every other month.

Anyway, in spite of the question mark about his reappearance in her life – at such a time, at such a place – it had been good to see David again. Part of him was still the same boy, or the man the boy would have become: there was the same easy smile and the depth in the eyes and the promise of the pleasantly unexpected, but of course there was something else. A touch of worldliness and secrecy, which comes from growing up and working with other people. It was that she found unsettling. After all, she hadn't changed much, had she? Or had she? Perhaps too little?

On the afternoon of the Monday she had fixed to see him, she redeemed the ring from the pawnbroker's, even though the recently completed gravestone for Felipe had made fresh inroads into her funds. Joe had very kindly offered to contribute to it but she had declined: it wouldn't have done.

In the shop, the old man smiled at her and said that he had had five offers for the ring but he had kept it for her, certain that she would come back. He did say, though, that he had had the ruby analysed by a friendly expert and that it was not an old ring. Indeed, it was a very new ring, with a very fine ruby in it. The design, of course, was ancient. Why would Middleburg have given her a very new ring, purporting to be old?

That night, she turned up at Gianni's on 9th Street, the place David had suggested, a smart Italian restaurant, even smarter than her usual because this was where the stars went. She recognised Rock Hudson, Frank Sinatra, Deborah Kerr and Lauren Bacall, all at different tables, all very lovely and elegant, but none of them wearing a golden ring purporting to come from a fifteenth-century design with the serpent of Laval engraved in ruby.

She was shown over to where David was sitting. He looked bronzed, handsome and prosperous. The three adjectives seemed to go together in LA, where only the unfashionable looked pallid, unprepossessing and down-at-heel. Everyone else shimmered like apples in a skin-care commercial. She noted that David had filled out a little, though no paunch was visible.

'Hi.'

He rose from his chair to greet her, and kissed her on the cheek.

She took the menu the waiter offered and looked across at her former lover. The last time but one that she had seen him had been on a cliff-top under the stars.

'You look good,' he said, 'better than ever.'

'You too. Put on a bit of weight. But in a good way. You seem bigger, taller.'

It was true, he had been a boy before. It was part of the glossy effect that LA seemed to have on people; everything was better. The waiter poured her a glass of wine from the bottle that sat in the cooler beside the table – a rather good Gewürtztraminer, drier than usual.

'So tell the story,' she said.

'No, you.'

'I asked first.'

'There isn't that much to tell. I went back home with my folks and then did post-grad stuff at Berkeley.'

'Where you did a paper on…?'

'Economics.'

'Good sound stuff.'

'I was determined to get a job and find myself somewhere to live. My father was especially … overwhelming.'

'So you moved back to San Diego after Berkeley?'

'Yes. It's a good place, but I got lonely. I knew no one there any more. And then I met this girl.'

'Did you ever think of me?' She asked it out of interest rather than affront.

'I thought of you a lot, but in that way of a hopeless dream. I had been warned off not just by my folks but by that man Prelati and the people round him. I had a letter from him telling me never to show my face again. You were off the menu.'

'And that put you off?'

'Yes. There just seemed too many things against us. Apart from the fact that we were only eighteen at the time...'

The waiter brought them each an insalata of lobster, not too much, not too little, and another waiter poured more wine.

'This wine is good,' she said. 'An exquisite and poignant wine.'

'It is, now you mention it. Anyway, it soon became apparent that we were after quite different things, luckily before we had any children. And then I found out that she was sleeping with a good friend of mine, and – you know what? – I was relieved, though I did strike my good friend off my tennis roster.'

She smiled but she was sorry she wasn't the only person who had lain with him under the stars. But perhaps he hadn't lain with anyone under the stars – only in very expensive penthouses. Time puts a patina on people, she thought, and the shine deflects from the real person that you once saw, and then the shine becomes thick shutters.

They chatted on. The lobster was replaced by tiny scaloppines of veal in marsala sauce served with fried zucchini. It was all delicious and rather sad. David understood it as well as she did. They tried valiantly but the kindling, which sometimes caught a spark and glowed and achieved a little smoke, never quite managed to catch fire. She couldn't tell what he was feeling, but the old hurt and disappointment came back to her, checking her instinct, fighting with her first reaction of excitement on seeing him.

'What about you?' he asked. 'What happened to you and how did you end up a Merrymaid in LA?'

Too much had happened in the intervening months and years. She felt the weight of it bearing down upon her. 'Do you mind if I keep that for next time,' she asked. 'I need to be in the right frame of mind for that, because some of it is strange – pretty depressing – something to do with my father who, as your parents pointed out, was a very bad lot. I felt I had bad blood.'

'You know, I never minded about that. It was my folks who…'

She reached across and clasped his wrist. 'I know,' she said. 'You weren't like that.'

But he had gone along with it. Sure, it had been hard for him, but he had shown his colours. When the meal was over, it was almost a relief. She could not tell him about the baby. It would only distress them both and there was nothing to be done. A sadness, possibly caused by tiredness, had settled on her. They were not going to get together. The baby was lost in any case, halfway to wherever it was that Fist took babies. The woman had said California, but she'd been told to lie.

Outside the restaurant they kissed briefly, as people do.

'Where do you live?' he asked.

'Oh, just down the street.' She wasn't going to ask him in for coffee. 'What about you?'

'Out in Beverly Hills.'

Cheek by jowly jowl with the Holdsworths and Middleburg, no doubt. She wondered for a moment if David was part of the plot, and then decided that would be paranoia.

'We must meet up again,' he said.

'We will always be friends.'

'Of course we will. Sure I can't give you a lift?'

'Quite sure.'

'I'll be back,' he said. 'You're not going to get rid of me this easily.'

'I don't want to get rid of you. I'm just not sure about *not* getting rid of you.'

'I never forgot you, you know. My wife used to tell me I was thinking about someone else.'

'You probably were, but I'm sure it wasn't me. I have to go now.'

'Say you'll see me again.'

'You'll see me again. Goodnight, David.'

They kissed again, the way a swallow drinks from a swimming pool. A butterfly, just a little skipper, stirred in her stomach and then it was gone and so was he. She felt that he might still be in love with her, but how did he feel about it? He had let her down. A rather horrible phrase that someone had said to her once, probably in Merrymaids, came to her mind: you can't warm up old meat. Anyway, she didn't want to be in love again. It would be a distraction when what she really needed to do was sort out the matter of her father.

And then she thought, no, David couldn't be going again. They had only just re-met.

'David,' she called, running after him. 'Mephistopheles…'

He was just about to hail a cab, but turned at the sound of his old name. And then he smiled at her and held his arms wide as she ran towards him.

'We had better go and get a coffee and start from the beginning,' he said, when the embrace was over.

They found a quiet corner in a quiet bar – it was a Monday night after all – her fatigue lifted and she told him all that had happened to her since they'd last met, only missing out a little bit of the wild week with the salesman – well, quite a lot of that, actually – and the bit about the baby. She wasn't ready to tell him about that yet. But what she did tell him about the rest of her experiences was enough to leave him open-mouthed.

'They killed the clock man and they actually kept you in a house here, drugged?' he exclaimed. 'Man, that's way over the top.'

'I couldn't really see any reason for trying to escape. I suppose that was the effect of the drug.'

'You should tell the police. But…'

'But what?'

'If your Middleburg is the same as the one I'm thinking of, he's pretty big round here. He's a major shareholder in TOJI with other irons in the fire. He's a German, some say a Nazi. What's he got over you?'

'He's sort of a guardian. He's a friend of my guardian in England. He looked after me when I was ill, then he wanted us to be engaged, to be my fiancé, but I think we can say that I've broken that off now. I ran away. I don't seem to have anyone else. I have no other family. My unfortunate father is dead. I don't even have a passport or a green card, so in theory – and in practice – he could have me put away or sent back to England. He can do what he likes with me. And I don't know how or why.'

'Is he generally kind?'

'He is always polite. He seems considerate, but I have the feeling there is some other game he's playing.'

'What makes you think that?'

'I wouldn't know where to start. Things happen out of the blue. He has this castle up in the hills. It seems to be connected with my family and my father's disgrace, but there's something weird about it. I think my father was framed. I was given this ancient family ruby ring but it turns out the ring is not ancient at all, though it is ruby. He gives with one hand and takes away with the other. There must be some purpose, some end to his game, and I feel I should find out

352

what it is. It's to do with my father, with the castle, with my being twenty-five. And something more – maybe not all about money at all…'

'They have been messing with you. It can only be about money. Power and money, especially money,' David said.

'I need to get into the castle and see what's happening,' she told him.

'I should come with you. How would you get in?' said David.

'I have a friend called Joe. He delivers wine there.'

'A friend or a good friend?' David's eyes were amused.

'A very good friend but not a lover,' she said. 'I met him in the course of my duties.'

David seemed saddened by her news. She realised that he too must have felt what a waste of time it had been for them to be separated. She decided to tell him about their baby.

'My God!' he exclaimed, almost shouting in his shock. 'Why didn't you tell me?'

It was shock, even concern – but not exactly paternal excitement.

'I didn't know where you were. And I didn't feel like being rejected again by your parents. They would have thought I was using you.'

'Of course, I understand. But how did you manage? I could have helped.'

'I don't think so. You were at Berkeley. The last thing you would have wanted was a baby on your hands.'

He shook his head and then he asked: 'Where is the baby now?'

She had thought she could cope with this question, but she had been wrong. Her eyes filled with tears. 'They took her away,' she said.

And then it all came out. The flight from London, the storm, the violent men, the house with its oppressive comfort and ruched curtains, the birth and then the ejection from the house, the shelter in the Peggotty hulk on the marshes, the fever and then the kindly man who took her under his wing.

David's eyes blazed with indignation and fury. 'He did all this to you and took our baby. My God, I'll make him suffer…'

'It's not as easy as that.'

'There are laws; there is justice. There is common humanity. However rich he is, he's going to pay.'

'You don't understand. He's not just a rich man. He is a sort of Prospero. A wicked Prospero.'

'I can understand how you would think that, but he's flesh and blood like you or me.'

'He is not like us. He has become something else. You will understand when you meet him.'

'You think he is evil?'

'He is on top of evil.'

Finally, David took her home to her little back street. 'You live here?' he asked incredulously. It had that effect on people from outside. He made a slight noise, a reflex to the place, almost an 'nf'.

'I live here, and I like it,' she said firmly.

Even if he disapproved of the location, he looked as if he wanted to be asked up for coffee, but she wasn't ready for that yet. He seemed disappointed.

'Hasten slowly,' she told him.

The nuns at school had been almost obsessively fond of the phrase. It was almost their motto.

'Ah yes,' he said. 'Good old *festina lente*. But I am going to darn well hasten when it comes to that man. He has kidnapped our child.'

She kissed him.

'I'm glad you told me,' he said. 'It was a bone of contention between me and my wife. She never wanted a child. And now I discover I already had one.'

'I'm *not* so glad I told you,' she said. 'He won't hurt me but he could easily dispose of you. It's no use going off like a bull in a Wedgwood display. Don't do anything. Have patience. In the short term, Lily is safe. I am sure she is alive. Much too valuable to him, don't you think, as a pawn? Poor little pawn. I try not to think about her except at night.'

'Of course, they're an awful lot of trouble,' he added, and then as an afterthought, 'as well as being a good thing.'

'What are?'

'Babies, you know.'

Of course, he didn't really mean it. It was just his way.

* * *

Two days later, in that coincidental way, Marie received a note from Middleburg, delivered with a bunch of roses to her tiny apartment. The fact that he knew her address was not a surprise; it had to happen. The note came in an official-looking envelope and was written on The Other Judas, Inc letterhead, couched in friendly terms as though the days of house arrest had never been and nothing had passed between them since they'd first met on an aeroplane returning home from Nice airport.

It invited her to come and see him at his offices in Wilshire Boulevard. He suggested Tuesday of the following week at an hour when he could give her 'some rather good English tea' and a chocolate Bath Oliver. If she would like to bring a friend he would be delighted to meet him, or her.

She showed the message both to Joe and to Margot – David was away in San Francisco on real-estate business – and asked them for their views. They each advised a cautious acceptance, to see what the man was up to and, since Joe was out on wine matters on the day in question, it was agreed that Margot should go with her.

That afternoon, she did a recce by herself on the The Other Judas, Inc – or TOJI – offices in downtown Wilshire Boulevard. It was a great, shining white edifice, proclaiming its power to those outside and, to those entering through the great swing doors, the prospect of impending entitlement. There was official bonhomie, there was welcome, there was also the coolness of formality – but above all was the impression of magnitude. This was the headquarters of a 'conglomerate', one of the new super-corporate entities of the sixties which had hardly existed before this decade. Discussed in the press, praised by some, feared by others, the subject of questions by politicians, TOJI embraced vast retinues of international brands, covering horizon-wide echelons of products.

Inside, through the swing doors, a beautifully coiffed and manicured receptionist called Jeannine held sway behind a high blond-oak desk. One look from her was enough to send the impertinent scrounger or curious intruder back to the outsider-land of the street. She was particularly hard on motorbike messengers and knew, just *knew*, who it was who had scratched FUCK on the elevators' graffiti-proof walls. She was just beginning to be aware that Marie had come in and was not doing anything constructive; she was not coming, she was not going and that always stirred the hypersensitive cilia in Jeannine's organs of reception propriety. Marie continued to gaze in exasperated awe at the assertive smoothness of Middleburg's citadel.

Beyond her, the elevators came and went with a deprecating noise like a butler's cough as the doors opened. When you stepped inside TOJI's head office, she observed, you knew you had arrived but you regretted that you had not checked your face for a smudge from breakfast, or a splatter from lunch. It made you regret the slightly worn suit you had put on that morning when the light was low, or the skirt that was too long and crumpled, because you had come to a place where everything was perfect.

'Can I help you?' said Jeannine.

Marie checked her mouth for a crumb, and left.

A week later, she and Margot went through similar emotions, though modified by a sense of entitlement since they were going to see the Big Cheese, as they entered the TOJI offices at the appointed hour. Margot had given her a biscuit she said she had made to give her confidence. Marie ate it with her coffee in the café before they set out. It began to make her feel rather odd, though not unpleasantly. In fact, she felt full of confidence walking up to Reception where Jeannine presided.

'Hello,' said Marie. 'We've come to…'

Jeannine held up her hand. It was a polite gesture but firm. Her telephone was ringing. She picked it up. 'Yes, Reception?' She held her hand up throughout her telephone conversation as though Marie were an approaching car which should not pass.

'Certainly, Mr Corvino. I understand. See to it myself. Bye now. Yes?'

This last was addressed to Marie.

'We have come to see Mr Middleburg.'

'You have an appointment?'

'Yes.'

357

'Of course.'

It was inconceivable to enter such a place without one.

'Forgive me one moment. Mercury.'

A motorbike messenger with the name on his bomber jacket had come through the door.

'You are late, Mercury. Take this package, please, to Tuggards. Mr Drench is waiting for it now. Yes?' She was addressing Marie once more.

'Lavell and Garraway. We have an appointment with Mr Middleburg,' Marie told her again.

'Ah yes. One moment.' She lifted her hand once more as if stopping an approaching express, and lifted another telephone. 'Tamara? Ah, good. I have a Miss Lavell and Miss…?'

'Garraway.'

'Miss Caraway. Yes? Very good. I'll send them up.'

She replaced the receiver and looked at Marie and Margot as if they were the luckiest people in the world. 'Mr Middleburg will see you now. Tenth floor, straight ahead.'

'Garraway,' said Margot.

As they left the lift, which ushered them in and ushered them out with the same deprecating cough, they were met with an apparition in the shortest skirt imaginable and legs that kept soaring higher than human ever climbed before. In fact, as Margot said afterwards, if you ever had the temerity to reach beyond the verges of the skirt, you would have to ensure a good supply of oxygen both for the climb and the descent. The apparition spoke.

'Hello, I'm Tamara,' she said, exuding Chanel. 'Very lovely to see you. This way, please.' She wafted them down a long, dark corridor, stopped at a heavy door with no name on it, and knocked.

'Come.'

Tamara opened the door and a great surge, a blast, of light from the huge window powered in upon them. They could not see. Only the light spoke. After a while, their eyes grew a little accustomed to the dazzle and they managed to discern their host. Maybe it was a trick of the light but Middleburg seemed to have grown, swelled, since Marie had last seen him. He sat, shining and prodigious, behind his vast desk which glimmered like a sea, a shining ocean. His head, bent low over something he was examining, seemed like a bathysphere about to plunge to unimaginable depths.

He looked up and smiled. 'Ah,' he said. 'My favourite person. Marie, how long has it been? And who is this?'

'An old friend,' she said. 'Margot Garraway.'

'Ah yes,' said Middleburg, not with a great deal of pleasure. 'I remember. Now, let me recall. Why are you here?'

'You asked me to come,' said Marie.

'Indeed. Your poor father's bequest to you must be activated on the occasion of your next birthday,' Middleburg continued. 'There will be a presentation to you. His share, of course, is less now than it was because of the expansion and capital enlargement of the business. It all started after the war with a company called Messinger which was a conduit, if you like, for one or two of the German scientists and doctors who had been working in Germany on the physiological, psychological and physical problems of aviation: altitude tolerance, cold endurance, the speed of sound, wound control, the limits of stress and so on. It fitted in very well with the research requirement of the Government which is why we came over here, but new opportunities arose, the longer we stayed. As a result of our focussed researches and experiments, quite different products were also suggested. Toothpastes, cosmetics, skincare, detergents, polishes, health products… And soon we found we needed a business distinct from the more serious activities of Messinger's to deal with the consumer side of things. That is where The Other Judas, Inc, or TOJI, came in.

'It started as a charitable non-profit organisation, which made us famous, but it was unsustainable. We had to become more commercial and we now range from household products and beauty care – our Bonjour Sagesse range sells all around the world – to automotive products, babycare, hotels and travel. Our search is on for the next best thing to eternal youth. These are the companies you are getting into.'

'I am not so much concerned with my share of anything as with the fate of my father and the interest you seem to have taken in my life.'

'Not interest so much as care. We have tried to take care of you because your father could not. After all, I am a second cousin, somewhat removed, but I am still your family. I am all the family you have.'

There seemed no point in pursuing the discussion at this particular point. Middleburg would only enjoy her discomfiture. She found herself holding her hand up to shade her eyes, so intense was the light she was looking into. She recalled a line of some poet, could it be Eliot, about looking into the heart of light. She thought, if only that light could be shed on one's heart! There was Joe and there was David. She rather doubted that Middleburg had a heart; rather, a huge, pulsating bank account.

'Do you think you could draw the blind a little?' she asked the new, inflated Middleburg.

'Of course.' He did not move. Nor did she. There was a knock at the door. 'Come.'

The lovely Tamara entered with a teapot and three cups, also a plate piled with chocolate Olivers.

'They come from Fortnums,' said Middleburg, noting their glances. 'As does the tea.'

'And Tamara as well?' asked Margot.

'Tamara comes from San Diego.'

Tamara busied herself pouring the tea and offering the Olivers, which Margot had no difficulty refusing although Marie was feeling slightly sick, which made her angry.

'Where is my father now?' asked Marie, trying to catch him out.

'Thank you, Tamara,' said Middleburg, clearly not wanting to air such matters in front of the girl.

'Could she…?' Could she draw the blind a little, Marie was going to say, but Tamara was halfway across the three-mile carpet. The apparition let herself out.

'We understand that your father died some time ago in prison, just as his friend, the jailbird Felipe, is now also dead. The privations they suffered finally killed them.'

The news of the certainty of her father's death came as no surprise to Marie but she would not let it show at this stage. It was difficult anyway to feel shock over someone she had never met, who had merely introduced his person to her mother whom she had not met either. She decided to ask Middleburg another question that had perplexed her.

'Why did you want to marry me?'

Margot looked at her curiously. Marie had told her much of her story, but not this.

'I had grown fond of you,' he said. 'You are an attractive young woman. After all I had done for you, I hoped that your affection might grow too, but it was not to be. You wanted to be free. At last you were well enough to go. I had to respect that. Though there are some pressing reasons why you might wish to review your decision. These I will divulge in due course.'

Marie clenched her fingers slightly and leant forwards in her chair. Why did he have to talk like the pedantic schoolmaster in *The Browning Version*?

'The papers I have been given suggest that someone systematically set out to rob my father, to lead him astray, to tempt him with drugs and finally to get him arrested and put away, so that they could control the money and the company,' said Marie.

'The papers you have been given were all forgeries.'

'What would be the point of such a fabrication?' asked Margot. 'Who would have done such a thing? To what end?'

'To make trouble. To cause confusion. To start a lawsuit. To divert your attention. To tell a good story. To make money. To blackmail. People are always forging papers. That's why forgers are so busy. Very popular in prison, I am told, is a forger.'

'But these were very specific papers, some of them very old, and all pointing to the fact that someone – possibly you yourself – had done my father out of his fortune, by hoodwinking him, by playing on his loneliness and scholarship, by surrounding him with evil people and feeding him the worst kind of drugs.'

'Well, well, well,' chuckled Middleburg, 'you've certainly been playing paranoia poker. Do you really think I, we, would go to those lengths to get a measly million or two from such an unreliable little bookworm as your father? He begged us to look after him. He begged us to look after you. He was in a bad way. That is why you are here, now, sitting in that chair, because I do not want to do you harm. I want you to take what is yours: a share in the company I have created. It is a bigger company now because we have an affiliation with an outfit in which the Government has an interest, a firm started here by German scientists like me who, at the war's end, were deemed by the army to be doing work of national importance. Because of government interest, it is vital that our shareholders and vice-presidents are well documented and everything is done by the book.'

'I've heard of companies like that,' said Margot. 'Wernher von Braun: what goes up must come down. When the US Army was briefed to gather these useful enemies in, it was called Operation Paperclip. That paperclip stuck in my mind.' You acquired a lot of information at Merrymaids if you kept your brain open.

'I'll tell you what,' said Middleburg, springing out of his chair like a pinball and pinging heavily about the room, almost sitting in this chair and now that, flirting with them before tearing himself away and round the room again. 'Come round in a week or two, and we'll drive you to Château Cauchemar and I'll give you the special guest tour of the castle. We do have coach tours that come by arrangement so we have a good presentation. Our French Bluebeard tour is remarkably popular, but our bestseller is the California Nightmare, a tour based on the horrors that went on in the beatnik days and hippie nights of the fifties and of course even today – we mustn't forget Mr Manson and his young ladies who cast a shadow.'

'Too close for comfort,' said Margot.

'You insist your daddy was not guilty,' Middleburg continued, still fixing Marie in his gaze, 'but please keep an open mind. Come along over and I'll give you something to think about. Like, who was your father, this wronged hero of yours? Did he ever exist? Is he perhaps not another myth, like Bluebeard and Red Riding Hood;

one of those things you pick up on the way through childhood, but have to let go along with fairies and Father Christmas as you grow to maturity. Yes, we have to leave the fairy stories behind and turn to the grown-up ones, as we ourselves grow up and grapple with the true nature of life. We are all engaged in an experiment, are we not? That is, this thing called existence. Here it is, spread out for us as on a table. Time is our Bunsen burner, experience and the world are our volatile ingredients and our bodies are the test tubes which we must take care of, for they are easily cracked. What is real and what is hearsay? What are we? Who are we? How much life can we take? What is the purpose of the experiment and will we ever find it out?'

He was more worked up than Marie had ever seen him. His face was flushed, his eyes blazed. The effect was serious and disturbing.

'I have evidence of my father,' said Marie. 'It proves he was real. I suspect you know very well who robbed him of his fortune, and used the money to start their own business.'

'You think you have evidence, but have you empirical proof? All you have is rumour, what people have written, and for what end? You follow a path of likelihood when the truth is that life can follow a path of unlikelihood, a path – how did he put it in the "The Road Not Taken"? – a road unfrequented, which is just as valid as the one you think you know, perhaps more so. We are all part of God's experiment, if you can call him God, and where it will end God knows. Don't assume … anything.'

Middleburg had finally arrived back at his own chair behind the desk. He vibrated for a moment and sank back between its arms like a ball finding home on a pinball machine.

'And now,' he said, 'it's back to work. The experiment, if we can call it that, goes on for all of us and I must say goodbye. Duty calls, as I am sure it does for you. I look forward to seeing you at Château Cauchemar. Ah, Tamara...'

The secretary entered as if summoned by magic – but perhaps he had pressed a button – and Marie and Margot got up from their chairs.

'Goodbye,' they said, as they left. 'Thank you for the tea.' Merrymaids set great store by politeness.

Tamara took them down the passage again with its carpets thick as a polar bear's pelt, pressed for the lift and, when the doors parted, smiled and invited them to have a nice day, which they duly echoed.

'Well...' they exclaimed simultaneously, and laughed like schoolchildren as the doors closed.

'Did you know your father?' Marie asked, finally.

'My father? Of course,' said Margot.

'What was he like?'

'He was around. Went off to work. Read stories at bedtime. Bought me a bike. Took us on holidays, that sort of thing. Dropped me off at parties. Sometimes even collected us.'

'Sometimes *collected* you?'

'I had a very ordinary childhood. Too ordinary, I used to think.'

'Lucky you.'

* * *

Next afternoon, she took tea in the Cake N Coffee on Olive Street with Joe and Margot. She had invited David to turn up as well, but he was late. She chatted to the other two while they waited and turned over recent events in her mind. Was she in love with David again or was she not? The memory of him letting her down still troubled her.

Eventually he arrived, untroubled by his unpunctuality and even giving, very slightly, the impression – which some people can do – that he was doing them a favour by coming.

At any rate, she wasn't sleeping with him again just yet. They sat in the café, drinking Jackson's English Afternoon Blend, served very weak the way the Americans like it, but out of a china teapot: the English way.

First, one subject had to be taken out and shaken.

'Never give me a hash biscuit without telling me again,' she told Margot.

'Gee, I thought you knew. Like, it would calm you down. Sorree.'

'Never mind it now. I wondered why Middleburg seemed so elusive. He looked strange, puffed up and amorphous like the Old Man of the Sea. Didn't you think?'

'That was the biscuit.'

'Oh. Well. Thanks a lot. First question, then: do I – or do we – go to Château Cauchemar to see whatever it is he has up his sleeve? He said he had evidence that made a compelling case against my father.'

'I think we should see what he's got,' said Joe. 'Although, with all his resources, he can turn evidence on its head. But let's see it anyway.'

'If I'm going to be part of this,' said David, 'wouldn't it be better if I introduced myself as soon as possible? Why don't I go up with Marie to the castle? Or would that confuse him?'

'I hope so. He's too damn unconfused at the moment. I think you should go with one of the boys,' Margot told Marie.

'Not me, I'm afraid,' said Joe. 'Next week's busy. Wine business again. Wine & Spirits Show in San Diego.'

'Thank you, anyway,' said Marie. 'You are all very kind.'

'Over to you, David?' asked Margot. 'Are you free?'

'I'll make myself free.'

Marie could see he was grumpy. She had been trying to make things up to Joe because she felt sorry for him now David was around. The contrariness of life made it certain that the less attention she paid David, the keener her old lover became. How little he knew her! And how easy it was to let misunderstanding grow from a thicket into a hedge and then an impenetrable wall ten foot high. How fragile life is, she thought, how precarious and alarming! Fate plays with people just as Middleburg plays with me: as if we are taking part in someone else's game, whose rules are unclear and whose outcome is dark, and we deal with the reality of uncertainty whichever choice we make. She felt sorry for David because he probably had thoughts like that too. She felt sorry for all of them, but not for Middleburg. He didn't have thoughts like that. He was above all that sort of thing, was Felix Middleburg, fishing away in the dark river.

'What do you think, Joe?' she asked.

'I'll do some sniffing around behind the scenes when I am next up there. I have wine to deliver and, as it's a major account, I usually turn up myself, so they won't be surprised to see me. The man is clever, he's powerful, he's devious and he wants something from you. There will be a moment of cards on the table, but I don't think we're quite there yet. That's when I want to be around.'

'How about you, Margot?'

'I think you should take David.'

Margot likes Joe, thought Marie. Now there's an idea.

* * *

Two days later, an invitation from The Other Judas, Inc arrived in an embossed envelope. It contained a card from Middleburg inviting her on Wednesday the following week to accompany him on a tour of the Château Cauchemar where she might be interested in certain things that had come to light. She was welcome to bring a fellow guest of her own choosing.

She replied giving the name of the guest of her choice. David had preened about it, forgetting his grump – since when had he become a preener? Was it wise to introduce him to Middleburg? It would give him another pawn to play with, but she wanted David to see him close up. *Festina lente*, that was the watchword. She felt bad about Joe because he was a good man and she really liked him – possibly better than David – but David had a part to play in all this and he was the father of her child. Let Margot have Joe if he liked her, it would be only fair.

Meanwhile, there was one thing that caused her slight concern. She was glad she had given David the news about the baby, their little lost girl, because there was just a chance that Middleburg would air the subject, whether out of carelessness, ignorance or malice – probably the latter. She would have felt guilty about not telling David if he then learnt about it from anyone else, even though he was the man who'd dumped her when she needed him. It still rankled. How different her life would have been if he had stood by her! Or maybe not.

Middleburg would know about that. Middleburg never dropped a catch.

* * *

On the appointed day, a large Mercedes appeared, bigger than the Red Indian's Rolls and with Middleburg sitting in the back. He greeted them with a kind of grave deference and indicated that Marie should sit next to him and David should sit on a plush pull-down seat opposite.

'I am glad you decided to come,' he announced to Marie as they made themselves comfortable in their respective quarters. 'I understand from my sources that you have seen certain documents purporting to have come from your father, Giles Lavell, deceased.'

He gave no indication that they had already spoken of the documents at his office. He motioned to the driver and the huge car surged forwards like a tidal wave.

'They do not purport,' replied Marie, calmly, 'they do come from him. He wrote them himself. They are vouched for by a very reliable witness.'

'They *were* vouched for but the very reliable witness is dead. Things aren't always what they seem, as Gilbert and Sullivan remind us. Skimmed milk masquerades as cream.'

'It is something I've come to expect, especially in my dealings with you and your company; there has been plenty of skimming and very little hard fact,' Marie told him. 'Nonetheless, I shall believe in the reliability of the documents unless there is some strong evidence to the contrary.'

'I am glad you say that, Marie, for that is exactly what I will show you at Cauchemar.'

'It had better be good,' said David, with a glance at Marie.

'Oh it will be, Mr um…'

'Drummond,' Marie told him.

'Drummond,' said David, almost simultaneously

'Ah yes. Mr Drummond. It will not just be good, it will be irrefutable.'

'I would like to remind you, before we get too comfortable,' Marie told him, 'that the time *before* the last time we met was when you were holding me against my will in your house in Beverly Hills.'

'Against your will? You were sick, Marie. You had had a breakdown. I personally had saved you from a situation where you were – I don't exaggerate – dying from complications following the stillbirth of your child.'

'Stillbirth? I don't think so,' said Marie. 'The little girl is called Lily and you are still cruelly holding her. You have kidnapped her. You have stolen her from her rightful mother. How cruel is that?'

'I didn't know that, Marie,' said David. 'You were dying? You didn't tell me that.'

It was true, she hadn't, but it was irritating of him to say so, nonetheless. It undermined the united front.

'There is plenty you don't know, Mr ah Drummond,' observed Middleburg, drily, communicating to David with a lift of the eyebrow that she harboured this *idée fixe*.

'Such as?' David was hot for information now, but Middleburg continued imperturbably as he fixed his eye on Marie.

'I took you in because I cared for you, brought you over to California to recuperate, found you the best doctors, paid for your medication, raised you from your sick bed ... and you were well on the way to recovery when you suddenly – with the help of a petty criminal who had been paid for his involvement – got it into your head that you must "escape". Maybe that too was part of your recovery and I am glad that we went along with it, since it seems to me that you are now, indeed, back to your old self. I became very fond of you, as you know, and, foolishly, I thought that you might reciprocate my feelings, but I realise that was just the fantasy of an older man. I am sure you won't blame me for that. You are a very bewitching young lady.'

Although she might have taken it as a compliment, he said it as though it were a slight misfortune.

The Mercedes had wafted them through the suburbs and was now cruising with imperceptible sensation – save the ticking of the clock – down the freeway and out of town while Middleburg proceeded with his plausible explanations. Now and then, David glanced at Marie to check her reactions and indeed his own.

At length, they pulled up outside the castle, as Marie had done with Joe some weeks back. It was high summer now and all around the hills looked parched and the trees in the valley were beginning to show the slight degree of listlessness that presages drought.

'Last time I was parked here,' she told Middleburg, 'someone took a pot shot at us.'

He seemed perplexed and concerned, though not altogether surprised. 'Really?' he queried, 'Are you sure?'

'The bullet went whizzing overhead.'

'Must've been the gamekeeper. He's a real old boy. We had some poachers earlier, out of season, and that really infuriates him. I'll have a word.'

The Mercedes now embarked on the silent ascent of the driveway, finally pulling up on a wide circle of gravel in front of the castle.

'I hope you've warned him we're coming,' said Marie.

'Please don't worry your head about anything. You are a guest of The Other Judas. We always use that name, that company, for PR purposes.'

'I understand he was the saint of hopeless causes,' said David.

'Very good,' replied Middleburg. 'Information is everything. In the quantum world, it is the one thing that cannot be destroyed. Now, may I suggest you leave the car and follow me? You will find the castle deserted today. No cleaning staff, no groundsmen, not even a gamekeeper. I have asked them all to stay away so we can have the place to ourselves. Your tour of the castle will take in the old story of Bluebeard and the more recent tales of California's very own nightmare.'

They followed him as he talked on. 'The papers in your possession say that your father was the victim of an elaborate deception while all he wanted to do was to study. Is that correct?'

'That is the general drift of them, yes,' Marie told him.

'What if I told you that he was deceiving himself as well as you? That he was the origin and perpetrator of the crimes and murders of which he was accused? That, in the end, the drugs that he was taking, particularly the LSD, began to turn his mind?'

Marie contained herself at the impertinence of the man. She felt comforted and reassured by David's presence by her side. 'I would want you to prove it.'

'I see you are more confident now with your old boyfriend by your side. But isn't his arrival at this particular juncture of your life another example of the unlikeliness of things?'

Middleburg was smiling gently, as he so often did, but Marie seethed with disquiet. What was he insinuating? That David's appearance at Merrymaids had not been coincidence at all? And if it was not, what had it been?

* * *

Middleburg led them up the front steps and into a hall typical of the kind of castle it was meant to be. It was tall, wide and designed to impress. On the wall were various heads of animals and one or two portraits of hairy-looking ancestors. There was armour and weaponry, there was a great bear, stuffed and rampant. Right down the middle of the hall was a long table and at one end stood another table slightly raised on a dais, the high table where the lord and lady would sit with special guests.

So this is the place that the old beatnik called Daddy, back in the squat off King's Cross, had spoken of, not with relish, he wouldn't have felt that, but with a kind of awe. How far away that seemed now, far away in time and place! She could hardly believe it had been her, living with those people. Where were they now? Where was Ivo? Wherever do good men go when the clocks stop ticking? And these in themselves were questions that now nagged at her with another thought. What if Daddy, his very name of Daddy, and his talk of castles and beatniks in California, had not been coincidental after all but had served as a disturbance, a foreshadowing? Brickville had been up there too in Kings Cross, ferreting around, and worse. What if she were part of a long conspiracy that had framed her entire life? It was too absurd, and yet, it all made sense. And if it were true – which we could hardly think possible – what purpose could it possibly have?

Middleburg now led them to the far end of the hall where there was a small side-chamber under a vaulted ceiling. He stopped at a circular grille in the floor and peered down. The two guests stepped forward beside him. Cold dank air and a smell of bones rose up to greet them.

'Down there are the dungeons,' Middleburg told them. 'That is where we tell the tourists some of the horrors took place. We will go down there in a moment but first I want to show you more of the floor we are on. Of course, I want you to remember that what we are speaking of all happened in France nearly six hundred years ago, though the walls seem to recall it as though it were yesterday. Some say that stone can receive and record the impressions that we force upon it. What you must also remember is that Gilles de Rais, whose castle this was, was a very plausible and powerful man, as well as being a Marshal of France and fellow general of Joan of Arc. One did not argue with Gilles de Rais.'

'What about my father?' she said.

'I am giving you the Bluebeard tour,' said Middleburg. 'Questions later.'

At that moment, Marie thought she heard, almost at the level of silence, a scream.

'Did you hear that?' she asked.

'What?'

Of course, it was a trick of the acoustics.

'Nothing,' she said. 'Just me.'

'I suspect you are a little bit psychic, Marie,' said Middleburg.

'She is impressionable, like myself,' said David. 'And who wouldn't be in a place like this?'

Middleburg held up a hand. 'Bear with me,' he said. 'All will be explained.' He moved them on through the building.

'There are various other service rooms here,' he continued, indicating the various directions, 'a butler's pantry, a scullery and a withdrawing room for the lord and lady and special guests which is here behind the hall.' He opened another door which disclosed a rather more comfortable chamber with no beasts on the wall but rather some hangings and even pictures. A stringed instrument lay against the wall. 'A rebeck,' Middleburg explained, 'a fifteenth century version of the viol which in turn pre-dated the violin.'

There were tourist leaflets on the table. Marie picked one up. It showed the design of a maze; she loved a maze so she slid it into her pocket. Middleburg did not seem to object. He was proud of his marketing for Cauchemar Castle.

'We have open days, banquets and feasts but only for privileged groups,' he said. 'People cannot just turn up – it would interfere with our work here – we are very strict about that. But people do indeed seem to have a macabre fascination with what went on here all those years ago. We shall now go down to the dungeons, always a popular port of call on party nights.'

'Doesn't that seem in rather bad taste?' asked Marie, crossly. Even if her father had not been involved, people had died within these walls, at some point or other.

'I suppose it may seem so to you, Marie. I can understand that. But Château Cauchemar is now a discreet commercial venture, it is a profit centre of its own in the TOJI empire and we have to go where the market is. What we do is far more demure than the proceedings of yesteryear when Gilles de Rais' preferences were what mattered. Non-stop parties, orgies, trials, beatings, breakdowns, magical practices, demon raising and, apparently, semi-ritual slaughter. That is what I should call bad taste, all with a considerable injection of drugs. We still allow weddings, balls and extensive functions to take place but all on the understanding that the proceedings are somewhat mitigated. Hallowe'en occasions are very popular. Human sacrifice is discouraged.' He smiled wintrily as if to indicate that he had made a joke.

David looked at Marie with the air of one who has heard more than he bargained for. 'Be that as it may,' he said, 'all these things are speculative, they are assertions, they do not prove that Marie's father was here too.'

'I am coming to that,' said Middleburg. 'For the moment, I am just giving you a *tour d'horizon*. It is important that you should feel the redolence of a place where so much evil happened. I will take you now to the tower where some of the scenes of horror were perpetrated and thence to the dungeons, which need no introduction since horror is implicit in the very word. After that we will proceed to the pleasaunce and the charnel house outside, which are also locations where offences took place. Bodies were thrown into the charnel house even before they were dead.

'Where the offences were *supposed* to have taken place,' corrected David.

'Quite so, quite so. You make the point again, Mr Drummond, but you will retract it, I believe, before the tour is finished. I will now take you to a secret room in the north tower where at least six young people of both sexes were violated and killed...'

He led them up a narrow, indeed claustrophobia-inducing, circular staircase whose stone walls appeared stained with some red substance. At length they stopped in a rounded chamber distinguished by narrow arrow-slits of windows and a number of iron hooks in the wall. For a moment a tableau of three figures – two young and one in full maturity – a boy and a girl of around thirteen years of age, cowering in front of a tall man with a whip, flooded her mind, and as quickly vanished.

'Here the victims were strung up,' Middleburg continued, 'and sodomized. Some were first killed and then raped, all perpetrated by Gilles de Rais in the years 1430 to 1440. There is a book here of illustrations if you wish to see... It is thought some aspects of the original were re-enacted in orgies here only fifteen years ago.' He started opening a venerable volume, bound in tooled leather.

'No, thank you,' exclaimed Marie, hastily. 'We are not ghouls. Is this what you show your escorted tours?'

'Indeed it is. It is always salutary to remind people of the depths of depravity to which the human race can fall, don't you think? They seem to have an appetite for such instruction. Let us now, talking of depth, visit the dungeons...' He led them down now, through the claustrophobic staircase, to the ground floor where, at the base of the stair, was another door set in the wall. Middleburg produced a key, suitably large and presumably mediaeval, with which to open it. The dank air floated up, laced (or was it her imagination) with suffering, hopelessness, tears and blood. He pressed a switch, which illuminated precipitous circular steps with a dim light, and led them down to another door at the bottom which he also unlocked.

'Do you have many accidents as you show people round?' asked David.

'Quite a few,' answered Middleburg casually.

'Could be expensive.'

'Not at all, Mr Drummond. Privileged visitors – and we only have privileged visitors – have to sign a form before they start saying that they waive all rights of recompense. And still they come! A night at the Château Cauchemar is often a prize in the product competitions the ad agency dreams up.'

'What happened here, according to you?' Marie asked.

'Girls and boys were sometimes locked up here for days, consigned to the care of a monstrous gaoler who appeared sometimes in the form of Gilles de Rais, otherwise known as Bluebeard. No one ever escaped. Imagine what they must have felt. Bribed with sweetmeats or money, and then … the cold, the hunger, the dread, the pain…'

The man could not disguise a certain quality in his voice that seemed almost gloating. Marie wondered whether it was he who, after all, had perpetrated the monstrosities he spoke of. Somebody must have done? Or must they…?

'And you really believe my father was behind some latter-day version of all this?' she asked.

'Patience, Marie. One of the last items I shall show you is a signed document in which he admits his guilt. But for the moment, the floor is held by Gilles de Rais. I have invited you here to impart my research into the life and crimes of that gentleman. If you will forgive me for one moment, I will just go and check that they have prepared the pleasaunce and the charnel house which will be our last ports of call before I end our tour in the withdrawing room. Look around meanwhile. Go on. Every corner will have its messages and memories…'

Marie started to move towards one of the cells with David and then she noticed that Felix was back on the stairs and already closing the bottom door behind him – *locking* the bottom door.

'Look out,' David shouted. But it was too late. The huge lock clicked and they were alone. David rushed to the door as if to hammer on it with his hands.

'Don't,' said Marie urgently. 'That is what he wants.'

'Fuck,' said David. 'What do we do now?'

'We wait.'

'He can't keep us here long. We have friends who know where we are.'

'He can keep us as long as he likes,' she told him. 'Everything they do is well thought out. But I don't think it would suit them.'

'Just as well I'm not claustrophobic,' David exclaimed, somewhat to her surprise, since it rather suggested that he was.

'Let's look around a bit. There's plenty of room,' she said. Indeed the dungeon seemed to stretch out further than the castle itself. There was a central 'office' where presumably the gaoler sat, a horribly plausible monster, and there were grilled partitions for the prisoners, at least thirty such chambers. The air was chill and damp and gave out that faint, nauseating aroma of decay. Something the size of a cat scuttled across a cell as they looked in. Messages of despair, fear and impotent hate were scribbled on the walls.

'If it wasn't so horrible, this place would be a joke,' she said.

Sounds again, this time just below the level of human hearing, now began to steal across the psychic barrier of the senses, weeping and lamentations, sudden cries of pain, implorings and hopeless despair. At the end of one of the corridors, there was a larger room with a table and a strange sort of bed with a hole cut out of its middle. Underneath was a large pail. The ghost of a scream made her start.

'I heard something then,' said David.

'What a hideous place,' said Marie. 'But you have to admire the showmanship. They have made a chamber of horrors out of nothing. They have invented their own legend. I am beginning to think that he is right; such horrors might have been contained in the fifteenth century, by a powerful lord, but this could not have happened here. It's all too … big. The Manson murders were horrible but they were ranch-sized not castle-sized.'

'You're right. They were essentially a suburban nightmare with their creepy-crawlings through people's houses while they were sleeping, and the murders mostly done by young girls.'

'Then why did I believe what they told me,' she asked, 'that my father was involved? He wasn't like that.'

'You didn't know anything about him until they told you something. Something is better than nothing if that's all you know. And another thing. I've been wanting to say I'm so sorry.'

'For what? It's not your fault.'

'For what I did to you.'

He squeezed her hand and she squeezed his back. Did he mean abandoning her, or making her pregnant? He really did seem sorry. At that point, just in time, before she could kiss him, a key could be heard turning in the lock.

'I do apologise,' exclaimed Middleburg, calmly stepping inside. 'Locked you in. Pure reflex, I'm afraid. We always lock up after showing people round. And then our receptionist buttonholed me.'

'Oh really?' said Marie. 'We didn't notice. Too busy exploring.'

'It opens your eyes as to what went on,' Middleburg said, sententiously, as they climbed back up the stairs after him. 'He made them play hide and seek all over the castle, of course. The games were some of the worst things, according to one boy who came forward as a witness. When you were found, you were killed.'

Middleburg led the way towards a large double back door which led out on to greenery beyond.

'And the last one left?' enquired David. 'Did he or she get a reward?'

'No. They were killed too.'

'And who was the boy, the witness? Did he come forward or was he pushed?' asked Marie.

Middleburg made a noise like a church organ running out of puff. She took it to be a hollow laugh.

'And now for the pleasaunce and the charnel house,' he said.

380

'What do you mean by the pleasaunce?' David asked.

'It is a part of the garden intended for enjoyment and recreation but in the days of mayhem it came to mean something between an open-air orgy and a place of shadows and secret terror. There is a summerhouse or gazebo there, which I shall show you, where we keep some of the documentation. And a maze where, I must warn you, it is better not to go. I do love a maze, don't you?'

He opened the door and disclosed an expanse of garden that seemed a profusion of colour painted against a background of green. 'Please,' Middleburg declared expansively, 'explore and enjoy. But bear in mind the use to which this place of enchantment has been put. Though today, I admit, the thought of such things seems distant.'

There were flowerbeds and climbing plants, trellises and bowers, pleached walks and quincunxes (which reminded Marie of the Holdsworths' feeble attempts at such things in Beverly Hills), statues (many of them erotic but undeniably old and original), rustic seats and purling streams. All these and more rendered the place a delight to the nose and a joy to the eye. Trees of various kinds provided enclosure before an ancient brick wall which ran around, and behind, the profusion of flowers and trees. There was a yew maze in one corner which especially pleased Marie.

'I cannot resist a maze,' she cried, as she peered down the beckoning pathway.

She had been given a book of mazes long before and had memorised many of them. There was something forbidden, secret and shy about them, as though they were protecting a heart.

'I should warn you, it may take some time,' said Middleburg. 'As I said, it is better not to go there. It is where some of the darkest things took place.'

'Perhaps later,' said Marie.

'Or maybe not,' said David.

'So ... what do you say happened here?' she asked Middleburg. 'It looks, it *feels*, too good to be the scene of another of your mythical horrors. Don't try and incriminate a garden any more than a person. Leave nature out of it.'

'I wish I could, Marie. But, alas, Gilles and his friends delighted to practise their debauches in such places. They loved to defile beauty. It is what men do. It was their way. As for the maze, don't you think it has been a place of terror as well as entertainment since classical days? Can you imagine finding yourself lost inside those dark green walls and being pursued by some nameless dread that finally turns into something at the centre, something worse than your worst fears?'

She looked at Middleburg with a new respect, though perhaps respect was the wrong word. It was interesting that she now thought of him as Middleburg. Felix had dropped out of the running. He was altogether too many-layered to be confined in a first name. She was becoming aware of dimensions in the man taking him beyond what she had thought him to be: an insistent, dangerous, meddling, voyeuristic interloper which was bad enough. But she now glimpsed something darker, and qualities she could not immediately give a name to. Perhaps that was why he seemed to have grown bigger. Fear was his food, he grew fat on it. Best not to show it or respond to it. He was like a visiting moon whose presence exerted dark tides.

'So you think that was what the maze was about?' she asked. 'Not a harmless diversion?'

'Maybe you should go in there, after all,' Middleburg suggested.

She was drawn to it. Perhaps there was something at the centre that might help her understand.

'No … don't…' David interrupted. 'Better not to meddle.'

'So you believe me?' Middleburg enquired, suavely.

'I just think we don't have much time,' said David. It was evident that something he had seen or heard had got to him.

'Then I think we had better proceed to the gazebo where we can examine some documentation,' said Middleburg. He now led them towards a substantial summerhouse positioned at the confluence of three grassy paths. On entering they found themselves facing a table on which was arranged a selection of papers and photographs.

'Here we have the evidence of a boy, Forel, who managed to escape from the castle during a game of hide and seek, or hide and kill as we now know it.' He continued, 'These are some photographs of exhumation taken on the premises here and other exhibits: a knife that was found on the premises with blood still encrusted on it and so forth.'

'They are certainly gruesome,' Marie declared, 'but they prove nothing.'

'Four children were dug up here,' exclaimed Middleburg, 'you surely don't dispute that.'

'I don't dispute that they were dug up if you say so,' replied Marie, stoutly, 'but the question is, who put them in there? Where did they come from?'

'To the charnel house, then,' he said.

'No,' said Marie, 'we have seen enough. I didn't come here like a ghoul to gloat over long-distant crimes. I came to find out about my father.'

'Come then. Let us sit and take a little wine,' said Middleburg, 'provided by your good friend Joe.'

They did as he suggested on the banquette that ran around the little summer house. In a recess, a tray was laid out with three glasses and a bottle of Domaines Ott waiting for them. It crossed Marie's mind that if he required some heavenly music, it would probably be on hand within barely a bar's rest. How did he know that Joe was her friend?

'So, then … my father…' she reminded him. 'What proof can you show me of his guilt? No need to spare my feelings. I've spent a lifetime being ashamed of what he did.'

'I think you will enjoy this,' said Middleburg, pouring wine from the Indian club-shaped bottle. 'We bought the domaine last year. I don't think there is a rosé to match it.'

He and David sipped and, judging by David's response, it was excellent. Marie drank too.

'As for your father, I'm afraid you have been misled about him. He wasn't here at all.'

Marie choked over her glass. 'Not here at all?' she asked, 'Then what…'

'Your father did not come here,' he continued, smoothly. 'You did not have a father called Lavell. That name belonged to an educated man who took to drugs and murdered young men and boys for his perverted gratification, out on a ranch in the desert, in the early fifties. It was a famous name at the time. Your father was German, a brilliant scientist and an SS doctor who might have been sentenced to death at Nuremberg for war crimes, but he was taken in by the US Army before other authorities could catch up with him. He couldn't have come here, immediately to this place, at that time. He was head of a small chemical laboratory doing useful work for national security in Seattle.'

Middleburg's bombshell, delivered so matter-of-factly, stopped

384

both of them in their tracks. David rocked slightly as if troubled by a shock wave. Marie was surprised by her reaction – it was indeed a shock, but anything was better than uncertainty. She had a father, at least. He was here, not very far away.

'He was what?' David almost shouted.

'Why was I encouraged to think of him as a latter-day Bluebeard?' she asked.

'Because it was less troubling for you than the truth. Your father was involved in supervising or personally conducting vital experiments on people in Nazi Germany. He made them lie in freezing water until they passed out or died, injected them with lethal bacteria and dangerous drugs from which they sometimes died in pain because the experiment was conducted in a hurry, corners had to be cut and the experiment had gone wrong. We thought that, growing up in Britain where people thought the very German language was like the devil talking, you would prefer a French Bluebeard for a father than a Nazi criminal – the lesser of two evils. Even so, as you will understand, we thought it best that you should grow up … somewhat apart.'

'But who are you to think best at all? What are you to me? What have you ever been? Why could you not say my father was a dear man who died in the war? Why did I have to grow up under a cloud? It was all a game, wasn't it? You think you can throw in unexpectedness like God, just when I am getting used to something…'

Middleburg turned on her abruptly. 'What you don't seem to understand is that you and I are alike. We come from a very dark background. I own you, Marie. I can do what I like.'

'Excuse me…' David protested. 'You can't say that.'

'I would pipe down if I were you, young man. I saw the way you looked when you heard her father was a Nazi murderer wanted for war crimes.'

David, to his credit, looked sheepish.

'Why did you lead me on with such lies?' Marie asked him. 'Lies, false clues, red herrings, wild geese ... What you are telling me may be more lies.' A thought struck her. 'My god, it was you, wasn't it? You are my father.'

He shook his head in amusement. 'On a huge hill, cragged and steep, Truth stands, and he that will reach her, about must and about must go – your poet John Donne, I believe.'

'It's no use quoting Donne at me. I will find out, you know,' she told him.

'You must understand, my dear, that, without me, you are nothing. I found you. I took you on when you were no more than a week old, when I was myself driven out of my own country. I arranged for you to be looked after as you grew up. You owe me your life. *With* me, you have all the money and power you could ever want. You are my ward. You could even be my heiress and rich beyond measure. *Without* me, you have no identity. You don't even have a surname let alone a passport. So ... I have my reasons for disclosing the truth by degrees...'

Marie was silent for a moment. David was clearly thinking about it too.

'What about all the evidence?' asked Marie, changing the subject, for she too had seen David's expression. 'What about the letters from my father – and the documents from Gilles himself?'

'All fake. Hollywood is full of scriptwriters and failed novelists. Some of them even Oxford graduates. We have every resource for make-believe here in Los Angeles. As I told you, this is a city of forgery. What are movies other than forgeries of real life?'

'Why should I believe you now after all the lies? You too could be a forgery.'

'I suspect you would argue with the Devil himself,' said Middleburg, jovially.

'You would know more about that than I do,' she replied.

Middleburg's cool cheeks showed just a hint of pink. His whole world had been broken in the fall of his country: what was there that could be worse? It took a great deal to unsettle him.

'You've made him cross,' whispered David. 'Is that wise under the circumstances?'

'Yes.'

* * *

Middleburg led them out of a door in the end wall surrounding the pleasaunce, explaining that the castle would originally have had a wide bailey of ten acres or so. Instead of this, the more modern concept of a walled garden had been applied by the original millionaire who had brought the castle over.

'In the light of our recent conversation, we will skip the charnel house,' Middleburg now announced. 'Today it is just a circular stone building furnished with some rather disturbing photographs. Instead we will visit the labs and living quarters of those of our technicians and researchers who are quartered here.'

They saw now that, outside the wall, a whole development of new buildings, masked by trees, had been erected in stone to match the colour of the castle but in a style that approximated to the cottages of some utilitarian German village, strung out on either side of a street going up the hill. They looked slightly, in that way some buildings do, as if they had been put up for a film set of *Escape from Colditz*. As Marie and David inspected more closely, they saw it was by no means a picture of rural Teutonic charm. Instead, there was a clinical precision about the scene. White-coated men could be observed, walking about, speaking together, taking the air and entering and leaving the dwellings.

'These are some of the very specialised laboratories of Messinger,' Middleburg told them. 'We try and follow tradition when we are here, admitting only special guests of the family. You, of course, are more special than most, untainted by your German father's business failure and his questionable clinic in Germany and inheritor of a portion of his estate. You are, in a sense, coming home.'

'A portion?' queried David.

It was a question Marie herself had been going to ask. It irked her just a little that David had asked it first. It was not his estate.

'Marie is entitled by a deed made by her Nazi father to a share in his estate, such as it was at the time the Executors took over the running of it. It was part of the agreement, signed by him, that this should be so. The executors, who became the investors, had to have a share – and a generous one – if they made a success of the enterprise which had been so severely run down by your father and his fatal enthusiasms.'

'And where did "The Other Judas" come from?' David asked. 'The name?'

'We called it that because St Jude – or Judas Thaddeus, as distinguished from Judas Iscariot – is the patron saint of lost causes. The Jewish association tickled us. It's not a bad thing in this funny country. And her father's business seemed to be a hopeless task indeed. He was a brilliant chemist but hopeless with money. We took it on as a charity, no less, and a non-profit charity it remained for some time, the appointed beneficiary being St Jude's, a home for orphaned children. We still support it, of course, and indeed we have opened further homes, although it no longer makes sense for TOJI as a consumer conglomerate to have a charitable status.'

'He was not just a hopeless businessman, my father,' Marie said. 'He was no good as a parent, either. How did he succeed in losing me after I was born?'

'The Russians were at the gates of Berlin. I could not contact your father. He was almost certainly busy destroying data that could fall into Russian hands. Bombs were falling all the time. I managed to get your six-month pregnant mother out of Berlin. He had made me promise to look after her and the baby if he was dead or out of action. I found her a farmhouse he had located where she could have her baby in reasonable peace. But, alas, there were few medical facilities around at that time, and when the time came, the midwife was sick, the doctor old and incompetent, there was no penicillin, and much to my grief, your mother died just after you were born. We managed to find another mother with milk and there you were – mewling and puking. And the rest is history. Your father only narrowly escaped the continuous shelling and air raids himself. He was trying to find your mother, but it was impossible at that stage. And then he was arrested by the Americans. It took some time for them to realise the value he represented to their defence programme. There you have it.'

'Mewling and puking? You seem keen on Shakespeare, for a German.'

'He was not for an age, but for all time. You can't keep him to yourself. And don't you English love Beethoven?'

He had a point, she supposed. They approached the nearest house and Middleburg turned to explain, 'These houses were built for Messinger's – which is our holding company and where all the greatest talents are accumulated – so that we could pursue the most important part of our activity in secure surroundings.'

'And what is that activity, Mr Middleburg?' asked David.

Marie couldn't help noticing that the more Middleburg talked money, the more politely David addressed him.

'Why, new product development, of course! And – what the Government likes best – contractual research that might help it in the ever-increasing Russian threat to United States security. Experiments too secret to show you, alas, but we can proceed at least to the consumer side which is the nearer part of the development. The workers live here for an allotted term. The rest-houses are those on the right hand side of the road. A little further up the hill are the labs where the most secret work is undertaken.'

'What sort of experiments are we going to see?' Marie asked.

'Oh, very small stuff, I'm afraid. Studies in poisons like botulism and campylobacter and poison dart frog and puffer fish. With quite extraordinary side effects and relevance for medicine. Experiments with mould and mould-deterrents…'

He opened the door of the nearest house and they walked past a lobby and washroom, straight into the lab itself. White-coated men were standing over lab tables. There was a smell of gas and disinfectant in the air. Middleburg stopped beside a bespectacled biochemist who was peering at a green growth on a Petri dish.

'What are you doing, Lorenz?'

The man replied, deferentially, in a strong German accent. 'This is a two weeks old pâté which has developed quite an efflorescence of aspergillus. If you look at this corner, however, you will see that the pâté is unaffected. It has been coated with a new edible retardant developed from lichen ... You could eat this now. I have some melba toast if you would like to try, Herr Middleburg...'

'Certainly, certainly,' said Middleburg, though the other two drew back. 'What is the purpose of experiment if you cannot enjoy its fruits?'

The chemist offered him a small knife with which he cut off a corner of the unvitiated pâté, and consumed it with apparent relish.

'Delicious!' he exclaimed, wiping his mouth with his handkerchief. 'Fresh as tomorrow morning. Come on, you two, no back-sliding.'

'I'm not a pâté-eater,' Marie told him.

'What about you, Mr Drummond?'

But David could not be persuaded. You could see Middleburg enjoying his discomfiture. In fact, since entering the lab, his whole demeanour had changed. His nostrils flared, his eyes flashed, his head was high. This was his stamping ground.

'Too bad. You have to enter into the spirit of experiment. I had the best time of my life in a laboratory. Yes, it was the best of times. We all were going somewhere together. There was nothing that could not be done.'

'What else is going on in this building?' Marie asked, eager to get away from the surrounding fungi cultures.

'The door will shut as we leave,' said Middleburg, and we will go through a special air-filtering chamber. 'We don't want spores drifting into our consumer product investigations.

They entered a new laboratory.

'Well, now, we have a man here, Reinhardt, experimenting with a revolutionary method of filling nutty honeycomb centres with a maximum quotient of air before they burst. Here Hilda is developing self-squeezing teabag technology. And this one is interesting ... Freddi here is examining the healing powers of honey versus treacle in our new range of honey-treated sticking plasters. See, this man's wound is being treated now! We are dependent on finding volunteers who are paid. No one is forced. We take no prisoners! Ho ho! And, moving on, here is how to turn beef into fruit, and vice versa, in our new molecular de-naturising scrambler...'

'Can you do that?' David asked.

'Of course not. Just checking to see if you're listening. There will be questions later. Come on in.'

Middleburg edged them close to a man who was doing something with a test tube and asked him something in German. The man replied in kind.

'He says he is experimenting with a new kind of toothpaste that fizzes in the mouth and attacks plaque. It is a biological compound that unfortunately keeps blowing the top off the toothpaste tube,' Middleburg told them. 'Now he must find out why.'

'Fascinating,' David said, though Marie couldn't tell whether he meant it.

They moved on: the toothpaste had a quite violent smell. The next man was trying to pasteurise a purée of fresh strawberries with a minimum of heat so that it still tasted like fresh fruit and did not distort the neck of the mini plastic milk churn for which it was destined. If that happened, air would get in and the fruit would ferment and explode if stored outside the store's chill cabinet. There was already evidence of his unsuccessful efforts.

Much German was expended on the workers here so that Middleburg could enlighten his visitors on the way. Middleburg cornered first one white-coat and then another. He commanded considerable respect.

'And here's another one,' he told Marie. 'This can and will interest you. This man is exploring the energy to be derived from food waste. See that clock above him. It is powered entirely by old blue cheese. The government is very keen. It is hot to trot.'

It was quite plain to Marie that the man was talking deliberate nonsense. This was not the kind of experiment he was interested in. He could not stop testing her out, prying and teasing. It enraged her.

'Is everyone here German?' she asked.

'I thought we would feel at home! Yes, mostly, in answer to your question. We find the Germans are better workers. Well, now you have seen some of the – how shall I say? – some of the foothills of our secrets, it is time to say goodbye. You have a birthday coming up, is it not so, Marie?'

'No. I have had it. On Midsummer's Day.'

'Oh dear. That is another thing I was meaning to tell you. I don't know where you got the idea of the twenty-fourth of June as your birthday. Our records show that in fact you were born on the twenty-fourth of August. Your mother was almost six months pregnant when the war ended on the eighth of May 1945. You were apparently over a week late. Your true birthday is on the twenty-fourth of August, a month or so from now. We will have a little celebration for you. I hope you will be able to come.'

A shift of a month in your birth date is no great issue in the scale of things, but Marie felt it was another assault on her identity. A birthday is one's own thing, nobody else's, and her old nanny had been very particular about celebrating it. Here was Middleburg pulling the rug from under her again. Her eyes pricked with tears. She could hardly speak. Was he mistaking her for someone else? Another girl unknown, without a name? If so, who was she? Where was she?

'I'm not sure…' she said. 'I…'

David wasn't helping at all. She looked at him, willing him to furnish her with an excuse.

'You must come,' said Middleburg. 'There are quite a lot of people anxious to see you take your inheritance.'

'Can I come?' asked David.

There it was. He was thinking of himself.

'Perhaps … as a spectator.'

'That's settled then. We can both go,' said David.

'Good. He is a good boy, your sweetheart, no?' said Middleburg.

Marie bit her lip. It was not David's business to put her in situations. But she would find out nothing if she didn't accept the invitation.

'I hope that will be enough to convince you of our goodwill towards you, which we will show in rather more tangible form on your twenty-fifth birthday. What do you say?'

'It sounds good,' said David, answering first again. 'Depends just how tangible it will be.'

'That remains to be seen,' said Middleburg, addressing Marie.

It's not at all right, Marie thought. There's something wrong, but I'm never going to prove it. David the Mephistopheles wants it all to go through so I inherit something of my father's money. Maybe I should just be happy with that, though I must remember Mephistopheles was a devil. Her thoughts chased each other round her brain like swallows round a clock-tower.

'I think we have seen enough,' said David. 'Perhaps we should take her home now. It's not every day you discover you have a Nazi father.'

'Which reminds me,' said Middleburg. 'Your father's name, your real name, is Messinger. That is the name under which you will be invited.'

Tact was evidently not David's strong point, but it wasn't the Nazis' either. Middleburg offered them refreshments in the castle as they walked back, which Marie politely refused. At length they were received back into the Rolls and sank gratefully into its cocoon of luxury. It had been a taxing day, at least for Marie. Every time she learned something new, fresh thickets appeared ahead of her. Most of the journey back to LA was spent in silence, with Middleburg, now and then, interjecting a conversation stopper like, 'We own that winery over there. They're starting to plant Zinfandel but I guess it'll never be a classic wine.'

She made the kind of small noise you make when there's nothing to say.

David said, 'I guess not, though I hear Mourvèdre is making a comeback.'

The car finally pulled up at the entrance to the little street that led to her studio. She got out and said goodbye.

'You must come again soon,' said Middelburg through his open window. 'We're opening a Manson annexe shortly, after they've found him guilty, of course, representing 1050 Cielo Drive, the place where Sharon Tate and her friends were knifed by Manson's girls last year. The ranch where the Family lived is not far away from the castle.'

It was probably his idea of a joke. 'I can't wait,' said Marie, and walked away, leaving them in the car. 'Thank you for the tour.'

She wanted to be alone. Only later did she wonder whether leaving David with Middleburg had been altogether wise.

* * *

Next morning, Marie woke out of a dream that her lost little girl had been calling her again. The shock of the loss assailed her once more as she lay with the unremitting sunshine of California pouring itself out, like the chorus of an American musical – intently, relentlessly – into her face. There was even a bright golden haze suffusing the bins across the street as a cleaner from the store next door poured in his daily sacrifice of dust and garbage.

Where was her little girl? What was she doing now, grown up and talking? Who was teaching her, and what? There was not a day when she did not think of her baby who would never know her mother. Marie wiped away a tear and hoped for things if not better then at least different. She got up, showered, dressed and felt more Californian. Luckily, she thought, the baby had been taken away before she could really bond with her. Then the loss would have been completely unbearable.

There was an envelope waiting for her, pushed through her studio letterbox. Inside was an invitation. It read:

You are invited to a Midsummer Celebration
given by The Board of Messinger's
on the occasion of the 25th birthday of
Miss Marie Messinger
on Saturday the 24th of August at 6.30pm
at Château Cauchemar
Dress: Smart Informal
RSVP

There was a crest of Laval, the serpent etched into a ruby background along with another device, of Mercury holding a retort.

She looked at the card as though it had been conjured out of air. Middleburg had stolen the crest and twinned it with his Messinger logo. She was beginning to feel quite dislocated under the burden of so many surnames. That, and the shifting date of her birthday, made the very ground she walked on seem to shimmy like the San Andreas fault.

* * *

It was too early for Margot – the rigours of the Merrymaid night were always considerable – so Marie first called Joe the Red Indian and then David and asked them both to meet her for coffee at Oliver's, Pershing Square, in an hour. There were protests about the earliness of the rendezvous – David had a meeting later that he couldn't miss – but she insisted it was important. When they were all three met together, she told them as briefly as she could anything more that seemed relevant about her past – not so many gaps, but a few to be filled in and a few more to be guarded – and then she showed them both the invitation.

'What does it mean?' she asked them. 'Apart from the obvious.'

'It means they want something,' said David.

'And they *have* something,' said Joe.

'Do you think I should go?' she asked.

'Only if one of us is right there with you,' said David.

'If not in the room, at least outside the door,' echoed Joe.

Nervousness made her impatient with the two men.

'They go to and fro in the evening: they grin like a dog, and run about the city,' she said, recalling a Psalm she had sung in the old school chapel; it had occasioned giggling among the girls.

397

Joe looked puzzled. David clearly thought she had gone mad.

'Psalms,' she told them. 'One choir sings the first half of the verse and then the second choir sings the second half which says the same thing in a different way. It's what we're doing now. We don't need to say the same thing in a different way. We need to move forward.'

David frowned. Joe laughed.

'Don't you just love the English when they say things like that,' said Joe. 'And it was sweet of you to say *we*, but it was David here and I saying the same thing.'

'Sorry,' she said. 'Don't mind me. So. What if they don't let you into the castle?'

'I shall be delivering wine. I'll say I made a mistake with the last order. David here can be my assistant for the day.'

'Thanks,' said David, rather grudgingly.

'There's no other way,' said Joe.

'Do we know anything more about The Other Judas?' she asked.

'The company's big,' Joe told her. 'I was running through some more background stuff. It's frighteningly big. But strangely enough, or perhaps naturally enough, no one knows much about it or who started it. Big companies, consortiums, like it that way. They don't like too many questions.

'But why do they think I should be interested in a big company?'

'It's the money,' said David.

'I think they are reckoning on your curiosity to come and find out, maybe they know that you'd like a family, a background. That feeling is very strong in people. We all like to know who we are,' said Joe. 'As for the tie-up with Messinger, it's really important to them. It was billed as a takeover but it was really Messinger who did the taking through another of their companies called Metromark. The government loved it. It allowed Messinger, which had government investment, to preserve its privacy and, at the same time, seem less sinister. There was a certain amount of protest from TOJI shareholders who didn't understand.'

'But why did they want me?' asked Marie. 'Middleburg keeps talking about it but he doesn't explain.'

'You're a PR dream. What could be less sinister than a young girl with the Messinger name reclaiming her place in the company?'

'Do we know anything of its background? Is it hiding something?' Marie asked Joe. 'I know it's a research company, and it's in chemicals, because we had the tour. What else?'

'I did some checking,' Joe told her. 'It was started after the war by the Government and CIA with, or for, a small group of naturalised Germans. It involved national security. There was talk of chemical warfare, drugs to boost or retard metabolism. It grew as the Cold War grew. Very big. But here's a funny thing. I can't swear to it, but it looks to me as if the group that started Messinger were the same as the people who started The Other Judas, in other words TOJI.

'Yes,' said Marie. 'They were. He told us that.'

'It's still privately owned,' concluded Joe. 'It means a very few people, including you, are sitting on a hell of a lot of money.'

'There is something about this that doesn't add up,' said David, trying to appear impartial. 'Marie says Middleburg always seems to be one step ahead of her. What is his secret? Is he afraid of us?'

She had noted a tendency in David to ask questions rather than state opinions. It gave him a way out. She wondered whether she was becoming ever so slightly irritated by his assumption of proprietorial rights.

'If they're afraid, it makes them more dangerous,' said Joe.

Good opinion, Joe, Marie thought. But wrong. Middleburg is not afraid.

'So what am I going to do?' she asked.

'We are going to drive to the castle on the appointed day,' said Joe.

'I am going to get out and enter the place from the front,' said Marie.

'And then Joe will enter the castle from the kitchens and serve tea...' said David.

'Behave, David. This is serious.'

'Kitchens are over to the left at the back,' said Joe. 'And then I'll put on one of the kitchen porters' white coats and make my way up to the great hall...'

'While I wait outside with the car, ready for a quick getaway,' said David. 'But he kind of said he'll let me in.'

Maybe he's thinking of a quick getaway just by himself if things are getting too hot, thought Marie. The school chapel came to her mind again. Our earthly friends may fail us ... Yes, she had discovered that. Funny how the old lessons kept coming back. The three of them reminded her of a group of children playing with a chemistry set, never sure which mixture would explode.

'Well, now we have all that sorted out, have we any idea what they are going to say?' asked Joe. 'Just give us a rundown of what we know.'

'I had been led by Middleburg to believe that my father was heir to a big family fortune, and was accused of terrible crimes in the fifties which echoed something that happened long ago in France to an ancestor of ours called Gilles de Rais. But, according to the papers and letters I have seen, my father was framed by people, cousins of his, who filled him with drugs and meanwhile accused him of the same kind of terrible things – linking him with the black magic and murders perpetrated by the wilder Californian communes – obscene crimes and murders, sometimes of children, like a Manson only worse. He was accused and brought to trial and imprisoned for life. There was some legal problem with the evidence, the Mexicans claimed him and kept him on death row while they sorted it out, but then it seems he died. I was brought up in the shadow of these accusations, but unaware of them, by old aunts and people who only hinted but never spoke out. And then when I reached eighteen or so, I found many of the people I trusted were in league with, or were employed by these same plotters. And now a few days ago, I discover from Middleburg that it was all baloney and that really I am the daughter of a Nazi war criminal. With some kind of perverted logic, he thought he would break me in to that idea by originally pretending I was the daughter of a multiple sex killer. Don't ask me why; something to do with a Nazi guilt complex. On the 24th August I shall be twenty-five according to their reckoning, I think that is the important moment for them. This huge company they have built on my father's money could perhaps, technically, be mine on that date. That is why they want me there. But there must be more to it than that. On the other hand, this could all be pantomime.'

'There is a whiff of the CIA about all this,' said David. 'It could be bigger than we thought.'

They looked at each other.

'It's the weirdest thing I ever heard,' said Joe, at last, 'and, believe me, I have heard weird.'

Marie thought of something.

'I don't think Felipe died at all. You remember Felipe, Joe? He was taken away in an ambulance. It was a sham. It's all down to Middleburg. He loves playing Prospero.'

'Well,' said David, 'we had better plan for this party. Only a fortnight away. What do we need?'

'Do you have a gun?' Joe asked him.

'Can't say I do.'

'I have,' said Joe, adding, with a cowboy accent, 'Took it off one of them cavalry boys.'

'Really?' asked Marie.

'Nope. At least, not the last bit. But I have a gun.'

'Do you think we'll need one?' asked David, with a hint (Marie thought) of alarm.

'Someone fired a warning shot when we went over to look at the place a few weeks ago,' said Joe. 'I'll bring it along.'

'If anybody's going to do any shooting, it should be me,' Marie said. 'It's my quarrel, my father, my life.'

'I have to go,' said David. 'Sorry. Late for a meeting.' He made a gesture with his arms of hopeless possibility as he left the room. He wasn't going to shoot.

Marie watched him leave. He was attractive: engaging, charming. She couldn't help loving the boy who had lain with her under the stars – but somehow she didn't quite trust the man. He had had the chance when they were together and he had taken the path well-frequented. Did she trust anyone? Joe drank his coffee and kept his counsel.

'Do you think I should reply?' she asked. 'It says RSVP.'

'No need,' said Joe. 'He knows the white squaw is coming. He hear the tom toms.'

* * *

Sitting together in the broad front seat of the delivery van as it chinked and rattled along, its back piled high with cases of wine, they discussed the evening ahead, how the boys could keep an eye on the proceedings without being caught, and the strange history of the castle itself. The boys were jolly. It was an adventure. She felt unprepared.

There was something constant, reassuring and helpful about Joe, but intuitive as well and full of surprises. She felt she could spend her life with someone like that, not David who she kept at arm's length. She loved the idea of him, he attracted her, but there was a question mark over his priorities. She could tell he loved the sniff of money with which Middleburg had surrounded her. What would David do if the money wasn't there? Would he grow cabbages with her or take to the open road?

'You're quiet,' he said, breaking in on her thoughts. 'Apprehensive?'

'Middleburg always likes to keep you on your toes. I don't know what to expect. I don't know what he wants. He feeds on uncertainty. That I *do* know.'

'At least his wine order is predictable,' Joe told them. 'He likes big Burgundies – and of course Alsace.'

The late summer evening was only just beginning to show signs of that liminal moment when, it is said, the other world impinges on the human one and the day turns to dusk, but the castle was already ablaze with lights as they drove up. The whole place was floodlit and the sound of a distant band could be heard as Joe's Chevy van settled its tyres onto the gravel. All the appearances of a party about to go into full swing were there. It lacked only one thing: people. No one else was on the steps. No other car was drawn up.

'I'll go in, as arranged,' said Marie.

Now the moment had come she felt understandably nervous. What

403

was she doing in this huge place called nightmare where so many horrifying things had supposedly been done so many centuries ago, and so many bones of boys and girls had supposedly been found a mere matter of a decade or so since? What did Middleburg call them? Privileged visitors. She felt like the little fly going up the spider's staircase.

She got out of the car and the two men watched and waited while she climbed the steps to the great front door. Her bones felt sullen and heavy as she dragged them up the flight. Nothing happened as she reached the top and waited, so she pushed the door, which swung open, and disappeared from their view inside the castle perilous.

A burst of music and party noise greeted her. She found herself once more in the large baronial hall with the various small chambers and cloakrooms leading off it. There were the same oaken chairs and table, the ancestral portraits and heads of various beasts killed by the castle's occupants, there was armour, there were swords and pikes, even one or two cannon balls. The party itself seemed to be going on beyond the two big double doors that faced her, leading to the refectory. She was glad that she had put on a pretty red dress, because she liked the dress, it went well with her bright hair, and of course she had worn it just in case the hosts really meant a party and were not just playing a trick. You could never tell with Middleburg and company. There was a notice on the door: *Presentation to Miss Marie Messinger on the Occasion of her 25th Birthday.*

She pushed open the door to find herself, not in a party surrounded by people and champagne, but alone on the refectory hall's elevated stage. She had been told it had been designed to be suitable for visitor and staff entertainments, presentations and shows. As well as stage curtains, it seemed to have a thick white sound-proof partition, rather like a fire curtain, so that the stage could become a chamber for small meetings and discussions, closed off from the main body of the hall. It was dove-white, a little like an operating theatre. Any time now, she thought, nurse will come, give me an injection, fit me into a surgical straitjacket and I'll wake up again in Beverly Hills. At that moment there was a further burst of laughter and chatter and snatches of conversation from the direction of the white fire curtain and she saw that a movie had been projected onto it from somewhere behind her.

It was showing, as she now perceived, a piece – or home movie – about an elegant party. Hollywood folk, she supposed. But as she looked, she thought she began to recognise some of the people it featured. It was like a dream. They were playing her a dream.

A chair had been considerately placed for her to sit and watch, with a table beside it on which stood a glass of champagne, but for now she remained on her feet, spellbound. It was, she felt, like the moment before dying when all your life comes back. She held on to the back of the chair, giddy.

The background music and party hubbub continued, but there were also half-heard snippets of conversation, voices she recognised. And there were, inevitably, the Holdsworths, lots of people from Merrymaids whom she knew, people from London, the squatters and, yes, even Daddy 'Oh, man', Mrs Izzard and Fist were there. Fist showed his fist and grinned hugely. The housekeeper and factor from Castle Fairlie were there, the well-fleshed and oily Prelati and the plump Francesca, reminding her of happiness and sorrow in Cannes, sex-mad Harvey too. Grindlay was there. David was there (why had he said nothing to her about it?) but not Joe. There was Mr Merriman, smiling the smile, a pretty girl on each arm – one of them, she saw, was Margot (who had also said nothing). There were executives. There was long-legged Tamara from TOJI's head office. There were expensive looking women and powerful men, at least two of them ambassadors if they weren't Hollywood bit part players, but at the head of them all were Middleburg and his faithful Ariel, Brickville, bathed in a kind of aura she had not associated with them before. They exuded power and dark magic. They seemed anointed with gold.

It was a trick, of course, a grotesque charade. At least, she thought, I might as well enjoy it. She sat down and drank from the glass, feeling a little like Alice in a strange new and not altogether appealing wonderland. She was surprised there wasn't a label on the glass saying 'Drink me'. Oh no, she was mistaken. There was, tucked under the flute. The champagne was excellent.

As soon as Marie sat down, everyone on screen stopped talking. And then they started clapping. Marie didn't know what to do so she stood up and curtseyed as she had been taught at school, then she sat down again. That seemed to go down well. Middleburg and Brickville advanced to centre screen.

'Here she is,' said Middleburg.

'The heiress,' intoned Brickville, psalmically.

Everything they said seemed to draw a reaction from the crowd.

'Stepping straight into Forbes Magazine,' said Brickville.

'Wow,' went the crowd.

'Sitting on the board,' said Middleburg.

'Attagirl.'

'Shaping the destiny of this great nation,' declaimed Brickville.

'Rah rah rah.'

'We are all friends here,' declaimed Middleburg, 'and we have drawn wide to bring some of you from your home across the pond, to our home here in the US of A…'

Cheers.

'…Take some champagne with us, Marie, lift high the glass, and in a few minutes we will drink your health, and ours…'

More cheers.

'But first mingle awhile, greet the long-lost faces, savour the moment, carpe the diem and be the most favoured guest of The Other Judas, Inc, Charity Extraordinary, known to the world as TOJI, the brand you feel at home with – TOJI at home, TOJI away, TOJI tomorrow, TOJI today! But … and it is a big but … we must never forget the name Messinger – the power behind the TOJI throne.'

Loudest cheers of all.

'The brand your father built and that from now on, you will share with us as our newest and youngest vice president.'

Cheers to lift the roof.

'You see how much they love you,' said Middleburg, 'but we had the party without you because you are so bad at turning up. Hold on, though, now. Stay where you are and I'll be with you in a minute.'

All well and good, she thought, if you like Marie Celeste presentations, but she could not tell whether she was in a ceremony or a charade.

The sound went off and the screen went blank. She got up from the chair. Far away, up the staircase at the end of the hall, she could hear someone calling her name.

'Marie … Marie…?'

She followed the voice up the flight until she came to a door that looked as if it were furnished with high-powered locks but which was, however, open. She entered the room because it seemed like an invitation but it almost immediately closed behind her. On the floor was an apparently unconscious woman in the uniform of a nurse, or medical security guard, or both. Was this for real or part of the play? She began to realise she had been asking herself this question most of her life. At this stage the play started to go wrong.

'Ah, there you are,' a man's voice said, suddenly, almost in her ear; a voice she seemed to recognise. 'She's not dead, you know. Yet.'

It was the kind of moment when you wish you were a ventriloquist's dummy with a head that goes round 180 degrees. She half-managed it to 90, when a blindfold was place over her eyes and she was pulled backwards onto the floor, with a pinion hold round her arms. Girls at school used to do this kind of thing to unpopular colleagues. It had happened to her.

'You don't know me,' the same voice went on, 'and I don't know you. That is the way I like it. You chose a bad day when you came here. Because…'

It was a thin, scholarly voice with a slight German accent.

'Because what?' she asked, fighting down panic tinged with anger.

The man sounded so civilised. He was standing very close to her and now started very slowly moving towards her like a steam-roller, pushing her backwards by the sheer force of the air between them.

She was back in the nightmare in the shed at the docks.

'…because … I can't remember,' he said.

'What are you doing here? Do you live here?' she asked, trying to play for time

'Of course I do, it's all mine.'

'What is it you want? I have been invited here.'

Would he be swayed by an appeal to his sense of hospitality? It was hard to control the tremor in her voice. The adrenalin was kicking in.

'Invited to meet me,' he said, as if it was the most obvious thing in the world.

'And who ... who are you?'

Her knees were shaking.

'I am a patient. I have been patient.'

'You are patient? You are a patient? You are not very kind to your nurse.'

She was saying whatever came into her head. It might rub him up the wrong way but she couldn't help it.

'Oh but I am kind. I am going to do to you what I do best.'

'And wh ... what is that?' she stammered.

'I'm going to measure you and then I am going to kill you. Or I might kill you first.' Oh my God. He said it so calmly, so plausibly, she could see exactly why it might make sense for him to do it.

'I would rather you didn't.'

'Of course you would. That is what they all say. Or words to that effect. But first I have to measure your sex. That is really my skill, my claim to fame as you might say.'

'How do you measure sex? It is surely something you cannot measure.'

'You're wrong. I can measure it very well. I have many interesting measurements in my files.'

He had produced a tape measure and spread it across her breasts. This was becoming annoying.

'Stop that at once! What has got into you?' she asked, but he sniggered: 'The more you resist, the better the result.'

Where were Joe and David when she needed them?

'I am a geneticist. I measure sex. It is tidier that way and more enjoyable. Your breasts are six and a half per cent larger than the Caucasian norm. Colour of eyes?'

'What has that go to do with it?'

409

'It is an added bonus if you have eyes of different colours. Do you have eyes of different colours?'

'Yes!' she said. She might as well have a look at this lunatic before he killed her.

Tearing her blindfold off, he gripped her shoulders and gazed deeply into her eyes. From a distance you would have thought the man was tall and distinguished-looking but close up the mouth was slack and the eyes glazed. There was a ghost of a bubble at the corner of his lips. It had become a nightmare castle indeed.

'Liar!' he screamed. 'You do not have eyes of different colours. Your eyes are the same colour. Do you understand? THE SAME COLOUR!'

'Please don't shout,' she said.

It seemed to calm him for a moment.

'You have no idea what the loss of your family, your city, your country, your beliefs, your very reason for living does to a man,' he said. 'It is absolutely shattering. In the end you lose your mind. Nothing can make up for that.'

He might have been pleasant-looking once, but there were stains on his waistcoat and now an odd look of hatred entered his own identical eyes of dusty, pale grey-blue.

'Now you'll see...' he threatened, kneeling down and raising his arm towards her. 'Now you'll see.'

'Stop it,' she cried. 'What do you think you're doing?'

He was just reaching up inside the hem of her dress with a hand on her thigh and his tape measure at the ready, when there was a sound like a pistol shot and the man fell to the ground where he crouched like Caliban. She looked round and a male nurse, who looked like a policeman trying to keep his identity secret, was curling up the tongue of a bullwhip which he had cracked within an inch of the man's face.

'I know who you are,' the man snarled. 'I'll send for you in the night and we'll start the tests in the small hours when you're at your lowest. Then we'll see who cracks the whip. First you'll cry like a baby and at the end you'll be howling like an animal. I have seen it happen, time and again.'

'He's one of Middleburg's lot,' said the secret policeman. 'He thinks he's Dr Mengele or someone. Quite possibly, he is. Sorry about that. I don't know how he got out. His room's normally locked and he's under twenty-four-hour surveillance, but they were going to move him for the presentation. He's been so quiet recently and he was meant to be sleeping now. He must've put his medication down the toilet. Or down her throat,' he indicated the prone figure.

'Is she all right?' Marie asked, thoroughly shaken.

The man examined the woman cursorily and took her pulse. 'She's fine. It looks as though she took the tranquillisers.'

'Someone should be spoken to,' said Marie, feeling not unreasonably angry. 'I could have been killed. Who did you say he was?'

Then the man said something, as he handcuffed her assailant, which completely took the breath out of her. 'He thinks he's your father.'

'My father?'

'Don't worry about that. He thinks he's everyone's father.'

'What is his name?'

'Ask him yourself.'

'OK. What is your name?'

The man who was her father seemed to have gone into a poached egg state but at that moment his eyes opened wide and he giggled.

'Daddy,' he said.

For a moment, she was so shocked she almost believed him.

'This is what comes of too much study,' said the secret policeman. 'It addles the wits.'

'Poor man. What have they done to you?' she asked the crouching figure.

'Best get out of here,' said the secret policeman. 'They say madness is catching. Go back down the stairs to the room you just left.'

The room was still there with the same seat beside the same little table, but the champagne had disappeared and there was now another chair set beside the original one. The same white partition, which served as a screen, was still in position. She gazed at the screen, waiting for something to happen. A stage seemed a funny place to have a meeting but nothing Middleburg did was without purpose. The stage was set.

The nurse left the way he had come and Middleburg entered, walked over to shake her hand and stroked her arm, making her flesh crawl.

'Not so long ago, when I left your house, I had hoped never to see you again,' she said, by way of conversation. 'But now hardly a day goes by but we meet once more.'

Middleburg smiled to humour her. 'I sometimes have that effect on people,' he said. 'Happy birthday.'

'It's not happy and it's not my birthday. You have gone to a lot of trouble to get me here.'

'Yes. That is what I have enjoyed about it.'

'I thought for a while I had escaped you,' she said.

'There is no escape. We can talk freely now as we are alone.'

Middleburg smiled. He motioned at the walls around them. There was no sign of the attendant spirit who had placed the chairs and taken away the champagne glass, replacing it with a carafe of water and a glass tumbler.

'We have had you under surveillance ever since you were born,' Middleburg said, 'and, maybe to your surprise, ever since you left us in Beverly Hills; ever since you thought you had left us. Mrs Holdsworth was beside herself with disappointment at your departure. I wondered where all the psychic energy was coming from. We do have séances. Hitler had them, you know.'

'I didn't know. But I imagine he'd do anything.'

Middleburg ignored her remark and continued, 'I think she has a crush on you.'

'Poor Mrs H. I think I would have had a crush on Quasimodo if I had been married to Mr Holdsworth.'

The evening seemed full of disagreeable thoughts.

'Mr Holdsworth is not so bad.'

'No, he is worse.'

As they spoke, the screen lit up with a picture of a large, beamed meeting-hall – the refectory, in fact – fitted with rows of long tables and benches. As she watched, a man in a white coat and surgical mask entered and sat down somewhere near the front. Then another came in. And another. The benches slowly filled up with more and more people in white coats and masks. The masks especially made them seem weird, unearthly. Gentle but insistent warbling from the organ – she had noticed the pipes above a console in the far wall – filled the empty spaces of the air and joined the walls together. The humans moved like goldfish between them. Nothing that happened under the authority of these people happened by chance. Cuckoo.

413

'Handel,' said Middleburg, indicating the music, 'you like it? "The Cuckoo and the Nightingale." A good German Englishman. Only I became a good German American.'

'Are you good?'

'Depends what you mean.'

'What are these people here for? Some kind of speech?'

'No, they have come to see you.'

'Me? Why would they want to do that?'

'Recently, as you know, The Other Judas combined forces with this big chemical and pharmaceutical company of ours called Messinger. Well, to be honest, Messinger took them over. They were having cash-flow problems while we had so much cash it was … well, we needed to do something with it. We were originally German prisoners – scientists and so forth whom the US Army thought could be useful to national security, otherwise they would fall into Russian hands – it was called Operation Paperclip as your friend Margot told you the other day.'

'I'd heard of that vaguely but didn't know what it was.'

'They were experimental physicists, biologists, geneticists, physicians and chemists like me.'

'And of course they'd had people to experiment on, in places like Dachau.'

'You have been reading too much of your *Daily Mail*,' he said.

'And you perhaps have not been reading it enough.'

There was a pause while they looked at one another.

'Why are they wearing masks?' she asked. 'The effect is disagreeable.'

'They work in a clean-room where there are no pathogens. When they go back inside, it is better that they take a minimum of pathogens with them.'

'What have I got to do with all this?'

'Your father helped us start the company – luckily it happened before he became confused ... or out of control as some said.'

'I thought my father was meant to have French connections, not German.'

Something Joe had said came to her mind. 'Nothing these people do is coincidental.'

'I explained that to you. Your father was German. He came from Alsace which is historically Germany, and which will be Germany again. He was heartbroken when your mother died. You should be grateful to him for thinking of your future and arranging to save your life before he went off the rails.'

'Do not remind me. I am ashamed to be alive.'

'That is ungrateful of you for it was your father providing for you that gave you a safe haven.'

'I am not grateful to him for leaving me in the dark all my life.'

'Your mother was half-German. Half-German and half-Scottish – genetically an unfortunate mix. The Celt and the Saxon have never been easy bedfellows.'

'What happened to me after she died?'

'You were saved and spirited away to your Scottish grandmother and her two sisters. I won't go into how you got there. I believe we arranged it via Sweden. Such a shame your grandmother died soon after you arrived.'

'And my father? Presumably he was in better form in those days?'

'Oh yes. He was very fit. As I told you, he was a top Nazi scientist and research professor. Aviation medicine, the study of what the body can stand in extremes of speed, height and cold. Physiology, biology, that sort of thing. Extremes of psychological stress. His department also studied genetics and the physics of ageing. He was, in fact, nominally in charge of Dr Mengele, a man with a second-rate mind. Your father was picked up by the Americans in West Germany, as I was, after the fall of Berlin.'

'You mean potential war criminals were given shelter by the Americans when they should have been at Nuremberg facing trial? How many were there?'

'Some say fifteen hundred, others estimate up to four thousand – but many of them were bona fide, not even Nazi Party members.'

'But that's ... that's a huge number. How many war criminals in that lot?'

'We do not call them criminals. They were patriots. The figure is not currently available.'

'Was there no shame? No feeling of guilt?'

'Here you betray your English education. We felt no guilt. It was considered necessary for national security. Stalin killed four times as many people as Hitler. The Soviets became the big threat as soon as the war ended. Many of these people still work here.'

'Do people outside know about it. In America?'

'Not very much. Openness is one thing, but national security is everything.'

'So all that stuff about Laval and those hideous crimes was untrue?'

'We had your great-aunts to think of too. We hit on it as a way of making them feel ashamed of your father and obliging them to bring you up under a cloud. They did not like it of course, but that way you could be an unperson, hidden for a time, and eventually returned to your real father as he wished. There had to be a reason why your father was not around. The next best thing to a Nazi scientist with a background in experimentation was a sex scandal. Don't get me wrong. I am an authority on Gilles de Laval, Baron de Rais and probably know as much about him as anyone living. The man fascinates me. I enjoyed playing that game. He was almost certainly guilty. But that was then, 500 years ago.'

'You were right. I'd rather have a killer sex maniac for a father than a Nazi who experimented on people and tortured and killed them in a concentration camp.'

Privately, she wondered if this were true, but it suited her argument to maintain it. It was bad enough to have either of them in her poisonous family tree.

'Exactly. Even so, I hope I may be able to change your mind. I have told you part of the story but not all. The truth is stranger still.'

All the while, to add to her sense of dislocation, the men in white masks and coats kept on coming and coming. The hall on the screen in front of Marie and Middleburg was now nearly half-full.

'I am not sure I want to hear any more,' she said. 'If they want to see me, why is it all on screen?'

'They have seen you. The only thing was, it wasn't you, was it? Or was it? Did you make the film with us or was it someone else, your *Doppelgänger*? As I have said, we never know if you are going to turn up.'

'They have seen me? How can that be?'

'Wait awhile and you will see. A glass of wine before the presentation?'

She made no response and sat like a wax doll. She wanted someone to pick up her arms and legs and waggle them about so she could walk. She wondered whether Middleburg had studied hypnosis.

Middleburg motioned her again to have a drink and indicated that she should sit down in the chair.. On the table, beside the jug of water and her tumbler, there now stood a bottle of wine in a cooler, along with two wineglasses – she noted that the wine was a 1963 Corton-Charlemagne, one of Joe's favourites. – They seemed to have appeared; she had not noticed them arrive. He opened the bottle and poured a glass of wine whose gorgeous, deep golden-yellow hue was positively mesmerising.

'You will have a little wine,' he said. It seemed more of a command than an invitation.

Marie hesitated for a moment, remembering the tricks that the Holdsworths used to play with drinks in Beverly Hills, but then she thought, why not? She could hear Joe advising that the man, though essentially suspect, had some superficial standards. He wasn't going to tinker with a Corton-Charlemagne.

'Yes, I will. Thank you.'

'The visitors come to the refectory here and unwind,' he told her. 'We have some good times here. It is good to have song and laughter and wine, no?'

Middleburg poured a glass for her, pushing the glass over to her on the polished wood as though in a game of chess, raising his own queen in salute. They looked at each other.

'To "Come What May",' he said.

'To "Come What May",' she agreed.

The wine was very good. She told him so. 'Like mother's milk,' she said. 'Not that I would know about that.'

'It is from an estate we own,' he said. 'It oozes its way around the buccal cavity, tickles the epiglottis, plays deliciously with the adenoids and lingers like a lover all the way down the larynx, ending in a curlicue of warmth around the oesophageal sphincter. Not my words, but those of a review in the Journal of Medical Science, out next week.'

'In spite of that, I still like it,' she said. He could play at being charming but she refused to be charmed. The script was not working out at all as she had imagined. Or was he once again giving her a tall story? The wine was stronger than she had thought. Drink me.

'About that other girl,' she said.

'What other girl?'

'That other girl pretending to be me.'

'Is there someone else? You sound like a jealous wife!' he laughed.

She thought it better not to air her doubts to him now. Her doubts were her weapons. Could it be that he had entrapped and groomed another girl like herself? Had he got the girl into his web, stirring like a half-dead fly, as she herself had stirred? How many had he got? And to what use was he putting them? Well, at least she had one answer to that. He was making this one pretend to be me.

Middleburg betrayed no emotion. He understood that she spoke, when she did speak, from a position of impotence. The web was tacky and her wings were pinned.

'The workforce is still arriving. All these people work for the firm I founded with your father,' he said, pointing at the screen.

'With my father's money?'

'We funded the firm with the help of the United States. They had the money. They wanted our genius.'

'And the name Messinger?'

'Our name was actually von Melder – my cousin's also, your father's. The name Melder in German can mean a messenger or an orderly. It has a military ring. The Germans like that. The symbol of the messenger is Hermes, the winged-heeled god – a sign today that denotes Messinger Research & Development to the Government and medics, and Messinger Chemistry and Bio-diversity or MCB, now making everything from toothpaste to detergents, skin rejuvenation creams and painkillers for the TOJI brands, as well as some very dangerous things for the Government. It is much simpler and more comforting for the shareholders and the government if some members of the family are still involved in the company. That is why you are going to be Messinger. And if you are going to be married to Mr Drummond, you will be Drummond-Messinger. It rolls off the tongue very nicely, don't you think?'

'So how come you're called Middleburg? Is that your real name?'

'Almost. I discarded the name von Melder when I left Berlin in 1945. I used Mittelberg for the Americans in Germany and changed it to Middleburg when I settled here. America is full of names like that.'

'Can I depend on anything you say?'

'Lies are no good unless there is a high proportion of truth.'

'So why did you take over The Other Judas?'

'We didn't take it over. We started it. Quite early on, we needed another name for the consumer division of Messinger's. We were a serious company making serious things like medication and pest control and fertilisers and even military materials of various kinds. A charity was the masterstroke. As long as you run a small part of the company for no profit, you can have it as a tax-deductible holding company. We needed something that sounded fun, something that gave people a lift when they were saying it, something that created goodwill. The Other Judas, Inc or TOJI for short. TOJI. You can like it without trying. Messinger was altogether too grim. You want to shoot the Messinger? Go ahead. No one wants to shoot TOJI – the company that grew and grew. Quite early on it had to stop being a charity for tax reasons.'

'So you had already started The Other Judas when you merged? It belonged to you anyway.'

'There is no law against buying something from yourself so long as the companies are separate. The companies are now together but separate. Everything is above board. Our shareholders are over the moon. Of course, we do have other companies.'

'And why did you spell Messenger with an i?'

'Because we couldn't register it with an e. Actually, the i makes it more distinctive. I am tempted to call myself Messinger. Middleburg does sound too European. But, hell, I've kind of got used to it now.'

* * *

'So you were a Nazi?' she asked.

She knew the answer to that one but she had to say it. He laughed.

'We all were. You had to be if you wanted to get on. That mad fellow, my cousin – your father – developed something quite unprecedented and of course he had plenty of helpers to work with him. The Nazis were really excited about his project – another month or two and who knows! We might have…'

Here he threw up his hands with a graphic, no-use-crying-over-spilt-milk gesture.

'We were not interested in your father's so-called crimes, only in his genius,' Middleburg continued. 'When he came over here to work on projects of national security, we promised to help him build a successful company to market some of his more peaceful ideas – cosmetics, anti-ageing creams, shampoos – so long as he helped us with other things. It all worked well for many years, but in the end he started to become ... well ... you have seen how it is with him. So we decided to merge the businesses.'

'You mean that man who tried to mess with me just now really is my father?'

'I do mean that. He is a man to be proud of. His whole world crashed about him and he made a new one. Why should he not be?'

'My father? I am dizzy with the things you tell me.'

'We came from a country in ruins. The kaleidoscope shook – and here we are again. You with a damaged father and I with a cousin. You should be overjoyed.'

All her life she had been looking for a father and a family but a father like this was not what she had ever imagined, missed or wanted. As for family, they appeared to be exclusively businessmen whom no one could call comforting, loving or cosy. All in all, the mixture of these considerations coupled with the events of the last half hour, to say nothing of the last few years, were suddenly taking their toll, breaking down her resistance. She felt weak, tearful, grateful, joyful, alarmed, suspicious.

'Someone suggested you work under the auspices of the CIA,' she said, reaching for something that did not directly concern her own journey of discovery – although she realised as she said it that perhaps it did, since she was the company mascot now: the pampered goat, or schnauzer.

'We never answer questions like that,' he said with an amused air, 'but it is right you ask questions now. That is why we are here. Soon your father will come down, heavily sedated, and acknowledge the workers' applause. It is a pity you see him now like this. He was a lion when he arrived here. Much untruth has been written about him. Those experiments people speak of were either conducted by Mengele, unauthorised, or were undertaken by your father himself for the good of humanity. Consider his work on antibiotics. In Germany, even before the war, he was right at the front in the development of sulphur drugs. And he was still developing antibiotics afterwards. You have probably been injected with Miramycin after a bug bite or wound that turned septic. It has saved tens of thousands of lives.'

'But he is still a monster. I am the daughter of a monster. Are you a monster too? A war criminal?'

'We don't use that word. The past is hidden. The workers do not talk about it. Many of them are Germans ... the families of those who have settled here.'

'And some of them are Nazis...'

'Only some. A little more wine before we start the presentation?'

'No more, thank you.'

She was still feeling the effects of her first two glasses, though her head was usually strong. Or was it simply her situation here and the nature of the story she was hearing that made her feel odd, displaced, as if she were taking part in a masque or charade, or what the Aunts used to call Dumb Crambo?

'Maybe a little water,' she said.

'I am presenting their co-founder's daughter to them, of course,' he told her, as he poured her a glass from the carafe. 'You are going to sign a document on the occasion of your twenty-fifth birthday and they are going to applaud you as a substantial shareholder in the company. They might even sing you one of their German songs. I think they will for I have heard them practising *"Guter Mond, du gehst so stille"*...'

'What project are they working on at the moment?'

'Can't say, I'm afraid.'

'But as a substantial shareholder surely I have a right to know.'

'Not if it is a matter of national security.'

'Who are the other shareholders?'

'Private individuals, big funds, nominees.'

'Who are?'

'Can't say, I'm afraid.'

'There is one other thing. Why have you been watching me? Why can't you leave me alone?'

He shrugged. 'We have to keep an eye on you. You are going to be a very big shareholder and you are the daughter of one of the founders. We did lose you for a time in London but we soon caught up with you. We really couldn't have you mixing too much with other people. Your father dreamed of meeting up with you one day and telling you his story. So we softened the background to make him seem more … sympathetic. We owed your father that. Thanks to him and people like him we have in this country, I don't say the largest, but the most effective stockpile of chemical and biological weapons in the world.'

'And that will be his legacy,' she said. 'But if I may speak of myself while we talk about the world that you seem so fond of, what do you think a childhood like that did to me?'

'You were looked after. You were fed. You had your old nurse to love. Many of Germany's orphans would have given an arm and a leg to be brought up like that. To you, your father's legacy will be enormous. You will be many times a millionairess. To the free world, his legacy is that it is a free world.'

'And who said national security takes precedence over morality? Was that a corporate decision?' Her mind was on fire.

424

'That was your father's decision,' he said.

'And why do you operate from a castle and not just your office?' she added.

'I love the castle. That is why I showed you round, not so much for you as for me. Every time I do it, I discover something new. And now I remember, that is why I called you Marie. That was the name of Gilles de Rais' daughter. I was interested in him even then. We had both lost so much. It made a kind of sense at the time.'

'I am glad it made sense to someone.'

'And his castle did too, you see. I found it by chance in earlier days when I was poking around. It's a good front for a laboratory working on government projects. It says history, continuity, respectability, you see,' he told her. 'All these things we cherish. The offices and labs are out beyond the pleasaunce that I showed you, away from the prying eyes of the public. We have many other factories and workshops of course, throughout the USA and the world.'

It was all to make America safe and free, Marie thought. You had to admire the duplicity of this man.

'And why did you go through the charade of showing us round the castle when you knew my father's so-called crimes were never committed? Why did you give out that they were?'

'Just to show you the care we've taken to conceal your true past. As you yourself have said, you would rather be the daughter of a sex-fiend than a Nazi. I didn't want to reveal the truth until we had this conversation. The castle and everything all fitted in rather well. We had Timothy Leary here, you know. And Manson in earlier days. He said there were messages in the stone. We had a séance here. Quite horrifying, actually.'

Her host now took her by the arm. He was keen on touching. He was one of those rare and disconcerting older men who seem to get younger every time you meet them. But it didn't make her like him more. It was part of his sinister and ever-growing pharmacopeia.

'Now,' he said. 'This is the bit that concerns you here.'

She shrugged his hand away. 'And why, after all the lies you've given me, should I believe one word that you say now? How do I know that this isn't another lie, another of your stories covering something even worse, though I am not sure that would be possible.'

'You do not have a choice.'

He pointed at the screen again, at the men in white coats, now fully gathered. A man appeared (it was Middleburg) piloting a Marie (it did indeed look like her) through a doorway and onto the stage. How many Maries did this man have? Had they somehow managed to hypnotize or drug her into this? It felt shameful to see herself doing something of which she had no recollection. What else had they made her do?

But it could not possibly be her.

A round of applause from the assembled throng greeted their appearance. A sleek, keen man in a white coat was already on the podium, speaking into a microphone.

'That is the Chief Executive of TOJI, the consumer side of the business,' whispered Middleburg, 'Martin Haldermann.'

'And now, ladies and gentlemen, a round of applause for Miss Marie Messinger and Mr Felix Middleburg, Founder Vice-President of Messinger Incorporated.'

The clapping of hands rose to a crescendo as the man urged the white-coats on, raising his arms the while like a conductor. Then with a downward sweep, as if his hands were daggers, he cut them instantly short.

'Thank you, ladies and gentlemen, fellow-workers in our great enterprise. I should like to pay tribute to our other famous founder, cousin of Felix here, none other than Marius von Melder or, as we now know him, Marius Messinger who, though stricken with age and illness, has come down to wish you well – and to meet again his daughter, Marie. Ladies and gentlemen, I give you Marie and her father Marius.'

'Come on, Marie,' Middleburg whispered at the screen. 'Give them a little wave and for chrissakes, smile.'

The Marie on screen did it. Marie found herself doing it too. There seemed no reason not to.

There was now a slight commotion in the action on film, the madman who had said he was her father was being shuffled up the steps to the stage on the arm of the security nurse. As he arrived, there was an enormous cheer and some 'heiling' from the serried ranks. He half-raised a feeble arm, and was led towards the microphone. It seemed he was going to make a speech. He stood like that for a while, stirring imperceptibly like a willow on a hot day, the air moving languidly above his brow.

The pause was pregnant. But then, just as Marie thought it must now be time for someone to do or say something, the figure that had once been her father clutched the microphone and addressed the throng.

'It's all...'

'What is it all, Founder?' asked the Middleburg on film.

'It's all...'

'Easy now,' said Middleburg, easing him along.

'*Ist alles ... Scheiße.*'

There was a great triumphant blast from the mighty organ and the audience erupted when they heard the great man say it was all shit. They had never heard anything better, or funnier. Her father smiled profoundly as though he had imparted the Secret of the Grail. The security-nurse now took him by the arm and led him back towards the stairs.

I should try and talk to him, Marie thought. Not now, but soon, when he's having a quiet moment.

'Speech! Speech!' the audience demanded.

'He is a good German,' she heard someone say, in German.

'Heil ... heil ... heil!'

We're having a rally, she thought.

Middleburg now strode forward and addressed the throng.

'This won't take long,' he said, 'for I know you will be thirsty and they are even now preparing beer, bread and *Wurst* in the kitchen and we have our very own *Bierkeller* and *Fräuleins* to serve in it. But I just wanted to add a word or two about Marie, only child of my cousin, Professor Marius Messinger. Because he is now somewhat incapacitated, he has asked us to transfer much of his very large share in Messinger Inc to her and I know that her arrival will coincide with a new golden age for TOJI-Messinger. She will now be working with us, taking an active interest in all of you and learning what each and every one of you is doing for the cause.'

More muted applause.

'Now,' he continued, 'I understand you have been rehearsing a good old German song that all of us know. I ask you now to sing *"Guter Mond du gehst so stille"* for Marie von Melder.'

A small, energetic choirmaster in shorts emerged and stood at the front. At a signal from him, the organ played a quiet tuning chord. And then they were off.

'Guter Mond, du gehst so stille
Durch die Abendwolken hin;
Deines Schöpfers weiser Wille
Hieß auf jene Bahn dich zieh 'n.
Leuchte freundlich jedem Müden
In das stille Kämmerlein
Und dein Schimmer gieße Frieden
Ins bedrängte Herz hinein!' *

It was one of those simple melodies that go straight to the heart. It brought a tear to Middleburg's compelling eye, though to Marie's mind the spectacle of so many white-coats singing nursery rhymes was surreal. The last thing she wanted was to spend more time with these people who duped and drugged and ran secret empires and sang nursery rhymes. How could they reconcile such innocent words with their chemical and research activities? She wiped away her own tear now, attached, it seemed, to Middleburg's eye, to the German people's eye, by an invisible mutual nerve. Her head felt heavy. Her legs and arms felt heavy. Was it the wine?

The image rose before her eyes of a long life spent under control – not her control but theirs – and she began to feel so heavy that she really did not mind; it was really quite welcome. It was the feeling

---

* *Dear Moon, you ride so quietly*
Through the evening clouds.
The wise will of your Creator
Directs you in your course.
Kindly shine for the weary one
In the quiet little room
And your light will pour peace
Into the oppressed heart!

she had had in the house in Beverly Hills after Mrs Holdsworth had brought her bedtime drink. At the corner of the screen, her eyes became drawn to movement at the side of the hall where a passage led off to a buttery or refectory or under-croft, or god knew what. Yes, it was Joe in his white coat. He seemed to be standing there, taking it all in. Or was he under some kind of guard? She could not quite see, but a man who did look uncommonly like Fist was standing next to him.

'And now,' said the Middleburg on screen, 'and now, pray silence for the signing of the document by our birthday girl.'

Screen-Marie sat down at the small table that was on the stage, complete with pen and blotter. A man who looked like a company accountant – no, it was Brickville – approached the table with a document, which he presented with a bow, and Marie's screen double took up the pen and signed. This was the signal for universal acclaim and a bombshell burst of clapping.

'There's more,' said the Middleburg on screen, and the crowd fell silent. 'As if that wasn't enough on her birthday, I am happy to announce the forthcoming marriage of our shareholder colleague and birthday princess to Mr David Drummond who is with us today. Although not a German…'

A group sigh arose from a hundred throats, not unlike the sound you hear when someone finds a kitten shivering in the rain. David was in on it, somewhere. She gazed round at the hall, at the people, the Germans in their working uniforms. Then she saw David, suited and spurred, fulfilling his role as a sort of Student Prince bridegroom elect, lurking at the head of the passageway leading to the castle's buttery.

'…he loves us almost as much as he loves Marie,' Middleburg

continued, 'and he is a fine young man of good family who will also be working with us as a marketing executive. Soon our heir will have an heir of her own.'

The shock of seeing David caught up in this charade made Marie gasp. How could he have the nerve to be so two-faced?

Middleburg beckoned someone forward out of the crowd, and David stepped out of the mass of white-coats to stand beside him.

'No,' the real Marie found herself saying now in a small voice, though it seemed to have become massively amplified. She *supposed* she was the real Marie, though by now she could not be sure – she could be anyone.

'No.' It is sometimes the quietest voice that carries furthest. There was a buzz from the audience of puzzlement, incredulity and, yes, something else: anger. It was absurd, but it seemed they could hear her.

All the while Middleburg was saying things that made no sense to her, but the audience appeared placated. The screen Marie went ahead and signed anyway.

'*Danke schön, meine Kinder,*' Middleburg said, finally, 'now go and enjoy. Bier und wurst in the bierkeller!'

The crowd on screen stirred as if a gale were running through a field of flax. They streamed out through the entrance to the broad corridor where David had been standing.

Marie had to get out; the air seemed heavy as chloroform, the light dazzling, making her feel like a rabbit in a headlight. She would faint if she did not get some air. Everything seemed to happen very slowly. There had indeed been something in the wine. Was it LSD? Why had she thought he wouldn't do that? He could and would do anything. But why?

The partition, with its projected film in front of her, rose and at the same time seemed to dissolve as though she were now actually walking through the image and down steps that had been placed to allow her to descend. The hall that she had been watching presented itself as real. Most of the white-coats had already gone but the remaining few turned towards her in amazement. She walked forward into the hall, with Middleburg behind her.

'Where have they all gone?' she asked. 'There were hundreds here and now just these?'

'All done with smoke and mirrors, we couldn't spare them all from their work, it is too important, besides you are such an unreliable guest,' said Middleburg. 'Look how many Maries there are.'

Look look look look look, the voices said, as if from a multitude of Middleburgs. She glanced aside and saw that she too was reflected in a myriad of crystals.

'And which is the real one?' he asked. 'Indeed, is there a real one? That is the question we have to ask. That is the question you are asking yourself. For you don't even have a name. Just … Marie … Marie … Marie…' Middleburg turned, like a weathercock spinning in the wind, to watch her as she ran, in slow motion as it seemed, down the aisle of the meeting-hall heading for the door out into the garden, while the residual whitecoats moved forward and some reached out to clutch at her as she passed. They appeared not hostile but intense.

'*Achtung*!' shouted Middleburg.

Now the drug was really taking over. She was aware, as she ran down the passage past the kitchens, towards the garden door, that the white-coats were after her. It was like the last scene in Alice when all the characters turn into cards and fall upon her. She burst out of the back door and ran out into the pleasaunce, gulping the evening air as if she were drowning and at the same time looking for somewhere to hide – the gazebo for instance, but her previous visit suggested it provided little secrecy.

As if at a signal, fireworks started – stranger, more inventive fireworks than she had ever seen. They soared, they crashed, they banged with a brilliance that kept nailing her shadow to the lawn. There was one series that looked like a champagne glass fizzing with effervescence, another set of the figure 25 in the heavens surrounded by writhing serpents, there was one of a girl in a firework version of the dress she herself was wearing, that bore a certain incendiary approximation to her own appearance. And then, all at once, there was the messenger god, Hermes, in his winged sandals, descended from the heavens and blazing like the day. All the while, an unseen choir and orchestra gave a rendition, *fortissimo*, of the spooky and harrowing 'Dies Irae' from Mozart's last Mass.

In the *son et lumière* of this celestial virtuosity, Marie was able to pause as the white-coats paused: first, to look up – the display could not be ignored – and at length, to look around.

She had thought that the pleasaunce was deserted but she now discovered other figures were there, statues, she thought as her eyes became used to the low lights and half-darkness, lovers everywhere, priapic fauns and shepherds, lovely girls, people entwined, now disengaging, statues that grasped at her as she ran, becoming alive, woken by the terrible secret that she carried, which wasn't the sin of her father but her own … which was that she didn't know, had never known, who or what she was, in a country where that is the biggest sin of all.

She had to be alone. Her eyes moved to the maze. It seemed as good a place as any to escape pursuit. She could at least hide in there and escape later round the back of the castle to find Joe and his car.

And if he wasn't there, he would follow her wherever she was because the Red Indians are good trackers. He had told her so.

She looked back. Men in white coats were streaming out after her, but not very efficiently. They seemed to flounder around, like robots. There was a *mêlée* by the gazebo. Joe appeared and fired his starting pistol into the air to distract them from her. There was indeed no sign of David. She heard another shot and saw Joe fall, but she was already running for the maze. She had taken the plan of it home after her first visit and traced its ways, so she would have the advantage over her pursuers – and there was Fist himself, his face contorted with rage, at the head of the hounds, shouting at her – sounds but no words. And now she was in the maze and the pursuit fell away. She had no idea what would happen when she reached the centre and found the classical temple. There would be somewhere to hide. They would not find her there. She ran on, deeper into the labyrinth, surrounded by the high box hedge, forgetting some of the maze-map in her confusion, and then she began to feel that she was being followed by something else. 'These sensations can easily happen in a maze,' she remembered reading somewhere. She had liked the thought of it on a hot summer day, with friends, but now…? Another false turn. Did they keep panthers here? Or unicorns? There was something bouncing the turf behind her. Or was it the demon Baron who still haunted Bluebeard's castle and would not go back into his box? She felt hot breath on the back of her neck, turned a corner, looked behind her in dread, tripped, fell over – and found herself at the centre of the maze where Middleburg had said you learnt what was the worst thing in the world.

The worst thing in the world was, in fact, Middleburg himself, sitting outside the little Doric temple on what looked like a sacrificial slab of white marble. Inscribed below the pediment of the temple, in Roman capitals, were the words *QUIS EST ISTE QUI VENIT*. On a tray beside Middleburg was a bottle of champagne and two glasses. In the middle of the glade, near at hand, was a sundial, which wasn't giving anyone the time of day. She got up, collected herself and tried to stop the tremor in her voice and the shaking in her legs.

'Who is this who comes?' he translated. 'Champagne?'

She shook her head but he poured her a glass all the same. He seemed to find it amusing. Her head was clearing now.

'I confess,' he said. 'I do have a machine that blows hot air into your neck just as you pass. It's located in the hedge on the last straight, to encourage the sensation of pursuit. A nice touch, don't you think?'

'How did you get here?' she asked.

'A secret passage,' he said. 'What else?'

'Oh.'

'I hope you enjoyed the show. I ordered our advertising agency's film company to produce it with a little help from one of the big studios that we own. Of course we supplied the extras.'

'It was somewhat baroque,' she told him.

'Time for cards on the table,' said Middleburg. 'Close your eyes.'

He leant over and put his hands on her forehead, shutting out the light.

'Now open them again.'

She did not know how much time, if any, had passed, but they were back in the original white room with the chairs and the table and a screen, now blank, in front of them. She felt no surprise. He had exhausted her capacity for it.

'Much of what you have seen here is the result of a little magic and a combination of certain Messinger drugs – quite harmless, I assure you. Positively beneficial, some would say. The characters you have met here were mostly actors. The maze was an illusion. The dungeons, the sinister turrets, the great hall, the battlements, the charnel house, the very castle itself – none of them belonged to Gilles de Rais. It is just a turn-of-the-century millionaire's whimsy. The world is an illusion. It only exists because we are looking at it. More to the point, you yourself are very largely a figment of my imagination because *I* am looking at you. You have to ask yourself – do you really exist?'

He paused.

'You said it was time for cards on the table,' she said. 'I didn't know I held any.'

'You don't. The cards are mine. For a start,' Middleburg said, adjusting his bottom on the chair, 'I know I have mentioned it already but I must ask you absolutely to get rid of any idea that your father was a sexual predator and killer or that he was related to the Laval family. And, indeed, dismiss the notion that that poor mad person, who you saw in the castle was your paternal progenitor. In fact, I must ask you to get rid of any idea that you have a father at all. That was all a smokescreen to hide what I am and what I have been. I wanted some mystery and shame to surround you because I, your guardian, was that one thing you thought worse than a killer paedophile. The truth is that I was the Nazi scientist, nominally in charge of that idiot Mengele – though in my defence I have to say I was not aware of the methodology of some of his investigations. It would have been enough, however, to get me the death penalty at Nuremberg. We were all tainted – better to keep you dark and secret where you would become accustomed to shame. So, yes, I acquired you as an infant. And since you are mine, I thought it would be interesting to watch a girl develop into a woman, a whole personality, thinking she is free, while all the time, watching her, playing with her strings. You became my marionette. Using various contacts, I found you somewhere to live and people to look after you. Somewhere nice and out of the way.'

A burst of cheering arose from the general party buzz beyond the box walls of the maze and a Bavarian brass band began to play. Oompah oompah.

Middleburg watched for her reaction.

'You might at least look grateful,' he told her.

'You have cruelly given me no time to think about it,' she said. 'I need time. I had a family and now I have none. I thought I had bad blood because I had a sex-crazed father who tortured and killed young people and next I find I have a Nazi famous for concentration camp experiments. And now you tell me I do not have a father at all, though I must have had someone. And you ... What are you really? My father or my guardian? Or was that the hateful Brickville?'

'You should not be hard on Brickville. He is my partner in charge of the UK and Europe, and wonderfully attentive. A very necessary man. He kept an eye on you for nearly twenty years. But I am, and always have been, your actual – if unofficial – guardian.'

'I prefer to call you my voyeur, peeping in at my life, stalking me and watching me as if I were your guinea pig. You have been throwing the dice. I suppose you got into the habit of experimenting on living people in the concentration camps. I have been your creature, haven't I? Running free but not free?'

He ignored her question. 'Your parents were good-looking, doubtless intelligent people,' continued Middleburg, almost as though he did not hear her, 'but they died. I do not even know their name. So really, you only have me. I have been more than a parent. I have been, if not God, at least your guardian angel. Your name, incidentally, is not Marie. It is Lily. You were born of destruction; so much was destroyed in Germany. You were the one thing I brought out, the only thing except my genius and my secrets. You think you are yours but you are mine. I invented you. I re-created you. You were indeed my creature, my Coppelia, my marionette. You cannot exist without me. You have no record, no name, no passport, no identity, no past and no future unless I say so. Nothing can happen to you unless I let it happen. I have been your undiscovered god.'

'I am Marie not Lily. Lily is my daughter's name.'

'You have no daughter. Where is she? Do you have her birth certificate? Her identification?'

'No. But she is here.' Marie's hand was on her heart as her eyes filled, against her will, with tears.

'You are mistaken. I have no knowledge of her.'

'You cannot do this,' she said. 'I will go to the police.'

'They will deport you – and to where? The puppet master can do anything he likes. The puppet cannot take a step, cannot move without him.'

'But where is the puppeteer without the puppet?' She thought she had scored there. His next words struck a shard of ice into her heart.

'I do have another ward. A little girl of six. She had no father or mother but as far as I could ascertain they were in good health and were handsome. I have arranged for her to be looked after in a remote castle by two elderly sisters and an affectionate nanny. Perhaps, in due course, if things work out, you might be interested in meeting her. Comparing notes, as it were.'

The full extent of her and Lily's predicament now fell upon her like a dog from an aeroplane. Whichever way she turned, the options were closing. David would extricate himself if he wanted to, he was good at that, and what about Joe? He was already walking wounded in all likelihood; maybe he wasn't even walking.

Middleburg, as usual, guessed what she was thinking.

'I am afraid you must give up any hopes of your vintner boyfriend, presently in hospital, he would lose the TOJI as well as the Messinger business if I gave the word and without that he would be reduced to scratching around or even bankruptcy. He has already invested more than he can afford in his company. The word would be out. The office and the Rolls would have to go and really he would be in no position to marry or even cohabit. Such a shame because he seems an honest fellow. And he loves the wine business.'

It seemed she did not have a choice. The only way to destroy Middleburg would be from inside. There was no point in asking what he wanted from her. He wanted everything.

'It sometimes happens to the ventriloquist that he develops a bond with his dummy,' he said. 'Or the puppet-master with his doll.'

Yes, she thought, and then maybe it is the dummy who haunts the handler, answers back and takes control. She had seen a short story about it. It gave her a flicker of hope.

'I propose to make you my heiress,' he continued, calmly. 'I love you now as if I had made you myself. Like a father, if you will.'

'You're clever enough to know that I must hate you. Why make me your heir? Keep your friends close and your enemies closer. Is that it?'

'I have heard it said.'

'Are you agreeing that I am your enemy?' she asked. 'Or that you are mine? What is it you want from me?'

'This is an experiment,' he told her. 'Not a romantic novel.'

'If you make me your heir, shall I be free to do as I wish?'

'Free to do as you think you wish,' he said.

'The Holdsworths must go.'

'They have gone already. I have hired the Grimshaws.'

'Do I have any choice?' she asked.

'What do you think? You have to marry David Drummond. That is part of the experiment.'

'Yours or mine?'

'Everyone's life is an experiment. But to be able to experiment with another person's life, that is unusual. Almost as interesting as the things I used to do in my laboratory outside Berlin.'

'And what is my real name?'

'I really couldn't tell you what your name was. It is Messinger now. It will be Drummond in three weeks' time.'

Truth with Middleburg was like a Russian doll; each lie had another one lying inside it. She wondered for a moment whether he really was in love with her. That would be a tragedy for both of them.

'You talk of an experiment. How will it end?'

'I cannot tell how it will end until it ends. That is the point of the experiment. The experiment has a life of its own. It has a kind of beauty. It is looking for a truth.'

She had a moment of inspiration. Perhaps he wasn't the head man after all? Perhaps there was another someone experimenting with him.

'Who commissioned the experiment?' she asked.

'You do not need to know that. The instructions were clear on that point.'

'When will it end?'

'It will end when it ends. Not a moment before.'

'And when will that be?'

'It will end when we have the information we need.'

'When I die? Is that it? Have you injected me with something? Do you mean to kill me?'

'Your date of death is not known at this stage. Only when it happens can we process the report and be able to answer the questions you have been asking.'

'I want to see my daughter.'

'You do not have a daughter. You were very ill, remember. You should worry about yourself. The experiment is entering the next stage. You must consider this next move. Come. We will find a car to take you to your apartment.'

'It's not an experiment at all,' she said, 'it's just a game. A horrible, cruel, despicable game. You just can't give it up.'

'It is a complex version of a game God invented called Snakes and Ladders,' he said. 'And an experiment as well. I think you should come and live with me until your marriage. Your old room is waiting.'

At this stage it seemed better neither to accept or refuse, just to acquiesce.

'I may come and go as I please? And keep my apartment in town?'

'Of course. You are well now, apart from the stress you feel. You must suit yourself.'

'I don't feel stress,' she lied.

'Ah, but you will find that you do.'

He said it with such certainty that she felt again that familiar pang of fear. It would have been easier if he had appeared wrathful, resentful, indignant, punitive or even simply cruel. It was the impassivity that was alarming.

Above all else, that was the duty of the observer in the experiment:

detachment. What she had to remember was, nothing that happened was random.

'Is that the whole truth, then, at last? Everything out in the open?'

'Oh,' he said, smiling, 'if you believe that, you'll believe anything.'

* * *

Marie turned up late next day at the house where she had lived that strange, passionless, inert half-life, until suddenly thrown into turmoil by a man with a letter – a man evidently introduced by Middleburg himself.

The shadows were lengthening and the house was bathed in the russet pink of sunset. She noticed that the wax-leaf privet needed trimming. Last time she had been here, they had been preparing for a wedding, her wedding to Middleburg. Now it was for her wedding to David. It seemed ludicrous to think of herself in captivity here now. Middleburg appeared to take her new emancipation all in his stride. Indeed, he walked out to greet her as if he were about to present her with an award. The new husband-and-wife team, the Grimshaws, were lined up to greet her too. Middleburg pumped her hand and introduced them to her and they extended their congratulations.

'So pleased to meet you … Anything we can do…'

'We've heard so much about you.'

She smiled back. Quite edible smells were wafting out through the hall from the kitchen, so unlike poor Mrs Holdsworth with her unrequited passion and her frozen Hostess *boeuf en croute*. The Grimshaws were no worse than the Holdsworths. Indeed, Mrs G was evidently a better cook.

Middleburg smothered Marie in questions, how she had made the journey, what sort of day had she had, was she thirsty, had she eaten, did she like oysters, would she like to go up to her room now and so forth. The house received her back like a roast come back for a crisping. The first thing she noticed when she did go to her bedroom was the wedding dress she had chosen for her marriage to Middleburg hanging in the wardrobe. There was something terribly plausible about it all.

She insisted to Middleburg that she keep on her old room in Echo Park as a bolt-hole. No one made any fuss about it; everyone quite understood. She even allowed David to make love to her there, but it wasn't as good as under the stars. Nothing ever would be. She cried about it after he had gone, but she was becoming quite reconciled to the idea of a rich life with a good-looking plausible husband whom she had once loved more than life itself. The father of her child.

After all, what would she do if she didn't marry David? She would have nothing, not even a name. But afterwards, as Mrs Drummond and with money in her purse and a passport, anything was possible. Indeed, as she thought about it, it was not only possible but probable.

* * *

A week later, she was walking down 6th Street with Margot. She had given up her job at Merrymaids because Middleburg had told her it was not appropriate for the heir of the Founder-Vice President of Messinger's to work in what was little better than a clip joint. And somewhat contrary to his expectation, she had agreed with him. It would give her more time to work on thwarting him. Meanwhile, she was exercising her freedom in the new Middleburg ménage.

Mr Merriman, though annoyed at first on hearing her news ('lousy drop-out'), was impressed by her report of the impending ceremony and wanted her to go on writing songs for him. She said she would be happy to do that.

She and Margot had been idly looking at clothes downtown, as one does. They were moving towards Bullock's on Wilshire and at the same time vaguely looking for somewhere to eat.

'Have you settled on a date yet?' asked Margot. Marie had told her that Middleburg wanted her to marry David.

'Three weeks or so, I think.'

'You shouldn't do it.'

'I am no one. I don't exist. I'll be deported if I make a fuss. But where to – England? Germany? Even there I have no records. I am an unperson. I only exist because of Middleburg. Once I am Mrs David, I will have a footing. I can start making plans…'

'But you don't love him.'

'I do in a way. I did. He can help me find my child. It's his child too.'

'Middleburg will still have a hold over you, because that's his game…'

There was a pause and Marie took advantage of it. 'Margot, why did you appear in that film?'

'What film?'

'You know, the party one.'

'Oh, that. They asked us to keep it quiet. It was meant to be a surprise.'

'Who asked you?'

'The film company. It seemed OK. Quite witty, actually.'

'Oh.' Marie wondered for the first time if she really completely trusted Margot.

'You might have told me,' she said.

But there was still one person she trusted.

* * *

The wedding preparations were even more elaborate than for her aborted wedding to Middleburg himself. All the details turned out to be much the same as on that previous occasion, only more extreme. There were swags, there were festoons, there was bunting, there were curlicues, there was – everywhere – what the French call *signes extérieurs de richesse*.

It was going to be a civil ceremony; Marie didn't want to make vows before a priest and David, being divorced, seemed to have no firm opinion on the matter.

'Anything you like, hon,' he told her.

'Don't call me hon. That's what we used to call the Nazis. Huns.'

'OK, hon … I mean darling.'

David couldn't believe his luck in marrying his childhood sweetheart – that's what he kept telling everyone – who also happened to be his passport to untold riches (which he mentioned only to one or two close associates). In anticipation of this, he had given her an engagement ring featuring a diamond of unusual opulence.

The wedding itself passed in a blur. Middleburg gave her away, David and she said 'I do', David produced a ring and David's now divorced parents, each with a new, almost identical partner, sat on the groom's side of the enormous Middleburg drawing-room where the ceremony was held and gave her a glad if somewhat guilty eye. He had not told them about the child, which in other circumstances they would have said could not possibly be his, but they were conscious of their role in having driven the young Romeo and Juliet apart.

The reception was long and gastronomically acclaimed. Speeches of great weight and length were made. Marie drank too much and David drank much too much, but finally, far too late, the tumult and the shouting died and they went upstairs to their suite in the Middleburg mansion (so christened by Marie) where they were staying the night. They were catching a flight to Nice first thing in the morning and Middleburg said it would be madness to sleep anywhere else.

David had insisted that they should honeymoon in Cannes where it had all started.

* * *

Cannes was little changed, but it seemed completely different.

There were small, inevitable alterations. Marguerite had gone from her *plage*. There was a new face in the bar at the Bristol and a monster yacht lay in the harbour. When she had last been here, the place had been suffused in the rosy glow of youth and love. Now she wasn't so young any more and love was off the menu.

They hired a car and drove up to St Paul de Vence and the Colombe d'Or with the lovely swimming pool and the even lovelier food. They went to Antibes and Mougins and looked at the lavender fields. They bought perfume for her and aftershave for him. David ate a great deal, drank a lot of red wine and became noticeably plumper. They swam in the sea and had lunch on the beach under the awning. They even took out a sailing boat and forgot about the

446

strong wind that blows up around noon, making it hard to come back, but they managed it. He made love to her a great deal, usually in the hotel. They tried once under the stars, but the pine-needles prickled. This time, she took precautions. She thought he enjoyed the honeymoon. She hoped so.

Every now and then she would take out her passport and look at it carefully.

On their return to LA, they moved into the new house in Beverly Hills that Middleburg had bought for them. It had a swimming pool and a privet hedge and a maid who came every day, and a gardener to take care of the pool and the lawn. David had his first day at the office in Wilshire and came back full of his new job and his colleagues. She could tell he had an attractive secretary with whom he would soon be unfaithful to her. But it didn't upset her. They had married because they both needed to be married and that was an end to it.

Marie was glad that she had kept her old studio apartment. She needed somewhere to be alone. Somewhere to work. She told them she was starting a children's book about a girl who had lost her mother. Middleburg expressed an interest in publishing the story. He had even thought of a good ending, he told her. She didn't ask what it was.

* * *

Three weeks after the wedding Middleburg had arranged a big welcome-back supper party – how he loved a party, or so he said – in aid of which he had ordered a reputedly amazing conjuror to entertain the guests: just a few friends, about forty in number, mostly David's, at home. Marie's only friends were Margot and a few girls from Merrymaids, who were considered unsuitable, but they came anyway.

The conjuror spoke with a mid-European accent and had a familiar face, yet Marie was sure she had never met him. Of course, sometimes one does meet someone new yet strangely familiar, just as occasionally someone smiles at you in the street as though you both belong to a secret club, just for a moment as you pass. So it was with this man.

Something strange happened during his act. He had said he was going to make a member of the audience disappear and invited volunteers for the role. Marie put her hand up because she rather wanted to disappear. A couple of other girls also volunteered. He invited them all up on stage and she stood there, with the two others, grinning foolishly. To each one, he asked the question: why do you want me to make you disappear?

The first girl, name of Annabel, said, 'I want to see what it feels like.' Lots of laughter, barracking and feely jokes, some going a little too far.

The second one called Suzanne said, 'I don't mind disappearing, but I want to come back.' More laughter and cries of 'why?' and 'but it's good on the other side'.

But to Marie, he whispered a message of his own.

'I don't have to make you disappear. You can do it perfectly well by yourself.' He said it as though he knew her. That is magicians for you.

'Whisper something to me. Anything,' he told her.

'Thank you very much,' she said. 'You are a good magician.'

'She says she doesn't want to disappear. She's having a great time as it is,' he announced to the gathering. There were cheers and whoops and all the sounds of wealthy America at play. Thinking about it later, it seemed as though the man had indeed passed her a message and it gave her an idea. No – it gave her determination.

* * *

That was why, a few days later, she stood on the kerb by a dusty road near a gas station somewhere on the outskirts on the wrong side of LA. She was holding a bag which contained her passport, *The Oxford Book of English Verse*, her toothbrush and toothpaste, a hairbrush and comb, some minimal make-up in a sponge-bag, a spare shirt and jeans, two spare pairs of knickers and what money she had – about a hundred and fifty dollars. The clothes she had bought in LA were all left behind. A suitcase would have been too noticeable, too heavy.

She had told Middleburg and the Grimshaws and her husband that she was going to spend the evening at Merrymaids, would probably be late as befitted her last appearance at the place and that she would therefore stay at her little apartment in Echo Park. They made no trouble. Why should they? She was married. Independence up to a point had been part of her bargain with Middleburg. It seemed to her prudent, however, not to spend the night at her studio, which they would be watching, but to book into a little hotel nearby where no questions would be asked and no answers given. She had been sorry to say goodbye to her studio. She had grown to love the place, it marked a new chapter in her life, and it was the closest she had ever come to having a home of her own.

She had left before dawn and where possible had kept to the side streets, walking in darkness. There was hardly anyone about. By the time the sun was rising she was well into the suburbs.

Half an hour later, things didn't look so good. The thought crossed her mind that maybe he was not going to come. She paused to look at her map. A sudden wind blew the dust on the sidewalk and it rattled the empty beer cans. She was in a part of town she didn't know; pale houses stretched away on either side. For a moment, insecurity swept over her, shaking her resolve. He'd had second thoughts. Middleburg had found a way to stop him.

Well, if he did not come, she would catch a bus which would take her to some other dusty place where she could disappear. But could she? Would she? Perhaps there could be no future without a past. She had a vision of her comfortable bed in her new home and the sleepy tranquillity of life in the house in Beverly Hills. It had been safe and undisturbed. She hadn't had to make decisions there. She could still go back. Middleburg and the Grimshaws would look after her and Fist, or something worse, would see she never strayed. It was the sort of thought she'd had when first diving off the high board in the (unheated) school swimming pool, the plunge into the unknown.

And then she thought how meagre it would be to wait around until Middleburg considered the experiment was over. It was not an option. Besides, was that what he really wanted – the end of the game? She was sure he did not and neither, certainly, did she. She still had a few pawns to play – maybe more. Was that what the experiment was really about? She felt her childhood detach and float away from her like a spent rocket.

And now she stood waiting. She was early. She kept her head down and the hood of her coat up.

A bus drew up a few yards away from her, with people looking idly out of the window. What did they see? Was she there at all? She made a decision. But was it her decision? Had any of her decisions really been hers? She climbed aboard, paid the driver five dollars and made her way towards an empty seat. The bus pulled out and accelerated down the road to nowhere. Houses and trees flew by; the world was all before her.

Marie settled back into her seat and prepared to be swallowed up by the vastness of America.

Three minutes later, a Chevrolet van arrived at the gas station. The driver – with a slightly Red Indian appearance, a Chumash if you were a connoisseur of such matters – looked around, waited, checked his watch and the details on the bus stop, walked into the gas station to use the telephone and called a number. He spoke briefly, nodded, returned to his van and drove off in the direction the bus had taken.

Soon he too was no more than a wriggle of dust on the road.

The Wraggle-Taggle Gypsies

Three gypsies stood at the castle gate,
They sang so high, they sang so low.
The lady sat in her chamber late,
Her heart it melted away like snow.

They sang so sweet, they sang so shrill,
That fast her tears began to flow,
And she cast down her silken gown,
Her golden rings and all her show.

She plucked off her high-heeled shoes
A-made of Spanish leather, O,
She would in the street with her bare, bare feet,
All out in the wind and weather, O.

O saddle to me my milk-white steed,
And go and fetch me my pony, O!
That I may ride and seek my bride,
Who is gone with the wraggle-taggle gypsies, O.

O he rode high and he rode low,
He rode through wood and copses too,
Until he came to a cold open field,
And there he espied his a-lady, O!

What makes you leave your house and land?
Your golden treasure for to go?
What makes you leave your new-wedded lord,
To follow the wraggle-taggle gypsies, O?

What care I for my house and land,
What care I for my treasure, O?
What care I for my new-wedded lord?
I'm off with the wraggle-taggle gypsies, O!

Last night you slept in a goose-feather bed,
With the sheet turned down so bravely, O.
Tonight you'll sleep in a cold, open field,
Along with the wraggle-taggle gypsies, O!

What care I for my goose-feather bed
With the sheet turned down so bravely, O?
For I shall sleep in a cold open field
Along with the wraggle-taggle gypsies, O!

Postscript

Annie Jacobsen's definitive work *Operation Paperclip: The Secret Intelligence Program that Brought Nazi Scientists to America* has been a constant recourse for me in providing a factual background to what is essentially fiction in T*he Experimentalist*.

My novel is much more romance than reality. I was a small child in the war and at the time the German language did indeed sound to us like the devil speaking. My grandfather's family were Jewish (though he himself married a girl who hailed from the Shetland Islands) and it was a matter of life and death for us who won the struggle against Germany. So I am on the side of those who regard Paperclip (as well as the British version of it) as deeply flawed and completely regrettable, but in terms of the reality of the Communist threat at the time, it was understandable. We have survived because of it. But, with our survival, we have taken on some of its poison.

Something happened in Germany to corrupt respected scientists and make them willing to experiment on human beings, to the point that some of those unwilling subjects died in pain, and to make others willing to drive slave labour to starvation, exhaustion and death in pursuit of their determination to further the ends of an evil regime. My anti-hero, Middleburg, simply could not, and cannot, get that sense of godlike superiority, power and control out of his system.

As someone remarks in the novel, once you let evil in, it thrives. The responsibility for that lies not just with those who carried out the Paperclip programme.

Acknowledgements

Anyone who wants to know about Los Angeles in 1970 and, of course, the trial of Charles Manson, could not do better than consult Vincent Bugliosi's brilliant book *Helter Skelter*. It has been a most revealing source of information, for my purposes especially, on the atmosphere in LA in 1970. Beyond that I am indebted to Graham Wade of that city (which I personally rather equate with Shakespeare's cities like Milan, Verona, Venice and Florence in his time – places of glamour and danger to onlookers from afar). My thanks to him for his perspicacious suggestions on: where my heroine should live, where Merrymaids should be located, where girls would go for a coffee downtown in 1970, where to find a good castle around LA, and what the weather is like in August. Google can furnish these things if you dig, but Graham has the eye of an artist.

Finally, I should like to thank my editor and publisher Rebecca Lloyd for her endless patience and editorial genius. I should also say that without Penny Hunter's beady eye a large number of errors and absurdities might well have been perpetrated. Any that remain are entirely down to me. *The Experimentalist* would have been a shard of a tale without their input, enthusiasm and belief. Also, I should like to express my appreciation to The Dome Press itself, my new publishers, who have had all the business and brouhaha of starting a major imprint, but have spared time and energy for myself and *The Experimentalist* from the start. My thanks, too, are very much due to my agent, Laura Morris who as usual has been tireless with her support and suggestions. And finally, of course, thanks to my wife Lyndsay whose patience during the research and writing of this work has been monumental.